D0540056

WID

Please return/renew this item by the last date shown on this label, or on your self-service receipt.

To renew this item, visit **www.librarieswest.org.uk** or contact your library

Your borrower number and PIN are required.

LibrariesWest

ONE NIGHT TO REMEMBER

KATE HARDY

THE MAYOR'S SECRET FORTUNE

JUDY DUARTE

MILLS & BOON

First Published in Great Britain 2020
by Mills & Boon, an imprint of HarperCollinsPublishers,
1 London Bridge Street, London, SE1 9GF

One Night to Remember © 2020 Pamela Brooks
The Mayor's Secret Fortune © 2020 Harlequin Books S.A.

Special thanks and acknowledgement are given to Judy Duarte for her contribution to *The Fortunes of Texas: Rambling Rose* continuity.

ISBN: 978-0-263-27871-2

0320

MIX
Paper from
responsible sources
FSC™ C007454

This book is produced from independently certified FSC™ paper to ensure responsible forest management.

For more information visit: www.harpercollins.co.uk/green

Printed and bound in Spain
by CPI, Barcelona

ONE NIGHT TO REMEMBER

KATE HARDY

For Julia, my editor—
who is simply a joy to work with—with love.

CHAPTER ONE

'THE BEST WAY to get over someone is to have a mad fling,' Natalie said.

'I don't need a fling,' Holly protested.

And it still felt too soon after Simon. Besides, how could a one-night stand take the place of eight years of being with someone? She'd thought their relationship was strong enough to cope with him being on secondment in New York for six months. Holly usually spent most of the summer away somewhere on a dig, coming home for weekends, and that had always been fine. She and Simon had rubbed along without any problems. They'd been happy.

Or so she'd believed. The more she thought about it, the more she realised how wrong she'd been.

Simon had met Fenella in New York, fallen hopelessly in love with her, and called off his wedding to Holly at the end of his secondment—only a month before they had been due to walk down the aisle together. He'd left it to Holly to cancel all the wedding preparations and send back the wedding gifts with an apologetic note, on the grounds that she was better at that sort of thing than he was; she'd gritted her teeth and done it simply so she knew everything had been sorted out rather than Simon dragging his feet and leaving something undone.

And, although his offer to buy out Holly's share of their house meant that she didn't have all the hassle of trying to sell the house, it hurt that he wanted to share *their* house with someone else. Plus she had had to find somewhere else to live, though Natalie had stepped in immediately with an offer of her spare room until Holly could find somewhere suitable.

The last fortnight had been particularly hideous. Holly had seemed to spend the whole time alternately apologising and squirming, knowing that everyone was gossiping about the situation behind her back. Some people were kind, though she'd hated being pigeonholed as the dumped fiancée. The pitying looks were hard to take. Thankfully the veneer of politeness stopped people actually asking what was wrong with her and why Simon had been so quick to fall for someone else, but she knew they were thinking it.

And she'd had to go through all their things and divvy them up; though, once she'd started, she'd realised how few of their joint belongings had been chosen by her, or even together. How had she let herself be such a doormat? Why hadn't she said no to Simon more often, or insisted on having more of *her* choices? What a fool she'd been.

Holly had honestly believed that Simon had loved her. She'd loved him, too. OK, so it hadn't been the big grand passion she'd read about in novels or seen at the movies, with rainbows and starbursts and fanfares every time he'd kissed her, but she knew she was plain and ordinary, so she'd never really expected to have that sort of relationship. She and Simon had liked each other at their first meeting and they'd got on well together. They'd dated, moved in together, bought a house. They'd been *happy*.

But not quite happy enough, it seemed.

Because in New York Simon had met the woman who really was his big grand passion, the one who made fireworks go off in his head when he kissed her—something that Holly had clearly never managed to do—and everything had fallen apart.

Maybe if Holly had been the real love of his life, they would've got married years ago, and they wouldn't have kept finding excuses to wait a bit longer before the wedding. Buying a house together rather than spending all that money on a party had seemed the sensible thing to do, given that house prices were going up so quickly. And then they'd both been busy with their careers. It was really only last year, when Simon's mum had asked some very pointed questions about just when her son was planning to settle down properly and produce some grandchildren, that Simon and Holly had set the date for their wedding. Even then, they'd set it for a year in the future rather than rushing into it.

As Fenella was apparently too green with morning sickness right now to get on a plane, Simon's mum was going to get her much-wanted grandchildren very soon, whereas Holly's mum would just have to make do with the grandchildren she had. And Holly wasn't going to let herself think about the children she and Simon might have had. The child she'd secretly started to want six months ago, when Simon had first gone to America. *The child Simon had made without her.*

'You need a holiday,' Natalie said.

'I'm fine.' Holly had cancelled her leave, not wanting to take the week's holiday that should've been her honeymoon. A honeymoon for one surely had to be the most unappealing thing ever. Or maybe it was better than going on honeymoon with someone who didn't really love you. Wasn't it better to be alone than to be with someone who didn't want you or value you?

And why hadn't she realised sooner that Simon had fallen out of love with her and that being together had become a habit instead of what they'd both really wanted?

'Anyway, it gives me time to concentrate on my career,' she said, trying to find a positive and damp down her feelings of misery and loneliness.

'Dry bones.' Natalie rolled her eyes.

'Sometimes they're wet,' Holly pointed out, 'if they're at the bottom of a rain-filled trench.'

Natalie shuddered. 'Cold, wet and muddy. Give me my nice warm kitchen at the magazine any day. Even if I do have an over-fussy art director wanting me to make a little tweak here and there that actually means making the whole dish all over again for the photographer.' She looked at Holly. 'Holls, if you're spending all your time with the bones of people who died centuries ago, you're never going to meet anyone else. Archaeologists aren't sexy.'

Holly laughed. 'Of course they are. What about Indiana Jones?'

'He's a fantasy.'

'All right, then. Brendan Fraser in *The Mummy*. You have to admit he's utterly gorgeous.'

'Fantasy again,' Natalie said. 'In real life, your male colleagues are either like Gandalf, muttering into their very grey, very straggly beards, or they're total nerds who are terrified at the thought of talking to a real live woman.'

'Apart from the fact that's a horrible sweeping generalisation, it's also not true. My male colleagues all talk to me,' Holly said.

'They work with you, so they see you as safe, not as a woman,' Natalie pointed out.

Which Holly knew was true. And she tried not to mind or let it make her feel even more inadequate than Simon had already made her feel. Why wasn't she the sort of woman that a man fell hopelessly in love with?

'You do need a break, though. I know you're not busy this weekend—' because it would've been her hen weekend, which Holly had also cancelled—'so let's go to Bath. It's the next best thing to Rome. You can drool over the curse tablets at the Roman Baths, and I can drag you off for afternoon tea in the Pump Room. And in between we can go and sigh over the lovely Georgian houses in the Circus.'

'And you can see how many Mr Darcy-alikes you can spot?' Holly teased, knowing her best friend well. Natalie was a complete Austen addict.

'Something like that,' Natalie said with a smile.

'All right. Actually, it'll be nice to go away with you,' Holly admitted. She hadn't been looking forward to moping at home this weekend. The last weekend in the house she'd shared with Simon, because next week she was moving her few possessions into a rented flat in Camden and he was moving back from his mother's to their house.

'Good, because I've already booked the hotel.'

Holly winced. 'That's a risky strategy, Nat. What if I'd said no?'

'Then I would've guilt-tripped you into coming with me,' Natalie said with a grin. 'Life's too short not to take the odd risk. We're staying in the middle of Bath, and according to all the review sites our hotel does the best breakfast ever. And this one is on me,' she added, 'because I know how much you were looking forward to Rome. It was the nearest thing I could think of, because I was guessing that Rome itself might have been too much to bear, even if I'd booked a different hotel.'

Holly hugged her. 'Thank you. That's really kind of you.'

'It's exactly what you would've done for me, if I'd been in your shoes,' Natalie reminded her. 'I still think Simon's the biggest idiot ever. The way he treated you— you deserved a lot better than that.'

Yeah. It would've been nice if he'd broken up with her *before* making Fenella pregnant. That was the bit that really hurt. Why had he kept stringing her along when he clearly didn't love her any more? Why had he let her believe that everything was just fine? Though it wasn't all him: why hadn't she seen the problems for herself?

And she hated the way people treated her as The Woman Who'd Been Cheated On. The whispered conversations that stopped when she walked into a room. The judgements. The friends taking sides. People they'd both known since university, who'd been her friends before she'd met Simon, had thrown in their lot with him; it had made her feel even more worthless, despite the fact she knew she was better off without them. She hadn't been enough as a partner, and she hadn't been enough as a friend.

How could she not have noticed their relationship unravelling? The signs must've been there before he'd gone to New York. She'd managed to snatch just one week-end with Simon during his secondment, quite early on, and he'd been distracted throughout it. He'd said it was work when she asked him; but now she knew it had been Fenella distracting him.

'At least he didn't dump me at the altar,' Holly said, keeping her tone light. 'It could've been a lot worse.'

'It could've been a lot *better*.' Natalie rolled her eyes. 'You're too nice for your own good.'

'Believe you me, I'm not being nice. I'm hurt and I'm angry, and bits of me want to punch him and yell and scream. But having a tantrum isn't going to change things,' Holly said. 'Simon doesn't love me any more, and having a hissy fit isn't going to make him decide he does love me after all. I don't want to be in a relation-ship where I'm the one who loves the other the most. I hate feeling so pathetic.'

'But you still love him.'

Bits of her did, and bits of her didn't. 'Eight years is a long time to be with someone,' Holly said. 'And most of them were good years.' But the other thing that nagged at her was how much of it had been her fault. If she'd made Simon feel loved and appreciated enough, instead of taking him for granted, maybe he would've acknowledged that he fancied Fenella but he wouldn't actually have done anything about it. Those six months of physical distance had turned all too quickly into emo-tional distance. 'I guess somewhere along the way we started drifting apart, and I should've been paying more attention to him.' It was the first time she'd acknowl-edged it to someone else, though the thoughts had kept her awake at night.

'He should've been paying just as much attention to *you*,' Natalie countered.

Maybe—but he hadn't. Holly shrugged. 'It feels pretty crap right now, but I'll live. Don't worry, I'm not going to turn into Miss Havisham or anything like that.'

'Good, because Simon isn't worth it.' Natalie squeezed her hand. 'OK. We'll get the train on Friday after work, do the Roman Baths first thing on Saturday morning, go for a walk to look at all the gorgeous houses, have afternoon tea at the Pump Room—and then, dear Cinders, you shall go to the ball.'

'Ball? What ball?' Holly asked.

'I got us tickets for a ball on Saturday night. It's just outside Bath—in an Elizabethan manor house, which you'll love. And it's Regency dress.'

'Regency dress?' Holly groaned. 'So this *is* all about your Darcy obsession.'

Natalie gave her an unrepentant grin. 'Asking you wouldn't have worked, so I'm dragging you out to have some fun.'

Holly grimaced. 'I love you, Nat, and I do appreciate what you've done for me, but a ball isn't really my idea of fun. I've got two left feet. And as for dressing up, the cost—'

'Problem solved, before you say you don't have a dress. I've already hired one for you,' Natalie informed her.

'What? How? It might not fit.'

Natalie coughed. 'If it fits me, it fits you. Someone on the magazine knows a really good hire place, and I went to see them yesterday. I tried on a few dresses and the ones I got for us are fabulous.'

'Uh-huh.'

'Holls, if nothing else, you'll enjoy the music. Apparently there's a brilliant string quartet who are going to play on a floating bandstand in the middle of the lake. So if you just want to sit and listen to them and sip Pimm's and watch the sunset and not even put a single foot into the ballroom, that's fine by me.'

Holly knew her best friend was trying to distract her from the train wreck of her personal life, coming up with ideas to keep her busy. And she appreciated it, because otherwise she rather thought she'd start to get really insecure and ask just what was so wrong with her that Simon hadn't wanted her any more. She'd always known she'd been punching well above her weight—Simon looked more like a film star than an accountant—and when Holly had stalked Fenella on social media she'd discovered that the other woman was super-glamorous.

Fenella was everything Holly herself wasn't. No wonder Simon had fallen head over heels with her. If you put a scruffy archaeologist who wore ancient jeans and T-shirts and usually had a smear of mud on her face from the trench she was working in next to someone with perfect hair and make-up and a designer suit, it was obvious who'd win in the gorgeousness stakes. Who'd be *enough*.

'I'll set foot in the ballroom,' Holly promised, 'so you get a chance to do some dancing. And I appreciate you having my back.'

'Always,' Natalie said fiercely. 'You've been my best friend since we were eleven. That's not going to change. I'm quite prepared to fly over to New York and beat Simon over the head with an umbrella—and threaten to baste Fenella in the stickiest marinade and barbecue her.'

Holly couldn't help smiling. 'Thank you, but there are better things to do in New York.'

Natalie gave her an 'are you insane?' stare. 'Can I at least make a mini-Simon out of modelling clay and stick pins into him?'

'That's money,' Holly said, 'you could spend more satisfyingly on posh gin.'

'Oh, the modelling clay and pins would be satisfying enough,' Natalie said. 'But you're right. Posh gin's a good idea. And we are *so* having posh gin at the ball. So I'll meet you at Paddington Station at four o'clock on Friday—next to the Paddington Bear bench—and we'll get the next train to Bath.' She smiled. 'I've got our tickets. I'll send you the email so you've got the PDF of our tickets, too, just in case something goes wrong with my phone.'

'It's more likely to be me forgetting to charge my phone. You know how hopeless I am,' Holly said wryly. 'You're the best friend ever. Thanks, Nat.'

'Roman archaeology, afternoon tea and a Regency ball. That's all our favourite things covered,' Natalie said with a smile.

'And no matchmaking,' Holly said, mindful of her best friend's views about how to get over a broken relationship. 'Just a nice girly weekend. You and me.'

'A nice girly weekend. You and me,' Natalie echoed.

Wine plus his parents really wasn't a good combination, Harry thought. He was really glad that that his brother Dominic, his sister Ellen and their partners were here, too. It was the only thing that made a visit to Beauchamp Abbey bearable. He wished the meal had been Sunday lunch rather than Saturday dinner, because having small children around might have dampened the sniping a bit.

Then again, the sniping had been there when he'd

been a small child, too. It had grown worse over the years, and it had been truly unbearable when Dom and Nell had both been at university. Harry hadn't been able to keep the peace between his parents and he'd hated all the conflict, so he'd escaped to his grandmother's as much as possible. His parents' behaviour had gone a long way to putting him off the idea of ever getting married.

At least Ellen had asked him to stay with her, so he didn't have to put up with a whole weekend of their parents. Now, with the cheese course over, his father was making inroads into the brandy and getting really snippy. 'You're thirty now, Harry. Isn't it about time you got married again and settled down properly?' George asked.

Trust his father not to pull his punches. And considering that Viscount Moran had made it very clear that Harry's ex-wife was much too lower class for his son... Harry damped down the anger. Having difficult in-laws wasn't the only reason, or even one of the main reasons, why he and Rochelle had broken up. But it hadn't helped.

'I'm a bit busy with my career, Pa,' he said as blandly as he could. 'It's not fair to ask someone to wait about for me when I'm touring so much.' And if marriage hadn't worked with someone who was in the same business and understood that you had to travel a lot to make a living out of music, it definitely wasn't going to work with someone who'd be left at home all the time.

'I think we've given you your head for quite long enough, letting you mess around with your cello for all these years,' George said. 'It's way past time you came back here, settled down and pulled your weight in the family business.'

'Messing around' wasn't quite how Harry would describe graduating from the Royal Academy of Music with first-class honours, or working with a renowned string quartet for the last six years. Not to mention the fact that he'd paid for the repairs of the conservatory roof at the abbey last year. He did his share of supporting the family estate, except he did it from as much distance as he thought he could get away with.

And it was getting harder and harder to bite his tongue. He knew his father resented the fact that Harry had gone his own way, but did George always have to bring it up and try to make his youngest son feel as if his career was worthless and he was a useless son? But, much as he wanted to stand up to his father's bullying and tell him where to get off, Harry didn't want to make life hard for his brother and sister. They were the ones who lived locally and would bear the brunt of George's temper, whereas Harry had the perfect excuse to escape to wherever the quartet was playing next.

'I still think my father would turn in his grave at the idea of people poking around the house,' George grumbled.

'Nobody will be poking around the house, Pa,' Dominic reassured him. 'They'll be following a defined visitor route. Nobody will go into areas we've roped off as private. And we've done Open Garden weekends for years without a problem; opening the house to visitors is just an extension of that.'

'The gift shop, the plant sales and the café we're going to set up in the Orangery will help to make the estate pay for itself,' Ellen added. 'We're developing an exclusive range of biscuits at the factory, based on some of the old recipes we found in the library, and we can sell all the gifts through our website as well.'

'Biscuits.' George's voice dripped with contempt.

Harry could see his sister-in-law Sally and his brother-in-law Tristan squirming, embarrassed by the escalating family row and not quite sure how to deal with Viscount Moran's uncertain temper, worried that anything they did or said would make things worse. With age, George had become more and more crusty, to the point where he was almost a caricature. One of these days he'd be in a satirical cartoon, with his mop of grey hair he couldn't be bothered to style, his jowls and his red cheeks, pointing a finger and shouting.

'Well, I don't want anything to do with it.' George swigged his brandy crossly. 'I don't see why you can't just wait for me to die before you start all this nonsense.'

'That can be arranged,' Barbara said, rolling her eyes at her husband.

George's temper flared. 'As for you, what do you care about Beauchamp? You grew up—'

Harry knew what was coming next: a pot-shot at his mother's background as the daughter of a local biscuit manufacturer. She was a commoner with her background in trade, not the gentry. And that in turn would escalate to comments from his mother that the Morans hadn't minded the money from Beckett's Biscuits rescuing them when George's father had drunk and gambled away the estate to near-penury, forty years before…

He stood up. 'Both of you. Please. Just *stop,*' he said quietly.

To his surprise, his parents did so.

It was a heady feeling that they were actually listening to the baby of the family for once. And maybe he'd drunk too much wine, because he found himself folding his arms and looking his father straight in the eye.

'Pa, Dom and Nell are absolutely right. This house eats money and it needs to start paying its way. You'll still have your private space and nobody's going to disturb that. We're simply letting people enjoy the garden and the artworks here, and it'll mean you won't have to sell yet another painting to pay for the next lot of repairs and work out how you're going to hide the faded patch on the walls because you can't afford to renovate the silk wall coverings.'

George stared at him in complete silence.

Warming to his theme, Harry said, 'A gift shop with plant sales and a café will create jobs and bring in visitors to help the local economy. Everyone wins. Dom, Sally, Nell and Tris all work really hard and they're doing a brilliant job. We all ought to appreciate that.'

More silence, and this time he could see that his brother and sister were squirming just as much as their partners.

He'd gone too far.

But he really wasn't going to apologise. Not this time. He hadn't said anything offensive. And he was so tired of treading on eggshells around his irascible father. Viscount Moran and his moods had dominated the family ever since Harry could remember, and it was way past time that changed. Harry was sick of having to kowtow to an entitled bully. 'Excuse me,' he said. 'I'll go and get some more water.' He picked up the jug from the centre of the table and headed for the kitchen.

Ellen followed him. 'Are you all right, Harry?'

'Yeah.' He sighed. 'Sorry, Nell. I didn't intend to stir things up. But I'm so sick of it. This is why I hardly ever come back to the abbey. I'm tired of Ma and Pa sniping at each other all the time. And I'm really tired of them treating you and Dom as if you're useless, when actually you're brilliant and without the pair of you Beauchamp Abbey would've collapsed under a pile of debt years and years ago.' He grimaced.

'In my professional life, I stand up to bullies. Especially if I see one of the older men trying to put the younger women down, or leering at them and trying to do the equivalent of the casting couch. It's absolutely *not* OK, and I'm not going to stand aside and watch it happen.' He sighed. 'I just wish I knew how to deal with Pa.'

'Just let it go,' Ellen advised. 'Pa can threaten whatever he likes, but he can't actually carry any of it out. Grandpa Beckett left the majority share in the biscuit business to me, so Pa can't sack me. The house is entailed, so Dom's the only one who can inherit it; and it'd take an Act of Parliament for Pa to make anyone other than Dom the next Viscount—which we all know isn't going to happen, because even people who've had a really good case for disinheriting their kids haven't been able to stop them inheriting the title and estate. Pa has absolutely no grounds for disinheriting Dom. He'd be laughed at if he tried.'

'I guess,' Harry said.

She hugged him. 'And ignore those stupid comments about your career. We're so proud of you.'

'Yes. Your quartet's booked up for two years in advance, which is pretty amazing,' Dominic said, walking into the kitchen, 'and what about the awards you've won? Plus whenever I play any of your recordings it takes me into another world. You're brilliant at what you do. Don't listen to Pa.'

'I was all ready to yell at him and tell him to stop being such a bully,' Harry said, 'but I stopped myself because I know I won't be the one who has to put up with the tantrums, and it isn't fair to make things worse for you. But I really, *really* hate the way he treats you all.'

'It is what it is,' Dominic said with a shrug. 'I don't think you're old enough to remember, but Grandpa Moran was even worse than Pa.'

'So why doesn't Pa think about how Grandpa Moran made him feel, and ask himself if that's how he wants his own children to think about him?' Harry asked.

'Because I don't think he can. He's too set in his ways,' Ellen said gently. 'But we love you, Harry. And we're hugely proud of you.'

'Seconded,' Dominic said, clapping him on the shoulder.

'Though,' Ellen added, 'he might have a point about letting someone back into your life. I know you were in pieces when Rochelle… Well.' She coughed. 'But that doesn't mean it wouldn't work with anyone else.'

Oh, but it would. Harry had faced a stark choice: his marriage or his career. And he'd chosen the thing built on solid foundations. The thing where he could be himself and not think about the might-have-beens: the little boy or girl who would've been five years old now.

'Thank you for your support,' he said, 'but I don't need anyone. I'm fine.'

'We worry about you,' Ellen said.

'I'm fine. Really,' he said. 'Just sick of the parents.' He grimaced. 'They loathe each other, but they'll never get divorced. They always bang on about divorce not being the done thing—' and they'd both gone on about it most when he could've done with a bit of support, in the middle of his own divorce '—but I think we all know Ma married Pa for his title, and Pa married Ma for Grandpa Beckett's money. Divorce means she'd lose the title and he'd lose the money. So they stay together and just make each other—and everyone around them—utterly miserable.'

'Which is why we don't live here with them.' Ellen ruffled his hair. 'Living in the village means there's just enough distance between us to protect the kids. But not all marriages are like theirs, Harry. Or like yours was, sweetheart. Look at me and Dom. I'm happy with Tris.'

'And I'm happy with Sal,' Dominic said. 'I know it was hard, what happened with Rochelle, but surely it's worth trying again?'

Harry sighed. The wreckage had proved that he should never have married Rochelle in the first place. Marriage wasn't for him. Not then and not now. 'The women who want to date me nowadays don't see the real me—they see either Harry the musician in the public eye, or Harry the younger son of Viscount Moran.'

'Then you're meeting the wrong women,' Ellen said. 'Why don't you let me—?'

'Thanks for the offer, but no,' Harry cut in gently. The last thing he wanted was for his sister to start matchmaking, even though he respected her judgement. He didn't want to fall in love again, only for it to go wrong. He couldn't face any more ultimatums with a woman saying he had to choose between her and his music. Clearly it was greedy to want love *and* his job. But at least his job never let him down, unlike love.

Ellen took a key from her pocket. 'Here. Escape back to ours, and get some fresh air. I'll tell the parents you've got a migraine.'

'You,' Harry said, 'are the best sister ever.'

She grinned. 'I hope so. Do you really have to dash off tomorrow?'

Harry nodded. 'Sorry, I have rehearsals.'

On Thursday evening, Holly was in the middle of packing her bag for the weekend when her phone shrilled.

'Hey, Nat,' she said, answering the call.

'Holls, I'm so sorry.' Natalie sounded thoroughly miserable. 'There's been a bug going round at work and I've picked it up—I've been throwing up all day and I feel like death warmed up.'

'You poor thing,' Holly said. 'Look, I'll ring the hotel and cancel, and then I'll come round and make you something with apples and rice that you might be able to keep down.'

'No, don't come here—you might go down with this bug, too,' Natalie said. 'And don't cancel. You picked up the dresses for us yesterday, so you can still go to Bath.'

'Without you? No way!'

'It's all paid for,' Natalie said, 'and at this late notice we wouldn't get a refund. It's daft to waste the money.'

'I can try asking,' Holly said, 'or see if they can reschedule.'

'No. You go without me,' Natalie urged. 'Have a good time and take lots of pictures for me.'

It wouldn't be the same on her own, but Holly didn't want to throw her best friend's kindness back in her face. 'Only,' she said, 'on condition that we reschedule a weekend away for both of us later in the summer, and it'll be *my* treat.'

'Deal,' Natalie said. 'And this time I'll try not to pick up any horrible sicky bugs.'

'I'll bring you back a Sally Lunn on Sunday evening,' Holly promised, knowing how much Natalie enjoyed the historic Bath speciality: a teacake that was a bit like a brioche, made from a recipe dating back to Restoration times.

'Jane Austen's favourite—and mine,' Natalie said. 'And I really hope I feel better by Sunday so I can do it justice!'

On Friday, Holly caught the train to Bath after work. Breakfast the next morning was as good as Natalie had promised; and then she headed to re-acquaint herself with the Roman Baths and drool over the lead curse tablets. She took a selfie while she drank a paper cup of the slightly warm and slightly disgusting water at the baths and sent it to Natalie, and followed it up with photographs of the gorgeous Georgian houses, tour guides walking around the city dressed up as Mr Darcy, and detailed pictures of the afternoon tea at the Pump Room. She called in at the ancient shop to buy a Sally Lunn, and picked up chocolates from the artisanal maker Natalie had been raving about since their last visit, then headed back to get ready for the ball.

She really didn't want to go.

But Natalie had paid for the tickets and Holly felt it would be churlish to deny her friend a few photographs to cheer her up.

The red dress Natalie had chosen for her fitted perfectly. It had a flattering Empire line bodice, short puff sleeves, a net overskirt and a silk underskirt, and Natalie had also hired a pair of long white gloves and a small reticule to go with it. Thankfully Holly had a pair of flat black suede pumps that would work as dance shoes.

She knew from the costume events her best friend

had attended in the past that she needed to put her hair up; she was used to wearing her hair tied back at the nape of her neck or in a braid for work, so it didn't take her long to put her hair up in a bun, braid a section that she could twist round the bun, and then curl the strands at the front. She added the bare minimum of make-up, then took a selfie in the full-length mirror.

She really didn't look like the scruffy archaeologist Simon had rejected; she barely recognised the woman in the photograph. So maybe tonight she could be whoever she wanted.

She sent the selfie to her best friend. 'OK?'

'More than OK. Utterly perfect,' was Natalie's verdict. 'Have fun!'

A ball wasn't Holly's idea of fun, but she duly took a taxi to the venue.

Natalie had been right to choose this dress. It made Holly feel amazing. How long had it been since she'd felt this confident in herself? She hadn't even felt confident when she'd tried on the wedding dress—which in itself should've been a sign that she had been doing the wrong thing. Maybe, she thought, Simon's defection actually meant she'd had a lucky escape from a marriage that would eventually have made her miserable.

And she wasn't going to think of her ex any more. She was going to enjoy the evening. She'd listen to good music, eat good food, and soak up the history.

The manor house was utterly gorgeous—built from mellow golden stone in the traditional Elizabethan 'E' shape, with pointed gables, ornate chimney stacks and stone mullioned windows. She smiled as she paid the driver and crunched along the gravel path to the front door; Nat was definitely right about her loving the house.

Inside was even better. There was a grand entrance hall and a library with an elaborate plaster ceiling, tall bookcases and oak panelling around huge windows. Better still was the first-floor gallery, which actually stretched the whole length of the house, and just off it was the ballroom where Regency dancing was already taking place. Holly took a few shots for Natalie, knowing her friend would love seeing all the costumes, then went through to the gallery and looked out into the gardens. Below was a perfect knot garden that echoed the design of the ceiling in the library; the framework of box hedge was filled in with lavender, rosemary and marjoram, with strategically placed alliums and roses. On a warm late spring evening like this, it would smell heavenly.

Behind the knot garden were lawns that sloped down to the lake, and she could see a bandstand in the middle with a small boat tied up just behind it. The string quartet was already in place; and hadn't Natalie suggested that she could just sit outside and listen to the music with a glass of Pimm's? Better that than being a wallflower in the ballroom, Holly thought, and headed out to listen to the music.

CHAPTER TWO

HARRY SETTLED INTO his chair on the bandstand; he'd checked the set-up beforehand, making sure there were four armless chairs and good overhead lighting for the musicians, and they'd all come across on the lake on the flat-bottomed motor launch. Thankfully it was warm enough to play outside without risking damage to their instruments; and actually he loved the idea of playing in the middle of a lake.

They'd been booked to play for two hours, and between them they'd come up with a mixture of classical music and film tunes that their audience should enjoy. Thankfully none of the others in the quartet was a music snob and they enjoyed playing the crowd-pleasers as much as he did, from Pachelbel to Bach to Mozart.

'I know we're already playing "The Swan",' Lucy, the quartet's viola player, said, 'but, since people have seen us get over here on a boat shaped like a swan, I think we ought to do "Dance of the Little Swans" as well.'

'Agreed,' Drew and Stella, the quartet's violinists, said.

'Or,' Harry suggested, 'a bit of T-Rex. "Ride a White Swan".' He plucked a couple of bars to illustrate his point. 'Or there's—'

'None of your experimental stuff tonight,' Lucy cut in with a grin, clearly having a good idea what he was going to suggest next. 'We're only playing music people know well. Traditional stuff.'

'"Dance of the Little Swans" it is,' Harry capitulated. 'Let's do that first.' The venue was beautiful and the event tonight made him think of all the things his family could do with Beauchamp Abbey, if his father wasn't so difficult. Though he shoved the thought away. Tonight wasn't about Viscount Moran. Harry was just going to enjoy the gorgeous late spring evening, and the joy of playing music he adored in such a fabulous setting.

They began with the Tchaikovsky, and segued into Harry's arrangement of Fauré's 'Sicilienne' before playing the first of the show tunes. People came to sit at the edge of the lake for a while, then drifted off again to go back for the dancing, while others took a break from the dancing and came to enjoy the quartet.

As the sun slowly went down, the sky turning amazing colours that were reflected in the lake, their audience grew smaller; but Harry noticed one woman in a red dress who seemed to be there for the entire performance. Usually people came to a ball in couples or in groups; he wondered why she was sitting alone. And it distracted him to the point where he nearly missed a note; cross with himself, he refocused and tried not to look at her.

But, despite his best efforts, something about the woman in red drew him. To the point where the only way he could concentrate was to promise himself that, as soon as he was back on dry land, he'd go in search of her and say hello.

* * *

Holly adored the music that the string quartet was playing. There was some really clever adaptation of music from shows and pieces that were usually performed by larger orchestral groups; she really loved Gershwin's 'Summertime', with the focus on the solo cello, and Bach's 'Air on a G String'. She could've listened to them play all night. Even though the sun had set and it was starting to get chilly, she really didn't want to go back inside the hall for the dancing.

She sat at the water's edge until the swan-shaped motor launch brought the quartet back to shore, then decided to go inside for just long enough to take a couple of pictures for Natalie before heading back to her hotel in the centre of Bath. She was about to haul herself to her feet when a man sat down beside her on the bank. 'Hello.'

He was absolutely gorgeous, with dark hair and midnight-blue eyes; and he was dressed like a Regency buck in white pantaloons, a white linen shirt with a fancy cravat, a cream silk waistcoat and a navy tailcoat. Holly was shocked to find that it was suddenly hard to breathe. She didn't react to men like this. Ever. She hadn't even felt like this when she'd met Simon. Oh, for pity's sake, what was wrong with her? She just about managed to reply with a shy, 'Hello.'

'I noticed you sitting here earlier. Would you mind if I joined you?'

Help. When was the last time anyone had chatted her up? Simon, eight years ago—and look how badly that had turned out. Holly was about to make a flimsy excuse to leave, but she could hear her best friend's voice in her head: *The best way to get over someone is to have a mad fling...*

She had no intention of doing that, but it wouldn't kill her to have a conversation with a handsome stranger. Though it would help if she didn't look at him, because those gorgeous blue eyes took her breath away. 'Sure.'

'Are you all right?'

'Yes. Why do you ask?'

'It's getting chillier out here, the music has stopped, and there's dancing inside,' he said.

'Dancing isn't really my thing,' she admitted.

'Which rather begs the question why you came to a ball.' Though he didn't look snooty. He looked intrigued. Interested. As if he wanted to know more about her.

'My best friend organised the tickets—except she went down with a tummy bug, and persuaded me to come anyway.'

'So you're here alone?' He grimaced. 'Sorry. That sounded a bit creepy, which really wasn't my intention.'

'It's fine.' Though she appreciated the fact he was sensitive. 'I was about to call a taxi back to my hotel.'

'Have you eaten tonight?' he asked.

'No,' she admitted.

'Neither have I. Come and have something at the buffet with me, and I'll give you a lift back into the city afterwards,' he invited. 'As long as you don't mind sitting in the front of the car with me—I'm afraid my cello takes up the entire back seat.'

Then Holly realised who he was. 'You were playing in the bandstand earlier.'

He inclined his head. 'The ball was organised by a close friend of Lucy, our viola player, so we agreed to play here tonight. Actually, it was fun—I haven't played in the middle of a lake before, and it's definitely the first time I've gone anywhere by swan.'

'I really enjoyed the music,' she said, and then was cross with herself for sounding so star-struck and gauche.

He smiled. 'I rather hoped that was why you were sitting there all evening.'

He'd noticed that? Then again, there weren't many women here wearing dresses the same colour as hers. Most were wearing cream or navy. 'Natalie, my best friend, said she thought I'd end up out here listening to the music rather than dancing.' She shivered, suddenly aware of the cold.

He noticed, because he shrugged off his tailcoat and placed it around her shoulders.

'Thank you. That's very gallant—and quite befitting a Regency gentleman,' she said.

'I'm Harry,' he said, holding his hand out to shake hers. 'Nice to meet you.'

'Holly. Often as prickly as my name,' she said. And how weird it was that her skin tingled when she took his hand to shake it. She'd never experienced that before either.

He grinned. 'I must remember that when I get accused of being overly pushy. Harry by name, harry by nature.'

Maybe it was a warning; but she instinctively liked him and he didn't strike her as being the difficult type. Then again, her intuition had been way off beam with Simon. Could she trust her intuition any more? On the other hand, he was a stranger. She could be whoever she wanted tonight: the woman in a red dress who stood out from the crowd.

Her confidence back, she pushed her doubts aside and walked back to the house with him. 'The music was so wonderful, I assume you've played together for some time.'

'Professionally, for about six years,' he said. 'We went to the same college and all hit it off, so it made sense to work together afterwards.'

'Six years? Are you quite well known, then?' The awkwardness came back. 'I apologise for not recognising you.'

'I'm not quite on the same level as Jacqueline du Pré or Steven Isserlis,' he said with a smile.

Meaning that he was actually rather well known but was modest about it, Holly thought. She liked the way he was so matter-of-fact.

'I don't actually care whether people recognise me or not, as long I get to play. The music is what really matters,' he said.

'Do what you love and love what you do,' she mused. 'My grandfather was fond of saying that.'

'Your grandfather was a wise man,' he said.

'Very,' she agreed.

She gave the tailcoat back to Harry as soon as they reached the house, then went in to the buffet with him. They watched the dancers while they ate.

'Are you sure I can't tempt you?' he asked, gesturing to the dance floor.

'I'm very sure,' she said with a smile, 'unless you're seriously good at Regency dancing and can teach me all the steps in about three seconds flat.'

'Or we could do the alternative—there's another room for those who enjoy dressing up in all the Regency finery but would rather stick to more modern dancing. One dance, and then I'll take you back to your hotel?' he suggested.

The sensible thing would be to say no, and get the taxi.

But something in his blue, blue eyes drew her.

'One dance,' Holly said. 'Though you'll still need to show me the steps.'

Simon had never really been into dancing, so she'd never actually learned how to do ballroom dancing—just the slightly awkward shuffle that most students did at discos and formal balls. She'd always thought that she had two left feet. But dancing with Harry the cellist was something else entirely. Especially because the next dance was a waltz, and Harry dipped and swayed and spun her, guiding her movements so she felt as if she was gliding on air, not putting a single foot wrong.

He swept her off her feet to the point where one dance led to two, then three.

And when the music changed from a formal ballroom dance to a soft, slow dance, Harry drew her closer and she found her arms were wrapped around him. They were so close together that she could feel his heart beating, strong and slightly fast—just like her own.

Dancing cheek to cheek.

So this was what it felt like.

Not the awkward and slightly embarrassing shuffle of her student years, but something that made her feel breathless and dizzy. The feeling increased as she realised that Harry had moved his head so that his lips were just touching the corner of her mouth. All she had to do was to move her head a tiny fraction and his lips would be against hers.

Could she?

Should she?

Her heart rate kicked up a notch as she shifted a tiny, tiny fraction. Suddenly the music and everything else around her vanished: all she was aware of was Harry, and the way he made her feel. Her lips touched his, and his arms tightened round her. He brushed his mouth against hers, almost as if asking permission, and then she kissed him lightly in response. And then they were really kissing, clinging to each other as if they were drowning.

When was the last time she'd been kissed like this, making her feel as if she were burning up from the inside out? She couldn't remember. All she could focus on was the feeling, right here, right now.

He broke the kiss and his gaze held hers. 'Shall we get out of here?'

Holly was shocked to realise that she'd completely blanked out her surroundings. She'd just let a total stranger sweep her off her feet and kiss her stupid in the middle of a crowded ballroom. This wasn't what she did. She was sensible Holly Weston, usually found in a lecture theatre or in a trench somewhere, wearing jeans and a sensible long-sleeved shirt and a hat to protect her from the sun and insects. The woman wearing a red Regency dress, dancing in a ballroom, felt like a completely different person.

Out of here, he'd suggested. She nodded, and he took her hand and led her out of the hall. They stopped to collect his cello, and Holly thought that her common sense was starting to come back—but then they got to his car and he kissed her again, and her common sense vanished once more at the speed of light.

He drove them back to Bath. Then, as they reached the outskirts of the city, he said, 'I can drop you at your hotel now. Or perhaps you'd like to come back to where I'm staying and have a drink with me?'

Holly opened her mouth, intending to tell him that dropping her by the train station was just fine, thank you—but her libido had clearly overpowered her common sense, because she found herself saying, 'I'd love to come back for a drink. Thank you.'

Was she *crazy*?

She didn't know this man at all.

OK, so he played the cello beautifully—but he was still a stranger, and they hadn't even swapped surnames. This was real life, where you didn't go off with someone you didn't know, no matter how amazing his kisses were or how brilliantly he played the cello. What on earth was she doing?

Then he pulled up outside a sweeping Georgian terrace, a building she recognised as one of Bath's landmarks.

'You're staying *here*?' She blinked in surprise. 'Are you telling me you own a flat in this building?'

'No, I'm borrowing it. It belongs to an old friend. Ferdy lives in London, but he spends most of his weekends here. As he's not here this particular weekend, he lent me the key to his *pied-à-terre*,' Harry said with a smile.

Clearly Harry the cellist was very well connected. She hadn't registered it before that moment, but his car was an expensive saloon. Top of the range. And a flat in this building would be eye-wateringly expensive for a main home, let alone a second. So either Harry was a lot more famous than he admitted to being, or he came from a really wealthy background. In both cases, she didn't measure up.

Par for the course.

She really ought to make an excuse and go back to her hotel. Except it would be rude, given that she'd already accepted his invitation. And he'd been so nice. And, actually, she wanted to spend more time with him.

'Come in,' he said, and retrieved his cello from the back of the car.

Once he'd unlocked the front door, he ushered her inside and tapped in the code to switch off the alarm.

'This is amazing,' she said, taking in the plasterwork on the ceiling, the deep cream-coloured walls and the elaborate doorframes. 'The perfect Georgian flat.' And how appropriate that both she and Harry were dressed in Georgian finery.

'Let me give you the grand tour,' Harry said. 'This is the sitting room.'

It had a high ceiling with a very elegant chandelier; the walls were painted a deep mustard colour and there were floor-to-ceiling sash windows dressed with dark blue velvet curtains, complementing the deep mustard velvet sofas. The black-leaded fireplace had deep blue tiles and a white marble surround, and the stripped wood floor had a rug in the centre in tones of blue and mustard. The whole thing felt distinctly Georgian; even the paintings looked appropriate to the era, with large portraits of women and children in Georgian clothing.

'Are they family portraits?' she asked.

'Probably. Knowing Ferdy, he most likely borrowed them from his gran,' Harry said.

She and Harry were from very different worlds; in hers, there might be a few photographs of great-great-grandparents if you were lucky, but actual painted portraits? She'd never met anyone like that.

He took off his jacket and laid it across the back of one of the sofas, then set his cello case down safely on the floor before ushering her to the next doorway. 'I think you can work this one out for yourself,' he said, gesturing to the kitchen-diner. Like the sitting room, the room had a stripped wooden floor, though the walls here were painted duck-egg blue. There were white painted cabinets, which she assumed also hid the fridge and freezer, and a discreet state-of-the-art cooker. At one end of the room there was a table with six chairs and a dresser with antique china plates, cups and saucers on display. More of his friend's family heirlooms? she wondered.

'Bedroom,' Harry said, gesturing to the one closed door. 'And the bathroom.'

The claw-footed free-standing bath was perfect, its outside a soft dove grey that toned with the darker grey walls and the white marble fireplace.

He ushered her back to the kitchen. 'Can I offer you coffee, tea or champagne?'

'Actually, a cup of tea would be really lovely, please,' she said.

He smiled at her, filled the kettle, and rummaged in the cupboard. 'Do you prefer builder's tea, Earl Grey, green tea, or something that looks like pot-pourri?' he asked.

'Builder's tea is perfect, thank you,' she said.

'I'll let you add your own milk,' he said. 'Um—would you mind if the milk was straight from the carton, or shall I try and find the milk jug?'

'Straight from the carton is fine,' she said. She was more used to drinking from a chipped mug balanced on the edge of a trench or among the papers on her desk, rather than from porcelain, and with the tea made from a tea-bag rather than loose leaves in a matching porcelain pot with what looked like a solid silver strainer.

'OK. Sugar?'

'No, thanks.'

He let the tea brew, then poured two cups and handed

her the carton of milk. 'To an unexpected evening,' he said, raising his tea cup in a toast.

'An unexpected evening,' she echoed, doing the same—no way would she risk chinking her cup against his and chipping it.

'Shall we go through to the sitting room?'

She followed him through, and couldn't resist looking out of the window. Even though it was dark, the street lights outside showed her how lovely the view must be in daylight.

'Ferdy gets a view of the sunset from here. It's gorgeous.' He paused. 'Holly. Just so you know, I never invite people back to wherever I'm staying, especially when I've only just met them. It's just…' He shook his head. 'I don't know. There's something about you.'

'I don't ever go off with total strangers either,' she said. 'But tonight…' It was the same for her. An instant connection she'd felt between them. Something strange and new and irresistible. Possibly much too soon, given that she'd only been officially single for three weeks; then again, if she looked back she could see the cracks in her relationship even before Simon's secondment to New York, and apart from that brief weekend she hadn't seen him for six months.

'Can I ask you something pushy?' she asked.

'Sure,' he said.

'Could I ask you to play something for me?'

'Of course.' He took the cello from its case, then checked the tuning and looked at her. 'What would you like me to play?'

'Anything you like. Your favourite piece,' she suggested.

'That rather changes with my mood,' he said.

'OK. Your favourite piece right now,' she said.

He grinned. 'Do you mind something really flashy and showy-offy?'

'Bring it on,' she said.

He proceeded to play something that was the equivalent of cello pyrotechnics; she recognised the tune but couldn't name it.

'That was amazing,' she said.

'Paganini's "Caprice No. 24"—it's a lot of fun to play,' he said. 'Given that you sat through our entire set, I assume you like classical music?'

'Yes, but I don't hear much live,' she said. 'I've been to a couple of Proms, but that's about it. This is a huge treat.'

He inclined his head in acknowledgement, and played something much slower for her.

'I really like that,' she said. 'What is it?'

'"Hushabye Mountain", from *Chitty Chitty Bang Bang*,' he said. 'It's a gorgeous arrangement.'

He followed up with a song she recognised as an eighties classic: 'Don't You Forget About Me'.

Harry was the least forgettable man she'd ever met. Not that she was gauche enough to say so. 'That was great, too,' she said when he'd finished.

He smiled and put his cello away. 'My turn to be pushy. Will you dance with me again?' he asked.

She nodded, and he connected his phone to Ferdy's audio system; then he dimmed the lights as soft music flooded into the room, and placed both of their cups on the low coffee table.

Again, he made her feel as if she was dancing on air. And this time, when they kissed, there was nothing to make her hold back.

'Holly.' His eyes were almost black in the low light. 'Stay with me tonight.'

A night with no strings. A night of pure pleasure. A bubble of time outside her real life. She could be sensible and call a taxi back to her hotel—or she could follow her impulses for once.

But she still had enough common sense to check something, first. Because she had no intention of hurting someone else, the way Simon had hurt her. 'There's no one who could be hurt by this? You're single?'

'I'm single,' he confirmed.

'Then, yes, I'll stay,' she said.

'Good,' he said, and led her out of the living room. Still holding her hand, he opened the door to the bedroom. The walls were painted deep red, but the thing that really drew her eye was the bed: a half-tester in dark wood with deep red and gold hangings. Her mouth went dry.

Then he lifted her up and carried her across the threshold, for all the world as if she really was a demure Regency maiden.

'Holly,' he whispered, setting her down on her feet. 'Are you quite sure about this? Because you can change your mind and it will be OK. I can drive you back to your hotel.'

The sensible thing to do would be to accept his offer of a lift home.

But right now she didn't feel very sensible. Right now, she could see the whole point of Natalie's view that the best way to get over someone was to have a fling with someone else. No strings, no promises—and nobody to get hurt, because she and Harry were both single.

'I'm sure,' she whispered back, wrapped her arms round his neck, and kissed him.

* * *

The next morning, Holly woke to the scent of coffee. Sunday morning. The memories of the previous night rushed through her head.

Oh, help. How did you behave the morning after a mad fling?

She could get dressed, creep along the hallway to grab her bag from where she'd left it... In the kitchen, where from the smell of coffee in the air she presumed that Harry was busy. Not to mention that this was an old building and, despite modernisation work, the floorboards probably creaked. Creeping out clearly wasn't an option.

Get dressed and brazen it out, pretending that she did this sort of thing all the time? Again, that wasn't an option, because she'd admitted to him the previous night that she didn't usually do this sort of thing.

Before she could worry about the situation any more, Harry leaned round the door. 'Good morning.'

'Good morning.' She gave him an awkward smile. He was wearing jeans and a T-shirt and his hair was damp, so clearly he'd already showered and dressed.

'I have coffee brewing and I just picked up some freshly baked croissants from the deli round the corner. Help yourself to anything you need in the bathroom. Ferdy keeps a bath robe for guests on the back of the bathroom door, if you need it.'

'Thank you.' So at least she wouldn't need to have breakfast in her Regency dress and risk spilling something on it and wrecking it before it went back to the hire place.

'And there's a spare toothbrush in the bathroom cabinet,' he added.

Harry's friend Ferdy kept his bathroom very well appointed, and Holly managed to shower without getting her hair wet. Wearing the borrowed bath robe, she padded barefoot into the kitchen.

'Help yourself to milk and sugar,' Harry said, pouring coffee into a mug and putting it in front of her.

He'd laid the table with a jug of freshly squeezed orange juice, a bowl of fresh strawberries, yoghurt, butter and jam, as well as a large glass jar of granola; he took the still-warm croissants from a paper bag and put them on a plate.

'This is really lovely,' she said shyly. 'Thank you.'

'My pleasure.' He smiled at her. 'I'm guessing right now that you feel as weird as I do.'

She nodded.

'I don't make a habit of this,' he said. 'But I don't regret last night.'

Neither, she discovered, did she. 'Snap.'

'Then let's just ignore the awkwardness,' he said. 'Are you busy today?'

'I'm due back in London this evening,' she said.

'So theoretically we could have lunch together, and maybe do something touristy? There's an amazing park not far from here, or we could follow in Jane Austen's footsteps and walk through Sydney Gardens to the canal.'

Meaning that last night might not be just a one-off?

Though Harry was a professional musician. He probably toured a lot. They might live hundreds of miles apart, and seeing each other could be difficult.

Then again, there was that connection between them. Maybe they should give it a chance and see where it took them. He'd told her last night that he was single; and, thanks to her broken engagement, so was she. There was no reason why they couldn't spend today together and see what happened.

'I'd like that,' she said. 'Though I really need to go back to my hotel and change first.'

'Of course. I can give you a lift, when you're ready to go,' he said.

'No, it's fine. I don't mind walking,' she said. 'So are you staying in Bath for a few days?'

'Sadly not. I'm driving to Birmingham tonight,' he said, 'because I'm recording tomorrow.'

Whereas she would going back to mark dissertations and be on hand to calm her students down before their exams. Their lives were very different. 'Uh-huh.'

'So do you know Bath well?' he asked.

She nodded. 'My best friend is a huge Jane Austen fan.'

'Have you been to the Roman Baths?' he asked.

'Yes,' she said, not wanting to admit that she'd also done some work on the site because it sounded a bit precious. 'And I've taken the waters.'

'They're absolutely vile. Or maybe I'm biased because the only time I ever tasted them I had a hangover, and Ferdy insisted on using the Bath cure.'

'Did it work?'

'No.' He grimaced, and then gave her a boyish grin that put the most appealing crinkles at the corners of his eyes. 'Though I'm pretty sure that Bath water tastes like bathwater, and Ferdy only told me it was a hangover cure so he could see my face when I tried it.'

She grinned back, enjoying the pun. Not only was she attracted to Harry the cellist physically, she *liked* him. And that ridiculous pun made her relax with him enough to really enjoy breakfast and just chat with him.

He insisted on clearing away while she changed back into her Regency dress.

'Are you quite sure I can't just drop you at your hotel?' he asked.

'Quite sure,' she said. 'I'll see you in an hour, outside the Pump Room.'

'Let's swap phone numbers in case either of us gets held up,' he suggested.

She took her phone from her bag, but it refused to switch on. She winced. 'Sorry, I'm utterly hopeless with my phone. It's out of charge—*again*.' She gave him her number and he tapped it into his own phone.

'See you in an hour,' he said, and kissed her at the door.

Back at the hotel, Holly put her phone on charge, and it started to beep with incoming texts. Most of them were from Natalie. Holly quickly texted her back.

Sorry, my phone went flat. Hope you're feeling better. I took your advice!!! Tell you more later. Love you. x

She sent a couple of the photographs she'd taken the previous evening, then changed into her normal clothes, packed, checked out, and left her luggage with the hotel's concierge to collect before she had to catch her train.

While she was walking down the High Street on the way to the Pump Room, she saw a sun hat blowing into the road, and seconds later a small child darted in front of her after it. The little boy's mum was frantically trying to find the brake on the baby's pram and screaming out to her son to leave the hat and come back.

There was a car zooming down the road, and the

driver clearly hadn't seen the child because he wasn't braking.

Acting purely on instinct, and because she was the nearest person to the little boy, Holly stepped into the road to grab him. She heard the screech of brakes, and everything seemed to happen in slow motion. Grabbing the child and pulling him out of danger. The car, moving closer and closer. The thud of the impact as the car hit her.

And then everything went black.

Harry glanced at his watch, frowning. They'd agreed to meet in an hour and he'd been a couple of minutes early. Maybe Holly had been held up. He'd give her a few minutes. From his spot outside the Pump Room he could see most of the area outside the cathedral door to his right, and then across part of the narrow street to his left, so whichever way she came from he'd see her quickly.

It was a gorgeous bright sunny day and he was looking forward to getting to know his mysterious lady in red a little bit better. He couldn't remember the last time he'd really clicked with someone like this; despite his usual reluctance to get involved, he found himself hoping that this might turn into more than just a weekend thing. Holly was very, very different from Rochelle. In fact, she was different from all the women he'd dated; he hadn't told her anything more than his first name, so refreshingly she hadn't seen him either as someone in the public eye or as the youngest son of Viscount Moran. She'd just seen him as one of the musicians at the ball. An equal. And definitely not a means to financial security.

He was dimly aware of the sound of a siren some-where beyond the cathedral, but didn't take much no-tice of it.

There was still no sign of Holly.

Harry waited for another half an hour.

OK, so he didn't actually know her very well, but he was pretty sure she wasn't the type of woman who would ghost someone. Maybe something had happened to hold her up. And, because her phone had died, she didn't have his number; so obviously he'd have to be the one to call her to see if she was OK.

One ring, two, three—

'Hello?'

That definitely wasn't Holly's voice; it was male and had a strong Glaswegian accent.

'I must have the wrong number. Sorry to have dis-turbed you,' Harry said, cut the connection, and tried again.

The phone rang twice before the Glaswegian man answered again.

'I'm sorry. I'm trying to get in touch with Holly.'

'I don't know anyone called Holly, pal,' the stranger said.

'This is the number she gave me this morning.' Harry had typed it in as she'd said it. 'Her phone had died so she gave me her number.'

The Scotsman laughed. 'It sounds as if she made it up, pal, and you're out of luck.'

'I guess. Sorry for bothering you.'

'No bother, pal. I'm sorry your girl let you down.'

Harry ended the call, flooded with disappointment and feeling thoroughly rejected. He'd never been ghosted before, and it made him feel as if he was worthless. Just like his dad always made him feel whenever George spoke about Harry's career.

Holly had been at pains last night to check that he was single and nobody could be hurt by them getting together; maybe it had been a warning sign that it hadn't been the case for her. He didn't think she seemed to be the cheating type, but then again it was now forty minutes since they'd been supposed to meet here, she hadn't shown up and the phone number she'd given him had turned out to be not hers.

No wonder she'd refused to let him drop her back at her hotel. Clearly she'd had no intention of actually meeting him.

He gritted his teeth. What an idiot he'd been. OK. He'd deal with his feelings the same way he always did—playing certain pieces of music to burn out the anger and disappointment—and then he'd drive to Birmingham now and start rehearsing. Last night had been a one-off, a bubble in time. His path was unlikely to cross hers again, and it was pointless trying to find her. Holly might not even have been her real name.

Holly. Often as prickly as my name.

She hadn't been prickly with him. She'd been warm and sweet and funny, and he'd really, really liked her.

Just a pity she clearly hadn't felt the same way about him.

And it would teach him not to give in to ridiculous impulses in future. He should've learned from his time with Rochelle that relationships weren't for him.

CHAPTER THREE

'Hi, there. How are you feeling?' a voice asked.

Sore, tired, and with a massive headache. Where on earth was she? Why was she in bed? The last thing she could remember...

...was a complete and utter blank.

'Where am I?' Holly asked, opening her eyes and wincing at the brightness of the light.

'Hospital.'

She'd already worked that one out herself from the nurse's uniform, but it wasn't fair to be rude to the woman. 'Which hospital?'

'Bath.'

'Why?' Double why: why was she in hospital, and why was she in Bath?

'Don't you remember?' the nurse asked.

'No.' And there was something important she needed to do, but she had no idea what it was.

'Can you remember your name?' the nurse asked gently.

'Yes, of course. It's...' She scrabbled in her memory to find her name and drew a blank. Panic flooded through her. 'I... I don't know. Why don't I know my name?'

'Try not to worry,' the nurse said. 'You've been in an

accident, and you hit your head. An ambulance brought you here.'

'Accident?' She didn't remember any accident.

And she didn't know her name.

'My phone. That will tell me who I am. If it's actually charged.' She remembered that. Everyone always nagged her about the fact she was terrible about keeping her phone charged. And that scared her even more. 'How do I know I'm hopeless about remembering to charge my phone, if I don't even know my own name?' What else wasn't she remembering? Would it all come back? Or did it mean that the accident—the one she didn't remember—had caused serious damage to her brain and her life would be completely changed?

'After a head injury, sometimes people have something called retrograde amnesia. The way memory is stored means you might not remember things that happened just before the accident, or even a couple of days before, but you can remember things from longer ago,' the nurse explained.

'So how come I can't remember my name?' Holly asked. 'Because my name has always been the same.' At least, she *thought* it had. But right now she couldn't be sure of anything and it felt as if she was teetering on a narrow path up a high cliff, the ground crumbling a little more beneath her with every step.

'Try not to worry too much. Memory can be a funny thing. We don't completely understand how it works,' the nurse said. She found Holly's phone and handed it to her.

'I'm sure I can't be on my own in Bath,' Holly said. 'I don't remember planning to come here in the first place, but if I'm here on holiday then I'm sure I'd be with my mum or my best friend.'

'There was nobody with you. The person who called the ambulance was the mum of the child you saved.'

'I saved a child?' She didn't remember that either.

The nurse nodded. 'A little boy. You got him out of the way of a car.'

So why hadn't someone been with her? She didn't understand—and her head hurt when she tried to think.

Her phone was charged, to her relief. But there were no notifications on the lock screen about missed calls or new text messages. If she'd been meeting her mum or her best friend and not turned up, they would've kept calling and texting her until they got an answer.

She didn't have any explanation, and it scared her even more.

What was her passcode?

She didn't know that either, Biting her lip, she looked at the nurse. 'I can't remember the code for my phone.'

'It might come back to you later,' the nurse said. 'But maybe you filled in the information on the medical emergency tab.'

Holly couldn't remember doing that either. Or how to access it. 'I'm sorry, could you help me, please?' she asked, trying to stem the growing panic.

'Of course.' The nurse took her phone and then read out loud, '"Holly Weston".'

Holly. She tested the name in her head. It felt right.

'It says you have no medical conditions,' the nurse said, handing the phone back to her, 'but it seems you're allergic to penicillin.'

Simon had made her put that in, for when she was on a dig. Just in case something happened.

Thank you, Simon, she thought gratefully, thinking of her fiancé.

Except Simon's name wasn't listed under the emergency contacts. Just her mum and her dad.

Memories came leaking back. Simon video-calling her to say he couldn't go through with the wedding. That he'd fallen in love with his colleague Fenella and she was pregnant...

And the misery felt almost as sharp as it had been the first time round.

OK. Separate issue, she told herself. That wasn't going to change. Deal with the important stuff—the urgent stuff—first. Why was she here?

'What day is it?' she asked.

'It's Sunday.'

Today and yesterday were both a complete blank, and the entire week before was spotty. She had no idea where she'd been staying or who she'd come here with or why she was even in Bath in the first place.

'Can I ring someone for you?' the nurse asked.

'Can I call my mum?' Holly asked.

'Yes.'

'Thank you.' Holly took a deep breath. 'Can I go home?'

'I can't discharge you,' the nurse said. 'You need to see one of the doctors.'

'But I feel absolutely fine,' Holly fibbed. There was an enormous gap in her memory that she'd try to fill in later, a headache that could be sorted with painkillers—and she'd ignore the soreness and tiredness because they'd go eventually. 'Can I see a doctor, please?'

The nurse narrowed her eyes, but said, 'I'll go and see if I can find a doctor.'

'Mum, there's been an accident,' Holly said when her mother answered. 'I'm all right, but I'm in hospital. In

Bath. Apparently I saved a child from being hit by a car,
but I don't remember anything.'

'Oh, my God. I'm on my way now,' Holly's mum said.

'You don't have to come,' Holly lied, really wanting to
see her mum; and how ridiculous was it that tears were
leaking down her face? This wasn't her. She was cool,
calm, efficient Holly Weston. Nothing fazed her, which
was why her colleagues had nicknamed her 'Lara Croft'.

And that was another bit of memory back. Please,
please let the rest of it return, too.

'You're in hospital, love. Of course I'm coming,'
Ginny Weston said.

'I don't even know if they're going to let me out today.'

'Then I'll find a hotel and I'll stay nearby until they
do,' Ginny said firmly. 'Love you, Holls. I'll be there
soon.'

'Love you, Mum. And thank you.'

By the time she'd finished the call and scrubbed the
tears from her face, the nurse had come back with a
doctor.

'I'm Anya Singh, consultant in the emergency department,' the doctor introduced herself. 'Janet here tells
me you can't remember anything from this morning.'

'I can't remember anything from the entire weekend,'
Holly admitted.

'OK. Well, you dashed out in front of a car and saved
a little boy from being harmed,' Anya said. 'The car hit
you, you hit your head, and you've been unconscious for
a while. Can I do some tests?'

'If it means I can go home, you can do anything you
like,' Holly said.

Anya grinned. 'That's what I like. Cooperative patients.'

Holly submitted to a barrage of tests.

'Now can I go home?' she asked, when they were all done.

'No,' Anya said. 'I want you kept in for observation. And I'm sending you for a CT scan just to check there isn't any brain injury we haven't picked up.'

'I'm fine. Isn't some memory loss after an accident like this normal?'

'Often it's just a couple of minutes before the moment of impact,' Anya said. 'And you were unconscious for long enough for me to worry that something might be brewing. I want you here in case it is.'

'If the scan's OK, can I go home?'

'Once I'm happy that you're not going to develop a brain injury, *then* you can go home,' Anya said firmly. 'Provided you have someone to keep an eye on you for at least the first twenty-four hours after we discharge you, and you need to rest.'

Holly thought about it. 'I live on my own.' At least, she assumed she did. 'But my mum will make me stay with her.'

'Good. I'll get that scan organised,' Anya said, and patted her hand. 'Don't be stubborn. Tell us if you're hurting anywhere. Otherwise you'll be staying here for a week.'

Holly grinned, liking the doctor's sense of humour. 'Got it.'

Three days later, Holly was back in London under her mother's watchful eye, and Natalie had called round to visit.

'I feel so guilty,' Natalie said. 'If I hadn't made you go to Bath on your own, it wouldn't have happened.'

'You'll drive yourself crazy, thinking like that. I'm

fine. No harm done,' Holly said. Just her lost memory; bits of the week before had come back, but the weekend remained a stubborn blank.

'So the accident means you didn't meet your fling,' Natalie said.

Holly frowned. 'What fling?'

Natalie showed Holly the text she'd sent. 'If you really *did* take my advice, that means you had a fling.'

'If I didn't turn up to meet this guy,' Holly pointed out, 'surely he would have called me?'

'Maybe he thought you deliberately stood him up,' Natalie countered. 'Why don't you ring him?'

'And say what? "Sorry I didn't turn up, but I got hit by a car, and I don't remember a thing about you"?' Holly asked wryly. 'I'm sure he'd be thrilled to find out he was so unmemorable. Not that he exists. I was probably just teasing you.'

'I don't think you were. Give me your phone.' Natalie checked the contact list. 'Oh,' she said, sounding disappointed. 'I know everyone in your phone list.'

'They're all either related to me, work with me or are very old friends,' Holly pointed out.

'You could just drop them all a text and ask if they accompanied you to Bath.'

'No,' Holly said firmly. 'Besides, if I'd agreed to meet anyone on that list, they would already have called me to see if I was OK.' She was solid, safe and reliable; or, from Simon's point of view, boring and unable to make his heart beat fast enough. The irony didn't escape her that his job—accountancy—was notorious for being boring.

'So no leads there to your mystery man, then,' Natalie said.

Holly shrugged. 'As I said, I was probably teasing you.'

'I'm not so sure. You didn't text me until Sunday morning—so my theory is you didn't actually go back to the hotel on Saturday night. You went somewhere with your fling.' Natalie flicked into the photographs. 'Oh. No selfies. At least, none of you with the mystery man.'

'I honestly think I must've been teasing. I'm too sensible to do anything else.' And too plain and ordinary for a stranger to sweep her off her feet.

'Maybe you're right.' Natalie looked disappointed. 'I'm still worried about you, though. You spent two days in hospital, and now you're staying with your mum under hospital orders.'

'It's only a precaution. I'm absolutely fine. I simply have a bit of a gap in my memory.' Holly said. 'If I'd missed anything urgent, someone would've reminded me about it by now.' She shrugged again. 'I guess we'll just have to put the last few days down as being my "lost weekend".'

'That's the fourth take you've messed up, Harry.' Lucy handed him a mug of coffee. 'Chug this down. It might wake you up a bit so you start playing the right notes in the right order.'

'Sorry.' Harry grimaced. 'I don't know why I'm playing so badly today.'

'You've had a really amazing job offer and you don't know how to tell us that we need to find another cellist to replace you?' she suggested.

'No.'

'What, then?' she asked. 'You haven't been the same since we played on that lake outside Bath.'

No. Because he couldn't quite get Holly out of his

head. Even though he knew it was ridiculous, because she'd stood him up and clearly wasn't interested.

'Harry—have you fallen for someone?'

'That's a bit out of left field,' he said, horrified that he was so transparent.

'So *that's* it. Spill.'

He sighed. Lucy had been one of his best friends for a decade and she knew him too well. If he didn't tell her, she'd nag until he did, so it was easier to give in. 'And it's ridiculous,' he finished. 'She obviously didn't want to see me again or she wouldn't have given me the wrong number.'

'Her battery was flat. Maybe the problem was with your typing,' Lucy pointed out.

'I don't think so.' He gave her a speaking look. 'If I can sight-read a complex score, then surely I'm capable of typing in a phone number.'

'Point taken,' Lucy said dryly. 'I wasn't saying that you were stupid—more that it's easy to accidentally type the wrong number. There must be another way of getting in touch with her.'

'How? I don't even know her last name. I know next to nothing about her; we didn't talk about personal stuff. The organisers of the event can't give me her name because of Data Protection rules.'

'True, but they could pass a message to her. Or you could put a message on social media. It'd go viral because it's the sort of mystery people love solving. I can see it now.' She drew a banner in the air with her hands and intoned, 'Help Harry find his Lady in Red.'

Harry couldn't think of anything more horrific than having his love life plastered all over the media. He'd been there and done that during his divorce, and he had no intention of repeating the experience. 'No, thanks.'

'There might be a good reason why she couldn't meet you,' Lucy said. 'And you said her phone battery was flat, so she didn't have your number. That's why she couldn't ring you.'

'And that's where your theory falls down,' Harry said. 'She knew I was playing at the hall on the Saturday night. If she'd looked up the details of the ball, she could've sent me a message through our website. She hasn't—so she's not interested. She ghosted me. It's not very nice.' It had made him feel horrible. 'But I just have to accept it and move on.'

'Oh, Harry.' Lucy ruffled his hair. 'I know it went wrong with Rochelle, but history isn't going to repeat itself.'

Absolutely—because he wasn't going to let that happen. Ever.

'I'm not being stubborn,' he fibbed. 'It's fine. And please don't do anything to embarrass me on social media, Lucy. I mean it.' He didn't need a relationship. And he'd make the same choice that he made last time: his career, rather than his love life. He knew where he was with music.

'OK, Holls. You know the drill from last year,' Shauna, the nurse at the university clinic, said. 'I ask you if you're pregnant, you tell me that you're not, and then I give you the malaria tablets and off you go on your trip to Egypt.'

Holly smiled. 'OK. I'm n—' She stopped. When had her last period been? She thought back. Two months.

Two months.

'Can being knocked over by a car stop your periods?' she asked. 'Because of shock or something like that?'

'It's possible, but it's not the most likely cause of a missed period.'

No. They both knew what *that* was.

Shauna looked at her. 'How many have you missed?'

'Two.' Holly had been so busy at work, she hadn't really thought about anything else.

'Could you be pregnant?'

She shook her head. Simon had been in America for months before he'd called off their wedding. She hadn't dated anyone since they'd split up. She couldn't even remember the last time she'd actually had sex.

The best way to get over someone is to have a fling. Natalie's advice slid into her head. Along with her own text: I took your advice.

Had she? Had she *really* had a mad fling during her lost weekend, rather than just simply teasing her best friend about it?

She couldn't remember even meeting anyone, let alone having sex with him or using birth control...

'Holly?'

'I don't know,' she said. But it was beginning to look like a possibility.

'Have you had any other early pregnancy symptoms?' Shauna asked. 'Sore boobs, feeling really tired, needing to pee more, feeling sick?'

'I've felt a bit tired, but I'm pretty sure that's because of the accident,' Holly said.

'OK. Have you been sensitive to smells, had any cravings, or had any mood swings?'

Holly shook her head.

'Then go and buy a pregnancy test, just to be sure.'

Shauna smiled at her. 'You're right, and it's probably the stress of the accident that's messed up your cycle, but I'm afraid we do need to make absolutely sure you're not pregnant before we can give you the malaria treatment. Which means you need to take a test—just to tick all the boxes.'

If the test said she was pregnant, that meant no malaria treatment. Which in turn meant no Egypt—and an awful lot to think about.

Holly took a deep breath. 'Go away and come back tomorrow, then?'

Shauna nodded. 'It's probably nothing to worry about. I'll book you in now.'

'OK. Thanks.' Holly walked out of the clinic and headed for the nearest supermarket to buy a pregnancy test.

She hadn't had even the slightest feeling of nausea. Her breasts felt completely normal. She'd put on a couple of pounds, but that was probably because she hadn't been to the gym since the accident. Her final check-up was next week and then life could go on as normal.

Pregnant?

Of course she wasn't.

But the idea niggled away at her. Supposing she *was* pregnant? Supposing she really *had* had a mad fling and they'd been so carried away that they hadn't thought about contraception, or maybe the condom had failed?

Then again, she had friends who'd been trying for months to get pregnant. One night, one baby? It wasn't that probable.

Though it *was* possible…

She took a deep breath, and headed for the toilets to skim-read the instructions.

She peed on the stick, then replaced the cap and stared at the screen. The hourglass symbol flashed to show that the test was working. Holly was sure it wasn't going to be positive, but somehow adrenaline seem to be coursing through her fingers, causing her hands to shake.

The hourglass stopped flashing.

Shockingly, the word 'Pregnant' was displayed on the screen. In bold. Very clear. But the hourglass was still flashing, so maybe it was waiting for the word 'not' to show up.

Holly squeezed her eyes tightly shut, just in case, then peered at the screen again. The word 'Pregnant' was still there, but this time there was some extra text. Not the 'not' she'd been hoping for, but '3+'—meaning that she was more than three weeks pregnant.

So she really *had* had a fling.

And now she was pregnant, with absolutely no idea who the father was and no way of getting in touch with him.

What on earth was she going to do?

She texted her best friend.

Need to meet you for lunch. Urgent.

To her relief, a text came back almost instantly, but dismay flooded through her when she read it.

Shooting today—no time for breaks—can meet you after?

Holly really wanted to talk about it now, but this evening would have to do.

Thanks. Meet you at your office. Let me know what time.

Just gone six?

Great. See you then.

Somehow Holly got through her lecture, and then a pastoral meeting with one of her students who was having a wobble and panicking about Finals. She spent the rest of the afternoon thinking about her situation and making lists of pros and cons; then, at six, she waited in the reception at Natalie's office.

Natalie came out, took one look at her and frowned. 'From the look on your face, gin is required—and lots of it.'

'No.' Gin wouldn't be good for the baby. 'Can we get something to eat?'

'Sure.' Natalie led her to a tucked-away pizzeria. Once they'd ordered, Natalie said, 'Out with it.'

There wasn't an easy way to say this, so Holly got straight to the point. 'It seems I wasn't teasing you and I *did* have a fling.'

Natalie blinked. 'He called you?'

'No.'

'Then how do you know?' She looked hopeful. 'You've got your memory back?'

'Unfortunately not.' Holly took a deep breath. 'I'm pregnant.'

Natalie was silent.

'Say something,' Holly begged.

'I don't know what to say. This was the last thing I expected you to tell me.' Natalie bit her lip. 'Are you all right?'

Holly nodded. 'No symptoms, apart from two missed periods—which I was too busy to notice. Shauna said I needed to do a pregnancy test before she could give me malaria tablets for the dig in Egypt. So I did.' She spread her hands. 'It was positive—which means no malaria tablets, and no Egypt.'

'What are you going to do?' Natalie asked.

'I don't know,' Holly said, trying to damp down the panic. 'I don't have a clue who the father is. I don't remember his name or even what he looked like.'

'Dark hair, blond, red? Blue eyes, grey, brown?'

'No idea,' Holly said.

'If your phone was out of charge,' Natalie said, 'maybe he wrote his number down for you?'

'I looked through my handbag. There was nothing with a phone number on it,' Holly said. It made her feel sick. 'He hasn't tried to ring me, so that proves he wasn't really interested.' She hadn't been enough to make her mystery man want more than a one-night stand.

She pushed her pizza away, no longer hungry. 'It's all I've really been able to think about this afternoon. So I made a list. My options are termination, adoption, or keeping the baby.'

'And have you decided what *you* want?' Natalie asked gently.

'I don't want a termination,' Holly said. 'I know it's mad, given I can't remember a thing about the baby's father. But it's not the baby's fault. And, if I'm honest, I was starting to get a bit broody when Simon left for New York.'

Natalie looked shocked. 'You never said.'

'I was hardly ready to admit it to myself, let alone to anyone else. Though I didn't get pregnant on purpose.'

Holly sighed. 'I'd never judge a woman for having a termination, because I think you should do what's right for *you*. Nobody else has the right to tell you what to do with your own body. But a termination doesn't feel right for me. Neither does adoption.'

'So does that mean you're going to keep the baby?'

Holly bit her lip. 'I was supposed to get married to Simon and then have a baby with him. Except I wasn't enough for Simon.' Or her mystery man.

'Simon is an utter...' Natalie growled a pithy description. 'Of course you were enough. *He* was the one who wasn't good enough for *you*.'

'Thank you.' Though Holly didn't believe her. 'I know it's not going to be easy, being a single mum. But I'll have the support of my family and closest friends. I can juggle childcare with my job, provided I stick to digs within driving distance of home.'

'I want to be the baby's godmother,' Natalie said. 'And you can count on me for babysitting and holding your hand on wobbly days. No matter what.'

Holly scrubbed away the tears that suddenly threatened to fall. 'Thank you.'

'That's what best friends are for,' Natalie said. 'But we need to try and find the baby's father.'

'How? That weekend's still almost a complete blank, and it's terrifying. I know some of what I did because there are photographs. But I don't remember doing any of it.'

'Maybe you could go and see a hypnotist to see if they can recover something?' Natalie suggested. 'Or ask the hall to put a message on their social media.'

'Saying what? "Gentlemen! Did you come to a ball here ten weeks ago and have sex with a woman in a red dress? Because she has some interesting news for you…"' Holly rolled her eyes.

'Well, maybe not quite that,' Natalie said with a grin. 'But how about, "Did you dance with a lady in red at the ball? She needs to get in touch." I bet it'd go viral.' She drew an invisible banner in the air. '"Help the Lady in Red find her mystery man."'

'I don't *want* it to go viral. I don't want to live my life in public,' Holly said. She wrinkled her nose. 'Let's say I gave him my number. It's two months and he hasn't got in touch. Which means he's not interested in me, so he's even less likely to be interested in the baby.'

'It's still worth a try,' Natalie said.

'I can manage on my own,' Holly insisted.

'You know, he must've been really amazing,' Natalie said. 'Because you're not the sort to have a fling for the sake of it.'

'If he was that amazing, surely I'd have remembered *something* about him by now?' Holly pointed out.

'You had a head injury,' Natalie reminded her. 'It might always be your lost weekend.' She paused. 'What about work?'

'The university will be fine about it,' Holly said. 'But I can't go to Egypt this summer. I also won't be able to do any work that involves radiology, because it isn't safe for the baby. I can do lectures, tutorials, and the desk side of things—and maybe the odd bit of work on a UK dig if I clear it with Health and Safety.' She rested her hand on her not-yet-showing bump. 'But hey. Nefertiti here—or Amenhotep—needs to come first.'

'You can't call that poor baby either of those names,' Natalie said, looking horrified.

'Nefertiti was allegedly the most beautiful woman

in the world, even more so than Cleopatra, and Amenhotep III is my favourite pharaoh—the one who made
his country prosperous and built amazing monuments,'
Holly pointed out.

'I thought it was Khufu who built the pyramids?'

'He did,' Holly said with a smile. 'One of them, anyway.'

'All your colleagues are going to call the bump Mini-
Lara or Mini-Indi,' Natalie said.

'And make jokes that instead of studying mummies,
I'm going to *be* a mummy.' Holly swallowed hard.
'Which is weird. It's not quite how I thought things were
going to turn out.'

'You don't have to make all your decisions now,' Natalie said.

'I kind of do. Two missed periods—that means I'm at
least ten weeks gone. I need to see my GP, get booked in
with the midwife, have a scan. And tell my family. And
work. And…' Suddenly, the decision she'd come to that
afternoon felt really, really daunting. Was she up to it?
Would she even make a decent mum?

She must've spoken aloud, because Natalie said
firmly, 'You're going to be brilliant. And you're not
alone. You've got your family, you've got me, and
you've got other friends who'll be there for you, too.
Even though this baby wasn't planned, he or she is going
to be really, really loved.' She grinned. 'And absolutely
not called Nefertiti or Amenhotep…'

CHAPTER FOUR

'So you've got a team doing a dig at the abbey?' Harry asked at Monday lunchtime as his sister parked her car on the gravel in front of the house.

'When we started doing the footings for the Orangery extension, the team discovered bones. Luckily they turned out to be really old ones so it wasn't a crime scene, but obviously the area needs to be excavated and then we'll have the bones reburied in consecrated ground,' Ellen explained. 'The kids are all beyond excited and desperate to help—and the archaeologist in charge is absolutely lovely. She's great with kids. She's let them use brushes to help her team reveal little bits and pieces, and they've all decided they want to be archaeologists when they grow up, even though she's warned them that half the time it means being on your knees and covered in mud and finding nothing but a couple of rusty nails.

'George has been begging her to go to the British Museum with them to see the mummies, and Henry's borrowed a book on hieroglyphics and he's been writing notes to everyone in them. Even Alice and Celia want to dress up as Cleopatra all the time.'

'It sounds as if the kids all have Egypt mania.' Harry smiled. 'Dare I ask if our parents are behaving?'

'Once Pa finished harrumphing about the disruption,' Ellen said, 'Dr Weston got talking to him about the past and she's drawn him sketches of what the abbey might have looked like. And he's eating out of her hand. So is Ma. It's incredible.'

'The main thing is that they're not giving you and Dom any grief.'

'Apart from grumbling about how much money it's costing to extend the Orangery for the tea rooms and shop, no,' Ellen said. 'And Dom pointed out that we'll get extra visitors coming to see the dig. I think the figures have finally made Pa see sense. Any day now, he'll start claiming it was all his idea.'

'That's terrible, Nell.'

Ellen grinned. 'I don't mind. If it means he lets us just get on with things, then he can claim just about anything he pleases.' She tucked her hand into the crook of his arm. 'Come and meet the team. And I can get to show off my brilliant baby brother. Thinking about it, we can use this for you, too. We could shoot a promo video of you playing something haunting among the ruins…'

Harry chuckled. 'Are you planning to give up the biscuit business and become my manager?' he teased. 'Or are you planning it to be a biscuit promo?'

'Now there's an idea. We can rename Bach's cello suite as the Beckett's Custard Cream suite…'

They were still laughing when they rounded the corner and Harry saw the full extent of the trenches cutting across the area around the Orangery. The lawn was a wreck. There was mud everywhere. And then, emerging from a trench, there she was.

His mysterious Lady in Red.

Holly, the woman who had spent the night with him in Bath and then vanished.

It felt as if someone had just punched him in the stomach. Hard.

What on earth was she doing here?

All he could do was stare as his sister said cheerfully, 'Holly, this is my baby brother, Harry Moran. Harry, this is Dr Holly Weston, who's leading the team in the dig.'

There wasn't even a flicker of recognition in Holly's face as she looked at him. 'Good afternoon, Mr Moran. Have you come to see the devastation we've wrought on your parents' garden?'

'I...' This was unbelievable. How could she just stand there and pretend they'd never met? He'd thought they'd had some kind of connection. For pity's sake, they'd spent the night together! Clearly he'd been wrong about there being anything between them. Lucy's theory about a good reason for his mysterious date not meeting him was completely wrong.

The truth was very obvious: Dr Holly Weston was a game-player, and their night together had meant absolutely nothing to her.

It left him reeling. He wasn't sure if he was more hurt or angry. But he sure as hell wasn't going to show it. If this was the way she wanted it, he would pretend she was a stranger, too. He forced himself to smile. 'Nice to meet you, Dr Weston,' he said coolly.

She wiped the dirt off her hand onto her T-shirt and held out her hand to shake his.

And Harry was horrified to realise that his palm was actually tingling when it touched hers. The attraction was still very much there on his part. He remembered

how she'd felt in his arms, and the warmth of her mouth
as it had touched his, and he really wanted to feel that
way again. But he'd just have to suppress the desire, because he didn't want to get involved with a game-player.
No matter if her hair was like ripened corn and her eyes
were an unusual amber colour. His heart had already
been broken, and he wasn't letting that happen again.

Ellen's younger brother was nothing like her or their
older brother, Dominic, Holly thought. There was no
warmth in Harry Moran's smile, only a tightness. Great.
Another member of the Moran family that she would
have to charm. Clearly Harry took after his parents
rather than his siblings when it came to being difficult.

'Harry's quite famous. He's a cellist,' Ellen said,
sounding every inch the proud sister. 'And he's absolutely brilliant.'

So *that* was it. Harry Moran was put out because
Holly hadn't recognised him. Poor little rich boy: tall,
dark and handsome, with those stunning midnight-blue
eyes, he was probably used to women falling at his feet,
all starry-eyed and thrilled to bits to meet him.

Well, tough. She didn't fall at people's feet. Especially someone as difficult and self-important as Harry
Moran seemed to be. Even though he was gorgeous and
her skin had actually tingled when he'd shaken her hand,
she wasn't going to do anything about the attraction. He
was way out of her league, and she wasn't in the market
for a relationship anyway.

'I'm sorry I didn't recognise you,' Holly said politely.
'Nice to meet you, too.'

Why was he looking at her as if he'd seen a ghost?

She was sure they'd never met before. Harry Moran was definitely not the sort of man you'd forget easily.

Sorry she didn't recognise him? Oh, for pity's sake. They'd spent the night together. Had breakfast together. Planned to have a touristy day together... Except then she hadn't turned up.

There wasn't the slightest hint of mockery in her eyes; but there was also no hint of acknowledging the night they'd spent together in Bath. Back then, he'd thought Holly was completely genuine, and his instincts were pretty good. So there had to be another explanation for why she was behaving as if she'd never seen him before in her life.

Did she have some kind of doppelgänger? A twin, perhaps? And, if so, was *this* Holly the good twin or the bad twin? Had he slept with a woman who looked like Holly but had borrowed her name for some reason?

'I'd better get on,' she said brightly. 'Do let me know if you'd like me to talk you through any of the findings, Mr Moran.'

Harry opened his mouth to ask her if she had a twin, but nothing came out. Which was probably just as well, because a question like that was very, very incriminating, and it wasn't something he wanted to discuss in front of his older sister.

'It's really interesting, Harry,' Ellen said, clearly oblivious to the fact that Harry felt as if he'd just been flattened by a steamroller.

'Holly! Holly! I made you a picture.' George, Ellen's eldest child, ran over and handed her a picture of a mummy. 'It's like the one you would've dug up in Egypt.'

'That's brilliant, George.' Holly crouched down beside him, and went through all the things he'd included in the picture. 'You remembered everything we talked about yesterday. Well done.'

'Can I take it to show Henry?'

'Great idea. And Henry might be able to do some hieroglyphics with you to help you label things. Have a think about what you're going to name your mummy,' Holly said. 'Remember what we said about how their names were formed?'

'Yay!' George said, and rushed off.

His sister was absolutely right: Holly Weston was good with kids.

Not that that was an issue for him. He wasn't planning on having a long-term relationship and children after his disaster with Rochelle.

But his nephew had raised an intriguing question. 'Were you meant to be in Egypt?' he asked Holly.

'I was supposed to be on a team working in Egypt over the summer,' she explained. 'For various reasons, someone else in the department needed to swap with me. Though please don't think I'll do a poor job or regard this as a second-rate substitute, because what we're finding here is utterly thrilling.'

'That's good,' Harry said. 'I'd better let you get on. Sorry for holding you up.'

'Pleasure,' she said, and her smile sent an unexpected surge of desire through him.

So inappropriate.

He needed to get a grip.

After a duty visit to his parents—who for once weren't fighting or finding fault with their youngest child—and seeing his brother and sister-in-law, Harry headed back to Ellen's house. He adored his nephew and

niece. Seeing them was always a tiny bit bitter-sweet, because if his own child had lived then he or she would've
been smack in between six-year-old George and four-
year-old Alice. Every so often Harry caught himself
wondering what his son or daughter would have been
like. What his marriage might have been like. He might
even have settled here in the village, so his child would
grow up with cousins, aunts and uncles as a large part
of his or her life...

He shoved the thought away. Not now. Instead, he
played a complicated game about pharaohs, mummies
and camels that George and Alice had made up together,
and after his sister and brother-in-law got back from
work he spent the evening chatting with them.

But he lay awake for a long time that night, thinking
about Holly Weston and wondering what to do about
the situation. The sensible thing would be to ignore it,
to behave as if they were complete strangers. But, at
the same time, Holly drew him more than any woman
he'd met before; despite his common sense warning him
that he didn't do relationships, he couldn't quite let it
go. Maybe if he could get to the bottom of why she was
behaving as if Bath had never happened, he could work
out what to do next.

What he needed was an excuse to talk to her.

'So are the archaeologists staying at the abbey?' he
asked Ellen casually over breakfast.

'No, they're staying at the Beauchamp Arms.'

So he could casually drop into the village pub this
evening for a drink... But that would only work if she
was sitting in the bar. She'd suggested talking through
their finds, so maybe that would be a better start. 'How

long is it likely to be before you can carry on with your Orangery development?'

'The end of the summer,' Ellen said. 'Though that's fine. We're not ready to open yet, and the delay gives us time to finalise the route, the guidebook, the gift shop and the website. If necessary, we can use marquees and make the café a pop-up tea tent until we can extend the Orangery.' She paused. 'I know your quartet is booked up for at least two years in advance, but do you think you'd be able to slot us in for the opening here?'

'I'm sure we can shuffle things round, if the dates don't work for you. But you're wise to plan it now,' he said. 'Let me know and I'll give the others the heads-up so we can pencil it in.'

'Next April?' she suggested. 'I love the sound of the Regency ball you played at. Maybe we can talk Pa into doing something like that at the abbey.'

'We didn't play the actual ball,' he reminded her. 'We were outside on the bandstand in the middle of the lake—and there isn't a lake at the abbey, let alone a bandstand in the middle.' The event where he'd met Holly, and she'd turned his world upside down. 'If you're thinking of holding a dance in the house, that's fine. Just tell me what sort of thing you want and we'll come up with some ideas for a workable playlist. Or if you want music to fireworks outside, overlooking the garden, we know some really good pyrotechnics people who can set it up.'

'Wonderful.' She smiled at him. 'So how long are you planning to stay?'

As long as he could, because he needed to talk to Holly and work out what was going on. 'I'm playing on Friday and Saturday night, so I'll need to head back to London on Friday morning; but I'd love to stay until then, if that's OK with you?'

'Of course it is. It's not often we get to see you.'

'Thanks.' He smiled at her. 'Actually, as you're putting me up, why don't I babysit for you tomorrow night and send you and Tris out for a posh dinner? My treat.'

'That'd be really nice.' She hugged him. 'It's good to have you home.'

'It's good to be back,' he said, meaning it.

After Ellen and Tristan had left for work and to drop off their children at their friends' houses for a play date, Harry headed down to the Orangery, and discovered Holly on her own in a trench. Fate was definitely on his side this morning. 'Good morning,' he said brightly.

Holly looked up at him, and his pulse rate speeded up a notch. Her eyes were incredible. 'Good morning,' she replied.

'Can I get you a cup of coffee or anything?' he asked.

'No, I'm fine with water, but thank you for asking.'

She was being scrupulously polite with him, and he could guess why: he'd been so shocked to see her yesterday that he'd behaved like an idiot. If he explained why, it would be really awkward. He still hadn't quite worked out how to broach the subject of their night together, and he needed to be careful not to alienate her. One thing he was clear about, though: he needed to apologise. 'I'm sorry I was a bit unwelcoming yesterday,' he said.

Her expression gave nothing away. 'It's understandable. We're intruding and our work is making a bit of a mess of the grounds.'

'It's not that. I'm pretty sure I came across as a celebrity whose nose was out of joint at not being recognised,' he said. 'Which isn't who I am. What I do is all

about the music, not about me. I'm incredibly lucky to
be able to do what I love most in the world for a living,
and it's not something I'd ever take for granted. So I
apologise for being bratty.'

She inclined her head in recognition. 'Ellen said you
play the cello.'

'I do, though my taste in music is a little broader than
what we tend to play.'

She gestured to the radio playing at the edge of the
trench. 'I work to old pop songs when I'm on a dig,
though I do like some classical music.'

'We play old pop songs, too.' He took a chance. 'One
of our popular ones is "Don't You Forget About Me".'

Not a flicker. He remembered playing that to her in
Ferdy's flat.

Why wasn't she responding? There must be an obvious reason, but he couldn't work it out.

'Hey, Lara. I brought your banana,' one of her students said, coming up to join them.

'Lara?' Harry asked.

Holly rolled her eyes. 'My students think it's funny
to call me Lara Croft.' She wagged her finger at the
younger man. 'It's Dr Weston to you, Jamal.'

But the smile in her face and the gleam in her eye told
Harry that she was teasing rather than being officious.

'Yeah, yeah—Lara,' Jamal said with a grin. He looked
at Harry. 'Actually, Dr Weston's way better than Lara
Croft. She's a real heroine.'

Holly squirmed. 'I'm perfectly ordinary.'

'You're a heroine,' Jamal repeated. 'Not many people
would do what you did. He looked at Harry. 'A couple
of months ago, she was in Bath.'

So this *was* his Holly, Harry thought, reeling.

'She rescued a little boy from the path of the car, but the car crashed into her, and she hit her head.'

'I'm absolutely fine,' Holly said, 'and I can assure you that I'll be absolutely meticulous about leading this dig.' She wrinkled her nose. 'The only real problem the accident caused was that I lost about a week's worth of memories.'

'You lost about a week's worth of memories,' Harry repeated, trying to take it in.

'Retrograde amnesia. It's when you lose memories from before your accident or traumatic event. It's the most recent memories that are generally a problem. I don't remember the accident, but from what I've been told I was lucky to get away with nothing more serious than a bit of bruising and memory loss,' Holly said.

The penny dropped.

If she'd been hit by the car when she'd been on the way to meet him, that explained why she hadn't turned up. It also explained why she hadn't got in touch with him that morning: she must've been in hospital, plus she hadn't had his phone number.

This was the missing piece of the puzzle. If Holly had lost a week's worth of memories before the accident, that would include the memory of meeting him. Which was a perfectly reasonable explanation for why she'd acted just now if she'd never met him before, and also for why she hadn't tried to find him via the hall and the string quartet's website. How could she try to find him if she couldn't remember him?

Relief flooded through him. So his instincts hadn't been wrong after all. Holly Weston *wasn't* a game-player; she simply had no memory of even meeting him, let alone spending the night with him.

'That's a pretty amazing thing to do, to rescue a child from the path of a car,' he said.

She shrugged it off. 'It's what anyone would've done. Anyway, I'm assuming you came here as there was something you wanted?'

'Yes—you offered to talk me through your findings yesterday, and I wondered when would be a good time for you?' he asked.

'I could do it now,' she began, but Jamal put a hand on her arm.

'Doc, I nearly forgot—Ricky needs you to come and check something.'

'OK. Later, then?' she said to Harry with a smile.

This was the perfect opportunity to get to know her again—and for her to get to know him. 'How about I bring us lunch?' he suggested.

'A sandwich would be nice. Thank you,' she said.

'See you here at one?'

'One,' she agreed. 'Sorry to be rude and rush off.'

He raised both hands. 'You're working and I'm interrupting. No apologies needed.'

He called into the deli and bakery at the village for picnic supplies, then headed back to Ellen's and spent the rest of the morning on his laptop, researching retrograde amnesia.

Amnesia actually seemed to be quite common after a head injury. Either it was retrograde, when the person couldn't remember the past, or anterograde, when the person had trouble forming a new memory. And Harry found the whole subject of memory itself fascinating, particularly when he clicked on an article about music and memory. It told him which areas of the brain lit up while someone listened to music, and how they were the same areas that involved memory. Studies showed that playing music helped people to remember things, and could spark memories even in people who had a brain injury.

So could he perhaps jog Holly's memory with music?

The evidence said that people who used songs and music while studying found it easier to remember things, such as the 'ABC' song helping people work out the position of a letter in the alphabet. So maybe if he played something from the set he and the quartet had played at the lake, Holly might remember meeting him. If he played one of the pieces he'd played to her in Ferdy's apartment, would it give her a flashback to the night they'd spent together?

He could try.

The next thing he needed to work out was how he could play something for her. He could hardly just turn up next to her trench and start playing his cello as she worked. She'd think he was either a maniac or a stalker.

He'd start with getting to know her a little better—or, rather, letting her get to know him again. And then perhaps together they could find a way forward.

Holly spent the rest of the morning feeling weirdly fluttery. And it was all because of Harry Moran. There was definitely something about him, and it felt as if she already knew him—which was ridiculous. She'd never met him before. And the attraction was so inappropriate. Nobody here at the abbey apart from her own team knew about the baby; but she couldn't possibly start thinking this way about one man when she was pregnant by a man she couldn't even remember. This was much too complicated.

Her heart actually skipped a beat when he came to her trench at one o'clock precisely, carrying a proper wicker picnic basket and a tartan rug. If she'd offered to bring someone a sandwich for a lunch meeting, it would've been a prepacked sandwich from the nearest supermarket; but, then, Harry Moran was the son of a viscount, so of course he'd go beyond that.

'Hi,' he said, looking faintly flustered.

Did he feel this weird spark of attraction, too? Her heart skipped another beat before her common sense kicked in. She was a scruffy archaeologist. She hadn't been enough for Simon, and she certainly wouldn't be enough for a famous cellist from a very posh family. 'Hi,' she said, and her voice actually squeaked. How pathetic was that? She sneaked a glance; either he hadn't noticed or he was in a similar state to her, because he didn't look as if he was laughing at her. 'That looks very nice—and a bit impressive.'

He winced. 'Sorry. I didn't mean to go over the top. It's just how...'

How people in his world did things. 'It's lovely,' she said. 'Thank you.'

She helped him spread out the tartan rug, and when her hands accidentally touched his she felt a zing like an electric shock. Oh, help. Right now, she was way out of her depth.

The wicker hamper contained china, proper cutlery and two glasses, plus a sourdough loaf, Brie—her favourite, though right now she couldn't eat it—a bowl of tiny plum tomatoes still on the vine, sliced chicken and watercress.

'This looks fabulous. I feel very spoiled,' she said.

'Pleasure.' He looked pleased, she noticed. 'I wasn't

sure whether you'd prefer wine or something soft, so I brought both.' He indicated the two bottles in the hamper.

'I'm working,' she said, glad of the excuse, 'so elderflower cordial is perfect.'

He clearly noticed that she didn't touch the Brie. 'Sorry. I should've thought to buy cheddar as well.'

Not wanting to explain that pregnant women shouldn't eat Brie, she said, 'Chicken, tomato and watercress is the best sandwich in the world. And this is one of the nicest picnics I've ever had.'

'I brought lemon drizzle cake as well,' he said.

'Oh, now you can *definitely* visit again,' she said with a grin. 'It's my favourite.'

This was so strange. Part of her was flustered by him, but part of her felt at ease with him, as if she'd known him for a while. 'Have we...?' she began, then stopped. There was no reason why their paths should have crossed before.

'Have we what?' he asked.

She shook her head. 'Ignore me. It just feels as if I know you. It's probably because I can see the resemblance between you, Dominic and Ellen.'

'Probably,' he agreed, though there was something in his expression she couldn't quite read.

'Well, I need to earn my lunch,' she said. 'I'm supposed to be telling you about the dig.'

'I know you've probably already explained this several times to different members of my family, but I'd love to know what you've uncovered about the abbey so far, he said. 'I always imagined the monks chanting plainsong, except none of us really know where the church once was.'

This was a safe subject. And if she concentrated on work she could push that swell of attraction to the back of her mind. 'Benedictine monasteries tend to be built to the same kind of layout. They had the church to the north, and they built the cloisters and the garth—that's the garden in the middle of the cloisters—on the south side of the church. The chapter house and dormitories would be on the east of the cloisters, the dining room and kitchen to the south, and the accommodation for visitors and the infirm to the west.' She grabbed her notepad and drew him a quick sketch.

'So where am I standing at the moment?'

'The west end of the church,' she said. 'Your house is roughly on the site of the chapter house, where they had meetings, and the living quarters of the monks.' She gestured to the building. 'I'm guessing there would be signs of the original building in the cellars, because the house obviously dates from after the Reformation. The cloisters run around the edge of the lawn, and the dining room and kitchen would be opposite us.' She gestured to the wall to their right. 'Your walled garden—a lot of the material was probably taken from the original west range.'

Holly Weston really knew what she was talking about. And her work was clearly her passion; she was lit up from the inside out as she talked to him, Harry thought.

Just like the gorgeous woman he'd met wearing a Regency dress.

And to think he'd asked her back then if she'd ever visited the Roman Baths. As an archaeologist, she'd probably done more than just visit the place; she'd probably studied the site. If she ever got her memory back, he rather hoped that little bit of embarrassment would stay quietly forgotten.

'That,' he said, 'is amazing.'

She looked pleased. 'You could've found any of that information on the Internet.'

'It's not the same as actually hearing it from someone who knows their subject. Someone who's passionate about their subject.'

She'd seemed almost on the cusp of getting her memory back when she'd started to ask if they knew each other. He should perhaps have told her then; but it hadn't felt like the right moment.

He couldn't think of a way to get back to the subject of her memory loss, when she said, 'It's a real thrill to be part of this. To put a story back together. To find things that haven't been seen for centuries.' She looked at him. 'Is it like that with what you do?'

He nodded. 'We're telling a story and painting pictures for the audience, pretty much interpreting what the composer felt when he or she wrote the music.' And this was perhaps his cue. 'Maybe I could play for you some time and show you what I mean.'

She looked wary. 'Maybe.'

Was she wary because she was single and thought he might be hitting on her, or because there was someone else in her life? But asking her directly felt too awkward. He needed to regroup. 'Cake,' he said, clearing away the remains of their picnic, 'and then I'd better get out of your hair. Though maybe I could drop in and be nosy again tomorrow?'

'I'd like that,' she said.

CHAPTER FIVE

THE NEXT DAY, Harry called in to the estate office to see his brother. 'I'm babysitting tonight for Nell and Tris,' he said, 'so how about tomorrow night I babysit for you and Sal and send you out to dinner? My treat. It means I get time to play with Henry and Celia, and I'll cook pizza for the three of us so you don't have to worry about feeding them before you go out.'

'That would be great,' Dominic said. 'How do I talk you into coming to stay more often?'

'I'll make more of an effort,' Harry said, meaning it. 'I'm just glad that you and Ellen both have your own houses rather than living in a wing at the abbey, so I don't have to stay *there*.'

'Actually, the parents have been a lot better since the dig started,' Dominic said.

'You mean they have to play nice in public,' Harry said with a wry smile, knowing that his parents were good at putting on a united front outside the family. 'So is it a huge disruption, having the dig here?'

'No. The archaeologists are a nice lot,' Dominic said. 'They work all hours, though.'

'They probably have to make the most of the good

weather,' Harry suggested, remembering what Holly had said the previous day.

'They put up a tarpaulin when it rains,' Dominic said. 'Holly's lovely, but she's as much of a workaholic as you are.'

Something else they had in common. And then he had a brilliant idea: the perfect way to get to know her but make her feel safe with him. 'Dom, can I ask someone to have supper with me and the kids tomorrow?' he asked.

Dominic looked surprised. 'Sure. Do we get to meet her?'

'It's not *that* sort of supper.' Which was only half the truth. 'I want to know more about the dig, but it isn't fair to stop the team working so they can talk to me. I was thinking about asking Dr Weston to have supper with us and tell me all about the dig at the same time.'

'Good idea,' Dominic said.

'Thanks. I'll go and have a quick word with her now.' He smiled.

'And you'll show your face in the house?' Dominic asked pointedly.

'So Pa can tell me yet again that I'm a wastrel and I don't contribute to the estate in the slightest?' Harry rolled his eyes. 'Which means I'll end up playing angry music all afternoon to get it out of my system.'

'The one that sounds like a wasp?'

'Bumblebee,' Harry corrected with a grin, knowing that his brother meant the Rimsky-Korsakov piece. The one Rochelle had played a lot on the flute as her audition piece, though weirdly playing it on the cello didn't bring back memories of his ex-wife. The speed of the piece always helped him to work out a bad mood. 'Yeah, that would do it. Fast and cross. A minute and a half. And then some Radiohead.'

Dominic grinned back. 'You mean the stuff the rest of the quartet won't let you play in public but I really like?'

'Yup. Stella says I'm just showing off, playing the cello like a guitar, but I love the music.'

'I'm almost tempted to skive off today, just to listen. I don't get to hear you play anywhere near as often as I'd like,' Dominic said.

Harry clapped his shoulder. 'All right. I promise I'll see the parents before I go. And I'll bring my cello with me tomorrow night and play whatever you want before you and Sal go out. Catch you later.'

He went out across the lawn to the dig site. Holly was working in a trench; as he drew nearer, he realised that she was humming along to something on the radio. Better still, it was a piece he knew—and it gave him the perfect opening to try jogging her memory. '*West Side Story* fan?' he asked.

She looked up and smiled. 'Absolutely. Apart from George Chakiris being impossibly gorgeous, how can anyone resist a song as lovely as "Somewhere"?'

'It's beautiful,' he said. 'So you're a fan of musicals?'

'Absolutely. I go to shows with my best friend as often as I can,' she said with a smile.

Just what he'd hoped she'd say. 'How about *Chitty Chitty Bang Bang*?'

Something flickered in the back of Holly's head. Not quite a memory or a feeling, but *something*. She couldn't quite put her finger on it. Maybe it was something she'd heard on the radio recently without really being aware of it. 'I think everyone knows the title song,' she said, and hummed it.

'"Hushabye Mountain" is my favourite piece from the film,' Harry said. 'Arranged for the cello.'

She frowned. 'I don't remember that one.'

'Maybe I can play it for you sometime,' he said.

Was he flirting with her? Her breath caught. She was starting to like the man she was getting to know. More than like: he really drew her. In other circumstances, she would've been really tempted to flirt back. But she had the baby to think about; besides, she'd already made the mistake of punching above her weight before with Simon. Harry was even more good looking than her ex. What on earth would he see in someone as ordinary as her? If she hadn't been good enough for Simon, she certainly wouldn't be good enough for Harry Moran.

Maybe she should tell him that her partner was coming down to see her tomorrow, to make him back off to a safe distance. Then again, if one of her team overheard, they'd be daft enough to start grilling her about her fake boyfriend, and then that would expose the lie to Harry, making her feel even more stupid.

Before she could make up an excuse, he said, 'Actually, I'm babysitting Henry and Celia for Dom and Sal tomorrow evening, and I promised to play something for Dom before they go out so I'll have my cello with me. If you're not busy tomorrow night and you'd like to join the kids and me for pizza, I'll play something for you after they've gone to bed, and in return perhaps you'll let me grill you a bit more about the dig.'

* * *

Holly was silent for so long that he thought she was going to refuse.

And then she smiled. It lit up her whole face, to the point where he felt his pulse start to leap. Oh, help. This was dangerous. She wasn't like Rochelle; he knew that. But he'd lost faith in his own judgement where relationships were concerned. Maybe he was being an idiot, seeking Holly out like this. Or maybe this was his chance to see if she could help fill the gap in his life that he'd been ignoring but which was becoming more and more obvious. 'All right. I'd like that. I'll bring pudding. What do you suggest?'

'Strawberries,' he said promptly. 'Because there's nothing better.' Would she remember that he'd given her strawberries for breakfast?

Apparently not, because there wasn't the slightest flicker of recognition in her face. 'Strawberries are fine by me,' she said.

'Great. The kids eat early, so shall we say half-past five tomorrow?' he asked.

'That'd be great.' Funny how the light in her eyes made the world feel suddenly bright.

'Good. I'll see you tomorrow,' he said.

Harry thoroughly enjoyed babysitting George and Alice that evening. He read them stories, he listened to them play what they'd been learning at their piano lessons, he played bits for them on the cello, and he taught them to do a round, playing 'Three Blind Mice' with them on the piano and himself on the cello. All the kind of things he'd once thought to do with his own child, but which he could still enjoy them with his nieces and nephews.

When they were finally asleep, Harry curled up in a chair and listened to music, a mug of peppermint tea by his side. Funny how his sister's house felt so much more of a home than his London flat did. There were photographs everywhere, well-loved books on the shelves, and a huge toy chest.

Despite their own upbringing, his sister was a brilliant mother, always having time for her children. His brother was the same. Harry had hoped to be like them when he'd come to terms with Rochelle's shock news about her pregnancy. Of course he'd done the right thing and married her. Except it had been the wrong thing.

How much of the break-up had been his fault?

It wasn't anyone's fault that she'd lost the baby. But he hadn't been there enough for her. He'd focused on his career, even though he'd known that cellists had a lot more openings than flautists. He should've made more compromises, let someone else take over from him in the quartet, and maybe taught instead of touring. Especially after the miscarriage, when he should have been there. You could replace a colleague a lot more easily than you could replace a partner.

But then, after that last fight, when Rochelle had told him that she'd got pregnant on purpose, and when he'd thought about her trying to persuade him to do less with his music and more with his family... Then he'd realised that she'd never really seen him for himself or loved him for himself. She'd wanted to be part of the aristocratic circles his family moved in, and when her career had stalled she'd been resentful that his was taking off. She'd wanted him to give up his music and work with his brother on the family estate.

Which wasn't what Harry had wanted at all. She'd

given him an ultimatum: his music or her. And Harry, completely disillusioned, had walked away.

Since his divorce, Harry had thrown himself into his music—the real love of his life—and he'd been lucky enough to be in the right place at the right time and able to take those opportunities.

Yet sometimes when he woke in the middle of the night, he felt that there was something missing. He could see how much happiness his siblings had found with their partners and children. Given Rochelle's revelation, the chances were that even if they hadn't lost the baby their marriage wouldn't have lasted. But still he wondered. Would he ever find someone who he could make happy and would make him happy, too?

Given that he hadn't been able to make a marriage work with someone who'd known him since he was eighteen—even though he realised with hindsight she hadn't really loved him—it seemed crazy to think that he could base any kind of future on something that had been literally a one-night stand. If Holly hadn't been in that accident, and they'd met up as planned, they might have had a chance to see where their relationship could go; and that might well have been a dead-end. A musician's life could be too peripatetic for a relationship to work.

On the other hand, he hadn't been able to get Holly out of his head, and he'd never felt like that about anyone else he'd ever met. Not even his ex-wife.

And then there was Holly's amnesia.

She only knew part of the truth. How would she react when he told her that he was part of the memories she'd lost? Would she back away? Would she be prepared to take a risk with him, especially as he didn't have a great track record with relationships? Would she think he was being creepy, or would she understand why he had held back from telling her the truth before now?

The thoughts went round and round in his head, and he just couldn't find a solution.

Harry couldn't settle to much on Thursday. And then finally it was time for him to go to Dominic and Sally's to babysit his niece and nephew. He'd bought pizza and salad earlier, as well as flowers for his sister-in-law.

'You really didn't need to, but thanks—they're gorgeous,' Sally said, kissing his cheek. 'Now, you know our number if—'

'—anything goes wrong. Which it won't,' he said firmly. 'Henry, Celia and I have plans. Which involves scoffing lots of pizza, playing lots of games, and a bit of music.'

'So Dom and I miss out on the music? That's so unfair.'

Harry smiled. 'That's why I came early. I promised Dom. I'll play something before you go. Your choice.'

'The bumblebee!' Henry shouted gleefully.

'You can choose something later,' Harry told his nephew. 'This one is all for your mum.'

'You know what I'm going to ask for,' Sally said.

Of course he did: the song he'd played in the church as she'd walked down the aisle to his brother. 'It's better as a duet so I have the lovely piano intro,' he pointed out.

'I don't care. I'll just pretend I can hear the piano,' she said with a grin.

He took his cello from its case, checked the tuning, and launched into Bryan Adams's 'Everything I Do (I Do it for You)'.

Dominic came downstairs and wrapped his arms

around his wife. 'This brings back memories. The best day of my life.'

'My joint favourite gig,' Harry said. 'Playing at your wedding and Nell and Tris's—it doesn't get any better than that.'

'You've played at the Royal Albert Hall. Surely that has to be the best?' Sally asked.

'No. Family all the way,' Harry said. He was beginning to realise how important family was to him, his parents excepted. 'Now go and have fun. Your children and I have plans.'

'Play some more, Uncle Harry. *Please*,' Celia begged.

'I will. After supper,' he said. 'But first we have games...'

They were halfway through a very rowdy board game when Holly arrived.

'Can I get you a cup of tea or something cold?' Harry asked.

'I'm fine,' she said, and her smile was so sweet that his heart actually skipped a beat. 'I brought strawberries and some ice cream. I hope that's OK?'

'It's perfect. Thank you.'

'Holly! Come and play with us,' Henry said, taking Holly's hand.

Once the game was finished, Harry said, 'I'm going to put the pizza on. Supper's in ten minutes. Celia, Henry, can you put the game away, wash your hands and lay the table for me, please?'

'Yes, Uncle Harry,' they chorused.

Harry Moran was completely different from the man she'd thought he was when they'd first met, Holly thought. Tonight he was smiling and relaxed, very much a hands-on uncle. And he was really good with the children.

It felt like being part of the family, with the children chattering and Harry encouraging them. For a second, Holly could almost imagine that this was how her future would be—a future she'd thought to have with Simon when she'd looked after her nephew and niece as a trial run for parenthood...

She pushed the thought away. Nothing could happen between her and Harry. She was pregnant with another man's baby; she didn't even know who the father was and she had no way of finding out. What man would want to take on that kind of complication?

Besides, he'd asked her here so she could tell him more about the dig.

He'd made it very clear that she was safe with him. This wasn't a date.

Though it was hard not to feel as if it was. His smile had made her heart feel as if it had done an anatomically impossible backflip.

Everything was fine until they sat down to eat. But Harry had made garlic bread, and the scent set off her nausea. She tried really hard to breathe shallowly so she couldn't smell the garlic, but it didn't work.

'I'm so sorry. Can you excuse me for a second, please?' she asked, and fled to the back door for fresh air.

Harry appeared beside her a few moments later. 'Are you all right?' he asked, looking concerned.

There was nothing for it. She was going to have to admit it. 'Just a touch of morning sickness. I thought I'd got away with it, but mine decided to start at ten weeks.' And she was sure it was psychosomatic: it had started on the very day she'd done the pregnancy test. 'I thought morning sickness was meant to stop at twelve weeks, but mine hasn't. It's just certain smells.' She grimaced. 'Normally I love garlic bread, but right now it doesn't love me.'

'Let me get you some water,' Harry said.

'But the children—'

'—are fine,' he said. 'Hopefully they'll have scoffed the garlic bread by the time you feel ready to go back in, but if they haven't I'll get rid of it.'

His kindness made her want to cry. It also made her feel sad, because now he knew about the baby the flirting would stop; anything else would be too complicated.

Holly was pregnant?

Harry's mind was in a whirl as he filled a glass with water. He'd thought he'd felt shocked enough by seeing her again, but finding out that she was pregnant… That was a huge thing. Really huge. So huge he couldn't think straight.

Just how pregnant was she? Her top was loose enough to hide any sign of a bump.

He counted backwards in his head. It was three months since they'd spent the night together, and Holly had just said she was still having morning sickness after twelve weeks.

So was the baby his?

The ground felt as if it had shifted under his feet—just as it had six years ago.

'Harry, I'm pregnant.' Rochelle's face, full of worry and panic.

The announcement had happened at the worst possible time for him, when the quartet had just been starting to take off and they'd had a massive tour booked. He couldn't possibly let his colleagues—his best friends—down by calling it all off.

Wanting to reassure Rochelle that he loved her and he'd do the right thing by her, he'd married her a month later. But he'd still gone on the tour, promising her that they'd have their honeymoon later. Looking back, he knew it really hadn't been the right way to start a marriage, but he'd been young and a bit clueless and so torn. If he'd let the quartet down, he would never have been able to forgive himself as they'd all worked so hard and they deserved their success.

If he'd stayed in London with Rochelle, and taught instead of playing, he knew he would probably have resented her for holding him back. He'd promised to come home at every opportunity; and he'd called Rochelle every single day. He'd sent her flowers and treats he'd thought she'd like. He'd tried to make *everything* work.

Then, two weeks after he'd left for the tour, the real nightmare had begun…

He shook himself. No. That had been then. This was now.

He knew he'd used contraception; he would never have been so reckless as to ignore that. This wasn't a repeat of the situation with Rochelle. He and Holly had never met before, and nobody would deliberately try to get pregnant by a complete stranger.

Another memory from that night flickered back. Holly been very careful to check that he was single, and he'd assumed that she was, too. Maybe his assumption had been wrong. Could she really have slept with him, knowing that she was already pregnant by another man?

Yet he was sure the woman he'd met in Bath wasn't like that. The woman he was getting to know all over again was lovely. Warm and sweet.

Then again, Rochelle had also been warm and sweet when they'd been students and after they'd started dating and moved in together. It had started out so well. But, oh, how quickly their love had turned sour.

Cross with himself, because she was his guest and he should be looking after her better instead of brooding, he handed her the glass of water, and waited for her to take a couple of sips. 'Better?' he asked.

She nodded. 'Thank you. I'm sorry.'

'Not a problem,' he said, wanting to reassure her. 'So you're through the first trimester?'

'Yes, I'm about fourteen weeks,' she said.

So the baby *had* to be his.

But knowing how complicated relationships could be, and wary from his experience with Rochelle, he couldn't help saying, 'Your partner must worry about you while you're working away.'

Her face shuttered. 'He isn't around.'

Meaning either the man had let her down—or he really was the father. It really wouldn't be tactful to probe any more right now. Besides, how exactly was he going to say to her, 'Hey, you don't remember me, but I'm very probably the father of your baby'? Especially when the children might come in and overhear. He was going to have to take this carefully. Tactfully. 'I'm sorry. I didn't mean to pry.'

'I know. I'm sorry. I didn't mean to snap.'

'Let me deal with the dining table, and then come back with us,' he said.

Thankfully the children *had* scoffed all the garlic bread, and he was able to call Holly back to the table to finish her pizza and salad.

'Now will you play for us, Uncle Harry?' Henry asked when supper was over. 'Please?'

'Do you mind?' Harry asked, looking at Holly.

'It would be lovely,' she said.

'Clear the table for me, please, guys. I'll sort out the dishwasher later,' Harry directed, and went to wash his hands.

Holly helped the children, and when they went back to the dining room Harry had moved a chair next to the piano.

'Yesterday, George and Alice showed me what they were learning at piano lessons first, and then we played a bit together,' he said. 'Shall we do that?'

The children agreed enthusiastically. Celia played 'Who Said Mice?' from *Cats*, and Harry played 'The March of the Lion' from *The Carnival of Animals*.

Both Holly and Harry clapped loudly.

'Uncle Harry plays the really famous one from *The Carnival of Animals*,' Henry said.

'Oh, please play that one! I love it,' Celia said imploringly.

Harry spread his hands. 'All right, guys. Here we go.'

Holly was totally transfixed when he played 'The Swan', and the piece actually moved her to tears.

'Don't cry, Holly!' Celia fetched her a box of tissues.

'Thank you.' She took the tissues gratefully. 'That was so beautiful. Sorry for being wet.'

'That piece makes a lot of people cry,' Harry said.

There was something intense and searching in the way he looked at her, but Holly couldn't work out what he was looking for. She also couldn't work out why she felt something so familiar about the situation. Nobody had ever played a cello for her in a family home, she was sure. What was she half remembering?

'Let's do something a bit more upbeat,' Harry said. 'Celia, this is what I want you to play for four bars, and repeat.' He showed her, then let her play the four bars until he was happy that she was comfortable with the piece. 'Brilliant. Henry, this is your bit.' He played the melody, and let Henry practise that. 'Right. Let's do it together. And what do we do if we mess up a note?'

'Smile and keep going,' the children chorused.

'Excellent.' He winked at them, counted them in, and together they played 'Heart and Soul'.

'That was wonderful,' Holly said.

Harry gave her a speculative look. 'Do you play the piano, by any chance?'

'No,' she said.

'Then we'll teach you,' he said. 'We're going to play a round. Something everyone knows. "Frère Jacques".'

'But—' she began.

'It's easy, Holly,' Celia said. 'And it's fun.'

'We'll have the three of you at the piano. Henry at the bottom, Celia at the top, and Holly in the middle. Or,' he said, 'if you'd rather sing than play, Holly?'

'No, I'll have a go at the piano,' she said, very aware of the expectant looks of the children. 'And if I miss a note…'

'Smile and keep going,' the children chorused.

She sat in the middle of the piano stool and Harry showed her the note pattern, breaking it down into man-

ageable chunks for her and correcting her gently so she
played the notes with the right fingers. He was kind, she
noticed, and gentle. Qualities she really valued. And it
made her blink back unexpected tears.

'Are we ready for this? Celia first, then Holly, then
Henry, then me,' Harry directed.

And then, before she knew it, the children were sitting either side of her and she was playing the round
with Harry and the children.

'That was amazing,' she said when they'd finished.
Totally absorbing. She could understand why Harry
loved what he did.

'Do you want to hear how amazing?' Harry waved
his phone at her.

'You recorded it?' she asked, shocked.

'Yup.' He smiled, and played the piece back.

To her surprise, all the notes were in the right places—
including hers. 'Nobody in my family has ever played an
instrument. This is…' She shook her head in disbelief.

Harry Moran was amazing. And he was brilliant with
children. It made her wonder why he wasn't married
with children of his own—though that was a question
she couldn't ask. It was way too rude and intrusive. Not
to mention being none of her business.

'More, please!' Henry begged.

Harry looked at his watch. 'One more. Then it's bedtime, or your mum and dad won't let me do this again.'

'Will you play "The Bumblebee"?' Henry asked.

'That's a bit excitable. I was looking for something
calming.'

Henry looked devastated. 'But you said earlier you'd
play it for me.'

'I know,' Celia said. '"The Bumblebee" is really short,

so if you do that first you'll have time to do another little one. The one I really like. "Sis..."' Her face screwed up in concentration as she tried to remember the name of the piece, and then she shook her head and hummed it.

'"Sicilienne",' Harry said, getting her to repeat the word, then he effortlessly zoomed through 'The Flight of the Bumblebee' for Henry before slowing down for Fauré's 'Sicilienne'.

'Now, bed. Or else I will be toast!'

'With jam!' Henry said, and squealed with delight as Harry chased him out of the room.

Harry returned just long enough to apologise to Holly. 'Do you mind if I read them just one chapter of Harry Potter?'

'Actually, I'd be happy to read the story, if you like,' she said. 'I do that with my niece and nephew.'

'Thank you. Then I'll sort out the dishwasher while you do that,' he said.

She was halfway through reading the chapter when Harry came up to join her. When she'd finished the chapter and Harry had kissed the children goodnight, they headed downstairs.

'You were very good with them,' he said. 'I think you'll be an amazing mum.'

There was something wistful in his expression. So did he have kids he didn't see, or did he perhaps want kids but couldn't have them and so he'd thrown himself into his music?

'Thank you. I hope that getting in some practice as an aunt will help,' she said lightly.

'I'm sure it will.'

She almost told him about her lost weekend, but she didn't want to risk spoiling things. Right now she felt safe with Harry. Cosseted. Valued, too. The way he looked at her... He made her feel attractive, something she wasn't used to, and she liked that feeling. Even though she knew it was wrong and it was selfish, she wanted more.

'Let me make us some tea, and then you can tell me all about the dig,' he said.

He made the tea just how she liked it—clearly, as a musician who played pieces without a score in front of him, he must have a good memory—and they settled in the living room at opposite ends of the sofa. She took him through what they'd found so far, and what she expected to find, and how they organised the work and catalogued the finds. And he did actually seem interested, asking questions every so often.

It was really easy to relax with Harry. She didn't know him very well, but she really liked what she'd seen of him so far. Plus he was gorgeous, even in jeans and a casual T-shirt; when he was dressed formally for work, no doubt all the women in the audience sighed over him.

Dressed maybe in historical costume: white pantaloons, a white shirt and cravat, a cream silk waistcoat and a navy tailcoat...

Where on earth had that come from?

She shook herself. How ridiculous.

'So what made you become an archaeologist?' he asked.

'My parents took me to the British Museum to see the mummies. And then there was an exhibition about Roman treasure—it was seeing the mosaic floors that thrilled me most,' she said. 'There was one with a peacock, and I just couldn't believe that someone had spent ages putting all those tiny tiles together to make a picture. And how amazing it must've been to discover it, to be the first person who'd seen it for centuries. From then on, I knew what I wanted to do.' She paused. 'Was it like that for you with music?'

'Granny Beckett—my mother's mother—played the piano,' he said. 'As soon as I could sit up, I used to point to the piano. She would let me sit on her lap and press the keys, and I loved it.' He smiled. 'Most kids like to watch cartoons and what have you, but I liked listening to music more than anything else in the world. I didn't care whether it was a recording or live. Granny Beckett had lots of Jacqueline du Pré records and she put one on. I was tiny—I must've been about five—and I was just transfixed when I heard du Pré playing the cello. Granny Beckett had a friend who taught the cello, and she came round one afternoon with a child-sized one so I could try it out. And that was it. The second I moved the bow across the strings, I'd found what I was born to do. I've never looked back.'

'Your grandmother sounds like a really special woman,' Holly said, seeing the way his face lit up as he talked about her.

'She was,' Harry agreed. 'If it wasn't for her, I would probably have ended up in the family business, hating every second of it. But she pointed out that Dom would always be the heir, Nell was the one with the head for business who'd do well in the biscuit business, and I had a gift so I should be allowed to bring people the joy of music.' He smiled. 'It's one of the reasons why I like playing joint pieces with the kids. I loved doing duets with Granny Beckett, and the kids like doing the same thing with me.'

'Do you think any of them will end up following in your footsteps?' she asked.

'Maybe Henry. He's got a real feel for the piano. And even though he's the oldest and he'll eventually take over from Dominic, I know Dom would let Henry follow his dreams without any fights.'

Which told her that there had been a few fights with Harry's parents over his choice of career. 'I'm glad your grandmother supported you,' she said. 'I loved what you played earlier.'

'Thank you. I'm so grateful that I've been able to do what I love most in the world for a living,' he said. 'And I was privileged to play both my sister and my sister-in-law down the aisle on their wedding days.'

'Would you play something for me, or will it wake Henry and Celia?' she asked.

'It's fine. What would you like?'

'You mentioned a piece of music to me the other day.'

'"Hushabye Mountain".' His midnight-blue eyes were almost black. 'OK.'

They went back into the dining room. He gestured to her to have a seat; then he moved a chair, sat down and checked the cello's tuning before he began to play.

The music was beautiful, and Holly closed her eyes, letting the sounds draw pictures in her head. It was slow and sweet and soothing; yet at the same time it made her tingle. As if it was a prelude to something. Weirdly she was filled with the sensation of déjà vu, though she didn't understand why. Where on earth could she have heard this before? And why was it making her feel breathless and tingly? Was it the music, or was it something else? 'That's incredibly beautiful,' she said.

'It's really popular on the quartet's set list,' he said.

He looked slightly sad, and she had no idea why, though she didn't want to be rude and ask.

'So you play at lots of different places?' she asked instead.

'Weddings, stately homes—we sometimes work with a company that does fireworks—and corporate events. We'll play pretty much any event, and we have a decent repertoire,' he said. 'Though my colleagues are more on the traditional side, and they get a bit cross with me when I mess about with radical arrangements.'

'What do you mean, radical?'

'Playing the cello like a guitar instead of with a bow,' he said.

'I don't get it,' she said.

'Neither,' he said with a sigh, 'do they.'

'No, I mean I don't get why they don't like it. Alan Rickman does it in *Truly Madly Deeply*, and it's one of my favourite film clips ever.'

'I know the one.' He looked at her. 'Do you know the words to that song?'

'Not all of them,' she admitted.

'Give me a sec.' He took his phone from his pocket, looked something up, and handed it to her. 'Here are the lyrics. Let's do it.' Then he picked up the cello and started to pluck the introduction to the song. It was just like the film. And all of a sudden Holly felt weak at the knees. This gorgeous, gorgeous man wanted to play a duet with her, mimicking one of the most romantic films she'd ever seen.

Her voice was a bit shaky at first as she began to sing 'The Sun Ain't Gonna Shine Any More', but grew stronger as he joined in. Even though he was a professional musician, he wasn't judging her or pointing out where she sang flat. He was singing with her, seeming to enjoy it as much as she was. This was *fun*.

And then, subtly, it changed. Every time she glanced up from the lyrics she noticed he was looking at her. Looking at her mouth, then catching her gaze: and it made her feel hot all over. By the end of the song she was actually quivering with yearning. Her gaze met his, and for a moment she thought he was going to lean over and kiss her.

If he did, there was no way she could stop herself kissing him back, baby or no baby. She wanted him. Really, really wanted him.

She felt her lips parting, and her skin tingled all over with anticipation. Her lower lip felt super-sensitive.

Moth to a flame.

He reached out and rubbed the pad of his thumb against her lower lip, and excitement coiled deep in her belly. Everything was forgotten except this moment, this feeling, this connection. She was dimly aware of Harry propping the cello against the piano, and then somehow he was sitting next to her on the piano stool, his arms were wrapped around her waist, her fingers were tangled in his hair and her wrists resting against the nape of his neck, and he was kissing her—*really* kissing her.

And it felt like fireworks going off overhead. Sparkles of silver and pink and gold.

When he broke the kiss, she was shaking. It felt really familiar—but how could it? She'd known him for a matter of days, not a lifetime. They'd never kissed before. This couldn't feel so right.

Oh, help. He'd really done it now. He'd rushed in and kissed her when he should've given her time. At the very least he should have told her about the night she'd forgotten. The night that the accident had wiped out of her memory.

Right now, she looked slightly dazed.

Did she remember what had happened in Bath? Had the kiss and the music he'd played her been enough to unlock her memories?

But she didn't say a word.

And Harry didn't know what to say.

'I'm sorry,' he said at last. 'I shouldn't have done that.'

She flushed. 'No.'

'I…' He blew out a breath. 'I don't usually behave like this. I know it's no excuse, but there's something about you that just draws me.'

She inclined her head. 'It wasn't just you. Look, let's just put it down to the music and the way it stirs up emotions.'

Tell her now.

Except he couldn't. Not when she was right in the middle of sticking up a huge wall between them. How did he tell her that he believed he was the father of her baby? She'd think he was crazy and he didn't want her to push away even more.

'I, um, I'd better go,' she said.

'Normally, I'd see you safely home. That was what I'd originally planned to do when Dom and Sal came home tonight.'

She shook her head. 'You can't leave the children. You're babysitting.'

'Exactly. So will you let me call you a taxi?' he asked.

'It's only a ten-minute walk to the Beauchamp Arms, and it's still light outside.'

'Even so.' The last time he'd let her go without seeing

her safely back to where she was staying, she'd been hit by a car. 'I'd feel happier. Please let me call you a taxi. And, just so you know, there are no strings, apart from the ones on the piano or my cello.'

She looked at him, smiling at his terrible pun; thankfully, it seemed he hadn't scared her off completely. 'All right. Thank you.'

He made a swift call. 'It's going to be twenty minutes,' he said. 'Which is long enough for me to make you another cup of tea, and maybe play something else. So my hands will be occupied and you can feel totally safe with me, because I don't want you to feel worried or uncomfortable.'

'Thank you,' she said.

He made the quickest cup of tea in history. And then he had to hope that he could play the cello well enough to move her to the point of agreeing to see him again. 'What would you like me to play?' he asked.

'Anything,' she said.

Just what she'd said that first time. Right. He'd take a risk and try to jog her memory. 'This is a bit flashy,' he said, and proceeded to play Paganini's 'Caprice No. 24'.

'I know this from somewhere,' she said.

He held his breath. Would she make the connection?

But then she said, 'I must've heard it on the radio or something.'

'Probably,' he agreed, damping down the disappointment. Instead, he played Bach and Elgar until her taxi arrived, things he knew he hadn't played for her before.

'Thank you for a lovely evening,' she said.

He couldn't quite let it go, and took her hand. 'Holly, I'm going back to London tomorrow for the weekend. I'm playing tomorrow night in London and at a wedding on Saturday evening, but—your university's in London, Dom says, so I assume you live there?'

'I do,' she confirmed. 'I stay here during the week, but I go home at weekends.'

'Would you consider having lunch with me in London on Sunday?'

'I…' She curved her hand over her barely-there bump and wrinkled her nose.

'I know,' he said softly. 'But it's not an issue for me.' And maybe on Sunday he could tell her about Bath and that he was the father of her baby. 'Have lunch with me. Please.'

For a moment he thought she was going to refuse, but then she nodded. 'All right. Where and what time?'

'What time is good for you?' he asked.

'Half-past twelve?' she suggested.

'Half-past twelve,' he repeated. 'Whereabouts are you?'

'Camden,' she said.

'Would you prefer to eat somewhere in Camden? Or I could book a table somewhere and pick you up?'

'I'll meet you at the restaurant,' she said. 'Anywhere you like.'

He'd been here before, arranging a date with her; and he was beginning to think that Lucy's theory was right and he *had* mistyped her number in his phone. He wasn't going to make a mistake like that again. 'Text me your number, and I'll let you know where I've managed to book,' he said.

She pulled her phone out of her bag. 'Oh. It's out of charge.' She grimaced. 'Sorry. Everyone nags me about this. It's a habit I need to break.'

He handed his phone to her. 'If you put your number in there, I'll text you later.'

And, while she was doing that, he scribbled his own number down on the back of his business card. 'Just in case I manage to break my phone or something before I text you,' he said. 'If you haven't heard from me by tomorrow morning, it means I've done something stupid with my phone, not that I've changed my mind and I'm ghosting you.' The way he'd once thought she'd ghosted him.

'Got it,' she said. And how sweet her smile was. It made him ache.

The more time he spent with her, the more he realised that he could be himself, with her. He really, really liked her.

But so much could go wrong. He'd thought that he and Rochelle would make a go of it, having so much in common and having known each other for years, but he'd been very wrong. Holly was nothing like Rochelle—and nothing like his parents with their constant fights—but he found it hard to ignore the past and how miserable relationships had made him.

He pulled himself together. 'All right. I'll see you on Sunday.'

He wanted to kiss her again. Really, *really* wanted to kiss her. But he didn't want to scare her away, so he let her go and finished clearing up before his brother and sister-in-law came home. He needed to tell Holly the truth about her lost weekend. But how?

Holly was thoughtful all the way back to the Beauchamp Arms. All evening, on and off, she'd felt this strange sense of déjà vu. As if she was on the cusp of something.

It absolutely wouldn't be fair of her to start any kind of relationship with Harry Moran. She was pregnant and she couldn't expect him to step into the place of the baby's father. Especially as she didn't even know who the baby's father was, which made her feel ashamed and guilty—though the sensible side of her knew that her amnesia wasn't her fault. And yet there was something about him. Something that drew her. He was nice. Kind. A real family man, clearly very fond of his nieces and nephews. Which rather begged the question of why he was still single and childless.

At the pub, she discovered that Harry had already paid for her taxi. That was definitely above and beyond. She texted him swiftly.

Thank you—though I could've paid for my own taxi.

It was the least I could do, as I wasn't able to drive you home myself.

An old-fashioned gallant gentleman.

Gallant…gentleman. Why was that familiar? Where had she heard that recently?

But it was like reaching out to grab mist on the surface of a pond, gone again before she could think about it.

She curled up in bed and looked him up on the Internet.

Harry Moran. Cellist. Part of the Quartus string quartet, though he'd also released solo music. The youngest son of Viscount Moran.

He kept his private life very private, she noticed. It seemed as if he'd been married briefly, a few years ago, but all the articles that talked about his marriage were from the kind of gossip magazines she disliked. She'd rather hear Harry's side of the story from Harry himself, if he wanted to tell her.

All his social media talked about music, not necessarily played by him. The posts that talked about his awards and accolades were all by other people, tagging him in; he clearly wasn't one to boast about his achievements.

After reading his entire website and all the non-gossipy articles she could find about him, she still knew no more about Harry himself. She didn't have a clue what drove him, other than a love of music.

He'd seemed to be of the opinion that her baby wasn't a barrier to a future relationship with her. Why? Was he perhaps unable to have children of his own, and her baby would give him a ready-made family? Was that why his marriage had broken up? Though those weren't the kind of questions you could ask straight out. She needed to get to know him better before she asked.

Was she making the right decision, agreeing to meet him for lunch on Sunday? OK, so he'd said no strings… But did he really mean that?

There was only one way to find out: and that was to meet him on Sunday.

CHAPTER SIX

'YOU'VE ACTUALLY FOUND your Lady in Red?' Lucy's eyes widened. 'Oh, my God! So did you find out why she didn't turn up?'

'She was in a car accident,' Harry said, 'which meant she lost all her memories from the week before it happened. Including meeting me.'

'Unbelievable! How did you find her?'

'She's leading the dig at the abbey.'

'Oh.' Lucy bit her lip. 'Awkward. So have you told her?'

Harry wrinkled his nose. 'Not yet.'

'Why not?'

'It's complicated,' Harry said and focused on tuning his cello, even though it didn't actually need it.

'How is it complicated?'

He couldn't quite bring himself to explain about Holly being pregnant. Particularly as Lucy knew all about why he'd married Rochelle, and how he'd felt when she'd lost the baby. He'd sobbed his heart out on Lucy's shoulder over both the miscarriage and the divorce, though he'd kept the bit that had really broken him to himself.

'How am I going to tell her, Luce? "Oh, by the way, you also met me a few months ago and we spent the night together.'" He rolled his eyes. 'That's going to go down well. Not.'

'If you don't tell her, when she finds out some other way—say she gets her memory back—it's going to be a whole lot worse,' Lucy warned. 'And don't fall back on the excuse that you're rubbish at emotional stuff because you're male and you're posh.'

'It's not an excuse. It's a fact.' It was one of the accusations Rochelle had hurled at him: that he backed away and lost himself in music rather than confronting anything. He'd grown up with his parents sniping at each other constantly and he'd hated the atmosphere, so he didn't seek out confrontations. And maybe deep down he'd used the tour as an excuse to stay away and avoid his own pain instead of coming back to comfort her.

The irony was that he'd won critical acclaim for his recording of Elgar's cello concerto later that year. He'd poured all his pain and his loss and the longing and the misery into his performance, letting the music comfort him.

When she'd finally told him the truth, it had hurt him so deeply that he hadn't let anyone else close since. How could he trust their motives for wanting to be close to him? How could he trust his own judgement, when he'd been so completely fooled? He'd loved her and he'd thought she'd loved him: but it had turned out he hadn't really known her at all.

He pushed the thought away. 'And you were right. When I put Holly's number in my phone, I got it wrong.'

'Told you so.' Lucy clapped him on the shoulder. 'You need to be honest with her. Yes, it's going to be awkward. But if you don't tell her, Harry, it'll come back to bite you.'

'I know.' He plucked the strings of the cello, sub-consciously playing the song he and Holly had sung to, right before he'd kissed her again. 'I didn't expect this to *matter*, Luce. I barely know her. And I don't believe in love at first sight.'

'You don't believe in love, full stop,' she said. 'But it's out there. Ignore your parents, because they're really not like normal people. Ignore Rochelle, too, because she was just as much to blame for your marriage break-ing up as you were.'

He knew that—they'd both been young, both made made decisions—but he still felt responsible.

'I have a long memory, and a good one,' she said softly. 'Yes, you could've done things differently. But so could she.'

Yeah. And Lucy didn't even know the worst of it. He hadn't told anyone about Rochelle deliberately getting pregnant. He didn't want to risk his heart to the care of anyone else ever again. Yes, he'd dated since his divorce; but he'd been wary since Rochelle's revelations, and he'd quickly discovered that his dates had seen him primarily either as Viscount Moran's youngest son or as Harry the up-and-coming celebrity musician. He just hadn't felt enough for any of them to want to break through the barriers and see if love could ever be real.

'Look at your brother and your sister,' Lucy contin-ued. 'That's real. Look at Stella and Drew—that's real. Look at me and Carina. That's real, and we make it work even though I tour a lot and she's here in London.'

But his relationship with Rochelle hadn't been real. It had turned out that she hadn't loved him the way he'd thought she had. She'd found herself struggling to get work and to move up the ladder, and she'd wanted financial security so, shortly after she'd persuaded him to let her move in with him, she'd deliberately got pregnant, knowing that Harry would insist on marrying her—and gambling that he'd give up touring and instead work on his family's estate.

He'd done half of it, giving her the financial security she'd wanted. But he hadn't given up his career. His music was who he was. And her ultimatum to him, making him choose between her and his music, had backfired on her spectacularly.

When he said nothing, Lucy continued, 'Love *is* out there, Harry. And your Lady in Red—'

'—Holly,' he supplied.

'Holly. Get to know her. Because she might just be The One.'

Even though he'd stopped believing in love, Holly Weston made him feel…

How did he feel? He wasn't sure, but it definitely wasn't like anything he'd felt before. It was unsettling and exhilarating at the same time. Was that love? Did she feel anything like that for him? Or, if she didn't feel that way now, could she learn to love him? Could this work out?

Dealing with emotional stuff always made him back away. It was terrifying. He gave Lucy his best smile. 'I get why Carina loves you so much. I love you, too. But now's not the time to discuss this. We have work to do.'

'Agreed. Love you, too, Harry.' She ruffled his hair. 'Let's go play the wedding.'

He'd play his best. He'd always do his best for the client.

But tonight he'd lie awake and wonder what was going to be best for Holly, for their baby, and for himself.

* * *

On Sunday morning, Holly couldn't settle to anything.

Was this a date, or wasn't it?

On the one hand, the way she'd felt when Harry had kissed her had been amazing. More than amazing. She'd never expected to feel like that.

On the other hand, she was pregnant with another man's baby. A man she couldn't even remember.

Harry had made it clear that the pregnancy wasn't an issue for him; but how could she start dating him, in the circumstances? Maybe she should've taken Natalie's advice and done something on social media to find her mystery man, because he had a right to know about the baby's existence—even though he hadn't contacted her at all since that weekend and she expected nothing from him.

She was still full of nerves when she took the tube to Clapham and found the restaurant where Harry had asked her to meet him. To her delight, it overlooked Clapham Common; the ceiling inside the restaurant was a canopy of flowers and there were fairy lights everywhere. The floors were stripped and sanded, the tables likewise, and the chairs were mismatched but somehow harmonious. She'd never seen anywhere so romantic and pretty.

Harry was already there, sitting at one of the tables, and he lifted his hand in acknowledgement as she scanned the room. When she walked over to join him, he stood up: an old-fashioned courtesy she really liked.

'Thank you for coming,' he said.

'Thank you for inviting me. This is lovely.' She gestured to the room.

'The food is amazing, too. On Sundays, they give you a choice of brunch or roast dinner.'

'Brunch for me, please,' she said. But there were so many things on the menu that she liked, she couldn't decide what to have.

'We could get a selection between us and share?' he suggested.

And suddenly everything was easy. 'That would be lovely.'

Once they'd ordered, she smiled at him. 'How did your concerts go?'

'Fine, thanks. We all enjoy playing weddings, and last night's set was fun. They chose "Rule the World" as the first dance, and the rest was a mix of pop songs—everything from the Beach Boys and the Beatles to Abba and Taylor Swift.' He grinned. 'Lucy was happy because she got a chance to show off her favourite Donna Summer track.'

'Did you get to use your cello as a guitar?'

He laughed. 'Sadly not. But it was a good night. Very different from the baroque pieces we played at St Martin's Church on Friday night, but I enjoyed playing those, too. I suppose I just love playing and sharing the sheer joy of music.' He smiled at her. 'How's the dig coming along?'

'It's fine. We're finding really interesting bits from where the original church was, under what's now your Orangery. Complete floor tiles, a couple of rather battered church vessels, some coins—and my absolute favourite, a tiny brass.' She took her phone from her pocket. 'I took some photos of the finds because I thought you might like to see them.'

'Absolutely.' He looked at the photographs with her

and asked tons of perceptive, intelligent questions; and he paid attention to her answers rather than just giving her a polite smile to conceal his boredom, as Simon often had.

Funny how easy it was to talk to Harry. She felt comfortable with him yet, at the same time, there was an undercurrent of excitement she couldn't remember feeling with anyone else before.

But she really needed to be fair to him rather than string him along.

She waited until they'd both finished their food and had a top-up of tea before saying, 'Harry, I need to be honest with you. I like you—' she liked him a lot '—but right now I'm not looking to date anyone. Given my circumstances, it isn't fair to let you think otherwise.'

'Thank you for being honest with me.' He took a deep breath. 'Have any of your memories from the week before your accident come back yet?'

'No, and it's been months now so they may never come back,' she said.

'Then I need to be honest with you, too,' he said.

Honest? Why? She looked at him, not understanding. 'What do you mean?'

'Quartus—my quartet—played an event just outside Bath a few months ago.'

She frowned. Her accident had happened in Bath. Was he saying…? It felt as if someone had just tipped a bucket of cold water onto her from a great height. 'Hang on. Are you telling me you played at the ball I had a ticket to but can't remember attending?'

He nodded.

'So you saw me there?' And, if he'd seen her, there was a chance that he'd also seen her mystery man and could help her track him down. 'And you saw the guy I was with?'

'You were on your own.'

'Oh.' Another blind avenue. Her stomach swooped in disappointment.

He looked really awkward now. 'Holly, I'm trying to tell you that you met *me*.'

She frowned. At Beauchamp Abbey, he hadn't mentioned that they'd met before. 'Why didn't you say something when your sister introduced us?'

'Because when I saw you again at the dig, you acted as if you'd never met me before.'

Now it suddenly made sense. That must be why he'd looked so put out when he'd met her again at Beauchamp Abbey and she hadn't acknowledged him. He must've thought she was playing some sort of game.

But if she'd been on her own when he'd met her...did that mean that *he* was her mystery man?

Knowing that she might be making a huge fool of herself but needing to know the truth, she asked, 'Are you saying that you and I did more than just talk? That we spent the night together?' Which would mean that he was the father of her baby. But she stopped processing that when a really nasty thought shoved it to one side. 'Were you there at the accident?' Oh, no. Had he been the man who'd driven the car that had hit her?

'Yes, you spent the night with me and, no, I wasn't there when the car hit you,' he said. 'I think it must have happened when you were on the way to meeting me.'

That led to a whole new raft of questions. 'So why didn't you ring me when I didn't meet you?' Had he been sulking, thinking that she'd stood him up?

'I did ring you. Well, I *tried* to,' he amended, 'but it

seems I'd taken your number down wrongly. I got a guy in Scotland instead.'

And that was it? He'd just given up? 'But you could've called the hotel, or tried to contact me through my work—there aren't exactly a lot of archaeologists in the world called Holly Weston.'

'But you wouldn't let me take you back to your hotel, so I didn't know where you were staying, and we didn't exchange surnames. I had no idea what you did for a living because we didn't talk about it. So I had no way of finding you—apart from putting something on social media that would've ended up embarrassing us both.'

Which was exactly why Holly had rejected Natalie's suggestion of using social media.

Shame seared through her, making her cheeks feel scorching hot. What the hell had she been thinking, going off with a stranger who surname she hadn't even known? Yes, she'd been hurt and angry at Simon's betrayal, but that didn't mean she could totally ignore common sense. Natalie hadn't really been serious in her suggestion that Holly should get over Simon by having a mad fling.

'So we spent the night together?' she asked again, just in case this was all some weird mistake.

'Yes.'

She felt sick. 'Didn't we use contraception?'

'No, we did,' he said. 'But no contraception is a hundred per cent reliable.'

'So you're the father of my baby.' It was a deduction rather than a question.

'Unless you'd slept with someone else that week—' At her withering glare, he added hastily, 'Then, yes. The dates tie up.'

No wonder he'd been so adamant that the baby wasn't an issue. *Because it was his baby.*

And she'd been feeling guilty about her attraction to him and tying herself in knots over it, while all along he'd known the truth. She'd even told him that she'd lost her memory, but he still hadn't bothered to enlighten her.

He'd lied to her. By omission, but it was still a lie.

And, after Simon, she'd had *enough* of men lying to her.

'Why didn't you say anything when you first saw me at the abbey?' she demanded.

'Because you didn't appear to recognise me at all. I thought you were…well, a player,' he admitted.

A player? She wasn't like that at all, and although she could sort of see where he was coming from, she also didn't agree. 'But Jamal told you about my accident and I told you about my memory loss. You could've said something then.'

'In front of your team?' He raised his eyebrows. 'Hardly. It was something I thought you'd rather discuss in private.'

'But you *did* see me in private. When you asked me to dinner.' When he'd played her that beautiful music and he'd kissed her and her head had felt as if it were full of rainbows. 'Why didn't you tell me then?'

'Because it was awkward and I didn't know how to tell you. Plus I'd just found out you were pregnant by me. I was reeling.' He blew out a breath. 'I'm trying to tell you now.'

In a public place—which went completely against what he'd just said about thinking she'd rather discuss this in private.

It made her want to cry. Big, fat, ugly tears. Anger and

misery and hopelessness, all rolled into one. She'd liked him so much. And he'd turned out to be another man like Simon. A man who'd lied and who'd let her down.

'I can't deal with this,' she said.

And, even though she knew she was behaving badly, she pushed her chair back and walked out of the restaurant, ignoring his soft, 'Holly, wait! Please.'

Right now, she needed fresh air. And she wanted to be on her own so she could start to process this.

Harry stared after Holly's retreating back, frozen by shock.

That really couldn't have gone any worse.

What did he do now?

He didn't have time to sit and think about it: he needed to go after her right now if he was to have any chance of salvaging this. He went over to the cash register, emptied his wallet and left more than enough notes to cover the bill, apologised, and dashed out after Holly.

She'd insisted on meeting him here rather than letting him pick her up, so he had no idea where she lived—other than it was somewhere in Camden—or which direction she would take on leaving the restaurant. He gazed around frantically, and saw her stepping into a black cab just down the street.

Where were all the taxis when you needed them? Why wasn't one coming along the street right now so he could flag it down, jump in and say, 'Follow that cab!'? Her taxi drove off, and there was no way he could follow her on foot.

Still, he had her mobile number. *If* her phone was charged. He called her and the connection went straight

through to her voicemail. 'Holly, it's Harry. I'm sorry.
Please call me. We need to talk about the baby,' he said.

He left his number at the end of the message, even
though he knew she had it. Then he started to send her
a text to back it up. Even though right now part of him
was annoyed that she hadn't given him a chance to explain and he thought she was being unreasonable, he had
to take into account the fact that she was pregnant and
full of hormones, and up until now she'd been dealing
with this on her own. Plus she'd had the accident that
had robbed her of her memory. His news would've been
a massive shock. He needed to cut her some slack.

Holly, please call me. We need to talk about the baby.

That sounded threatening, which wasn't his intention.

And about how I can support you, he added, hoping
that she wouldn't take that the wrong way. That was the
problem with words on a screen. It was all too easy to
mistake the tone. He would so much rather do this face
to face, but she hadn't left him any choice.

As soon as her phone shrilled, Holly knew who was calling her without having to check the screen. She ignored
it and let the call go to her voicemail. A few moments
later, her phone pinged to signal an incoming text.

Right now, she didn't want to talk to Harry Moran
or hear what he had to say. She wanted to get her head
around the situation first.

The one person she would have discussed the situation with was Natalie, but her best friend was away for
the weekend. And, much as Holly loved her mum and
her sister, this wasn't something she wanted to discuss

with them. Part of her was ashamed of having a wild fling with a stranger, and she didn't want her mum and her sister to think less of her.

She asked the driver to drop her at the next tube station and headed for Regent's Park. A walk in a green space was what she needed to help her analyse this like the scientist she was, unpicking the layers and working things out for herself. She switched her phone off completely, not wanting anyone to disturb her, and wandered amongst the roses while she pondered the situation.

Harry Moran was the father of her baby.

So why did she still not remember a thing about that night? When he'd kissed her the other night, it had felt like fireworks going off in her head. Had it been the same that night in Bath? And, if so, *how* could she still have no memories of it?

And why hadn't he told her about this before? Why had he waited the best part of a week?

Pushing the hurt and anger aside, she tried to think about it from his point of view and piece together what had happened in Bath.

They'd spent the night together. It was out of character for her to have that kind of wild fling, and she had a feeling that Harry wasn't the sort to sleep around either. She didn't remember their fling—but she'd felt a huge pull of attraction towards him when she'd met him again at Beauchamp, even when she hadn't known that he was the man she'd had a fling with. He'd clearly felt it, too, or he wouldn't have kissed her again.

Harry didn't know where she was staying, so that meant they must have gone to wherever he was staying after the ball, rather than to her hotel. She still had no idea where that was, but it must've been within walking distance of her hotel. And she'd agreed to meet him later that morning—except on the way she'd rescued the little boy and been hit by the car, none of which she remembered.

He hadn't known about the accident and had obviously waited for her at wherever they'd agreed to meet. When she hadn't turned up, he'd tried to call her—but he'd got someone else's number.

According to him, they hadn't even exchanged surnames. How could she have gone off with someone whose name she didn't even know? How could *he*?

Heat flared through her cheeks again. She never, ever got swept away like that. The one *grand passion* moment in her life, and she couldn't even remember it. How ironic was that? And yet she'd felt swept away again that night when they'd sung together and he'd played for her. She'd had butterflies in her stomach when she'd got ready to meet him for lunch today.

He'd known nothing at all about her. Not her surname, not where she lived, not what she did for a living. So, realistically, the only way he could have traced her was if he'd put a 'find the mystery girl' type post on social media. Why hadn't he done that? He had a reasonably high profile in the classical music world. People would have picked it up and tried to help.

Then again, looking at it from his point of view: he'd waited for her and she'd stood him up. When he'd called her, it was the wrong number. Logically, he must have believed she'd given him the wrong number on purpose so he couldn't get in touch with her, that she'd ghosted him.

And then, the next time he'd met her, she'd behaved as if she'd never met him before. From her point of view, she *hadn't* met him before. But he wasn't privy to that information. If it had been the other way round, how would she have felt? She thought about it. She would have assumed he was a player and would've been furious with him. It kind of fitted with the way he'd reacted to her, all starchy and cold.

But there was an explanation. One that he'd learned pretty quickly. As soon as Jamal had told him about the accident and she'd filled in the gap, he must've realised that was why she hadn't turned up, and that she had no memory of him.

What would she have done, in his shoes?

How did you tell someone that they had forgotten you—and forgotten your wild fling, too?

For all Harry knew, Holly could have met someone else and fallen in love in the weeks between their fling and then meeting him again—just as he could have done. So his choices would've been to pretend their fling had never happened at all, or to choose his time carefully and talk to her about it in private.

Harry had clearly done the maths and worked out for himself that the date of her baby's conception tied in with the date of the fling she couldn't remember. Clearly that was why he'd asked her to Sunday lunch in a quiet restaurant, on neutral territory; it was the nearest he could get to talking in private without discussing it at either of their homes.

Had she just been massively unfair to him?

Very probably, she had to admit.

So what were they going to do about it?

As the father of their baby, Harry had had rights. Morally, if not legally, he could share in decisions about the baby's upbringing, and see the baby.

Would he want that?

Given how she'd seen Harry behave with his nieces and nephews, she was pretty sure he would want to be a hands-on father. But she also knew that his job involved a lot of travelling. The logistics would need to be worked out carefully.

And what about her?

Harry remembered her 'lost weekend'. He knew what had happened between them—and he'd kissed her again since then. Did that mean he wanted the relationship to continue? And was it because he wanted her, or did he feel obliged because of the baby?

She'd been in a relationship where her partner had settled for her and then discovered she really wasn't enough for him. She'd learned from the experience, and no way did she want to be in that situation again.

So where did that leave them?

She could hardly avoid Harry, given that the dig she was leading was at his parents' home. Anyone who had the grit and determination to make a successful career in the arts wouldn't let something like this just drop. If she refused to speak to him, he'd probably come and sit in her trench and refuse to move until she *did* talk to him. Meaning the whole mess would become very public and embarrass everyone.

With a sigh, she switched her phone back on. One missed call, one voicemail and one text—and they were all from Harry.

She listened to the voicemail first.

'Holly, I'm sorry. Please call me. We need to talk about the baby.'

Guilt flooded through her. She'd been the one to walk

out and she'd left him to settle the bill, yet he was the one apologising.

She read his text.

Holly, please call me. We need to talk about the baby. And how I can support you.

It was all very calm, very polite, and very reasonable. And it left her feeling very much in the wrong.

She bit her lip. Right now, she owed Harry Moran an apology. And he was right: they did need to talk about the baby.

She dialled his number.

'Holly?' He sounded wary when he answered.

'Sorry for walking out on you,' she said. 'You're right. We need to talk about the baby.'

'It's your decision,' he said. 'Tell me where and when.'

He was being so nice that it brought tears to her eyes. 'I don't know.' Which was stupid. For pity's sake, she had a PhD. She wasn't stupid. Why couldn't she answer a simple question about where and when to meet him?

'When are you going back to the abbey?' he asked.

'Tomorrow morning.'

'Are you free this afternoon?'

'Yes.' She swallowed hard.

'Where are you?'

'In Regent's Park, by the roses. Where are you?'

'Still in Clapham, walking on the Common.'

Walking and thinking, like she was? Even though they had very different backgrounds and very different jobs, they seemed to react the same way to things. Perhaps that was a good sign.

'I'll jump in a cab and come to you,' he suggested.

'Find somewhere to sit, and text me to let me know exactly where you are. I'll be there as soon as I can.'

'All right. I'll meet you by the waterfall in the Japanese Garden,' she said.

'I'm on my way,' he said, and hung up.

CHAPTER SEVEN

THIS MEETING WAS going to be more crucial than the most important audition he'd ever had in his life, Harry thought. And he really needed to get it right. Holly had agreed to meet him to talk about the baby; if he messed that up, he wouldn't get a second chance.

He still hadn't quite got his head round the fact that he was going to be a father. He'd been here before, and it had gone so badly wrong; it scared him that it could go wrong again. Then again, if it went right it would still be scary. He adored his nieces and nephews, playing with them, spending quality time with them and playing music with them; but he'd never had to deal with sickness or tantrums or being so bone-deep tired that he couldn't think straight, the way his brother and sister had. Babysitting a child for a few hours was a far cry from being completely responsible for a child.

If the baby made it through the pregnancy.

His and Rochelle's baby hadn't. OK, so it didn't mean that history would repeat itself, but this time round he was more aware of the risks.

And then there was Holly herself.

How did you make a success of a relationship with someone you barely knew? He liked the woman he'd got to know so far, and the physical attraction was most definitely still there. But they barely knew each other, and he wasn't great at relationships. He'd adored Granny and Grandpa Beckett—his father's parents had died when Harry was small, so he couldn't remember them—and he loved his siblings. But his relationship with his parents was strained to the point where he avoided them as much as possible. His marriage had been a disaster and he hadn't let anyone close to him since.

He had no idea how this thing between himself and Holly would work. But he did know that they needed to have a very honest and potentially very painful discussion.

He checked his phone to find out exactly where the Japanese Garden was in Regent's Park. After the taxi had dropped him at the entrance to the park, he headed through the Jubilee Gates and down a narrow path.

Just as she'd promised, Holly was waiting by the waterfall.

'Good choice,' he said, glad she'd found a quiet spot in the park. 'Thank you for agreeing to meet me. I'm sorry about earlier. I really don't want to fight.'

'I'm sorry, too,' she said. 'I shouldn't have walked out on you.'

Hormones, probably, though he wasn't quite stupid enough to say that out loud.

'And I owe you for lunch,' she continued.

He flapped his hand. 'No, you don't. My suggestion, my bill.' He took a deep breath. 'I've been thinking about things from your point of view and you're right. I should've told you as soon as I met you again.'

She gave him a wry smile. 'I've been thinking about it from your point of view, too. When I didn't turn up and the number you'd taken down turned out not to be mine, you must've thought I'd ghosted you.'

'I did.' He looked rueful. 'But now I know you couldn't remember a thing about me, so how could you possibly have got in contact with me?'

'I still don't remember anything from the few days before the accident,' she said. 'I think it's always going to be my lost weekend. And that's terrifying—reaching out for something and it's just not there.'

'It must be a horrible feeling. I read up about retrograde amnesia. That's why I tried playing you some of the music from that night, in case it made a connection for you and helped you to remember.' He wrinkled his nose. 'I'm sorry. Perhaps I should've come straight out with it.'

'What were you going to say? "Hello, you don't remember me, but I'm the father of your baby."? I would've run a mile,' she said. 'I'm sorry for throwing a hissy fit.'

'I think we're on the same side,' he said. And there was one mistake he'd learned from. 'The first thing I want you to know is that I'll support you.'

She gave him a level stare. 'You don't want me to do a DNA test to prove the baby's yours?'

'No need. The dates tie up,' he said. 'And you give the impression that you're not in the habit of sleeping around.'

Her smile was wry. 'That's correct. I'm much too beige for that.'

He frowned, not understanding. 'Beige?'

She gestured to her hair and her eyes. 'Beige. And most of the time I'm covered in mud, also beige.'

He smiled. '"Beige" isn't how I'd describe you. Besides, you were wearing a red dress when I first met you. A Regency dress.'

* * *

A dress she couldn't remember wearing, but she'd taken a mirror selfie for Natalie, so she knew that bit was true.

'I think,' Holly said, 'I'd like to start by filling in the gaps in my memory, if you wouldn't mind.'

'Do you trust me to tell you the truth?' he asked.

She nodded. 'What reason do you have to lie to me about what happened?'

'None whatsoever,' he confirmed. 'I have no idea what you did during the day before you arrived at the ball, but I noticed you sitting on the bank, watching us, wearing your red dress. I don't normally even see the audience when I play, because I'm always so focused on the music, but I kept seeing you. So, when the set ended and we were back on dry land, I came to talk to you. It was getting a bit chilly, so I lent you my jacket. And you said I was very gallant.'

His jacket. *Gallant.* Goosebumps prickled over her skin. 'Were you wearing Regency clothes, too?'

'You remember?' His voice held a note of hope.

'No.' Not quite. But she'd had that idea of him wearing a tailcoat and pantaloons. Was it the beginning of a memory resurfacing, or just coincidence?

'We went into the house, where we stopped at the buffet table and then we watched the Regency dancers.'

She smiled. 'I have two left feet, so I know we didn't join them.'

'Actually, we did,' he corrected. 'Not the Regency stuff—we went to the other ballroom, where they were playing slightly more modern dance music. We danced quite a lot. And then it all slowed down.'

Dancing with him. 'I don't remember,' she whispered. 'Did I tread on your toes?'

'No. You followed my lead. It felt like dancing on air. The perfect fit. I've done a lot of formal dancing, in my time, and that kind of chemistry's rare. And then...' He took a breath. 'I kissed you, and you kissed me back.'

His eyes had gone very, very dark. So did that mean he still felt that pull of attraction towards her? The same attraction that had sent fireworks flaring through her head the last time he'd kissed her?

'Then we decided to get out of there. I drove you back to Bath, and I asked you to come back for a drink to the place where I was staying.'

Which was where his story stopped making sense. 'I never go off with strangers.'

'A stranger and his cello,' he said. 'Though I know what you mean. I don't go off with strangers either, or ask them to go off with me. Just...' He shook his head as if trying to find an explanation. 'There was something about you. I can't explain it. This doesn't normally happen to me. But I didn't want to say goodnight.'

She knew she must have felt the same, because she'd felt drawn to him ever since she'd seen him again. Even the first day, when he'd been formal and stuffy and cold, she'd *noticed* him.

'One of my old school friends has a flat in the Circus. We went back there and I made you a cup of tea. Builders' tea, no sugar.'

The bit about tea sounded accurate. But where they'd gone... 'A flat in the Circus?' She shook her head. 'No way could I forget something like that. Nat—my best friend—is a huge Jane Austen fan. I would've told her all about it. Texted her. Taken a photo, at the very least.'

He coughed. 'Neither of us looked at our phones. When we did, the next morning, your battery was flat.'

'Uh-huh.' That sounded accurate, too. Everyone nagged her about keeping her phone charged.

'You asked me to play something for you.'

'"Hushabye Mountain".'

His eyes widened. 'You remember?'

'No. You played that for me at your brother's house, and you just told me you tried to jog my memory with music, so I assume that was one of the pieces you played for me in Bath.'

'But you didn't remember it,' he said.

'It's not your fault.' Her breath caught. 'And then I stayed the night.' She'd had the fling she couldn't remember. The thing that had changed her life. And, even though she knew intellectually how retrograde amnesia worked, emotionally she couldn't quite get it. How could she possibly have forgotten the kind of feeling that was strong enough to make her act so far out of character?

He nodded. 'I went out to buy croissants for breakfast. And strawberries. I asked if we could do something together. We planned to meet outside the Pump Room—but you wouldn't let me drop you at your hotel. You insisted on walking.'

That sounded like her, too. Her mother always grumbled that Holly was too independent.

'Because your phone was flat, you gave me your number. Except obviously I didn't take it down correctly,' he finished.

'And then, on the way to meet you, I rescued a little boy from the road and got hit by a car. None of which I remember.'

'Which must be really scary.'

He understood. He wasn't judging her; he was trying to put himself in her shoes. 'It is,' she admitted. 'It's like a black hole. One that I'm probably never going to be able to fill. The more time that passes, the less likely it is I'll remember.'

He took her hand and squeezed it briefly. 'That's hard. But it isn't your fault, Holly.'

'It doesn't matter whether it's my fault or not. It's still a blank. And I hate it.' She grimaced. He'd filled in some of the gaps, and right now she didn't know what to think or what to feel. Everything was mixed-up and crazy. She rested her hand on her bump to ground herself.

'It must've been a real shock when you realised you were pregnant,' he said. 'When did you find out?'

'Two months later. I was busy at work—it was exam season—so I'd barely even registered the missed periods. I was all ready to pick up my malaria tablets for the Egypt trip, but the practice nurse asked me if I was pregnant. It was a routine question. Even then, I thought it must be the accident messing up my cycle—plus I didn't remember you or anything else about that weekend.' She swallowed hard. 'She said I needed to take a test, just to rule it out. And I discovered that I'd forgotten even more than I'd thought I had.'

'So you were prepared to bring up the baby on your own?'

'I looked at all the options, and that was the one that worked for me. My family, friends and colleagues are all supportive.' She paused. 'Now we're both up to speed with the situation, I guess.'

He raked a hand through his hair, and the dishevelled look suited him. It made him look younger and more approachable. 'I want to support you and the baby. The tricky thing is my job, because I'm away quite a lot. But I think we can make it work if we both compromise a bit.'

Compromise? She was glad he'd said he'd be there for the baby—but what about her? How did he feel about her? She narrowed her eyes at him. 'What sort of compromise did you have in mind?'

'I don't want to be a distant parent.' He blew out a breath. 'I really wasn't expecting to be a parent. Obviously you weren't either.'

'No. But I've had more time than you to get used to the idea.'

'I've had a couple of days to think about it. And here we are. Near strangers. Expecting a baby together in about five and a half months.' He looked at her. 'I intend to be a good father. But I should warn you that I don't usually do relationships.'

Which meant what, exactly?

He took a deep breath. 'I'm divorced.'

She winced. 'I know.'

His face shuttered. 'You've seen the media?'

'Obviously I looked you up on the Internet,' she said. 'I saw the headlines, yes, but I didn't go into those sites to read the details because it felt like prying. I thought if you wanted me to know, you'd tell me.'

'Give that today's all about honesty,' he said, 'then, yes, you need to know. I met Rochelle when I was eighteen, when we were studying at the Academy, though we didn't get together until after we graduated.' He sighed. 'She was a flautist. There are a lot more opportunities for cellists than there are for flautists. When you start out, you have to go wherever the work is. Although we were both based in London, if she had the chance of playing for a touring opera or ballet company, she had to go. She might've been playing in Glasgow while I had a contract down in, say, Truro.' He shrugged. 'If we'd both managed to play for the same orchestra, or seen each other for more than a snatched day here or there, maybe we could've made it work. But we didn't. I was offered a lot more work than she was, so even when we were in London she didn't see that much of me.'

'I'm sorry.'

'It was messy,' he admitted. 'And I didn't do enough to save my marriage. The quartet had started to take off, and we were getting regular bookings. I said I'd support Rochelle—I had family money—so she didn't have to worry about struggling to find work. I said that maybe she could teach or something, be based in London all the time so we weren't at opposite sides of the country and might see more of each other. And she accused me of putting my career before hers.' A muscle worked in his jaw. 'Up to a point, that's true. I could've offered to stay in London and teach and let her be the one to go touring.'

'But playing's what makes you feel alive,' she said. 'I see your face when you play. It's your heart and soul coming out of your fingers into the music.'

'Thank you,' he said, 'for understanding that. Rochelle didn't, even though she was a musician as well. Or maybe it was because we ended up in competition, instead of supporting each other. Though it must've been hard for her. She was just as good a musician as I was, and it must've felt bad to be the one who was struggling.' He looked sad. 'So it didn't work out.'

Holly had a feeling that there was more to it than that. Those blue, blue eyes had darkened with pain, as if it hadn't been an amicable split. Had his ex maybe had an affair? Though it would be unkind to probe. 'I'm sorry.'

'She wanted me to give it up and work on my fam-

ily's estate. Which meant I had a choice,' he said. 'My
career or my marriage. I chose my career.'

Was that a warning? Or was it something he regretted?

He looked at her. 'The night we first met—the night
you don't remember—you asked me if I was single.
Which sounds to me as if maybe you've been let down
by someone.'

'Dated someone who turned out to be married, you
mean? Not quite.' She grimaced. 'I was supposed to get
married a couple of weeks after Bath.'

He looked horrified. 'Are you telling me that you
went off with me while you were engaged to—?' He
stopped. 'No. Of course not. That's not who you are. I
don't need you to confirm that. I apologise. I'm letting
what happened with Rochelle get in the way, and that's
not fair to you.'

That definitely sounded like an affair. She knew how
it felt to be cheated on. And she appreciated that he didn't
think she was the type to cheat. 'Thank you,' she said.
'No. I was single, but I had been in a relationship for
eight years. Simon went on secondment to New York for
six months; and while he was there he fell in love with
someone else. He called off the wedding three weeks
before I went to Bath. I was supposed to go to Rome
for my hen weekend that weekend, but obviously I cancelled that, too.'

He took her hand. 'I'm sorry about your ex. That's a
really horrible thing to happen.'

'I seemed to spend all my time either apologising to
people or feeling like the world's biggest failure,' she
admitted. 'I never want to go through that again.' She
paused. 'Fenella—the woman Simon fell in love with—
was pregnant. Which is why he called it off between us.'

Harry winced. 'That's rough.'

'It could've been worse. He could've left me at the altar,' she said, 'or told me after we'd got married. And then things would've been even more complicated.'

'I'm so sorry someone treated you like that.' Harry frowned. 'Are you telling me that, even though he was the one to end things, he made you unpick all the arrangements?'

'For someone who had to be so precise in his job, he was hopeless when it came to organising things at home. If I'd left it to him, it... Well, things would've been forgotten or not cancelled properly, and...' She grimaced. 'It was just easier to sort it out myself.'

'I'd call that adding insult to injury.'

'It is what it is.' She shrugged. 'But I think it's why I reacted so badly to you not telling me the truth. My tolerance for lies is pretty much at zero after Simon.' She looked at him. 'You didn't tell me an untruth, but it was a lie by omission.'

'Noted, and I apologise again. You deserve better than that. And you deserved better than that from Simon as well.'

'My best friend said that, too. She wanted to do something nice for me, and she knew how much I'd been looking forward to Rome. The Roman Baths in Bath were her idea of the nearest substitute. And it was nice of her.'

He smiled wryly. 'And to think I asked you if you'd visited the Baths.'

She smiled back. 'Obviously I didn't tell you I'd worked on the site as a student, or you would have had an idea what I did for a living and been able to look me up on the Internet.'

'Indeed.' He paused. 'So where do we go from here?'

What did he want? she wondered. For that matter, what did *she* want?

'Whatever you decide, I'll support you and the baby. Though that doesn't mean you're tied to me,' he added hastily.

So did that mean he wanted to try and make some kind of future with her, or not? Right now they were supposed to be being honest with each other. So she'd get this out in the open. 'If I'd met you outside the Pump Room that morning—and I'm fairly sure I did intend to meet you, because otherwise I would've made an excuse and told you I had to get back to London,' she said, 'what do you think would've happened?'

'We would've had a nice day doing touristy things,' he said. 'And, if we'd had the chance to get to know each other a bit more, I might have suggested meeting up with you in London and seeing where things took us.'

'And now?'

'We've kind of skipped a step. We've made a baby without having a real relationship first.' He paused. 'Maybe we can rewind a little bit and get to know each other properly. Go on dates, as if the baby isn't part of the equation.'

It all sounded sensible.

But he hadn't said how he felt about her, or asked how she felt about him. She had the distinct feeling that Harry Moran kept his heart under armed guard. It was understandable, given that his marriage had ended badly, but it was frustrating. If he wasn't prepared to take a chance, open up to her as she'd try to open up to him, it wouldn't work between them.

'There's only one thing,' he said. 'Weekends are pretty busy for me at the moment. The quartet has a wedding booked for just about every Saturday between now and the end of the summer, and we have other commitments in between. I'm based in London, but we travel around a fair bit.' He paused. 'Which means Sunday lunchtimes are probably the best time for me to see you, and London's the easiest place to meet. Does that work for you?'

This felt more like a business arrangement than a relationship.

And even though Holly had told herself she didn't want any more relationships after Simon's betrayal, she realised that actually she did. And Harry's view on the whole thing felt lukewarm.

Did she really want to get involved with someone who was emotionally unavailable—to risk falling for someone who might not ever be able to feel the same way about her as she was starting to feel about him? She'd spent eight years in a relationship where she had been the one who'd loved the other the most, and she didn't want to repeat that.

The alternative was to cut him out of her life, which wasn't fair. This was his baby, too. And the baby deserved to know both parents.

At her continued silence, Harry said softly, 'I know that probably sounds like too little, too late. But I don't want to make any promises I can't keep.'

'It feels a bit clinical,' she admitted. 'OK, so I don't remember our fling, but...' But she wasn't the sort of person to have a fling. Harry wasn't either; so surely the fact that they'd both acted so out of character *meant* something? 'Plus we made a baby. Unintentionally.'

'I like you,' he said. 'At least I like the bit of you I've got to know so far.' There was a glint of amusement in his eyes as he said, 'Except possibly the hormonal version of you that stomps off in a huff.'

'That,' she said, 'isn't fair.' Then she thought about it. 'Or maybe it is. I don't usually stomp off in a huff.'

'Your colleagues call you Lara Croft—which I'm guessing is because you're not scared of anything and you just roll your sleeves up and sort things out, quietly and methodically. I like that.'

'And you make people *feel* things,' she said. 'I like hearing you play.'

'That's a good place to start from,' he said. 'I can't promise you this is going to work out between us, because I don't have a good track record.'

Was he trying to tell her that there was more than one divorce in his past?

The question must've shown on her face, because he said, 'I've only been married once, and there haven't been a string of long-term girlfriends. Or even much of a string of short-term ones. It took me a while to put myself back together after the divorce, and my work schedule means I'm not very available.'

'Uh-huh.' She didn't know what to say. He was sounding more and more emotionally distant.

'But I'll try my hardest. And, whatever happens between you and me, I want to be a decent dad to our child.'

So her *grand passion* had fizzled out. Disappointment flooded through her. He didn't want a relationship and he was clearly going to see her as an obligation. That wasn't what she wanted. At all.

It must have shown on her face, because he said, 'Holly, you need to know I'm not good at emotional stuff. I grew up with my parents fighting constantly and I used to escape into my music—which is an explanation, not an excuse, because I'll take the blame where it's due and I made a mess of my marriage. I know you've been hurt and your ex lied to you, and I don't want to make a promise to you that I'm scared I won't be able to keep.'

'So are you saying you want to be with me, or not?' she asked.

'I'm saying I'd like to try. Neither of us usually does mad things, but we still had that fling. My head's all over the place right now, but I want to get to know you better. Not just on Sundays,' he said. 'It's not that far a drive from London to Beauchamp. I could maybe come and see you during the week. I could take you out for dinner or into Cambridge and we could go punting on the river.'

So he *did* want to try. He was just scared that it would all go wrong. She could understand that, and it made her feel a bit less awkward. And, because he was offering something, she felt it was her turn to offer something, too. 'Because I was a bit late finding out about the baby, I'm late for everything else, too. I've got a dating scan in London on Wednesday, if you're free.'

'I'll make sure I'm free,' he said. 'Thank you.' He paused. 'Would you mind if we kept this to ourselves for now?'

'To ourselves,' she repeated. Was this his way of telling her that he didn't think she was good enough for his family and he'd have to talk them round?

'Dominic and Ellen will be thrilled,' he said, as if guessing what she was worrying about. 'My parents see the world in a very different way from most, and I don't want them upsetting you.'

'Oh.' So it kind of was that he didn't think she was good enough.

'Right now,' he said softly, 'I need to get my head around the idea of being a parent. And it's easier to do that at a distance from my own parents. You've met them, so you know they can be difficult. Even though Nell says they're both eating out of your hand.'

'I think they accept me now,' she said. 'At least, as the head of the dig.'

'For what it's worth,' he said, 'Dom and Nell like you. A lot. And Granny Beckett would definitely have approved of you.'

'I see.'

He reached over and took her hand. 'Let's just give ourselves some time to get to know each other without any outside pressure.'

Even though she still felt insecure, there was the baby to consider. And they had to start somewhere.

'Perhaps,' he said, 'I could offer you tea and cake at my place.'

He was inviting her into his private space. Given that he'd told her he wasn't good at emotional stuff, it couldn't be easy for him to ask her there; he was making the effort and she appreciated that. 'That,' she said, 'would be nice.'

Harry's flat was the top floor of a Victorian three-storey house, and it was much smaller than Holly had expected. Everything was neat and tidy, but it felt more like a hotel apartment than a real home. The only personal things in evidence were the framed photographs on the mantelpiece and the top of his piano: wedding pictures of his siblings, pictures of his nieces and nephews, and a photograph of what was clearly the quartet at an award ceremony.

He made her a mug of tea just how she liked it, and sat next to her on the sofa.

'So you're a minimalist, then,' she said.

'I'm away a lot. It makes sense to keep everything very tidy,' he said. 'I'm assuming that means you're not?'

'Let's just say I have a few overflowing bookcases, lots of maps, and a collection of fossils on display, not to mention the fact that I often work on my knees in mud,' she said. 'And I was expecting you to have a lot of music.'

'It's mainly in digital format,' he explained, 'though I do have a cupboard full of Granny Beckett's vinyl.'

That was what worried her. Everything was a little bit *too* neat and tidy. How would he cope with it being disordered? 'Babies make a lot of chaos,' she said.

He grinned. 'Having two nephews and two nieces, I already have a rough idea about that.'

'And you don't mind?'

'No.' He looked at her. 'So tell me about you.'

'There isn't that much to tell. I'm the younger of two girls. Our parents are both on the cusp of retiring and planning to travel a lot; my sister has a son and a daughter. I don't have any pets, because if I'm on a dig that would mean putting a dog in kennels or getting my mum or sister to dog-sit, which doesn't seem fair.' She spread her hands. 'That's about it.'

'Maybe we ought to find a list of speed dating questions,' he suggested. 'It'll be a quick way of getting to know each other.' When she nodded, he did a quick search on his phone. 'Right. What makes you happy?'

'Work,' she said promptly. 'And my family and friends.'

'Snap,' he said. 'Next: do you prefer the city or the country?'

'Both,' she said. 'I love living in London—but I also enjoy it when a dig is in the middle of nowhere and all I can hear is birdsong. You?'

'Both,' he said. 'I love living in London, too, but I like punting down to Grantchester and wandering through the meadows.'

'Sounds nice,' she said.

'I'll take you there,' he promised, and consulted the list again. 'What are you reading at the moment?'

She winced. 'Something really nerdy. A book about facial reconstruction.'

'I think I've seen an article about that in one of the Sunday supplements. Isn't that where you find a skeleton and the artist can work out what the person actually looked like when they were alive?' he asked.

'Yes. It's fascinating. They make a 3D model of the skull, import it to a virtual sculpture system, and the artist then reconstructs the facial muscles. There's an amazing one at the Johns Hopkins in America—the Cohen Mummy. For decades, everyone thought it was a boy, but it turned out to be a woman.' She grabbed her own phone and found the pictures for him. 'And they managed to do that from a partial skull—the jawbone was missing.'

'That's absolutely amazing.' He looked at her. 'I can see why you love your subject.'

Simon had always zoned out a bit when she'd talked about work. Having a partner who was actually interested in what she did felt strange—though in a good way. 'What are you reading?' she asked.

'A biography of Bach,' he said. 'Though I also like crime novels. Not the gore-fests—I like the ones where you get inside the characters' heads.'

'Me, too,' she said. 'There's a brilliant series about a

forensic archaeologist. I'll lend it to you, if you haven't already read it.'

He smiled at her. 'Thanks.'

'What about TV?' she asked.

'I don't bother very much. I'd rather be at a concert,' he said. 'How about you?'

'Costume drama,' she said. 'My best friend absolutely loves Jane Austen, so I've seen every adaptation going.'

He looked at his phone. 'Lark or owl?'

'Lark,' she said.

He wrinkled his nose. 'I'm an owl. I think we're both going to have to compromise a bit there.' He checked the screen again. 'What makes you laugh?'

'Bad puns.' She looked at him. 'What's an archaeologist's favourite sort of joke?' At his shrug, she said, 'Pre-hysterical.'

He laughed. 'Love it. What's the difference between a fish and a piano?' When she shook her head, he said, 'You can't tuna fish...'

'I think,' she said, 'our nieces and nephews are all about to double their joke stock.'

'Sounds good to me,' he said. 'What's your ideal holiday?'

'Somewhere with lots of ruins and museums to explore,' she said promptly. 'Yours?'

'Somewhere with lots of concerts.'

'So not a beach holiday?'

He shuddered. 'That's my idea of a nightmare.'

'Mine, too.' She looked at him. 'So we have a lot of things in common.'

'Which is a really good start.'

True, but she wanted more. She wanted him to want her, not to feel obliged because of the baby.

'What time is the scan on Wednesday?' he asked.

'Half-past nine. I'll text you the details,' she said.

'Thank you. And are you going straight back to Beauchamp afterwards?'

'Possibly.'

'Or maybe you could come to a lunchtime concert with me first? Some of my friends are playing Mozart at St Martin's on Wednesday. We could grab something to eat in the crypt beforehand.'

He was asking her on a real date? Something that was both reassuring and exciting. Maybe he wasn't going to see her as an obligation after all. 'I'd like that,' she said. 'And maybe we can take your nephew and nieces to see the mummies at the British Museum at the weekend, if you're around on Sunday.'

'I'd like that,' he said. His eyes crinkled at the corners. 'We could make a list of all the things that you would like to do, and work our way through it.'

A list. He was really beginning to sound like a man after her own heart, which gave her hope. 'You're a planner?' she checked.

'Lists are my guilty pleasure,' he admitted.

'Mine, too.'

He persuaded her to stay a bit longer by playing the piano for her, some of the pieces that he'd already played her on the cello, and then he drove her back to her flat.

'I'll see you on Wednesday,' he said on her doorstep. 'Maybe I can pick you up from here and we can go in to the hospital together.'

Like a real couple.

Funny how that made her feel so warm inside.

'Goodnight, Holly.' He looked at her and his eyes darkened.

Was he going to kiss her?

For a moment, she thought he was going to take a step backwards. And then he cupped her face in his hands, his touch gentle. Her skin tingled where it made contact with his, and as he stared at her mouth she felt her lips parting.

Slowly, slowly, he dipped his head and his mouth brushed against hers. And it felt as if the dull evening suddenly turned Technicolor, with the brightness and the saturation both turned up to the max.

By the time he broke the kiss, she was shaking—and she could see a slash of colour across his cheekbones. He might not be saying it, but she knew that he was affected by this thing between them just as much as she was.

'See you on Wednesday,' he said, and stole another kiss—as if he was finding it as hard to tear himself away from her as she was finding it to let him go.

CHAPTER EIGHT

AND JUST LIKE that Holly found herself in a relationship again. Except this wasn't safe and familiar, like it had been with Simon. Even seeing Harry's name on her phone screen made her heart beat faster.

She imagined this was what dating was supposed to be like in your teens—not that she'd dated much back then. The headiness, the excitement. Not being able to stop thinking about him and how it felt when he kissed her. Was it the same for him? She was beginning to think that it might be, because on Monday Harry texted her a photograph of the church where he and the quartet were playing Haydn. On Tuesday he called her, just to say hello. And on Wednesday her doorbell rang at a quarter to eight in the morning, when they'd arranged to meet at half past to go to the hospital.

'Good morning.' Harry handed her a beautiful bouquet of roses. 'I know you're not going to be here to enjoy them again until Saturday, but I couldn't let today go without bringing you flowers.' He kissed her lightly. 'And I brought us breakfast.'

Which turned out to be freshly squeezed orange juice and still-warm croissants. 'Thank you. That's so lovel—' To her horror, Holly felt a tear slide down her

cheek. She brushed it away with the back of her hand.
'Sorry. Hormones. I'm really not one of these women
who cries buckets at every little thing.' But she wasn't
used to feeling as if someone cherished her, and it threw
her.

'I know you're not a weeper.' He kissed her again, his
mouth warm and sweet and reassuring, yet at the same
time it sent her pulse rate soaring. 'So are you OK?'

She nodded. 'I've just put the kettle on. I'm supposed
to drink loads of water—'

'—before the scan,' he finished. 'I've been reading
up on things.'

He ended up making the tea while she put the flowers in water.

When had someone last brought her flowers?

Apart from the ones all her visitors had brought her
after the accident, she thought it was probably her mum
on her birthday. Simon hadn't been one for romantic gestures. And Holly was discovering that she liked romantic
gestures. She liked them very much indeed.

Harry held her hand all the way to the tube station,
all the way on the tube journey, and all the way to the
hospital. And he kept his fingers laced tightly through
her own in the waiting room, after he'd checked that she
was comfortable and had water. Was he maybe nervous
of hospitals? she wondered.

Harry felt sick. Adrenaline was speeding through his
bloodstream. It was way, way worse than the nerves
he always felt just as he walked onto the stage. But on
a stage he knew what he was doing, plus he had his
cello to cling to. Here, he had no control over whether
things would go well or not. He was holding Holly's

hand, and he knew he was holding it way too tightly, but he couldn't help himself.

The last time he'd been a prospective father, it had all gone so badly wrong. He hadn't even got to the stage of having the first scan with Rochelle, because she'd lost the baby two days before their appointment. Even if today turned out to be fine, so many things could still go wrong. Maybe it had been a mistake to search the Internet to find out what to expect at each stage of the pregnancy. Holly was past twelve weeks, so in theory she was out of the major danger zone, and the dating scan would give them an accurate figure. But supposing the sonographer couldn't find a heartbeat? Supposing, instead of happy tears, there was just despair, like last time?

He was older now. Wiser. He would handle things very differently if this turned out to be a crisis.

But until he heard the magic words, he wasn't taking anything for granted.

'Are you all right, Harry?' Holly asked.

'I'm fine,' he lied.

'Just... I can't feel my fingers.'

'Sorry.' He swallowed hard and forced himself to loosen his grip. 'I'm just a bit nervous. Which is ridiculous, I know, because you're the one actually carrying the baby and you're—'

'Harry,' she said softly, 'shut up.'

And then she kissed him.

It wasn't a passionate, earthy, no-holds-barred kiss. It was sweet and gentle and reassuring. Letting him know that, whatever happened, it would be just fine in the end because they were both in this together.

And for the first time Harry found himself starting to

think that this was actually going to work out. Holly—his nerdy, practical, quiet archaeologist—made his world feel a better place simply because she was in it. She made him feel grounded.

This was crazy. They barely knew each other. She didn't even remember the night they'd spent together in Bath, thanks to her accident the day after. They'd been dating officially for all of three days. He couldn't possibly feel this way about her.

But just as she'd drawn his attention while he'd been playing the set at Bath, she drew him now. She made him feel centred.

'Sorry.' He kissed her back.

'First-time dad?' the woman next to them asked, an indulgent smile on her fact.

No. Not that he wanted to discuss that now. 'Yes,' he said. It wasn't a complete untruth. He and Rochelle hadn't made it as far as this stage.

'Don't worry. The scan won't hurt the baby, love, and it won't hurt your wife.' She patted her own bump. 'This one's our third. But my partner is still going to be here any minute now because nothing beats seeing your baby for the first time. It's magical.'

As if on cue, her partner arrived, but before she could introduce Harry and Holly to him, they were called into the ultrasound scan room.

'This is it.' Harry forced himself to hold Holly's hand in a supportive way rather than clutching it for dear life, and walked with her into the dimly lit ultrasound suite.

The sonographer talked them through the test; then Holly lay on the couch, lowered the waistband of her skirt and pulled up her top to expose the bump. The sonographer spread gel over Holly's stomach, and pressed the head of the probe against her abdomen.

And there, on the screen, was their baby.

'Say hello to your baby, Mr and Mrs Weston,' the sonographer said with a smile.

Harry didn't correct her that Holly was actually Dr Weston and he was Mr Moran. All he could see was a black and white screen, the baby's head and the curved spine.

'That's just one baby,' the sonographer said, then she took some measurements. 'When was your last menstrual period, Mrs Weston?'

Holly told her.

The sonographer smiled. 'Wonderful. It all ties up nicely with the measurements. You're fifteen weeks, so the baby is due at the end of February.'

Harry still couldn't speak. He just stared in wonder at the image on the screen.

'There are ten fingers and ten toes,' the sonographer continued. 'The heart is beating nice and strongly. I can't see anything that worries me at this stage, but I'll measure the fluid at the back of the baby's neck as part of the screening test.'

'Thank you,' Holly said.

She squeezed Harry's hand, and he realised he was meant to speak. 'Sorry. Thank you,' he mumbled. 'Sorry. I'm just...'

'The first time they see the baby blows most dads away,' the sonographer said kindly. 'Would you both like a photograph?'

'Yes, please,' he said. 'Our baby. I just...' He shook his head, as if barely able to believe what he was seeing. *'Our baby.'*

* * *

Harry actually had tears in his eyes, Holly realised, and her heart melted. She smiled at him. 'It's pretty amazing.'

'Fifteen weeks. So the baby is about the size of an apple, lanugo is covering the baby's skin, and they can hear your voice.'

The sonographer grinned. 'It sounds as if someone's been doing some bedtime reading, then.'

'A little bit,' Harry admitted.

When Holly had found out that she was pregnant, she'd been so sure that the baby's father wouldn't be in the slightest bit interested. From Harry's reaction just now, she knew that he was very much going to be a hands-on parent. They were in this together. She squeezed his hand again. 'That's good.'

The sonographer finished doing the measurements, printed out two photographs, and then Holly wiped off the gel and restored order to her clothes.

Harry couldn't stop looking at the photograph. 'Our baby,' he said again, his gorgeous blue eyes wide with wonder. Would their baby have his eyes? she wondered. What would their baby inherit from each of them? And she loved the idea that maybe they'd grow together as a family, see bits of themselves reflected in their child.

They headed for Trafalgar Square and through the National Gallery, discovering that their tastes in art were similar. After a quick lunch, they took their seats in St Martin's Church, and Holly thoroughly enjoyed the Mozart piano trios. Afterwards, Harry introduced her to his friends the performers, calling her his partner; it sent a weird little thrill through her veins.

'Are you going back to Beauchamp this afternoon?' he asked.

'This evening. I want to see my mum first, and show her the picture of the baby,' Holly said. She looked at him. Was this rushing things too much? Then again, she and Simon had taken things really slowly and that hadn't worked out. Maybe she needed to be less cautious and do the opposite. 'If you don't have to rush off anywhere, then you're welcome to come with me.'

'I'd like that. And maybe I can drive you back to Beauchamp.'

'Thanks, but I'd rather have my car handy.'

'Then, if you don't mind giving me a lift, I'll get the train back from Cambridge tomorrow.' He paused. 'Right now, I want to tell the world about you and our baby, but I'll be guided by you on this.'

'We've been dating officially for all of three days,' she pointed out.

'We would've been dating for three months by now,' he countered, 'if things had gone according to our original plan.'

She looked at him. 'So you intend to be in this for the long haul?'

'We're still getting to know each other, and I made a mess of my marriage, so I don't want to make a promise and let you down,' he said, 'but whatever happens between you and me I intend to support you through pregnancy. And I'll be a hands-on dad.'

'You work away a lot,' she said. 'You can't be hands on from a distance.'

'As hands on as I can,' he amended. 'But, yes. If your parents want to know, my intentions towards you are entirely honourable. We're both capable of sorting out the complicated stuff between us, even if it takes a little time.' He kissed her lightly. 'I don't think either of us expected this. But we'll make it work.'

'It scares the hell out of me,' she admitted. 'I knew Simon for years. I thought we were fine. And it all went wrong.'

'Whereas we've done everything the wrong way round,' he said. 'So maybe this time it'll go right.'

How could she explain that she was punching so far above her weight, being with him? She hadn't been enough for Simon, and he was a dull accountant. How could she possibly be enough for an award-winning musician who led an incredibly glamorous life crisis-crossing the globe?

To her horror, she realised she'd spoken some of it aloud, because Harry raised an eyebrow.

'Let me unpick this for you. Firstly, your ex doesn't sound like a very nice guy, so don't look at yourself through his eyes. Secondly, my life isn't that glamorous. Although I dress up for a performance, there's a lot of time spent travelling, checking lighting and seating, waiting around, and practising scales. Thirdly, I never get distracted when I'm working, with the exception of Bath—so there's something about you that's special. The more time I spend with you, the more I like you. So stop worrying about whether you're enough, because you *are*.'

It brought a lump in her throat, to the point where she couldn't answer.

He kissed her again. 'If it makes you feel any better, I'm pretty nervous about meeting your mum. In her shoes, I'd want to know exactly why this gadabout, flaky guy made my daughter pregnant and deserted her.'

'I didn't remember anything about you and you didn't have enough information to get in touch with me,' she reminded him. 'So it's not quite desertion.'

'It is, if you think about it. I could've tried to search for you on social media.'

'I would've *hated* that,' she said. 'So I'm glad you didn't.'

'Even so. I'm meeting your mum for the first time, and I can't possibly go without flowers—seriously nice flowers,' he said, and insisted on stopping at a florist's on the way back to Camden.

Ginny Weston was delighted by the flowers, but even more so by the way Harry behaved towards her younger daughter. 'The way he looks at you—Simon never looked at you like that,' she said quietly to Holly in the kitchen.

Holly flushed. 'Mum!'

'I know, I know. It's early days, and you've both got the baby to think about—and he must still be coming to terms with the fact that he's going to be a dad. But the way he looks at you... That's exactly how I want your partner to look at you,' she said. 'If he hadn't taken your number down wrong, he would've been there at your bedside the whole time while you were in hospital.'

'No, he wouldn't. He was working the next day.'

'I have a feeling he would've made some alternative arrangements to make sure he was there by your side,' Ginny said. 'I like him.'

They stopped long enough that Harry ended up meeting Holly's father and sister, too. And Natalie, who had texted to ask about the scan and dropped in on her way home from work. So it was much, much later than Holly had intended by the time they got to Beauchamp.

'You've been a hit with my family and my best friend,' she said. She swallowed hard. 'But although yours seem to like me in my professional capacity—'

'—they'll love you as my partner and the mother of my child,' Harry finished. 'Ellen and Dominic are lovely. My parents are difficult, yes, but you might already have worked out for yourself that the trick to dealing with them is to ignore whatever they say.' He paused. 'Granny Beckett would've asked you a lot of questions. And then she would've smiled and given you the biggest hug.' He smiled. 'So don't worry. My family and closest friends will approve of you.'

Just for a second, there was something in his expression that she couldn't read. What wasn't he telling her?

'It's your choice,' he said, squeezing her hand. 'You can drop me here outside Nell's and we'll tell her tomorrow if you want to get some rest. Or we can tell her now, if you're going to lie awake worrying about it all night.'

'I wasn't a worrier until the hormones started,' she said.

'Are they going to keep you awake tonight?'

She nodded ruefully.

'Then let's face the music tonight,' he said, 'because you need to rest properly.'

He held her hand all the way down the garden path, and he was still holding her hand when his sister answered the door.

'Harry! We weren't expecting you tonight.' Then Ellen noticed him holding hands with Holly. 'Oh. Nice to see you, too, Holly.'

'Can we come in?' Harry asked.

'Of course. I'll put the kettle on.' She smiled at them. 'I wish I'd known you were going to call in tonight.

George and Alice are asleep and they'll be so upset to have missed you.'

'They'll see me tomorrow, if you don't mind me scrounging a bed,' Harry said.

'Of course not.' She rolled her eyes at him. 'You know we always have room for you.'

'I have news,' Harry said, and proceeded to tell Ellen everything.

Holly's breathing grew more and more shallow, and adrenaline rather than blood seem to be flowing through her veins.

But when Harry had finished, Ellen just grinned and hugged her. 'Well, obviously it's all a big surprise and it's a bit complicated—but I'm so pleased for you both and I really hope you've got a scan picture of my niece-or nephew-to-be, because I'm dying to see it!'

And from that moment on it was all easy. Ellen persuaded Harry to video-call Dominic and Sally and explain it to them, and they seemed just as pleased as Ellen and Tristan were.

'One thing, though,' Sally said. 'If you two decide to get married, you really need to have "Don't You Forget About Me" as your first dance.'

'Or anything from Radiohead's *Amnesiac*,' Dominic chipped in.

Harry groaned. 'This one is going to run and run, isn't it?'

'Absolutely. Oh, and you need forget-me-nots in your bouquet. Welcome to the family, Holly,' Dominic said. 'So when are you telling the parents, Harry?'

'Tomorrow,' Harry said.

'If they say anything vile, Holly, just ignore them,'

Dominic said. 'And be assured that we'll all have your back when Harry's not here.'

'So you don't all think I'm...' Holly's voice faded.

'We think,' Ellen said, 'you're sensible, you're lovely, the kids adore you, and you're perfect for our baby brother.'

The Viscount and Viscountess were too taken aback to say anything rude when Harry told them the news the next morning. And Harry forwarded a slew of texts from the rest of the quartet to Holly, saying they were looking forward to meeting Harry's mysterious Lady in Red at last. The fact that he'd clearly talked about her to his closes friends, even when he hadn't known who she was, reassured her.

Although Harry had to head off on Thursday, he called Holly every single day, texted her snippets about what new developments their baby would have that week, sent her a photograph of the gorgeous hotel where the quartet we are playing on the Saturday, and picked her up on Sunday to take her to lunch at Lucy and Carina's so she could meet his closest friends and colleagues.

'This is just brilliant,' Lucy said, hugging her warmly. 'I'm so glad he's met someone like you.'

'The woman who forgot him the very next day?' Holly asked wryly.

'That wasn't your fault. What were you supposed to do, let that idiot drive straight into a little boy? Actually, I think you were really brave, scooping him up like that.'

'Instinct,' Holly said. 'Anyone would've done the same.'

'Actually, a lot of people wouldn't have had the nerve.' Lucy tucked her arm through Holly's. 'Right. Let's get you a drink, a decent seat, and something to eat. Do you play an instrument at all?'

'I'm sorry, no. I just listen to music.'

'Don't apologise.' Lucy smiled brightly.

Was it her imagination, Holly wondered, or did Lucy look relieved?

'Though Harry taught me to do a round of "Frère Jacques" at the piano with his niece and nephew. And he got me to sing—you know, the bit in *Truly Madly Deeply*.'

'I love that film. It makes me cry buckets,' Lucy said. 'But if you're encouraging him to play the cello like a guitar…'

Holly bit her lip, remembering what Harry had said about how his colleagues viewed that style of playing. 'Sorry.'

Lucy chuckled. 'I'm teasing. Our Harry doesn't need encouragement. Actually, I've seen a huge difference him over the last week—a difference that makes us all very happy—and it's all thanks to you.'

The next couple of weeks were more of the same: seeing Harry in London on Sundays and on the occasional evening if he could get down to Beauchamp.

'You're my Sunday girl,' he teased, the evening when they were curled up together on his sofa, and hummed the middle section of Blondie's 'Sunday Girl'.

'If you start playing that on the cello, the quartet will have my guts for garters,' she said with a grin.

'Are you kidding? They adore you.' He paused.

Her heart skipped a beat. Was he going to say he adored her, too?

'Holly, I…' Then he stopped.

What was holding him back? Worry that she didn't feel the same?

'I don't want to rush you,' he said, 'but I can't help myself. I apologise in advance. But I...' He rolled his eyes. 'Sorry. I'm usually good with words.'

But not when it came to emotional stuff? Maybe it would help if she said it first. 'You're adorable,' she said. Though she wasn't going to say the L word. It was too soon. Though she knew she was falling harder for Harry with every day that passed.

'That's how I feel about you, too,' he said, as if she'd spoken her thoughts aloud. 'Do you have to go home tonight?'

Her pulse leapt. 'You're asking me to stay?'

'Yes. And I'll drive you home tomorrow. Whatever time you like,' he said. 'Though if I'm rushing you, I'll wait.' He stroked her hair. 'I just don't want to say goodnight.'

She didn't either. She missed him hugely when they weren't together, and it was good to know that he felt the same.

Yes, this was rushing it. Then again, she was carrying his baby. So maybe none of the conventions mattered any more. 'I'll stay,' she said.

He kissed her lingeringly. 'Good. Because I want to wake up with you in my arms.'

Just as she presumed they'd done in Bath.

'I really hate the fact,' she said, 'that I don't remember Bath. That I don't remember making our baby.'

Colour slashed through his face. 'Obviously I didn't know we were making a baby at the time, but I definitely remember making love with you.' His eyes held a bright, almost febrile glitter. 'Maybe if we repeat it, your memory will come back.'

She didn't think it would. Not now.

Clearly it showed in her expression, because he said, 'Even if it doesn't, I'll do my best to make it the same.'

It didn't bring her memory back, but Holly loved the way that Harry let her undress him, clearly keeping himself in check. Even in jeans, he was gorgeous; out of them, he was even more so, his musculature sculpted and his abdomen flat.

'You're so beautiful,' she whispered.

'Thank you. But I'm feeling a bit underdressed now. My turn?' Harry asked.

Feeling ridiculously shy, she nodded and let him undress her. He took it slowly, caressing every centimetre of skin he uncovered, until her whole body felt heated. He lingered particularly over her abdomen. 'I can see the changes in you,' he said, 'and you're gorgeous.'

'I'm very ordinary,' she corrected.

'Are you, hell,' he said. He scooped her up and carried her to his bed. 'Simon might have had blinkers, but I don't. You once told me you were beige. Well, you're not. You're gold and honey—the colour of your hair, the colour of your eyes, the way the sun kisses your skin.'

And then he proceeded to show her just how gorgeous he thought she was.

Afterwards, she lay curled in his arms, sated. 'I still don't see how a bang on the head could make me forget something as amazing as that. Someone as amazing as you.'

'Memory is a funny thing. And it's bound up in all the senses. Like Proust and his madeleines,' he said thoughtfully, 'the scent and taste bringing the memory back.'

'I guess.' She kissed him. 'I'm just sorry I forgot you. Because you're not at all forgettable.'

'And I'm sorry I didn't just suck it up and do the whole "Help me find my Lady in Red" thing on social media,' he said. 'Because I hate to think you believed I would ever desert you.'

'That isn't who you are,' she said. 'You know I'm glad you didn't do the social media stuff! I'd hate to have people gawping over my private life.'

'Then it's just as well I work in the area I do, rather than rock or pop,' Harry said. 'We get a lot less press intrusion.' He curled his hand round her abdomen. 'Right now, all I can think of is you, me and our baby.'

She stilled.

'What's wrong?' Harry asked.

'I think,' she said, 'I just felt the baby move. Like bubbles inside me.'

'I read that it could happen around this time,' he said thoughtfully. 'But it will be a while before I can feel the baby move.'

'You really have been reading up,' she said, smiling.

'I have. And I'm hoping you'll let me come to your antenatal classes. I mean it about supporting you.' He kissed her again. 'And I'd like to start playing music to our baby. Music is meant to be good for helping you relax and bond with the baby, and for the structure of the baby's brain. Plus studies show the that babies actually remember the music they hear in the womb.'

'Sounds good to me. And I'd like to read those studies, too,' she said. 'Let me have the link.'

'I will.' He smiled. 'Thank you for indulging me in the nerdy stuff.'

'No problem. I'm sure Amenhotep or Nefertiti will enjoy you playing to them.'

He stared at her. 'Amenhotep and Nefertiti? They're the names you've picked out?'

'But of course. My favourite pharaoh and the most beautiful woman in the world,' she said, enjoying the expression on his face—a mingled look of horror and a desperate attempt to be supportive.

'Amen...' He blew out a breath. Then the penny clearly dropped. 'All right. Ammy or Nef it is.'

He'd even worked out the diminutives?

'As long as we have a middle name of Camille for a boy and Hildegard for a girl,' he added.

He'd lost her as much as she'd lost him. 'Camille?' she asked.

'Saint-Saëns,' he explained.

The composer of one of the most famous cello pieces, she remembered. 'And Hildegard?'

'Of Bingen. She was a twelfth-century Benedictine abbess, composer, writer and philosopher,' he explained.

Holly laughed. 'I've already horrified my best friend. I'm so looking forward to seeing her face when she hears *your* suggestions.'

He laughed and kissed her. 'I guess we have some more serious decisions to make, but we have plenty of time. For now, I want to enjoy just being with you.'

CHAPTER NINE

By the middle of October, Holly began to believe that this was going to work out. Although Harry's schedule was hectic, he was scrupulous about coming to antenatal classes and appointments with her. He saw her every Sunday and as many other days in the week as he could, and on the days when he was away working he video-called her and played a lullaby to the baby.

The day he felt the baby kick for the first time, Harry went uncharacteristically quiet. Holly reminded herself that they were still getting to know each other, still getting used to their back-to-front situation. Just because she was starting to fall in love with him, it didn't mean that he was falling in love with her. And, although Harry had been vocal on the subject of Simon's behaviour towards her, deep inside Holly still worried that she wasn't going to be enough for him. Would he grow bored? Would he feel that she was holding him back? Would he expect her to put her career second to his—especially as he'd already warned her that he'd put his career before his marriage?

Once she'd let herself think, the worries multiplied. She didn't know where to start unpicking them and discussing them with Harry so, not wanting to rock the boat, she said nothing.

But if there was a time to say those three little words, when emotion was bubbling high, she thought it would be the moment after he felt the baby kick. The fact that he hadn't said it… Was he with her because he felt obliged to be there, rather than wanting to be with her?

The thought wouldn't go away. She needed to be careful. Last time round, she'd loved Simon more than he'd loved her and she'd ended up hurt. She couldn't let herself love Harry until he was sure how she felt he felt about her. And she certainly wasn't going to be the one to say it first. She had her pride.

This was a tightrope, Harry thought. One he'd negotiated before and he'd fallen off. Been badly hurt.

Could he take the risk that this time he would stay sure-footed?

But the parallels between the past and the present worried him. He'd married Rochelle because she'd been pregnant. It had been a knee-jerk reaction because he'd loved her and had wanted to support her. He and Rochelle had had a lot in common, similar careers, had known each other for years and had always got on well, and the sex had been good. So on paper their marriage should've worked out. They should've been strong enough to cope with the miscarriage, help each other through it.

Instead, everything had collapsed. He'd discovered that she hadn't really loved him—she'd loved the idea of being part of an aristocratic family, but she hadn't loved him for himself.

This time round, the way he felt about Holly was

nothing like he'd ever felt for anyone before. OK, so they hadn't known each other long, and for a lot of that time she'd forgotten he even existed, thanks to her amnesia, but they were working on it. It wasn't just sexual attraction: he really liked the woman he was getting to know. He was pretty sure he was in love with her. And he'd almost told her that when he'd felt the baby kick.

But how could he be sure that it would work this time?

He didn't want to upset Holly with his doubts, so he said nothing. Maybe his doubts would go. Maybe he just needed a little more time.

On Sunday, the quartet was due to fly to Berlin to play three nights of Mozart. They had arranged to have a late lunch at Lucy's house before the flight, and both Carina and Holly planned to wave the quartet off at the airport.

'You're really blooming, Holly,' Lucy said, 'and Harry looks so happy. It's lovely to see that. Especially after Roch—' She stopped abruptly, her eyes widening with obvious horror. 'I'm so sorry. I didn't mean to put my foot in it.'

'It's OK. I know about Rochelle,' Holly reassured her. She was beginning to think that the divorce was one of the reasons why Harry might be holding back, scared of repeating a mistake.

'I'm glad he told you. Though I did worry a bit when he first told us about you.' Lucy bit her lip. 'Especially because of the baby. It was so sad.'

Sad? What was sad? What baby? Was Lucy telling her that Harry had a child he didn't see? Holly stared at her, shocked. 'Baby?' she asked finally.

Lucy winced. 'Just ignore me. I'm talking rubbish.'

'I don't think you are. And I'd rather know the truth,'

Holly said. 'Otherwise my imagination will blow it up into something far worse.'

'Sorry.' Lucy squeezed her hand. 'I don't know how to say this without upsetting you. It's just about the worst thing you can possibly say to a pregnant woman. Rochelle, um, had a miscarriage, just before the dating scan.'

Holly went cold. A miscarriage. OK, so she was beyond the twelve-week mark now, so the risk was an awful lot lower; but was this why Harry was holding back, because he was scared that history might repeat itself?

And why hadn't he told her? It was another lie of omission, and it made her wonder what else he was keeping from her. When she thought about it, it hadn't been just an omission; he'd out-and-out lied about it, telling the woman in the waiting room at the scan that he was a first-time father.

Clearly he that wasn't true.

Now she was going to question everything he said to her, and that wasn't good.

'Holly? Are you all right?' Lucy asked, looking concerned.

'I'm fine,' Holly fibbed. 'Just a bit tired.'

'If you want to go and have a lie down, you're welcome to have a nap in our spare bedroom,' Lucy said.

What Holly really wanted was her own space. Time to think about what she'd just learned and what it meant for her future. If Harry wasn't going to trust her with the whole truth of his past, it wasn't going to work between them. Was he really over his ex and the loss of their child? Was he only with *her* because she was expecting his baby and he felt obliged to stay with her?

'That's really kind of you,' she said, 'but I'll be fine.'

Somehow she managed to make small talk with Harry's friends during the rest of lunch, and then she insisted that she and Harry would do the washing up together.

'Can we have a quiet word?' she asked when they were halfway through.

He frowned. 'Sure. What's wrong?'

There was no point in pussyfooting about. She needed to know the truth. 'When were you going to tell me about Rochelle's baby?'

He blanched. 'Oh, Christ. Who told you?'

'It doesn't matter—the person concerned thought I already knew. And you should've told me a long time ago.' She scrubbed the last few plates a bit too hard. 'Harry, you're clearly with me just because you feel obliged to be with me.'

He looked aghast. 'That's not true.'

But she didn't believe him. And she didn't want to be with someone who was selective with the truth. Been there, done that, and worn the T-shirt. 'I'm going home to my flat when I've done the washing up,' she said. 'On my own. Maybe we'll talk when you get back from Berlin and you've had time to think about what you really want.'

'But—'

'No buts,' she cut in, as gently as she could. 'I don't know what else you've been keeping from me.'

'I haven't kept anything from you.'

'Lies of omission are still lies, Harry. I had enough lies from Simon to last me a lifetime, and I can't spend the rest of my days wondering if you're keeping me in the dark about something.'

'Holly, I'm—'

'When you're back from Berlin,' she cut in. 'We'll talk then. But right now I don't want to see you. I need some space. Please thank Lucy and Carina for their hospitality. I'm going now, without any fuss.' Even though it was ripping her apart. Even though she'd planned to go to the airport with Harry and wave him off, she couldn't bear to do that now.

And just like that Harry's world switched into monochrome. Even though it was an unseasonably warm autumn afternoon, it felt like a dull winter's evening.

How could this all have gone so wrong?'

One thing he did know: there was no way he was letting Holly go.

He went to find Lucy. 'Holly's a bit tired,' he said, 'so she's slipped off home, but she wanted me to say thank you for her.'

'I'm really sorry that I dropped you in it,' Lucy said, biting her lip. 'I thought you'd told her about Rochelle.'

'Not about the miscarriage,' Harry said. 'Given that Holly's pregnant, it's not exactly a good subject.'

'I'm sorry if I caused a row between you.

'You didn't do it on purpose,' Harry said.

'But?' she asked.

He sighed. 'But she said she doesn't want to talk to me until we get back from Berlin. Lucy, I know this is all last minute, but—'

'You don't want to go to Berlin with us,' she finished.

'Holly's not like Rochelle. She didn't give me any ultimatums,' he said. 'But I really can't go until I've fixed this.'

'Our flight's this evening,' Lucy reminded him.

'But we're not actually playing until tomorrow evening. I can book another flight for me for tomorrow morning,' Harry said. 'I know it's going to mess up rehearsals, and I'm sorry.'

'I guess it'll mess things up more if your head's all over the place. We'll manage. Go after her,' Lucy advised. 'But just keep us posted about what's happening tomorrow.'

'I will.' He hugged her. 'Thanks.'

Except, when Harry turned up at Holly's flat, she wasn't there. And her phone went straight through to voicemail.

He sat on her doorstep. She'd told him that she was going back to her flat. Where else would she have gone? The most likely places were to her parents or to Natalie, but he didn't want to risk going to the wrong place and missing her.

He pulled out his phone and called Natalie. As he'd half expected, she didn't pick up.

She might be able to ignore a call, but she'd see a message. And hopefully she'd pass it on.

Please tell Holly I'm sitting on her doorstep and I've cancelled my flight.

He waited.

No response.

He gave it another ten minutes before he sent a second text.

And I'm not moving until she talks to me, even if I have to sit here for the entire night.

That did the trick, because his phone shrilled and

Holly's name came up on the screen. 'You're being melo-dramatic and ridiculous,' she said crossly.

'No,' he said quietly. 'Actually, I'm just desperate. And I'll do whatever it takes so you'll talk to me about this. Preferably face to face.'

'Go home, Harry.'

'I don't want to go to Berlin and leave things like this between us. Please. Come and talk to me, Holly.'

'Is there any point?'

'I think so. But how will you know unless you hear what I have to say?'

There was a long, long pause, and for a nasty moment Harry thought he'd pushed her too far and she'd call the whole thing off. But finally she said, 'I'll give you twenty minutes.'

'Thank you.'

It was forty minutes until the black cab dropped her outside.

'Why are you doing this?' she asked.

'I can't go to Berlin and leave things like this between us,' he said.

'It's your *job*,' she pointed out. 'You're supposed to play for three nights. You can't just not turn up.'

'I'll get the redeye flight tomorrow—*if* we've sorted this out.'

'Then I suppose you'd better come in.' She unlocked the door and ushered him inside.

'I'm sorry,' he said. 'I know how you feel about lying. I honestly didn't intend to hide anything from you.' He grimaced. 'I didn't tell you about the miscarriage be-cause you're pregnant and I didn't want to worry you. I did intend to tell you about it—but there never seemed to be a good time.'

* * *

Holly folded her arms. 'Try now. I'm listening.'

'I'll tell you the truth. All of it. But this isn't very nice,' he warned. 'I told you I was married. What I didn't tell you was that although I thought I loved Rochelle at the time, the main reason I married her was because she told me she was pregnant. The baby wasn't planned.'

Just like *their* baby. No wonder Harry hadn't let her close. He'd obviously thought he was making the same mistake all over again.

She swallowed hard and kept listening.

'Rochelle was having trouble finding work, and I knew she wanted security for the baby, so we got a licence and married as soon as possible in the registry office. It wasn't a big do: just the two of us and a couple of strangers who agreed to be our witnesses. I went on tour, promising to do the honeymoon bit and whisk her away when I got back. Except I didn't because, two days before the dating scan—while I was still away—she lost the baby.'

'I'm sorry,' Holly said. 'That must've been horrible for both of you.'

'It was.' He dragged in a breath. 'I wasn't there for her. The quartet was only just taking off so I couldn't just ask someone else to play in my stead. I didn't want to let the others down, and I knew her mum was there with her so I thought it would be OK to carry on with the tour.' He raked a hand through his hair. 'It seems absolutely insane to me now. Why on earth didn't I catch the first flight home? It was terrible of me. To be honest, I don't think I knew how to confront my own grief about it all. But that marked the beginning of the end for us.'

Holly's heart bled for him and for his ex. It sounded as

if they'd married in haste and really repented at leisure—
and they'd both had to deal with losing a baby, too. Without realising what she was doing, she splayed her fingers
protectively against her abdomen.

'Exactly,' Harry said wryly, clearly noticing what
she'd done. 'That's why I didn't tell you. I knew it would
upset you.'

It wasn't just that. He hadn't been honest about the
end of his marriage either. 'You led to me to believe it
was the pressure of your careers that drove you apart,'
she said.

'It was, in part.' Harry looked at her. 'Losing the baby
just made the cracks wider. She wanted me to give up
my music and go to work in the family business.'

'But you would've *hated* that.'

He nodded. 'It just got worse and worse. We had a
massive fight and she told me to choose between her and
the quartet. I couldn't believe she was actually asking
me to give up who I am.' He swallowed hard. 'I've never
told anyone this bit before, but that was when she told
me the truth. Something that hurt like hell, but ironically
made it easy for me to make the decision. She told me
that she'd deliberately got pregnant because she knew
it'd make me marry her. She thought it would give her
financial security and make her part of an aristocratic
family.' He closed his eyes briefly. 'She didn't love me
for *me*. She loved the youngest son of Viscount Moran.
My career wasn't enough for her; she wanted all the glitz
and glamour that went with my family, or so she thought.
So that made the decision easy. I said I was a musician
first. And she said she wanted a divorce.'

Holly absorbed the news. Rochelle had deliberately
got pregnant? She'd seen Harry as a means of security,

rather than him being the love of her life? That put a whole new spin on things. No wonder Harry was shy of relationships. Maybe, just like her, he thought he wasn't enough for anyone.

But she also knew the last thing he wanted was pity. She'd hated all the pity, too. 'That's rough,' she said. 'And I'm sorry she saw you like that. You're worth a lot more. And that's not pity talking, by the way.'

'I know. You've been there yourself.' He looked away for a moment. 'You can't get divorced in England on the grounds of irreconcilable differences. We went to a solicitor. Neither of us had committed adultery, so that left us with the option of citing unreasonable behaviour.' He grimaced. 'Mine.'

'That's not fair,' she said.

He shrugged. 'It was that, or agreeing to separate and then waiting for two years. Besides, she had a point. I hadn't behaved well. I should've been there for her when she lost the baby instead of wrapping myself in the security of my music.'

'She didn't exactly behave well, either,' Holly pointed out.

He shook his head. 'I'm not playing the blame game. I've seen my parents do that too many times and it doesn't end well for anyone. Maybe she feels guilty now about the way she treated me—I don't know. But we were both to blame. And we both wanted out of the marriage. But after that I swore I'd never get involved with anyone again.' He looked at her. 'What I didn't expect was to meet you. To fall in love with you.'

She felt her eyes widen. '*Do* you love me?'

'I love you,' he confirmed.

He'd said it first. But he didn't look happy about it.

'And it scares the hell out of me,' he added.

'Because you're in almost the same situation again—an unplanned baby, but this time with someone you haven't known for years?'

'No,' he said. 'It doesn't matter about not knowing you for very long and it doesn't matter that we didn't plan the baby. What scares me is that something might go wrong with our baby like it did with mine and Rochelle's baby. With music, I know what I'm doing and how to fix problems, but with a baby... I have no control over what happens.'

'I'm past the most dangerous trimester,' she said gently. 'And, despite the horror stories you see in the news, most pregnancies and births are straightforward.' She looked at him. She knew she was going to have to ask the hardest question, for her own peace of mind. 'Do you still love Rochelle?'

'No. I did, back then. At least, I thought I did at the time. But now I'm not sure I did, because the way I feel about you isn't the same as I felt about her. I love you. I know I do. You make the world feel grounded. But I'm still scared.' He looked anguished. 'What if I'm a terrible father?'

'Because your own parents weren't great with you, you mean?'

'Yes.'

'You're not them, Harry. You'll do things differently.'

'How can you know?'

'Because of your grandmother,' she said. 'I think that's the sort of parenting that will stick with you. Someone who notices, someone who makes a difference. Someone who gives, someone who guides without being pushy. And from what I've seen, you're an excellent uncle.'

He inclined his head in acknowledgement. 'Thank you, but there's a huge difference between looking after my nieces and nephews for a little while and being responsible for a baby full time. What if I get things wrong?'

'You muddle through and you work it out.' She looked at him. 'Just like you said to Henry and Celia when they were playing for you—if you make a mistake, you smile and keep going. You learn not to make the same mistake next time.'

'I know I'm not making the same mistake I made with Rochelle. I love you, Holly. I want to be with you. I want to live with you and make a family with you. But I'm scared you'll think I'm only saying that because of the baby.'

She knew they needed to face that one head on. 'Are you?'

He shook his head. 'We didn't plan our baby, but he or she definitely isn't unwanted. I want to be a good dad and I want to be there for our baby—but I'm asking you to marry me for *my* sake. I want to be with you, Holly, but I'm trying not to pressure you.' He paused. 'So I'll ask you: what do you want?'

'I still don't remember meeting you for the first time, and maybe I never will,' she said. 'And when I met you at Beauchamp I thought you were a spoiled poor little rich boy.'

'And then?'

'Then I started getting to know you. And I liked the man I was spending time with. You're good with children, you're fun to be around, and you play the cello so beautifully that you make me cry.' She took a deep breath. 'I'm scared that you only want to marry me because you feel you ought to. I'm ordinary. If I wasn't enough for Simon, how can I possibly be enough for you?'

He walked over to her and wrapped his arms round her. 'Because you're everything I want. You make me feel as if the world's a good place. You're the only woman I've ever noticed while I'm playing—and until now music has been my main focus in life.' He stole a kiss.

'But now I want more. I want you, and I want to be a family with you. And I know I've messed up twice now by not telling you something because I was trying to protect you, but I've learnt from my mistakes. You don't need me to be your knight in shining armour. You're perfectly capable of sorting everything out yourself—except you don't have to. I'll be there with you. All the way. I'll tell you everything, even if I have to warn you first that it's the wrong time or the wrong place or I'm concerned that it might hurt you. Because I know how much you value honesty—and I honestly, honestly love you, Holly.'

'I love you, too,' she said. 'And I'm never going to make you choose between me and your music.'

'So what do you want?' he asked.

'Love. Honesty. Fairness,' she said. 'I'm not expecting the future to be easy. You're away a lot, and my job's going to take me away from London from time to time. I want the baby and my career.'

'That's what I want, too. So we'll compromise,' he said. 'I'll tour less. I could teach.'

'Would you be happy teaching?' she asked. 'Because

there's a big difference between finding a workable compromise and making yourself unhappy. And I can definitely assure you that I don't want you to give things up and work at Beauchamp. I like your family—even your parents, actually, because they're all right with me—but it's not the right place for you. You're a musician.'

'Thank you,' he said, 'for understanding. I don't know if teaching's for me, but this is a good point to rethink the direction of my career.' He looked thoughtful. 'I'd like to try composing. Writing music for films. I could do that from home and we can share the baby's care between us—and make time for us, too.'

'We could schedule it,' she said. 'The baby. Work. Date night.'

There was a distinct twinkle in his eyes. 'Says my gorgeously nerdy academic. I like that idea.'

'So we're going to live together, as a family?'

'Yes. Though we need to find a house. My flat's too small for the three of us.'

'So's mine,' she said.

'So we'll go house-hunting tomorrow.'

'We'll go house-hunting,' she said, 'when you're back from Berlin. Speaking of which, you really do need to go. You'll miss your flight.'

'I already cancelled it. I can book the first flight out tomorrow morning,' he said, 'or I could try to find someone else to take my place in Berlin.'

'That isn't fair on Lucy, Stella or Drew,' she pointed out. 'Go to Berlin.'

'Provided you forgive me for not telling you about the baby earlier?'

'Only because I hope you've learnt not to lie by omission.'

'I have,' he said. 'So now that's cleared up, can we go for a walk?'

She folded her arms. '*After* you've booked your flight.'

'Give me ten minutes,' he said, and grabbed his phone from his pocket. He booked the flight and tapped in his credit card details. 'All organised. It's the first flight tomorrow. If I check in an hour before the flight, I need to leave here by about half-past four in the morning.'

'I'll drive you to the airport,' she said.

'You need your sleep.'

She shook her head. 'I'll be awake anyway. Amenhotep seems to wake up at half-past three to do a bit of baby gymnastics.'

'Noted,' he said. 'And I'll do my share of night feeds for Amenhotep Camille.'

'I'll hold you to that,' she said with a grin.

'Now can we go for that walk?'

'What's so special about a walk?'

'Humour me?' he asked softly.

She rolled her eyes, but let him lead her out of the house and out to Primrose Hill. At the top, they paused to look at the view.

'The whole of London before us,' he said softly.

And then he dropped to one knee.

'Holly Weston, I love you. I think I might even have fallen in love with you before you remembered knowing me. It scares the hell out of me because I've never felt this way about anyone before, but not having you in my life is an even more scary prospect. I'm not promising that it's going to be easy, but I'll be honest with you and I'll love you for the rest of my days, and I'll try to be the best husband and father I can possibly be. Will you marry me?'

'I love you, too,' she said. 'Even if I did forget you the day after I met you. Yes, I'll marry you.'

EPILOGUE

April

'YOU'RE READY FOR THIS?' Holly's father checked.

'I'm ready,' she said with a smile. 'Mum's got Eliot?'

'And he's sound asleep,' her father said, smiling back.

'I still can't believe you're making everyone wear Regency dress. And that you're getting married in a red dress, too,' Natalie said, making a last-minute adjustment to Holly's bonnet and veil.

'It's where it all started,' Holly said. 'I don't remember wearing a dress like this—and, anyway, Harry looks amazing in full Regency garb. We kind of had to.' Just as she'd insisted on having forget-me-nots in her bouquet and woven into her hair.

Natalie grinned. 'I'm not complaining! I love my dress. And the children all look so cute.'

Alice and Celia were flower girls, and Henry and George were ushers, all taking their duties incredibly seriously.

The wedding was in the family's private chapel at Beauchamp Abbey. As Holly's father opened the door and led her inside, Holly could see that Lucy, Drew and Stella were waiting to play her down the aisle. She suppressed a grin. Harry had thought she'd asked for Pachelbel's Canon; the rest of the quartet had had other ideas, aided and abetted by Harry's sister-in-law.

Celia and Alice walked down the aisle in front of the bride and her father, scattering rose petals, and at Holly's nod the trio switched from Pachelbel and started playing 'Don't You Forget About Me'.

Harry turned to watch her walk down the aisle to him, grinning broadly as he recognised the tune, and there was a ripple of amusement and love throughout the congregation, who all knew exactly why she was walking down the aisle to that particular tune.

In a red Regency dress, to a man wearing a tailcoat and pantaloons.

And then it hit her.

She remembered.

She remembered Harry wearing the Regency outfit and striding across the lawn to her. She remembered him putting his jacket round her shoulders. She remembered him walking her to the house and dancing with her, making her feel as if she were floating on air. She remembered him playing the cello to her, playing this exact tune, then dancing with her again. Asking her to stay with him. Carrying her across the threshold of his bedroom, making her feel precious and cherished and gorgeous.

Every step she took down the aisle towards him brought back another memory, another feeling, until her head was full of rainbows and she was close to tears of joy.

'Holly?' he asked, looking concerned when she joined him at the aisle.

'I remember,' she said. 'I remember the first time I

met you, and you played me this exact song in Ferdy's wonderful Georgian flat. I was wearing a red dress, like this one, and you were wearing Regency clothes, just like you are now, and you made me feel amazing. I *remember*.' She blinked back the tears.

'I'm glad I made you feel amazing, because you *are* amazing.' He dipped his head and stole a kiss. 'And I'm glad you remember. Because right now my heart's beating as fast as it did the very first time I saw you, and I can't wait to marry you—because I really, really love you.'

'I really, really love you, too—and I won't forget you again,' she promised.

The vicar, who had baptised Harry as a baby—and who'd baptised Harry and Holly's baby the previous Sunday—smiled at them both. 'That's good to hear. Now, your guests are waiting.' He coughed, and raised his voice. 'Dearly beloved, we are gathered here...'

* * * * *

THE MAYOR'S
SECRET FORTUNE

JUDY DUARTE

To the amazing authors who took part
in The Fortunes of Texas: Rambling Rose—
Michelle Major, Stella Bagwell, Marie Ferrarella,
Nancy Robards Thompson and Allison Leigh.

You ladies rock!
Thank you for making my book a joy to write.

Chapter One

Rain splattered the windshield as Ellie Hernandez maneuvered her recently detailed red Honda through the wet city streets, trying to get to the ribbon-cutting ceremony on time. She was the mayor of Rambling Rose, for goodness' sake. And she always made it a point to arrive at a meeting or an event early. Hopefully, today wasn't the exception.

She glanced at the clock on the dash and rolled her eyes. In fifteen minutes she was supposed to be on hand for the grand opening of the Shoppes, a collection of high-end stores that would cater to the wealthy, a swarm of which had been moving to Rambling Rose in recent months. They'd begun to infiltrate the small town she loved, threatening to make the community in which she'd been raised unrecognizable. And she found the whole thing unsettling.

Not that she didn't want the community to grow and prosper. She believed that growth should be organic, the result of Rambling Rose's quaint, small-town appeal, and not fabricated commercialism.

As the wipers swished and swooshed across the windshield, a big black Dodge Ram passed her on the left, its right rear tire hitting a puddle and splashing a wave of muddy water at the side of her car so high that it struck the windshield with a vengeance.

"Hey, jerk! Watch where you're going." She didn't recognize the fancy, late-model vehicle, so she assumed it was one of the rich newcomers, no doubt in a hurry to join in the excitement of yet another one of Fortune Brothers Construction's grand openings.

Callum, Steven and Dillon Fortune had come to Texas eager to make their mark in real estate renovation. Sure, Ellie could appreciate them renovating the old foundling hospital, which was now the Rambling Rose Pediatric Center. And the new veterinary clinic they'd opened last month would benefit the community, too. But the locals, the people

who'd made their homes here long before the big
real estate boom, weren't into wearing designer
clothing. Nor were the small-town masses interested in dining in a five-star restaurant, another of
the Fortune Brothers Construction projects.

The rain had stopped, so she shut off her windshield wipers. Moments later, she pulled into the
parking lot, just behind the guy driving the black
pickup. After finding a spot and shutting off the
ignition, she reached for her purse and grabbed
her compact red umbrella. Earlier, on the morning news, the weatherman had said the storm was
moving south today, but Ellie wasn't going to take
any chances.

She climbed out of the car just as the pickup
driver—a corporate cowboy, if that fancy black
hat was a clue—got out of his vehicle, too. She
paid him little mind. Being on time, to her, meant
arriving at least fifteen minutes early, and the
clock was ticking relentlessly.

Still, her late arrival couldn't be helped. She'd
had a doctor's appointment at ten o'clock, but he
was running behind. And now she was, too. Running, that is.

As she hurried toward the entrance, making her
way around a couple of puddles, she wished she'd
worn something more sensible than heels, like the
pair of sneakers packed in the gym bag she always kept in her trunk. But she favored business

attire while working on behalf of city hall, and even when she'd had to squeeze in a visit to the doctor, she hadn't wanted to take the extra time to change shoes.

In her peripheral vision, she spotted the approaching cowboy, all tall and lean and...

Fortune.

Steven, to be exact.

She'd known that he and his brothers, Callum and Dillon, would be here today. The Florida developers had moved to Rambling Rose last fall with visions of grandeur that had already begun to change the once blue-collar town for good. And the Shoppes was another one of their fixer-upper projects.

She couldn't help but glance to her right, and when she did, Steven tipped the brim of his black Stetson and tossed a dazzling smile her way.

She offered him a polite but forced smile of her own and picked up her pace, her heels clicking on the newly paved blacktop in a don't-be-late cadence. But she couldn't seem to shake him.

"Good afternoon, Mayor," he said, his voice deep and almost booming. "What's your hurry? We're nearly ten minutes early."

"I know, but that feels late to me." She tried to ignore his tall, dark and handsome presence, but that was nearly impossible to do, especially when it seemed that those big blue eyes of his had a permanent spark in them.

In the five or six months since Steven had moved to town, he seemed to always stand out in the crowd. He'd also acquired a sexy cowboy swagger. If she didn't know better, she'd think he'd been born and bred in Texas rather than in Florida.

Now, as he moved beside her, close enough for her to catch a whiff of his musky aftershave, one of his long strides matching two of hers, people were going to think they'd arrived together. Maybe even in the same vehicle.

Great. Just great. Not that any of the Fortune brothers was her nemesis. It's just that they didn't see eye to eye with her on much of anything, and she had a responsibility to the people who'd voted her into office—the hardworking citizens who'd lived here for years and weren't comfortable with the influx of wealthy newcomers. So, needless to say, arriving with Steven at her side made it look as if she and Fortune Brothers Construction were in cahoots. And that wasn't the case.

Still as much as she hated to admit it, rich or poor, Steven was far more attractive than a man had a right to be. And a misplaced attraction like that was the last thing she needed today.

No, there were more important things to think about than the sexy man sauntering next to her—like the short speech she had to make in a few minutes. On top of that, she had a lot to ponder after today's exam at the doctor's office. As a result, she wasn't paying attention to the rain-slicked ground, and her foot slipped on something wet and hard—a small rock or stone? She let out a little shriek as she lost her balance.

Steven reached out to catch her. Before the wannabe hero could save the day—or prevent her from making a clumsy fool of herself—she landed on her backside with a wet, muddy thud that sent her hair clip flying across the ground as cold, dirty water soaked through her slacks to her panties.

"Are you okay?" Steven asked.

"I'm fine." She brushed a loose strand of hair from her face and tucked it behind her ear. For a moment, her tummy flip-flopped, and she feared she'd be sick. But she sucked in a breath of fresh air, and the feeling soon passed.

Steven reached down to take her hand, his brow furrowed, his eyes...

Dammit. The sympathetic gaze and the sky-blue color were almost enough to chase the clouds away. Almost.

In spite of her reluctance to accept his help, she took his hand, feeling the warmth as it embraced hers. Work roughened, yet soft and gentle at the same time.

From her position on the ground, he appeared much taller than six foot something. The moment he pulled her to a stand, her legs wobbled, and her heart rate, already escalated, skipped to a zippity-do-dah beat.

"There you go," he said, his smile as nice as it could be—yet, under the circumstances, annoying all the same.

She drew her hand from his and cleared her throat. "Thank you."

"Are you sure you're okay?" he asked.

Ellie blew out a sigh. "I'm actually more humiliated than hurt."

Could anything else go wrong today? It didn't seem likely.

She brushed her wet derriere and realized she couldn't get on a stage looking like a drowned rat—and no doubt, one of the last to leave a sinking ship. Her town was a-changin', and there wasn't one darn thing she could do about it.

As she turned to head back to her car, where she kept her handy-dandy Ellie Hernandez Emergency Preparedness Kit, a sharp twinge shot through her ankle. Her steps faltered, and she swore under her breath.

"Let me help." Steven took her by the arm, his grip strong and steady, yet tender.

Another woman might appreciate the gallant gesture—or be flattered by it—but Ellie pulled away and waved him off. "Thanks, but I've got this."

All she had to do was figure out where the nearest bathroom was so she could change into one of the two spare outfits she always had with her. As she limped back toward her car, past the vehicles that had arrived earlier, she reached into her purse, pulled out her key fob and, using the remote, popped open her trunk.

"What are you doing?" he asked.

"Getting something to change into." She removed a neatly folded pair of slacks and a matching blouse she kept in the car for spur-of-the-moment business meetings or unscheduled events, then grabbed her gym bag.

Steven let out a slow whistle. "Would you look at that? You keep a traveling wardrobe on hand. I'm impressed."

"I like being prepared." The irony, though, struck her with a low blow. She could count a handful of times in recent months that she hadn't been the least bit prepared for the unexpected.

"Where do you plan to change clothes?" he asked.

She shot him an incredulous look. "In a bathroom. Why?"

"I have a much better idea—and one that's quicker. Our construction trailer is about fifty yards from here. Think you can make it?"

She paused only a moment before nodding and falling into step beside him.

As much as she hated to accept any help from one of the Fortune brothers, she'd much rather change in a trailer than one of the nearby porta-potties, which would be her only alternative if she didn't want to do so in her car or, God forbid, trek through the gathering crowd with wet pants and dirty hands to search for a restroom inside the Shoppes.

She glanced at her bangle wristwatch. "I can't believe this is happening. I'm never late."

"Relax," he said. "They're not going to start the grand opening without either one of us."

He was right, of course. But all Ellie needed was for someone to see them enter that blasted trailer together and think the worst. Talk about sleeping with the enemy. How was she going to spin her way out of this?

After Steven unlocked the door to the trailer to let Ellie inside, she turned to him and scrunched her pretty face.

"You're going to wait out here, right?"

"Of course. If you feel more comfortable, use the lock."

She stepped inside, and the door snapped shut. The sound of the dead bolt followed.

"Seriously?" Steven muttered.

"I heard that!"

Steven slowly shook his head as he stood on the wooden porch steps, holding the company keys and waiting for the pretty but disheveled mayor to change. He sucked in a deep breath of the rain-scented air and scanned the sky. Storm clouds, once dark and threatening, had lightened and begun to move on, giving way to small patches of blue. Thank goodness the people who'd shown up for today's ceremony wouldn't get drenched.

He'd been looking forward to the ribbon-cutting ceremony at the Shoppes at Rambling Rose for months. It was the third grand opening Fortune Brothers Construction had held this year. And with each one, their reputation back in Florida, as well as in Texas, grew stronger and more impressive.

Too bad that wasn't the case here, in Rambling Rose. You'd think the town council and Mayor Ellie Hernandez would be happy that Steven and his brothers had remodeled the old five-and-dime. Once an eyesore that had been abandoned and neglected for more than twenty years, it was now an elegant two-story building that housed a variety of upscale boutiques. But for some damned reason, she didn't consider their contribution to the community.

Last month, at the fund-raiser for the new Paws and Claws Animal Clinic, Ellie had made it clear that she wasn't impressed with the progressive changes he and his brothers had made, or were making, to the town.

Steven lifted his left wrist and glanced at his Rolex, a birthday gift from his father. It was nearly time to get the show on the road, although he'd meant what he'd told Ellie when they arrived—the ribbon cutting wouldn't take place without them. Still, her little misstep was bound to be a setback.

She might keep spare clothing packed neatly in her trunk, but that didn't mean she'd change faster than any other woman who made it a point to have every hair in place. And as far as Steven was concerned, the tall, willowy brunette looked damn near perfect each time he saw her.

A slow grin stretched across his face. Seeing Ms. Perfection seated in a mud puddle, her hair hanging wild and loose instead of contained in a neat twist, her sable eyes wide and lips parted in disbelief, was a pretty sight to behold. And a far cry from the image the good folks of Rambling Rose had come to know and love.

From what he'd gathered, Ellie had been an only child, her mama and daddy's pride and joy. She'd sold more cookies than any of the others in her Girl Scout troop, sung solos in the church choir and helped the women's club serve meals at the home-less shelter. She'd gone on to become the valedictorian of her senior class before earning a master's in public policy. So it wasn't just her pretty face that was impressive.

Still, she seemed a little too good to be true, too damn perfect. He wondered what flaws might be lurking beneath the surface. There had to be something, if only he could find it. He also needed to get on her good side, but so far, he hadn't had any luck with either of those tasks.

Steven leaned against the wooden porch railing, prepared to wait it out. When the door squeaked open, taking him a bit by surprise, Ellie breezed out of the trailer, smiling as if she'd never suffered a setback. The only sign of being flustered was her flushed cheeks, which merely added a rosy tint to her olive complexion and made her brown eyes pop.

"Thank you," she said. "Changing in the Fortune Brothers Construction man cave was a lot nicer than using one of the porta-potties."

"You're welcome." He tossed her a disarming smile, which seemed to escape her notice. On the other hand, her appearance didn't escape his.

She'd come outside different—not just from when she went in, but from when she'd arrived. She'd combed her hair, leaving it down instead of in her customary updo, and she'd changed out of the dressy black pants she'd had on, trading them for khaki slacks. She'd shed her tailored jacket and the crisply pressed white blouse, too. Instead she wore a cream-colored sweater accessorized with a red plaid scarf.

"Just look at you," he said. "A little more casual and down-to-earth than when you arrived, but as professionally dressed as ever."

He'd meant it as a compliment, but she never seemed to be sure about him or his true intentions, so it didn't surprise him when she rolled her eyes and clicked her tongue. "Under the circumstances, it's the best I could do."

"Nicely done, then."

"Thank you," she said, "but let's *go*."

At that, she took off, walking past him while he locked up and leaving him to catch an intriguing hint of her citrus-blossom scent.

After slipping the keys into his jeans pocket, he followed her, enjoying the sway of her hips and the way her long, dark hair swished across her back—a very nice change. She really ought to wear it down more often.

He shook off his thoughts and caught up with her.

In spite of a slight limp the pair of gym shoes couldn't mask, she never broke stride.

"What time is it?" she asked.

"Like I said, they'll wait."

She let out a huff. "That's *not* the point."

They stopped by her car long enough for her to toss her gym bag into the back seat, the hasty effort a sign of her inner frustration.

"Why do I get the distinct feeling you don't like me?" he asked.

At that, her movements finally stilled. "I don't have any reason to dislike *you*. It's just that the changes you and your brothers have been making in Rambling Rose aren't helping the community at large. And it's clear that you don't know the townspeople well enough to give a damn what they want."

"You're wrong. My brothers and I care about the residents of Rambling Rose."

Ellie chuffed. "You only care about the newcomers. Now that the homes in Rambling Rose Estates have gone on the market, we've had an influx of millionaires move in. And the longtime residents feel pushed out. Unappreciated."

"The locals might not like the idea of new residents moving in—wealthy or not. But you can't blame Fortune Brothers Construction for the hard feelings."

She didn't respond in words, but her arched brow clearly said, *Oh no? Who else is to blame?*

"When Bradley Industries came in with big dreams and then went belly-up, my brother and I picked up the pieces and finished projects in rec-

ord time. I'd think you'd be happy that someone
was able to complete them."

She didn't comment. But what could she say?

The way Steven saw it, Fortune Brothers Construction had stepped in and made the community
a better place. "You have to admit that our recent
renovations of the pediatric center and the animal
clinic will benefit everyone in Rambling Rose."

"Maybe so." She nodded toward the elegant,
two-story glass-front entrance to the Shoppes. "But
what about this? Just look at this place."

"What's wrong with it? It looks great." And
hell, why wouldn't he think that? He'd helped design it.

She slapped her hands on her hips. "The people
who live in Rambling Rose, the ones who were
born and raised here, aren't that fancy. They don't
shop in stores like this. Nor do they appreciate the
fact that, thanks to all the wealthy newcomers, the
owners stand to turn a big enough profit to allow
them to afford the rent in a luxurious setting. And
that will create larger social and economic divi-
sions in our communities, something we've never
had before, which is my point."

"I appreciate your loyalty to your constituents
and your desire to keep things the way they've always been, but the world is changing, Ellie. The
technology-savvy millennials prefer specialty

shops over department stores—or else they're shopping online."

The attractive mayor, Ms. Perfection, practically snorted. "I'm a millennial, Steven. And I'm not impressed by fancy buildings and expensive specialty shops."

He merely studied her. He admired her passion for the town as it used to be. And he found her more than a little intriguing. He wasn't exactly sure how old she was—late twenties, he assumed. Either way, she seemed too young to be a mayor, even of a small town like Rambling Rose.

When he didn't respond right away, she took a deep breath and slowly let it out. "I'm sorry. I didn't mean to put us at odds before the ceremony."

"No worries. I'm not the least bit offended." In spite of their difference of opinion, he actually enjoyed their banter.

He'd grown up as the oldest son of a very wealthy man, and while he and his siblings were all accomplished, the brothers had built the construction company to the point that they'd each become financially successful in their own rights. So Steven was used to being catered to, flirted with and pursued by attractive women.

But that wasn't the case with Ellie, and he found that refreshing. She intrigued him. Yet it was more than her spunky attitude he found appealing. He'd always been attracted to brunettes, and this one had caught his interest the very first time he'd laid eyes her.

"We can talk later," she said. "We need to climb up on that stage and get this event over with." And with that, she was off once again.

A car door slammed shut, and Steven glanced across the parking lot, where several men and women had gathered around a white SUV, its rear door lifted high. There didn't seem to be anything unusual about the vehicle, but there was something out of sync about the people.

When one guy reached into the back and began to hand out signs, Steven realized why.

Protesters. That's all they needed.

Had Ellie spotted them? Apparently not, since she continued toward the makeshift dais, where a red ribbon stretched across the front of the glass doors.

Then again, maybe she had inside information and had known they'd be here. If she didn't have to attend the grand opening in an official capacity, she might have held one of the protest signs herself. She clearly shared their sentiments. But if there was one thing Steven had come to know about Ellie Hernandez, it was that she took her job as mayor seriously.

That being the case, would she go so far as to shut down the protesters or call in law enforcement?

Another car door slammed, and three more people joined the first group. He suspected all hell was about to break loose. Steven and his brothers could handle anything they might throw their way. But how was the pretty young mayor of Rambling Rose going to respond, especially if things were to blow sky-high and a fight broke out?

Steven hated to admit it, but he couldn't wait to find out.

Chapter Two

Ellie had been tempted to suggest that Steven wait in the parking lot for a minute or two so they could stagger their arrival, but since he seemed determined to stick by her side, she figured he'd refuse. So she gave up her efforts to shake the sexy man who looked more like a fancy cowboy than a slick businessman.

As they neared the front of the Shoppes, her steps slowed to a casual pace, and she tucked a loose strand of hair behind her ear. Up ahead, a crowd had gathered around the portable dais, where a well-dressed Callum Fortune stood off to the side, near a small table, checking his watch.

Two women in their mid- to late fifties turned when they heard approaching footsteps and eyed Ellie and Steven carefully, as if connecting imaginary dots and jumping to the wrong conclusion.

"Great," Ellie uttered softly. "I knew they'd think we'd arrived together."

"So what?" he asked. "Who cares?"

"I do. It's bad enough that I have to stand next to you and your brother on that dais as if we were all in agreement."

"Sleeping with the enemy, huh?"

That thought had crossed her mind more than once, and while the thought of sleeping with a man like Steven Fortune knocked her a little off stride, she stopped to set him straight.

"I'm a city official," she said, "and my loyalty lies with my constituents."

He flashed a dazzling, heart-strumming grin. "I moved to Rambling Rose back in October, so that makes me one of your constituents."

"Point taken, but for now, we have a grand opening to officiate." She offered the two women gawking at them a polite smile, then hurried toward the portable dais, with Steven matching her strides.

The moment Callum noticed them, he motioned for them to join him and Dillon on stage. Ellie blew out a sigh. Did they have to make a big Broadway production out of everything? Not that there hadn't been other grand openings in town, but the folks in Rambling Rose kept things simple, and they served punch and cookies at the end.

As she and Steven climbed the side steps to the dais, her stomach pitched. She sucked in another comforting breath, which served to settle her nerves, as well as her tummy.

Callum removed a handheld microphone from a small table and addressed the crowd. "On behalf of Fortune Brothers Construction and all the store owners, I'd like to welcome you to the grand opening of the Shoppes at Rambling Rose."

Several people clapped heartily, most of them newcomers. But the ones Ellie recognized in the small crowd had a more reserved response.

"My brothers and I are happy to be a part of Rambling Rose's renaissance," Callum said as he handed the mic to Steven. Ellie, who'd taken her place to the left of the men, slapped on another polite smile and stood with her hands clasped behind her back.

"I've only been in town for the past four or five months," Steven said, "but in that short period of time, I feel as though I've become part of the community." He glanced at Ellie as if hoping she'd back him up, but she'd already gone above and beyond to do her job today—and to keep her thoughts and opinions to herself.

Most of them, anyway. She hadn't wanted to

put a damper on the festivities, especially since the rain had stopped.

Callum handed Steven a stack of gold-trimmed envelopes, then picked up the scissors Ellie would use to cut the red ribbon that stretched across the doorway leading to the stores.

"As a gift from Fortune Brothers Construction," Steven said, "as well as the store owners and eateries, each of you will be given coupons for discounts on today's purchases and a chance to win prizes."

At that, the crowd cheered and clapped.

"So without further ado," Steven said, "we'll ask Mayor Hernandez to cut the ribbon so you can go inside and meet the newest members of the Rambling Rose Chamber of Commerce."

Steven gave Callum the mic, exchanging it for the scissors, but before he could pass them to Ellie, a male voice shouted, "Fortunes, go home!"

She didn't have to see the man who'd interrupted the grand opening. She recognized Mel Sullivan's graveled voice. The woolly, white-haired man was one of the older townspeople and a regular at the Roadside Diner, as well as at Mariana's Market. Mel had been voicing his opinions loud and clear for months, and since he stood front and center of the group of protesters, he appeared to be the ringleader. She also recognized the others with him, six to the right and four to the left, all carrying hand-painted signs as they moved forward and approached the dais.

"Rambling Rose doesn't need any more of those highfalutin rich people parading around town and showing off their wealth," Carl Wagner shouted. "Send 'em packing, and tell them to take their money with 'em."

Ruthanne Garrison cried out, "Save our town, Mayor!"

That's it. Enough was enough. Ellie snatched the microphone from Steven and took center stage. "Friends, neighbors, I understand your concern, and I support your First Amendment rights, but the people gathered here today have every right to go shopping without any trouble or turmoil."

Ellie handed the mic to Steven. "You cut the ribbon. I'm going to talk to them."

"Want me to go with you?" he asked.

She slowly shook her head. "That would only make things worse." Then she turned and made her way down the steps to speak to the people she considered her friends and, hopefully, convince them to get into their cars and go home.

Mel, Carl, Ruthanne and the others were all good people—and well-intentioned. She'd known them all her life, and they'd watched her grow up. They trusted her to send the Fortunes packing and to save their quaint town from further ruin.

Hopefully, she wouldn't let them down. At least,

not with respect to the Fortunes. But the time was coming when she'd have to humbly face the community at large and reveal her secret.

She cringed at the thought of letting them down, of admitting that she'd failed to live up to everyone's expectations. Ever since childhood, she'd tried to be perfect and had worked hard to develop a respectable reputation. And up until now, she'd succeeded. But she'd recently made a big mistake, and she would soon have to deal with the repercussions.

A few of the townspeople might not give it another thought. Yet some would be shocked and others disappointed to learn that in five short months, Ellie Hernandez, hometown superstar, would become an unwed mother with no husband in sight.

The glass-enclosed lobby of the Shoppes wasn't especially large, but it was certainly fancy, boasting a colorful Spanish-tile waterfall in the center of the room that had been created by a Texas artisan. Even the floor tile provided a rich look that would appeal to the wealthy newcomers.

The Fortunes had gone to great lengths to lay out a remarkable welcome to the potential shoppers. They'd set a variety of refreshments on several linen-draped tables, each adorned with orchids and other exotic floral arrangements that had been provided by Tropical Paradise, the new flower shop located on the lower level.

Servers dressed in black slacks and crisply-pressed, tailored white shirts carried silver trays, some of which held flutes filled with champagne or sparkling apple cider, while others displayed a variety of fancy hors d'oeuvres. Ellie chose to pass on everything, especially since she hadn't quite kicked the morning sickness that had plagued her early in her pregnancy.

A woman in her thirties, who stood with a group of friends, opened her gold-lined envelope and let out a happy shriek. "Oh my gosh! I won a pair of jade earrings from Sebastian's Fine Jewelry."

The server carrying the goose-liver pâté walked by, close enough for Ellie to get a tummy-swirling whiff. She quickly took a step back and turned toward the fountain, hoping she wouldn't have to run to the restroom. She swallowed hard, took a deep breath of fresh air, cooled and cleansed by gurgling water, then stepped to the side and turned her back to the server.

"There you are."

Ellie looked up and spotted Steven sauntering toward her, carrying two flutes of champagne. He handed one to her, but she slowly shook her head. "Thank you, but I'll pass."

"Seriously?" he asked.

She actually liked champagne and would have accepted a glass, had she not been pregnant. She also could have held on to it, pretending to take part in the festivities, but she wasn't in the mood to fake it.

"Come on, Ellie. Lighten up. Can't you think of anything to celebrate?"

"I'm here, aren't I?" She offered him a smile that was more sincere than any of the others she'd managed on prior occasions when their paths had crossed.

Steven's smile faded, as if he might be slightly offended—or bothered. Or…?

Oh, for heaven's sake. Who knew what a rich man like Steven Fortune ever really had on his mind? Even his last name screamed wealth.

"It's not what you think," she said. "It's just that I need to keep a clear head while I'm on the job."

At that, his grin returned, recreating a pair of dimples that threatened to unravel her. And Ellie rarely let things get to her. She glanced at her wristwatch. Had she stayed at the grand opening long enough? Could she find an excuse to cut out now?

As one of the servers walked by with several more flutes, Steven motioned for the man to come over.

"Here," he told the server, as he placed one of the glasses back on the silver tray. "Can I trade you for one of the apple ciders?"

"Absolutely, Mr. Fortune." He reached for a single flute, its contents a bit darker than the rest, and gave it to him. "Here you go, sir."

Steven thanked him, then handed the sparkling juice to Ellie and lifted his glass of champagne in a toast. "To Rambling Rose."

She would have been hard-pressed to join him in celebrating the Fortune brothers' latest venture, but how could she not drink to the town she loved?

She clinked her glass to his, setting off the rich, resonating sound of fine crystal, which only served to remind her of the wealth that threatened to turn her beloved Rambling Rose into a metropolis.

Still, she took a sip of the sweet bubbly.

What would Steven say if she told him the real reason she'd passed on an alcoholic drink? Not that it mattered. He'd find out soon enough. And so would her parents.

Her gut clenched at the thought of the loving couple she'd tried so hard to make proud. It would kill her to see the disappointment in their eyes.

"Hey," Steven said, "what's with the turned-up nose? Did you get a bad pour? Bitter champagne instead of sweet cider?"

Ellie hadn't meant to let her thoughts alter her expression, let alone her demeanor, especially at a public event. So she forced a carefree grin and tried to laugh it off. "No, the drink is fine. *I'm* fine. It's just that I... Well, a weird thought crossed my mind, and I drifted off for a moment. That's all. No big deal."

But it wasn't just a fleeting thought that had stolen her away from the present and set off a flurry of concern. It was cold, hard reality. And once her tummy bulge turned into a full-on baby bump, it was actually going to be a big deal. A *huge* one.

Ellie had never backed down from a challenge, but this one scared her silly. After the truth came out and she experienced her fall from grace, there'd be more than a few awkward or embarrassing moments. Sure, they'd soon fade and life would go on. But there was something else she found troubling, something she'd need to deal with. Because, when push came to shove, she wasn't sure if she could handle the mayorship and motherhood. But that's the last thing in the world she'd ever reveal to Steven.

"I want to show you something," he said.

Huh? Her brow twitched, and her head tilted. As their gazes met and locked, something stirred inside her, drawing her out of her uneasy thoughts and—

"Come with me." He nodded toward the farthest corner of the festive lobby, where three large brass easels held a couple of fancy poster boards displaying several other projects Fortune Brothers Construction had in the works.

She couldn't very well refuse to look at the exhibit of their future renovations, so she followed him to the impressive, professional presentation.

Steven pointed to the first poster. "This is Paz, the wellness spa we'll be opening soon."

Ellie studied the sketch of the exterior of a beautiful building.

"It's going to be finished with reclaimed wood and other natural materials," he added.

"Nice."

"That's it?" He feigned disbelief. "You can't tell me that a busy mayor like you wouldn't need to unwind once in a while at a luxurious spa."

Of course she would. And she'd love it. But she didn't want him to think he'd won her over, so she gave a little shrug. "I'm really not what you'd call the luxurious type."

"I don't believe that. Everyone needs a good massage once in a while." He lifted his hands and moved his fingers in a kneading fashion, as if they were working their magic on an invisible body. "I'm sure you have plenty of stress built up and have a few knots. Or maybe you just need to relax. If not, you should just be pampered."

The thought of his hands on her body sent her senses reeling and her imagination soaring.

Oh, for Pete's sake, Ellie. Cut it out. What's the matter with you?

No way would she let those hands anywhere

near her—no matter how good she imagined they'd feel.

She moved to the middle easel, hoping to dispel any pampering thoughts—his or hers—and studied the next drawing.

"That's the restaurant," Steven said. "Callum found the property in January."

"The old feed store?"

"Yes. Ashley, Megan and Nicole were in town for Callum and Becky's wedding, and when they saw the building and property, they jumped on the idea. We've already started the renovations. They're going to call it Provisions. They have a lot of experience in upscale restaurants, so I know it's going to be popular."

"When will it open?"

"If all goes well, it should open in May, so they're eager to move to Rambling Rose so they can get busy."

Great. More Fortunes would be moving to town. Not that Ellie had anything against the family—especially the sisters she'd never met. It's just that there'd be three more wealthy people moving here.

Unable to help herself, Ellie asked, "How many sisters do you have?"

"Four. Stephanie is already here and working at Paws and Claws. And the triplets make four."

Triplets? Ellie nearly rolled her eyes. Goodness. They came in multiples. Her hand slipped to her tummy. Thank goodness she was only expecting one baby. What would she do with three?

She shook off the overwhelming thought, then took a step to her right and focused on the last easel, which displayed the plans for and a sketch of the Fortune Hotel.

"I'm surprised you and your brothers decided to promote the sketches of this project," she said.

"Why?" Steven crossed his arms, shifted his weight to one hip and tossed her a dazzling grin. "Just because we've met a little resistance from the Rambling Rose planning commission?"

"A *little*?" She returned his smile, although hers was smug.

"Let's just call that a snag," he said. "And a little inconvenience for the time being. We'll break ground soon, and it'll be up and running before you know it. Think of the property taxes that'll be coming in. Believe me, once local business owners begin to see the increased revenue brought in by tourists and visitors, the community will not only accept it, but they'll be proud of it, too."

"Don't be too sure about that," she said.

"Why?"

"Because it's not just about the money. The locals aren't happy about the way you and your family are trying to change our way of life. I told you and your brother as much at the fund-raiser for the new animal clinic, but my words and the point I was trying to make obviously fell on deaf ears."

"Oh, we heard you. Loud and clear. But no one succeeds by thinking small."

She was tempted to call him on the conceit hidden within his statement, but she bit her tongue and addressed the project that wasn't likely to pass the planning commission—*ever*. At least, as long as she was mayor, even if the length of her term was questionable at best.

She turned toward Steven, crossed her arms and strengthened her stance. "You're going to have difficulty getting that project to pass, because it's not going to benefit many of my constituents."

"Change is good."

"That's sometimes true. Just for the record, I'm not opposed to progress, but only if a project maintains Rambling Rose's character. And a sprawling hotel complex fits our town like a pair of Mommy's high heels on a preschooler playing house."

Steven glanced down at her feet, then looked up and grinned. "Or like a pair of sneakers on the mayor?"

"Very funny."

"Like it or not," he said, "the town's character is changing, Ellie. And I think you'd better try to grow with the times. Your constituents will appreciate it in the long run."

She blew out a sigh that released only a bit of

her frustration. "What do you know about the people who voted me into office? I doubt that you've met any of them while living in that big fancy mansion of yours."

"That's probably true."

Instead of a response, she continued to stare at him, although the longer she gazed into those big blue eyes, the less she felt like arguing her point.

Damn him. Steven Fortune might be one gorgeous hunk, but he had a way of blowing the wind out of her sails. In fact, he'd become a real pain in her backside. And the fact that he seemed to enjoy their banter didn't help.

Footsteps sounded, and she glanced over her shoulder to see Steven's brother Callum approach. Other than their six feet or more height and close-cropped dark hair, the two men didn't really resemble each other. They were, however, business partners and shared the same vision.

"Am I interrupting something?" Callum asked, his brown eyes glimmering with mirth.

"Only a stalemate, it seems." Steven winked at Ellie, the playful gesture tempting her to punch him in the arm.

"Why don't you take the mayor on a private tour?" Callum suggested.

Steven gave his brother a cursory glance before locking his gaze on Ellie. "I don't think she wants one. She's not happy about the new stores opening up."

At that, Ellie bristled and felt the need to defend her stance. "I have nothing against the businesses or their owners. It's just that the locals, the ones who were born and raised here, aren't into designer handbags, five-hundred-dollar outfits, French pastries or artisanal cheeses."

"That's yet to be seen," Steven said. "I'll bet some of those folks will end up surprising you."

The man just wasn't getting it. She turned to appeal to his brother instead. "I'll admit that Fortune Brothers Construction has made some improvements to the town, like renovating the old foundling hospital and turning it into a pediatric clinic." In fact, Ellie would be taking her baby boy for checkups with one of the doctors there before she knew it.

"Don't forget about Paws and Claws," Steven said.

"We do have a lot of animal owners," Ellie said. "In fact, last month, at the Valentine's Day fundraiser, my best friend and roommate spent most of the evening checking out the pets available for adoption that night and felt sorry for a scraggly dog with feet that were too big for its little body. So she brought him home right then and there. She named him Tank because of his big paws, but he's practically doubled in size already and has been chewing up everything in the house, including my new sunglasses."

Steven laughed, a mesmerizing sound that lightened Ellie's mood considerably.

"Your friend didn't know she'd adopted a puppy? I'd think someone from Paws and Claws would have made it clear that Tank wouldn't stay small before letting her take him home."

"I'm sure Daria was told—or had figured it out herself. But knowing her, she just didn't care."

"I'd like to meet Tank. And Daria."

Yeah. Right. As if Ellie would invite the irritating but sexy hunk to her home.

"Why would you want to meet that sweet, goofy pup?" she asked. "Is it because he's been creating havoc in my peaceful house?"

"Yep. That's exactly why. It sounds like Tank and I have something in common. We both annoy you, but if you give us a chance, you'll probably find us likable."

Callum laughed and gave his brother a pat on the back. "I don't know about that. Puppies can be trained. And I'm not so sure about you."

"I'd tend to agree with you about that," Ellie said, unable to stifle a smile.

"Becky just arrived." Callum nodded toward the lobby entrance. "Our sitter was running late, so we had to drive over here separately. I'll leave you two to fight it out on your own."

Ellie watched Callum's new wife, a pediatric nurse, step through the glass doorway. Becky had been a single mom—to one-year-old twins. Surely if she'd been able to handle two babies at once, Ellie could handle one. Right?

A little niggle that felt a lot like panic began to stir inside her. Babies were small and vulnerable. And as an only child, she'd never been around them.

She'd only held one once, a long time ago, but the mother had hovered around her as if she was going to drop it or do something wrong. What if she...?

No, Ellie. Chill. You've got this.

As Callum sauntered toward his wife, Steven seemed intent upon returning to the conversation they'd been having.

"You've already admitted that some of our projects have benefited the community," he said.

"Yes, but you and your brother bought up every piece of property you could, and from all outward appearances, you're only focused on what the newest residents want."

"I beg to differ."

Of course he did. She wouldn't expect anything less.

"I'm afraid we'll have to agree to disagree," Ellie said.

"Good idea." His grin morphed into a dimpled

smile. "But if you could do anything—pie in the sky—what changes would you like to see in Rambling Rose?"

She paused for a moment, but not because she didn't have a response, but because the question came from him, and he seemed to be interested in what she had to say.

"I'd start by building a community center that would cover a lot of needs for those who are on a limited income, like senior citizens and single parents. I'd love to see us offer after-school care for latchkey kids, as well as tutoring. And it would be awesome if we could provide classes that would appeal to adults, too, like computer basics, flower arranging, cake decorating, financial planning, yoga, line dancing, pickle ball, which I hear is all the rage. Anyway, you get the idea."

"I do. And I can't make promises without talking to my brothers, but I think we'd all be better off—Rambling Rose, Fortune Brothers Construction—if we could find a way to meet in the middle."

Ellie knew he might be blowing smoke as a way to appease her, so she studied the man, his expression sincere, hopeful. His face so blasted handsome. And she couldn't help but wish that they could find some common ground, but so far, it hadn't seemed possible.

"Would you be willing to meet a few of the

locals and get to know them on their own turf?"
she asked. "If so, that would be meeting me in
the middle."

"You bet I will. Maybe you can set up a com-
mittee—"

She held up the palm of her hand like a traffic
cop, stopping him in midthought, and shook her
head. "No way. I'm not talking about a meeting
down at city hall. I didn't get to be the mayor by
forming committees. If you really want to know
what makes Rambling Rose tick, you'll need to go
where the locals go."

Steven cocked his head slightly. "All right. I'm
game. Where do you suggest I meet them? The
Grange Hall? The local church?"

"If you really want to get to know the folks who
live here, you'll need to go to Mariana's Market
on a Saturday morning."

"I've heard about it. Vaguely. But I don't know
where that is. Or what it is. Help me out, okay?"

Darn him. He couldn't pull off a meet-and-greet
like that without her, and the fact that he was willing to take a field trip away from his fancy home
and busy office actually made her eager to facili-
tate the little excursion.

"You won't find Mariana's Market on your
GPS," she said. "Just meet me at my office on
Saturday and I'll take you there. Bring your broth-
ers, too."

"All right. You've got a deal." He reached out to shake her hand, and as his long fingers slipped around hers in a warm, firm grip, her senses reeled as if...

As if *nothing*, she admonished herself.

Ellie glanced at her wristwatch while trying to come up with a plausible reason to cut out and go home.

"As much as I'm enjoying our chat," she said, "I really need to go. I promised my roommate that I'd puppy-sit."

"And I really should greet my sister-in-law, as well as the other guests and shopkeepers. But I'll see you on Saturday." He tossed her another dazzling smile that darn near melted her in place. Then he turned and sauntered away.

Ellie watched him go, torn between admiration for the guy and frustration with his plans to ruin her town.

Too bad the Fortunes hadn't remained in Fort Lauderdale, doing whatever the rich and famous did there. Yacht races, maybe. Sunning themselves on the white sands of the Atlantic. And what a sight that would be for tourists and Floridians alike.

Unable to stop herself, she sought Steven in the crowd once again.

Unlike Callum, Steven had quickly shed his no-worries, Tommy Bahama style. And with each week he remained in Texas, the more he seemed to have acquired a cowboy persona—albeit a cowboy with more money than he knew what to do with.

And now it seemed she'd have to come face-to-face with him on a regular basis, especially if the construction company continued to have ribbon-cutting ceremonies every time she turned around. She'd take Steven and his brothers to Mariana's, although she wasn't sure that would have the desired effect on any of the Fortunes.

But try as she might, she couldn't quite shake the desire or the effect Steven Fortune threatened to have on her.

Chapter Three

On Saturday morning, Steven rode shotgun in Ellie's Honda while his brother Dillon sat in the back, a rather nondescript expression on his face. At twenty-nine, the fair-haired, blue-eyed Fortune brother was the kind of man most women would find attractive. At least, when he smiled. But he hadn't been doing too much of that lately.

Steven had invited Callum to join them on the expedition to Mariana's Market, but Callum had passed. He and Becky had taken the twins to the Austin Zoo today. Steven thought the toddlers were a little too young for a trip like that, but both

Callum and Becky had seemed excited about the family outing.

Of course, that just went to show you how little Steven knew about babies—or modern parenting. Their father, David Fortune, might have been a good dad and a great financial provider, but he'd left the daily child-rearing tasks to their mom. And when their mother's health issues struck with a vengeance, the boys had had to look after their younger sisters. Callum had made it clear that he'd grown tired of the responsibility. That fact coupled with a rocky first marriage that ended in divorce, he'd been reluctant to have a family of his own and had been hesitant to get involved with a single mother.

Before meeting Becky, Callum had put the construction company and business first. But he fell in love with the pretty, kindhearted nurse, and she'd left her mark on him, making him a new man. Not that the change wasn't a good one. It's just that Steven was still getting used to seeing his brother carrying toddlers, wiping noses and changing diapers. The guy even seemed to enjoy it.

Steven wasn't going to swear off having kids or a family, but if and when the day came, he wasn't going to take such a hands-on approach to fatherhood.

He glanced over his shoulder at Dillon, who looked a bit cramped sitting in back. Dillon hadn't complained, but then again, he hadn't said much of anything this morning.

"You doing okay back there?" Steven asked.

"Yeah. Why?"

"You're pretty quiet."

Dillon shrugged a single shoulder. "I don't have anything to say."

Steven shouldn't find that unusual. His brother had been pretty tight-lipped since moving to Rambling Rose. Probably because he'd loved living in Florida and seemed to be having a hard time adjusting to life in Texas.

He occasionally seemed to retreat into himself about something, but on the whole he was a pretty quiet guy, and his brothers hadn't wanted to poke too much.

"You want me to move my seat forward to give you more room?" Steven asked.

"No need. I'm doing all right."

Maybe so. But as Steven turned around and faced the front, he wished he'd insisted that they take his Cadillac Escalade instead of Ellie's sedan. At least the SUV would have provided his brother with more leg room. But Ellie had made it clear that she was running the show today, so he'd let her take the lead.

As they drove down a long rural road, he spotted an abandoned factory up ahead, where a wide variety of trucks and cars parked in an adjacent graveled lot.

Ellie turned on her blinker, indicating a turn into the place, and Steven's brow furrowed. *Seriously?* This was the place where all the locals hung out?

He wasn't sure what he'd expected Mariana's to be—a coffee shop, maybe—but it looked as if Ellie was taking them to a flea market. He scanned the periphery, the shaded tables, the trucks parked with open tailgates that displayed their wares. If these were the locals Ellie had wanted him to meet, he'd have to agree—her constituents weren't likely to shop at high-end stores.

As they got out of the car, Steven turned to his lovely tour director for the day, who'd dressed casually in a pink T-shirt, black jeans and a pair of sneakers. "So this is Mariana's?"

She nodded, a bit smugly.

"I never would have guessed."

At that, she smiled, a bit of pride glimmering in her eyes. "Mariana's Market has been around for as long as the town has. And this is the real deal. Rambling Rose at its best. I wanted you to meet some of the people who've lived here for years, the folks who keep everything running smoothly—mechanics, handymen, waitresses, farmers. You'll even see some of the ranchers who live nearby."

"I live on a ranch," Steven reminded her.

Ellie laughed. "Is *that* what you call it?"

"Okay, so the Fame and Fortune isn't actually a working ranch, if that's what you mean. But we have a stable and horses."

Ellie clicked her tongue. "Oh, come on, Steven. That isn't a house you live in. It's a sprawling mansion with enough space for your entire family to live on the property and still maintain their privacy."

All right. He had to give her that.

As they neared the open-air marketplace, Steven spotted a couple of vendors along the edge, their tables shaded by colorful canopies, as well as a variety of shoppers, all of whom seemed to know each other.

"Mariana's has sure drawn a crowd," Steven said. "What do they sell here?"

"All kinds of things. Vintage clothing, discount perfumes and even some homemade goop that's guaranteed to clean oil leaks off the driveway. You can also buy used furniture and handmade crafts and baked goods. Frances Elliot makes these great hand-knit scarves and sweaters. And Alice McKinley's quilts are amazing. In fact, she's making one to order for me, a shabby-chic style for my bed." Ellie tossed him an enthusiastic smile that put a spark in her pretty brown eyes.

Damn, he could get lost in that sparkly expression.

Were they somehow becoming friends? He hoped so. And not just for business or political reasons.

"Looks like the high school cheerleaders turned out." Dillon pointed to a table where a couple of teenage girls were selling tickets of some kind.

"Rambling Rose High School is having a talent show next week," Ellie said. "It would be a good idea if you and your brothers bought a few tickets in support of the kids."

Steven wasn't so sure he wanted to attend an event like that, but she was right. It would probably help if people saw him and his brothers getting involved in the community, and especially with the youth. So what the hell. "Sure, I'll buy some tickets."

Ellie's face brightened, and he had to admit, it was worth the cost of the tickets just to see it. So he reached into his pocket, pulled out a money clip and removed a hundred-dollar bill.

"How much are the tickets?" he asked one of the teens.

"Five dollars each."

"Then I'll take twenty."

While the teenager counted out the tickets, Steven turned to Ellie. "Are you going?"

"I wouldn't miss it."

Then neither would he.

"You won't be sorry," Ellie said as he pocketed

the tickets. "Some of those kids are incredibly talented. I really enjoyed it last year."

Steven had planned to give away the tickets he'd just purchased, but maybe he ought to actually attend, especially if it would help him get on the mayor's good side.

As they strolled through the open-air marketplace, Steven and Dillon were met with more than a few wary stares. One guy wearing a red plaid shirt and a pair of denim overalls narrowed his eyes and studied them suspiciously. The obvious distrust in the older man's gaze didn't seem to bother Dillon, but it troubled Steven—probably more than it should.

Back in Fort Lauderdale, the Fortune family had a stellar reputation. Their father had made millions by getting in on the ground floor of the video game industry. And after he married Steven's mother, Marci, the couple soon got involved in several charities and philanthropic projects that had benefited the entire city. People appreciated them there.

But that wasn't the case here in Rambling Rose, and Steven found the locals' animosity unsettling and bothersome.

When David Fortune married Marci, he'd had two sons of his own, Callum and Dillon. Soon after, he adopted her sons, Steven and his younger brother Wiley. The couple then went on to have four daughters together.

Ever since he was a boy, Steven had been proud of the family name and had tried his best to prove himself worthy of it. His father might have treated all of his children the same, but Steven couldn't seem to forget that he wasn't a Fortune by blood. But that didn't make him any less loyal.

Ellie strode toward the scowling older man and reached out her hand to greet him. "How's it going, Frank? Did you and Helen take that trip to Oklahoma last weekend to visit the kids?"

"We sure did." Frank's expression morphed from suspicion to outright pride and joy. "We drove up there last Friday. And on Saturday afternoon, we got to see Billy play basketball. I have to tell you, Ellie. That boy isn't too tall, but he's got a good eye and quick hands. He's fast on his feet, too, and he's becoming a dang good player. I hate to brag, but it wouldn't surprise me if the college scouts got wind of him and started banging on his door before the end of the season."

"That's awesome, Frank. I don't blame you for being a proud grandpa." Ellie turned to Steven and Dillon. "Frank, have you met Dillon and Steven Fortune yet?"

A slight scowl returned to the older man's face. "Can't say I have."

"They're eager to meet some of the people

who've lived in town for years," she said. "They'd like to get your take on their plans to open that new hotel."

Frank waited a couple of beats, then extended his arm and greeted each brother with a work-roughened hand. "I won't pull any punches. Most of us don't like the idea of that hotel one little bit."

"What don't you like about it?" Steven asked.

Frank chuffed. "It's too damned big and fancy for a town like Rambling Rose." He studied Steven for a beat, then folded his arms across his chest. "I suspect that's why you boys are having trouble getting the planning commission's approval."

That was true. The commission seemed to be split right down the middle, with very little sign of yielding.

"They have a few concerns," Steven admitted, "and we're trying to work them out."

"No surprise there," Frank said. "If you ask me—and practically everyone else you'll find here at Mariana's Market—you'd be a heck of a lot more successful if you were building a motel instead of a five-star hotel, although some folks are opposed to any additional lodging in town that would attract more tourists."

Yeah. Right. There was no way Steven or his brothers would even consider downsizing to a motel. But he didn't want to stir up trouble before they'd taken more than ten steps into the market.

"Thanks for the suggestion, Frank. I'll keep that in mind."

"We'd best be moving along," Ellie said. "Give Helen my best."

Once they'd gotten out of earshot, Dillon let out a soft whistle, followed by a half chuckle and an elbow nudge. "You're going to think about it, huh? There's no way you or Callum would agree to a project like that."

Steven shot his brother a look meant to suggest he should keep his mouth shut. He was making some headway with Ellie and didn't want to risk losing what little they'd gained. Besides, the longtime Rambling Rose residents might not trust the Fortunes or any other newcomers, but it didn't take long for Steven to realize they adored their young mayor.

Up ahead, a middle-aged man wearing a straw hat with a torn brim and a green apron stood behind a produce stand. When the ruddy-cheeked fellow spotted Ellie, he called out, "Good morning, Mayor. I got some of those sweet strawberries you like. They go pretty fast, so I put a couple of boxes under my table for you."

Ellie brightened, and while her smile was directed at the produce vendor, just seeing it turned Steven's heart on end. "Thank you, Pete. I'll come back to get them before I leave. And I'd like some of your broccoli, too."

"You got it!"

As they made their way through the market, Dillon asked, "So who's Mariana? What's her claim to fame?"

"She has a food truck in the center of the market. It's been there for years, but over time, as she and her menu gained popularity, other people who had stuff to sell began showing up. And that's how this became known as Mariana's Market."

"Sounds like an interesting beginning to an unusual business," Steven said.

"Yes, and it's a little mysterious, too. Even though she's been around for ages and is loved and well-known in the community, I don't think Mariana is her given name. She's a bit of an enigma, especially when it comes to her roots. When she and her mother first acquired that food truck, it had *Mariana's* painted on the side. So she took on the moniker herself for promotional purposes. Since she never talks about her past, some of the locals think she had a personal reason for a name change. No one knows for sure, and she won't confirm anything. So people keep guessing."

"She sounds like an intriguing character," Steven said. "I'd like to meet her."

"You will." Ellie tossed him a bright-eyed smile that turned him inside out. "A trip to Mariana's Market wouldn't be the same without stopping by and ordering one of her meat-loaf sandwiches or the chicken fried steak and potato salad."

"So she specializes in down-home cooking," Steven said.

"For the most part. She also includes a couple of southwestern specialties on her menu, which vary. But on the weekends, she always has menudo. People claim she makes the best in town, but I'd have to disagree. When it comes to Mexican food, Alma Hernandez—my mother—is the best cook in all of Texas. But don't tell Mariana."

"Menudo?" Dillon scrunched his brow. "Is that the spicy soup made out of tripe? If so, I think I'll pass."

Ellie gave Steven a playful nudge with her arm, as if they'd become friends. "What about you? Are you braver and more adventurous than your brother?"

"I don't know about that," Steven replied. "Dillon's not afraid of much. But if you say it's good, I'll give it a try."

As they ventured on, Ellie stopped to introduce Steven and Dillon to some of the vendors and several shoppers. As long as the brothers had the pretty young mayor to vouch for them, most of the people seemed to accept them.

Next up was a group of senior citizens who met every Saturday morning at the community center and caught a shuttle van to the market. Some came looking for knickknacks or arts and crafts, but most seemed to consider the outing a social event.

Steven had to admit he'd met a lot of colorful but likable characters, but none of them was likely to venture to the Shoppes to purchase a bespoke suit, a Louis Vuitton purse or gourmet vegan cuisine. And when asked, not a one was in favor of the hotel development.

No wonder the planning commission had been giving Fortune Brothers Construction such a hard time. But Steven wasn't one to shy from a fight.

They paused when they came upon a card table with four older men playing gin rummy.

An older man with a head of thick white hair looked up from his cards with a smug grin. "Well, I'll be damned. Would you look at this?"

"Oh, for cripe's sake." A balding fellow sitting next to him furrowed his brow. "Don't give me that, Cotton Head. You can't possibly have gin now. I just dealt the cards."

Another guy said, "Norm, you didn't shuffle them very good, so if he does, I wouldn't be surprised."

"Oh yeah?" Norm let out a snort. "Cotton Head, if you can call gin now, I'll give you two hours to gather a crowd in town square, then I'll kiss your ass."

Cotton Head offered up a big gap-toothed grin,

laid down his hand and said, "Then you'd better pucker up, Norm."

At that, Dillon let out a laugh. A bright smile, once a familiar sight Steven hadn't seen in a while, stretched across his face and glimmered in his eyes. "Those guys are a hoot."

"Aren't they?" Ellie lowered her voice. "And you haven't seen anything yet. But they're more than a couple of funny old men hanging out at a flea market and poking fun at each other. They're actually veterans who do a lot for the town. In fact, twice a week, they drive out to Austin and volunteer at a soup kitchen. They don't just dish out plates of food and pat themselves on the back for doing a good deed. They actually sit down and eat at the tables, talking to people and treating them like old friends."

"Do you think they'd mind if I watched for a while?" Dillon asked Ellie.

"No, not at all. They always draw a crowd and seem to like it."

As Dillon lingered behind, Steven and Ellie continued to walk through the market.

"It's good to hear my brother laugh," Steven said. "He's been pretty quiet and low-key ever since we moved here."

"Sounds to me as if your brother misses his life in Florida."

"Maybe so. But he's a big part of Fortune Brothers. And he's adjusting."

Ellie's pace slowed as she approached a weathered brown-and-white motor home with an outstretched blue canopy. Various pieces of antique furniture had been placed in front of it, while a rectangular table displayed smaller items for sale.

"I love antiques," Ellie said. "And my mom collects old jewelry. Do you mind if I look around for a minute or two?"

"Not at all. Take your time."

As Ellie picked up an elaborate necklace with blue, green and purple stones set in a peacock design, Steven made his way to the left of her to look at a couple of old books and magazines that rested at the edge of the table.

He spotted a fragile brown copy of *The Poetical Works of Sir Walter Scott* that had to be more than a hundred and fifty years old. He was about to pick it up when a faded red scrapbook caught his eye. He opened it instead. "Wow."

"What did you find?" Ellie asked.

"This." He pointed to the old newspaper clippings someone had carefully glued inside. "It's a bunch of articles about Rambling Rose. Some of them date back to the early 1900s."

He carefully paged through it. "I can't believe this, Ellie. There's even a feature about Fortune's Foundling Hospital."

"That's awesome."

"I'm going to buy it." He glanced over his shoulder and motioned to the dark-haired vendor. "How much do you want for this?"

She shrugged. "Twenty dollars?"

He might have haggled, just for the fun of it, but he was too intent upon owning the scrapbook and taking his time to catch up on more of Rambling Rose's history.

Moments after they'd purchased both the peacock necklace and the scrapbook, Ellie said, "Should we head over to Mariana's now or wait for Dillon?"

"I can go back and tell him we're ready to eat."

In all honesty, though, Steven preferred to have more time with Ellie on his own, without his brother or the business or the family name to get in the way. He liked having the chance to get to know her better—not as the mayor, but as a young woman the town loved and admired.

Ellie might think that she was just like her neighbors, but there was more to her than that. A lot more. Something seemed to be happening between them, and while he wasn't sure what it was, it went beyond politics and business deadlines.

She'd shown him a side of the town she'd grown up in, and he wanted to introduce her to his world, too.

As they walked back to the card game, her

shoulder brushed against his arm, and he felt the strangest compulsion to take a hold of her hand, which would have been totally inappropriate. And stupid. But for some crazy reason, he felt more and more drawn to Ellie Hernandez as a person.

And worse, he was tempted to act on it before the day was done.

After taking Dillon away from his VIP seat at the weekly gin rummy game, Ellie led the two Fortune brothers to the center of the marketplace, where Mariana's food truck was parked. It was quite the experience, she supposed—being flanked by two gorgeous hunks, both muscular and at least six feet tall. They also had the same blue eye color, with only slight variations in the shade.

But there were more than a few subtle differences. Dillon's dirty-blond locks were slightly tousled, while Steven's dark, short-cropped hair was often covered by the black Stetson that seemed to have become a part of him since he'd moved to Texas.

Several times over the past hour or so, when the brothers weren't looking, Ellie had stolen a peek at them, just to check them out. Surprisingly, she hadn't been able to spot a family resemblance. Not that it mattered, she supposed. Some siblings took after different relatives.

Still, they were both eye candy in their own

right. And she hadn't been the only one checking them out, either. The brothers had caught the attention of just about every woman shopping at Mariana's Market today, drawing smiles from most of them. But it was Steven who'd captured Ellie's interest—and not just because of his sexy swagger, his damn good looks or the way those fancy jeans molded to his butt.

No, there was more to Steven Fortune that Ellie found appealing. His charm, she supposed. He also exuded confidence without any sign of pride or arrogance. And he was bright, too. Whenever she challenged him, he held his own.

Unlike a lot of men Ellie knew, Steven wasn't intimidated by her brains and political success. She had to admit that she found it refreshing.

Unable to help herself, she stole another glance at him, only to find him gazing at her in a way that set off a dizzying flutter in her chest. For a couple of beats, something stirred between them, and even though they continued to move through the crowd, the marketplace seemed to stand still.

Oh, for Pete's sake, Ellie. You didn't read any romantic interest in his eyes.

And even if she had, she'd better get over it. In a few short months, she'd be a mother with her hands full. It was going to be tough enough for her to put her baby boy first while trying to handle her job as mayor. So she'd be absolutely crazy to consider a romantic relationship—and a complicated one like this one would no doubt be. Her day planner was full enough as it was.

Besides, if Steven actually had dating on his mind, a rich, handsome man like him would run for the hills as soon as he learned she was pregnant.

Ellie shook off the foolhardy thought and pointed ahead at the food truck, where several people had already begun to fill the seats at the folding picnic tables set up out front. The red, black and white vehicle with chrome trim had gotten a fresh coat of paint since the last time she'd been here, as had the green swirly letters on the side that spelled out *Mariana's* in a fancy cursive font.

She pointed ahead. "There it is. We'd better place our orders while we can find a place to sit."

"Something sure smells good." Steven took a second whiff. "All of a sudden, I'm starving."

"I agree," Dillon said.

Mariana, a matronly woman with ruddy cheeks, warm brown eyes and bleached blond hair pulled into a bun, popped her head out the open window where she took orders and passed out food. She gave Ellie a little wave, then, in a graveled voice that was loud even when she whispered, she yelled, "Fred Willingham! Your meat-loaf sandwich is ready."

"That has to be Mariana," Steven said to Ellie.

"You've got that right."

As they got within five feet of the food truck, Fred said something to Mariana as he picked up his meal. The tall, slender man usually spoke in a soft tone, so Ellie couldn't hear what he said, but it must have been funny, because Mariana let out a raucous laugh.

Before Ellie had a chance to say hello to Fred, he turned to the left and walked away holding a foil-covered paper plate. But the matronly woman remained at the open window and broke into a big ol' grin. "Howdy, Mayor. What do you think of the new paint job?"

"It looks good." Ellie glanced at each of the brothers, then back to Mariana. "I'd like to introduce you to Steven and Dillon Fortune."

"Well, now." Mariana crossed her arms and eyed both men carefully. "This is a surprise. You fellows have been the talk of the town, and I don't mean just among the gossipmongers. But I gotta say, you two don't look like rich vermin to me."

"Actually," Steven said, offering her a charming smile, "my brothers and I are pretty harmless."

"Good to know. But just in case one of you should get a wild hair, I keep a shotgun near the cash register, and I know how to use it." Mariana waited a beat, then winked at the men, who hadn't quite figured out how to take her, and let out another hearty laugh.

"I've been telling them about the locals," Ellie told Mariana. "About the people who've called Rambling Rose home for years. It's hard for them to understand that we're simple folk with big hearts and a strong work ethic. So I brought them to the marketplace so they could see for themselves just how special this town really is."

Mariana arched a brow and studied the men. "So now you're here. What do you think of us?"

"You're all pretty colorful and likable, especially Norm and the boys playing gin rummy." Steven cracked a grin and nodded his head toward Dillon. "I was afraid my brother was going to sit down and join the game."

"They'd welcome a newbie like you," Mariana said, "but if you take 'em up on it, you'd better hold on to your wallet. Losing to those guys won't be cheap."

"I'll keep that in mind," Dillon said.

"So what'll it be?" Mariana asked. "I've got meat loaf and fried chicken on the menu today. And the southwestern special is green chili and homemade tortillas."

"How about the menudo?" Ellie asked.

"Sorry. I'm afraid you're out of luck. I got off to a slow start this morning and didn't get a chance to cook up a new batch."

"That's too bad." Steven winked and jabbed an elbow at Dillon's arm. "My brother and I had our hearts set on having a great big bowl of it."

"If you come back next weekend, I'll have it for sure. And your first bowl is on the house." Mariana glanced at Ellie. "You guys gonna eat? Or did you just stop by to hold up the food line?"

Ellie couldn't help but laugh. "I'll have the fried chicken."

"Me, too," Steven added.

Dillon said, "Make that three."

Twenty minutes later, after they'd eaten their fill of some of the best fried chicken and homemade potato salad in Texas, they called it a day and returned to the car.

As Dillon climbed into the back seat, Ellie paused before opening the driver's door. She probably could've waited to question the brothers until the drive back to town, but Dillon hadn't done much talking today. And she couldn't quell her growing curiosity.

"So what did you think?" she asked Steven.

"About what?" A crooked smile tweaked one side of his lips and dimpled his right cheek. "The people we met here?"

She nodded.

"I'll admit, it's been eye-opening. Up until a couple of days ago, when we had that run-in with the protesters at the grand opening of the Shoppes, I had no idea how much local resistance we were facing."

Ellie's hands hung at her sides, and she fought the urge to cross her fingers. "Does that mean you'll reconsider your plans to build that big luxury hotel?"

"Not really. You and the people who frequent Mariana's Market might not like it, but the newcomers in town will welcome a nice place for their friends and family to stay while visiting. On the other hand, the tour has given me a lot to think about and consider. So thank you for bringing us here today."

"You're welcome. Were you surprised to see this side of Rambling Rose?"

"Yes, but I saw something else that I hadn't expected to see. And that's making me reconsider a lot of things."

"Like what?" she asked, wanting to hear him out.

He scanned her from head to toe and back again, his gaze practically caressing her. Then he offered her a smile.

Her cheeks warmed, and she wondered what he was getting at. And what that appreciative grin meant. Instead, she pushed for a different response. "Aren't you going to answer my question? What did you see that gave you pause?"

"I saw the way you relate to the people—and

vice versa. They love and respect you as much as you love and respect them."

"There's a reason for that. I haven't lived in Rambling Rose my entire life. I was adopted when I was six. But it wasn't just my parents who took in a scared, awkward little girl in pigtails. Everyone in town adopted me, too. So I consider them all part of my family."

"You're lucky."

"Don't I know it."

Sometimes it seemed as if Ellie had grown up as a princess in a fairy-tale life. Once upon a time, she'd been a neglected, frightened and malnourished little girl who'd been rescued from a crack house by a king and queen who weren't able to have children of their own. And she'd never forgotten that. So for that reason, she'd spent the last twenty-two years trying to make her adoptive parents proud and to prove to them, as well as the entire community, that they'd made a wise choice in accepting her as one of their own. And for that reason alone, she dreaded having to tell them that she was about to be an unwed mother.

But that was way too much to share with anyone, especially one of the new, rich residents.

"The Rambling Rose locals trust me," she said. "Not a day goes by that I don't know that, that I don't respect it. And I feel the weight of that trust every day."

He nodded and smiled. "I'm sure you do."

She inadvertently placed a hand on her tummy and stopped short of giving it a loving caress. What had been a small bulge last week was developing into an actual baby bump, which meant her secret would be out soon enough. It was time to tell her parents. And then she'd have to make an announcement to the community.

Maybe it would be in her best interest to tell Steven first. She could practice her confession on him, and once she'd done that, she wouldn't be able to drag her feet any longer on telling the people she loved.

Actually, that would solve another mounting problem. Once she'd told Steven she was pregnant, neither of them would waste another minute thinking about wacky romantic ideas.

Satisfied with her new game plan, she turned toward the driver's door.

"How about having dinner with me tonight?" Steven asked.

Even though she'd half expected him to ask a question like that, her lips parted, and she slowly turned back to face him. "I…uh… Thank you, but I don't think that's a good idea."

"Why not?"

She glanced to her right and then to her left. Several other people had followed them out to the parking lot.

"I don't want to explain in public," she said. "I'll tell you when we're alone."

"Then a private dinner it is." He tossed her a boyish grin. "How about tonight, at the Fame and Fortune Ranch?"

Chapter Four

The drive back to town seemed to take a lot longer than the ride out to Mariana's Market. It was a lot quieter, too. If Ellie hadn't been nearly drowning in remorse for accepting Steven's dinner invitation, she might have tried to break the awkward silence.

Steven had assured her that the Fame and Fortune Ranch was the best place for them to speak confidentially, but the more she thought about the logistics, the more she doubted his claim. After all, his entire family lived on the property. Well, at least those who'd moved to Rambling Rose from Fort Lauderdale.

She'd heard through the grapevine that the fancy-schmancy house was laid out in a way that provided them all with a certain amount of privacy, but she found that hard to believe. And what about household help? Maids, butlers and cooks—oh my!

By the time she reached the city limits, she decided to ask him for a rain check—one she'd never use.

Since Dillon hadn't been privy to Steven's invitation, she wouldn't mention it until after she dropped off the brothers at their pickup. Then she'd take Steven aside and tell him she'd just remembered her plans to go out with her friend Daria this evening, so she'd have to pass.

But by the time they arrived at city hall, she'd changed her mind yet again. Everyone in Rambling Rose had been talking about the Fortunes' renovated, ranch-style home. From what she'd heard, the sprawling estate would boggle the mind of a common person. So Ellie actually would like to see it. On top of that, it might be a good idea—politically speaking, of course—for her to interact with Steven and his family on their own turf. Then, after dinner, she'd ask him to walk her out to her car. That's when she'd tell him about the baby.

Granted, it would be a difficult conversation to have, a rather embarrassing one. But once she'd gotten that out of the way, she'd go to her parents' house and give them the news.

Eventually, the community would learn her secret, too. At that point, she'd deal with any repercussions that might arise.

One day at a time, she told herself, *one good deed after another.* That had been her mantra for as long as she could remember, and it had led her to becoming a perfectionist, an overachiever and a leader.

Only trouble was, Ellie wasn't perfect. Deep down, she felt like an impostor. And now everyone in Rambling Rose would know it.

The whispers would eventually die down, she supposed, and everything would fall into place. Then she'd finally be able to openly celebrate the upcoming birth of her baby. Her son. A tiny human being who'd need her to look after him, to encourage him and to love him with all her heart.

When she stopped next to the pickup to let both Fortune brothers out of her car, she told them goodbye.

Dillon got out of the car first and shut the passenger door, but Steven remained seated beside her, holding the brown paper sack that held the old scrapbook he'd purchased and looking at her. A slow smile stretched across his gorgeous face. "I'll see you later."

Still, he didn't reach for the door. His eyes lingered on her for a beat. As their gazes locked, her breath caught, and her pulse kicked up a notch.

"Does six o'clock work for you?" he asked.

For some reason, the words jammed up in her throat, making it impossible to utter a sound, so she nodded her agreement.

"Great." Then he got out of the car.

Once the passenger door snapped shut, Ellie didn't wait for him to get into his own vehicle. Instead, she drove off, hoping she hadn't made another big mistake. But they seemed to be tiptoeing around attraction, pondering whether to act upon it. And that needed to stop.

Once Steven knew she was pregnant, her life would take a slow turn to normal. The flirtatious smiles, as well as her heart flips and flutters, would soon be a thing of the past.

Minutes later, she turned down Pumpernickel Court, a small subdivision that was built near the elementary school in the 1960s. She pulled into the driveway. Using the remote on her sun visor, she opened the garage door and parked next to Daria's late-model Prius.

Three months ago, Daria had been working for an accounting firm in Austin, but the company downsized and she was let go. Knowing Daria, she would've taken the layoff in stride, calling it a little inconvenience. But she'd just gone through a major breakup, so it hadn't taken much to knock her off balance. She'd called Ellie that evening in tears.

"Rent a U-Haul trailer," Ellie had said. "Then pack up your stuff and come to Rambling Rose. I've got a spare bedroom, and it's yours for as long as you need it."

Two days later, Daria arrived. The timing had worked perfectly. Ellie and Mike had recently split, so the two new roommates had shared their disappointment and pain caused by men who were all hat and no cattle. And now the roomies were relieved and glad to be single.

Ellie closed the garage door and entered the house through the outdated kitchen.

"I'm home," she called out as she set her purse on the kitchen counter.

Tank bounded toward her, greeting her with a happy whimper and a wagging tail. He miscalculated his speed and tried to slow his pace, but he tripped over his big paws and tumbled to a stop at her feet.

"You silly guy. What're we going to do with you?" Ellie gave him a scratch behind his floppy ears.

"Hey," Daria said from the doorway. "You're home."

"Yep." Ellie straightened but continued to study the rascally pup. "I swear Tank has doubled in size in the past couple of weeks. The lease allows us to have one small pet, but that puppy is going to outgrow anyone's definition of 'small' before we know it. The landlords are going to freak when they see him."

"You're probably right." Daria crossed the kitchen, opened up the pantry, removed a dog biscuit from the box and handed it to Tank.

Ellie scanned the floral wallpaper, yellowed and faded from age, the pink Formica countertops, and outdated white appliances. The entire house could have used a major renovation decades ago, but the owners hadn't wanted to spend the money.

Even though the house was a rental, Ellie planned to buy new blinds and paint the third bedroom and turn it into a nursery.

"If the landlord doesn't want Tank here," Daria said, "I'll have to look for a new place."

That might sound like an easy solution, but Daria's part-time job as a bookkeeper at the car wash didn't pay much, so she wouldn't be able to afford a dog-friendly place until she found a better position.

"How's the housebreaking coming along?" Ellie asked.

"Awesome. Tank's doing great. He hasn't had an accident all day. Every time I take him outside, he goes potty."

"Sounds like you're the one who's being trained."

Daria laughed. "Yeah, you're right."

If the landlord did complain about Tank, Ellie

and Daria might have to house hunt together. They'd both gotten attached to the rascally pup. He was a little goofy but lovable. He was also a little troublesome. "Did he chew up anything today?"

"Nothing but his toys. But then, I've been following him around like a coyote circling a chicken coop."

"That's good to hear. I don't want to lose another pair of heels."

"Sorry about that." Daria reached for another dog biscuit and handed it to Tank.

As she did, Ellie took a moment to watch her friend, who was the prettiest woman she'd ever known. Daria's biracial father had been in the military and stationed in Hawaii when he met and married her mother, who was a Pacific Islander. Daria seemed to have inherited all the best qualities of every race and culture represented on her family tree, including long dark curly hair, blue-green eyes and tanned skin. The men in town had noticed, too, but Daria claimed she wasn't interested in dipping her toes back in the dating pool.

After giving Tank a pat on the head, Daria straightened and brushed her hands against her slacks. "So, how'd the tour of Mariana's Market go?"

"Okay, I guess. But I don't think the Fortune brothers will alter their plans for that fancy hotel. So I'm not sure how helpful it was in the long run."

"By the way," Daria said, "I took some chicken out of the freezer. I thought I'd add some barbecue sauce and bake it. How's that sound?"

Ellie took a deep breath, then slowly let it out. "It sounds good, but I'm not eating at home tonight."

"You have another meeting? On Saturday night?"

"Sort of. I'm having dinner with Steven at the Fame and Fortune Ranch."

Daria's jaw dropped. "No kidding? Does he know about…?"

"The baby? Not yet. So far, you're the only one I've told. But I'm going to let him know tonight."

Daria leaned against the kitchen counter and crossed her arms. "Before you tell your mom and dad?"

"That's my plan. He seems to be interested in me—romantically. So tonight, when we're alone, I'll tell him I'm pregnant. That ought to cool his heels. And it'll force me to quit dragging my feet and finally face my parents with the news."

Daria let out a little whistle. "You might want to rethink that."

"Telling my parents?"

"No. You *need* to do that. And sooner rather than later. But it just seems weird to share that news with Steven first." Daria eyed Ellie carefully, then blew out a slow whistle. "OMG. He's not the only one having a few romantic thoughts, is he?"

Ellie might have waved her off, told her she was wrong. But Daria knew her almost as well as she knew herself. "All right. I find him attractive. But even if he were interested in dating a pregnant woman—and I'm one hundred percent sure he wouldn't be!—I'd never go out with him. We have too many opposing ideas."

"I've always believed the old adage that opposites attract."

"Maybe. But they don't make for lasting relationships. We both learned that the hard way." Ellie nodded toward the doorway. "Come on. Let's go into the living room. I've been walking all over Mariana's Market, and I want to get off my feet."

As Daria followed her out of the kitchen with Tank on their heels, Ellie added, "On top of that, what would the community say if they thought I'd gone to the dark side?"

"Seriously?" Daria laughed. "You see Steven Fortune as Lord Vader? Come on, he's not that bad."

"Maybe not." Ellie plopped down in the brown recliner and kicked off her shoes. "But I'll have enough community disappointment to worry about within the next couple of days. I'm not going to throw a can of lighter fluid onto the flames.

Besides, I really need to focus on getting ready for the baby."

"I can't wait to help you. We'll have to plan several shopping trips. You're going to need a small dresser, a crib and some cute bedding. And once your parents find out, I'll bet your mom will want to convert one of their spare rooms into a nursery, too."

"True." There was no argument there. George and Alma Hernandez loved children, especially babies. They'd make awesome grandparents. "But it might take them a little while to get used to the idea. They're pretty conservative. I don't think they'll like me running around town barefoot and pregnant."

"Then wear your shoes." Daria smiled and slowly shook her head. "Come on, Ellie. You've never been an embarrassment to them. And you won't be now."

"I hope you're right. It's just that…"

"Your parents *adore* you. They'll get over any disappointment they may feel real quick. And in this day and age, that should take all of five minutes."

"You've got a point. It's just…" Ellie didn't keep much from Daria, but she'd never told anyone about the conversation she'd overheard when she was only six. Maybe now was the time to share it. "A couple of weeks after they first took me in as a foster child, I stood outside the kitchen door and heard my father ask my mom if she was sure she wanted to go through with their plan to adopt me."

"You can't blame him for that. Adoption is a big step. It's only natural that a couple would talk it over and make sure they're on the same page."

"I know. But he said something else. He asked if she thought I might have inherited any bad genes from my biological parents. I didn't understand all the words he'd used, but I knew what he meant. My biological father was a gang member serving a life sentence. And my mom was a druggie who cared more about her next fix than she did me." Ellie took a deep, fortifying breath, then slowly let it out. "Papa was afraid that, even if they provided me with love and a solid upbringing, I could turn out to be just like my birth parents."

"But you didn't."

"I know." Ellie gave a little shrug, hoping her friend could piece it all together—the insecurity that still lingered inside, popping out every now and then, the fear of failure that sometimes dogged her.

"How did your mother respond to that?"

"She told him they'd just have to take it one day at a time."

"Apparently, those days went by without a hitch."

"Only because I made up my mind to prove to them that I wasn't a bad seed."

"You don't think your parents know that?" Daria asked.

Ellie's shoulders slumped. "Yes. But for the record, my birth mom was never married to my dad. And she used to entertain a lot of men, if you know what I mean."

"Come on, Ellie. So you had sex with Mike. When you realized the relationship wasn't working, you split up. That's what a smart woman does. Your parents can't blame you for that. Dang, girl. The guy's a freelance photographer whose new job requires him to fly from country to country on photo shoots. He'd never be around. And, on top of that, he didn't want kids. Ever."

"You're right. I'd hoped he'd change his mind in time, so I respected that. But then I got bronchitis, and the antibiotic must have made my birth control pills ineffective. We used a condom, but he wasn't happy about it and got a little careless."

Mike had been a bad choice from the get-go. And Ellie should have been smarter, should have picked up on his flaws earlier.

"Ditch the pity party," Daria said. "Let's focus on the upside. You're going to have a sweet baby boy, and I'm going to be a godmother and an honorary auntie."

Ellie blessed her friend with a smile. "He's going to be a lucky little boy, one who's well loved from the day he arrives."

"You got that right. That little peanut isn't going to want for anything."

Except a father.

Ellie rested her head against the backrest and closed her eyes as she recalled the day she'd told Mike she was pregnant.

"You gotta be kidding," he'd said.

"I'd never joke about something like this."

They'd already broken up for several reasons, his new job assignment for one, and she'd known he wouldn't be happy with the news.

"I'm not ready for a kid, Ellie. And you just got elected mayor. You don't need to be burdened with one now, either. How soon can you schedule an abortion?"

She'd cringed at the thought of the solution he'd suggested. The baby might be unplanned, but unlike her parents had done to her, she'd never put her needs and desires over those of her child.

"I won't take that route," she'd told him.

"Don't expect me to take that journey with you. I'm flying out to South America in two weeks."

And he'd done just that.

What would Steven think when she told *him* tonight? Not that it mattered. Mike hadn't had a problem walking away from his own flesh and blood. No way would a man, especially one as rich and handsome as Steven Fortune, want to deal with someone else's baby.

And Ellie had better not let another fruitless thought like that cross her mind again.

As Steven drove Dillon home, he made a mental list of what he'd need to do before Ellie arrived— and the top of that list was to figure out what kind of groceries to buy.

Manny, the family cook and ranch caretaker, was off this weekend, which was just as well. Steven preferred to prepare dinner for her in his private quarters.

"Hey," Dillon said, "aren't you listening to me?"

Had he said something? "Sorry, I was deep in thought."

"Me, too," Dillon said. "About the hotel. If the people we met today are a good representation of the community at large, we're going to have a hard time getting the project approved. Maybe we ought to scrap the original plan."

Steven shook off his thoughts about his date with Ellie and got back to business. "No way am I going to roll over. That hotel, as planned, will be good for the town as a whole. I'll just have to use a little more charm and finesse."

"With whom?" Dillon cut a glance across the seat and cracked a smile. "The planning commission? Or the beautiful mayor?"

Steven didn't respond.

"Cat got your tongue?" Dillon asked. "You can't deny it. I saw fireworks between the two of you today."

"They were probably one-sided."

"No, it went both ways. Ellie might consider you an opponent, but she's attracted to you, too."

Thoughts about Ellie always kicked up Steven's pulse a notch. He'd suspected that she felt something for him, but realizing that his brother had picked up on those vibes, too, validated his suspicion and sent his blood pumping.

Silence filled the cab as they neared the ranch, then Dillon spoke again. "Did you see the way she interacted with the people at Mariana's Market?"

"How could I miss it? She's like a rock star to them." In fact, Steven was a bit dazzled by her himself, not that he'd admit it. "It's not likely that she'll change her mind about the hotel. She still thinks it's too big, fancy and expensive for the common folk."

"Since when have you ever let a stubborn politician stop you?"

"Never." And Steven wasn't about to let one stop him now. He'd work on Ellie a little more at dinner. "By the way, Dillon, I hope you have plans tonight."

"Why's that?"

"I invited Ellie to come over."

"I knew it."

"You don't know squat. It's just a business meeting."

"The hell it is." Dillon chuckled. "You've got more than business on your mind, brother."

Maybe so. He had to admit he was eager to spend more time with her. But no matter how big the Fame and Fortune Ranch was, he wanted to entertain her in private. And since Callum and Becky were spending the night in Austin with the twins and Stephanie had recently fallen in love with Acton Donovan and was now living with him on his ranch, tonight was Steven's best chance of having Ellie to himself.

"Don't worry," Dillon said. "I'll make myself scarce. I've got a kitchen in my quarters, just like you do. So give it your best shot."

Four hours later, the doorbell rang, sparking a rush of excitement as Steven headed to the foyer. He'd already fired up the grill on his private patio. A couple of filets, seasoned just right, were waiting in the fridge, and he'd completed all the prep work for a salad.

He swung open the door, and while he'd known the pretty mayor would be standing on the stoop, he hadn't been prepared to see her looking so… amazing. Her glossy black hair hung loose and down her back, allowing him to see how long it actually was. Her brown eyes were larger and more luminous than usual, and a shy smile stretched across her pink-glossed lips.

"Come in," he said as he stepped aside and watched her enter the house rocking a pair of dark jeans and a funky T-shirt with a Rosie the Riveter print. The woman who looked hot in whatever she wore never ceased to surprise him.

He led her through the foyer, with its travertine flooring, floor-to-ceiling windows and Southwestern artwork, and to the east, toward his private quarters.

"You have a nice house," she said, her gaze taking in the decor. "Or should I say estate?"

"*House* works for me." He offered her a disarming smile. "We didn't all live together in Florida, but we got a good deal on this place. Another developer built it for himself and his fiancée. But the couple split up before they moved in, so Callum, Dillon and I snatched it up."

"Hmm. That seems to be your MO. You just pick up projects that were abandoned prior to completion."

"Can you blame us?"

"No, I suppose not." Ellie's steps slowed as she took a moment to scan the expansive living room that was rarely used. "It does seem like a luxurious mansion."

"I guess you're right. There are two guest houses and enough land for us to build more, if the need should arise."

"Not to mention the guard at the gate who let me in."

"The gatehouse is a new addition to the property." And only a precaution. The disgruntled people who'd formed protest groups were probably harmless, but Steven and his brothers decided a little extra security wouldn't hurt.

"I didn't expect the Fame and Fortune Ranch to be a luxurious compound."

"I prefer to call it a ranch. You'll have to check out the stable."

"I'm sure it's impressive," she said.

Right now, the only one he wanted to impress was her.

"So where is everyone?" she asked.

"It's just you and me tonight."

Her gaze zeroed in on his, setting off a flurry of pheromones that damn near took him out at the knees. Talk about fireworks. Dillon had been right. Those colorful sparks were going both ways.

He was half tempted to reach for her, to pull her into his arms, but it was too soon. And he wasn't about to push when they had the whole evening in front of them.

"I thought I'd grill a couple of steaks—filet mignon. But if you're not into red meat, we can have chicken or salmon."

"No, that's fine. Steak sounds good." Her head tilted slightly, and a playful glimmer lit her eyes.

"What's the matter?"

"It's just that I never pegged you for a chef."

"I'm not. But I can whip up a decent meal when I want to. My sisters, the triplets, are super foodies. That's why they're going to open Provisions, the restaurant we're building."

"I hope they have some business experience. Restaurants take a lot of work."

"Actually, Ashley, Megan, and Nicole have a lot of experience working in restaurants. They've been cooking, waiting tables and working front of the house since they were in high school. And Nicole might be self-taught, but she's worked her way up to sous chef. She knows what she's doing."

Ellie scrunched her brow in the cutest way, and her head cocked slightly to the side.

"I know what you're probably thinking," he said. "A lot of people find it surprising that a man who'd made a fortune in the video game industry would insist that his children get jobs once they turned sixteen. But my dad figured it would build character. And that working would keep us out of trouble."

"You're right. I find it surprising. But it's also an admirable philosophy."

"It didn't hurt any of us," Steven said. "It taught us how to work for someone else, a boss who wasn't a parent or relative. And then, once we turned twenty-one, he gifted each one of us with a sizable check, something to add to our coffers."

"A bonus, huh?"

"Yes. If I ever have kids, I'm going to make them get jobs, too. I mean, once they're old enough."

She seemed to ponder that for a beat, then asked, "When are the girls coming to Rambling Rose?"

"Soon. Now that Stephanie has moved out, they'll take over her quarters on the other side of the house."

"I'll look forward to meeting them. And to trying out the food at Provisions."

Since Ellie had made it clear she wasn't into glitz or glamour, Steven feigned mock surprise and placed a hand on his chest. "Seriously? You'd actually eat at an upscale restaurant?"

"Believe it or not, I'm a bit of a foodie myself, whether it's down-home cooking prepared in a food truck or a five-star French restaurant in the city."

Apparently, there was a lot more to Ellie Hernandez than he'd once thought. She wasn't just a small-town girl doing her best to dig in her heels when it came to change. She wasn't just beautiful and savvy. She also had a heart, not just for Rambling Rose, but for the people she considered her tribe.

The more Steven talked to her, away from city hall and grand openings, the more she intrigued him. And tonight he looked forward to learning a lot more about her on his private patio.

And under a new moon and a starlit sky.

Chapter Five

Ellie sat at a glass-top table on Steven's small private patio, settling into the romantic ambiance he'd created this evening. He'd thought of everything. Twinkly lights on the trees and shrubs in the surrounding yard. An outdoor heater to chase the chill from the evening air. A yellow rose in a bud vase placed in the center of the table set for two. An uncorked bottle of red wine. A crystal decanter of water.

There was no way he had the time to set a scene like this unless he'd used hired help. Of course, he certainly could afford it. In fact, an estate this large probably required a full staff, some of whom might even live on the premises.

But then again, an ultrarich, handsome bachelor like Steven might have created this secluded spot, with lights in the trees, for him to use as a permanent romantic prop for the women he brought home.

Even the night sky seemed to have fallen under his magical orchestration, as if he'd snapped his fingers to chase away the clouds and reveal a big yellow moon surrounded by a million shining stars.

When Steven walked through the open sliding glass door and dazzled her with a smile, Ellie darn near fell under his spell, too. He carried two crystal wine goblets and set them on the table. "I thought a zinfandel would go best with the filet mignon, but if you'd rather have white, there's a sauvignon blanc chilling in the fridge."

"Thank you, but I'd prefer water." She probably should have explained why she was avoiding alcohol. It would have been a good segue into her announcement. But she wasn't quite ready to drop the bomb on him.

Or maybe she just didn't want to see a curtain come crashing down on the magical scene.

Whatever the actual reason, she added, "I'm driving."

He nodded, filled her goblet with water then poured the zinfandel for himself.

Eager to change the subject to one that was safer

and more comfortable, she asked, "So how many brothers and sisters do you have? And which one is oldest?"

"There are eight of us. I'm the oldest."

She'd suspected as much. He seemed to have taken a leadership position within the family.

He took a seat across from her. His gorgeous eyes studied her so intensely that she could feel him watching her. For a moment, she wished things were different, that her life wasn't complicated. That he wasn't so good-looking, so charming... And even more than that, she wished she wasn't expecting another man's baby.

Steven lifted his goblet and, after giving the zinfandel a little swirl that tinted the glass, he took a sip. "I was three and Wiley was two when our mom met David Fortune. They fell in love, and when they got married, David adopted me and my brother. And our mom adopted Callum and Dillon. So we're a blended family. Then Stephanie and the triplets came along."

"Yours, mine and ours. That's nice."

"It is now. We've all grown to love and respect each other, but it wasn't that nice at first. Callum and I didn't hit it off. He was used to being the top dog in his family, and then I came along, usurped his position and became his big brother."

"I can see where there'd be problems blending

two families," she said, "but you're lucky to have siblings. I'm an only child."

"There were times I wished I'd been one, too. But eventually things changed, especially when we began to play sports in high school and worked together in construction. Admiration and respect grew, and now we're not only brothers but business partners."

"That's cool."

"I think so." Steven pushed back his chair. "If you'll excuse me, I'm going to put the steaks on."

A few minutes later, while the meat was grilling, he returned to the table. Instead of taking his seat, he placed a hand on her shoulder, setting off a spiral of heat. "So what about you, Ellie?"

What about her? What was she feeling? How did his gentle touch affect her? Where were her wayward thoughts going?

"What do you mean?"

His fingers trailed off her shoulder, and he stepped to the right and took his seat. "What was it like being an only child?"

Aw. A safe topic. She could handle that. "Actually, you and I have one thing in common. The circumstances were a lot different, but I was adopted, too."

She fingered the stem of the water goblet. She wouldn't reveal where she'd come from or how she'd ended up in foster care at the home of a hardworking mechanic and a devoted schoolteacher. Or that her new parents, an older, childless couple, had once questioned whether she was a bad seed or a blessing.

"But being adopted is the only thing we have in common," she added. "I didn't grow up in the lap of luxury. And my parents believed that doing well in school was the only job I needed."

He took another slow sip of wine, clearly enjoying the taste. "So what about your plans for the future?"

"There's not much to tell." Her cheeks warmed at the lie, and her mouth went dry. She lifted her glass and took a cool, refreshing drink.

The conversation stalled while Steven finished grilling the steaks. Then he returned to the house and brought out two green salads. As he set one in front of Ellie, she caught an alluring whiff of his woodland-scented aftershave that trailed away as he took his seat, leaving her in a dreamy fog.

As they began to eat, her conscience rose up like a finger with an acrylic nail, poking her chest, insisting that she tell him now. Yet a rebellious spirit rose up, which suggested there might be some genetics at play after all, and insisted that she wait a bit longer.

She'd planned to tell him after dinner, right before she went home. Why change it up now?

"I know you and your brothers are business partners," Ellie said. "Who's the boss?"

"We're pretty much equal. I ran the main part of the construction/development firm in Florida. Dillon's big on details, so he's always been the nuts and bolts guy. And Callum took on the expansion and remote projects. I'd been chomping at the bit to get into the commercial side, and Callum said I'd get that opportunity in Rambling Rose. So here I am."

"Yes. Turning out one project after another."

"True. But we didn't start from scratch. We bought half-completed projects, which is why we were able to finish them in record time. That's probably what bothers you. It looks as if we're making a lot of changes all at once."

"Maybe so."

As much as she hated to admit it, she found herself admiring Steven, not just the adopted little boy, the high school student who worked construction, but the man he'd become.

"Just so you know," Steven said, "Callum handled the pediatric center and I took a big interest in the veterinary clinic, since I'm a real animal lover."

"Did you have pets as a kid?"

"No. My mom was allergic to pet dander. We might have been able to have outdoor animals, but since she also had a lot of health issues, my dad refused to consider it."

"That's too bad. I had a dog named Sweetie Pie when I was a growing up. I think pets enrich a child's life."

"My sister Stephanie loves animals, too. She became a vet assistant back in Florida and has the same job here in Texas. She also has a houseful of pets, including a rabbit and Acton's one-eyed cat."

"And you have a ranch and horses." No wonder Steven had morphed into a cowboy so easily.

"I enjoy riding in my free time, but I'm pretty busy." He took another sip of wine. "You may have figured this out already, but I'm the one taking charge of the hotel."

"And that's why you take any criticism of the blueprints personally."

"I try not to." Steven flashed a charming cowboy grin, then stood to clear the table.

Ellie scooted her chair back, intending to help with the cleanup.

"Don't get up," he said. "I've got this."

"Me, too." She offered him a smile of her own, then carried her dishes inside and to the small kitchen.

They worked well together and had the counters wiped down and the dishwasher running in short order.

"Ready for dessert?" he asked.

"I'm pretty full."

"Maybe something light? I have raspberry sorbet."

"Sounds good."

Moments later, he served them both. Instead of returning to the patio or finding a seat in the house, they stood at the counter and ate the sweet treat—a perfect ending to a filling meal.

As Ellie took the last bite of her sorbet, Steven said, "It's been a great evening. Thanks for driving out here tonight. But you still haven't told me what you were afraid to say in public."

Um. Yeah. That. How could it have slipped her mind?

Probably because she'd blocked it out so she could have one last hour to pretend there wasn't anything stopping her and Steven from becoming more than two people who clashed over ideas and goals. Only they didn't seem to be clashing now. They seemed to have become friends. And the possibility of becoming more than that lingered on the horizon.

"Did you forget what you wanted to tell me?"

No, she hadn't. But before she could find the words to speak, he reached out and cupped her jaw. His thumb stroked her cheek, caressing it and sending a shiver of excitement from her head to her toes.

Her lips parted, and her breath caught.

"Maybe this will jog your memory," he whispered.

His touch, his heated gaze jogged more than her memory. She ought to take a step back, but she was so caught up in the moment, the woodsy scent of his cologne, the blasted romantic mood that had been growing all evening, that she couldn't seem to think, let alone move.

Steven brushed his mouth across Ellie's, softly, tentatively. The cool, sweet taste of raspberry sorbet lingered on her lips, and he was dying for more.

She leaned into him for a moment, kissing him back, but before he could slip his arms around her and draw her close, she pulled her mouth away from him and stepped to the side.

"What's the matter?" he asked.

"I'm sorry. I…" She tucked a glossy strand of dark hair behind her ear, revealing a small diamond stud. "I didn't mean for that to happen."

"You don't owe me an apology. We didn't do anything wrong. Something's been building between us for quite a while. And I'd be surprised if you claimed you weren't feeling it, too."

"Yes, I've felt it. But kissing wasn't a good idea."

He tossed her what he hoped was a disarming smile. "It seemed like a good one to me."

She slowly shook her head and blew out a ragged breath.

He studied her carefully, waiting for a response. When she didn't explain, he said, "I don't often get my signals mixed, and you were giving off some I'm-interested vibes."

"You're right. I don't blame you for picking up on them. And acting on them. But…" She bit down on her bottom lip, clearly wrestling with whatever she had on her mind.

When she didn't continue, he pressed her to go on. "Is it because of our different backgrounds?" If so, that would be a new one for him. Most women fell all over themselves to date a rich and success-ful man.

"No," Ellie said. "That's not it."

Good. If his wealth didn't impress her, that made her all the more appealing to him.

"I hope you're not worried about our political dif-ferences," he said. "Or the potential conflict down at city hall. Because, believe it or not, you and I both want what's best for Rambling Rose."

"I'll admit that's a factor, but it's not the biggest one."

Then there was only one other reason. "Are you involved with someone else?"

"No. Not really. It's just…" She stood tall, sucked in a deep breath and blew out the words. "I'm pregnant."

Pregnant.

The word reverberated in the small kitchen, bouncing off the walls like the little ball in a pin-ball machine.

Wow. He hadn't seen that coming. He probably ought to respond, but he'd be damned if he knew what to say.

Congratulations?

Who's the lucky guy?

It sure as hell wasn't him.

And what was with her response to his question about there being someone else? *No. Not really?*

What the hell did that mean?

Steven might be dazed, even stupefied, but he couldn't very well just stand there. He had to say something. "I didn't realize… I mean, I might catch a lot of buzz from the Rambling Rose grapevine, but no one ever indicated you were…involved. Or dating."

"I try to be discreet when it comes to my private life. I dated a guy for quite a while, but we broke up about four months ago." She paused, clicked her tongue and closed her eyes.

Steven had no idea what to say. *I'm sorry?*

"And the guy…?" he asked.

She sucked in a deep breath, then slowly blew it out. "The relationship hadn't been working for either of us for a while, and I'm the one who finally called it quits. He knows about the baby, but he's not interested in being a father. In fact, he left the country."

From her frown and the twitch in her eye, he suspected she might not be happy about that.

"Are you sure you're over him?" Steven asked.

"Absolutely. His character flaws came out when I told him about the baby. I'm just sorry I didn't pick up on them earlier."

"So what's troubling you?"

"When the news gets out, and everyone finds out that I'm pregnant with no husband in sight…"

There'd be talk. That was for sure.

Ellie leaned a hip against the counter. "Things will probably get… Well, I'm not sure *ugly* is the right word, but it won't be cool." She looked at him, her eyes pleading. "Please keep that bit of news to yourself until I've made an announcement. My parents don't even know yet." She combed her fingers through her hair, mussing it in an oddly pretty way.

As he tried to sort through his thoughts, silence filled the room.

She studied him intently. Her brow furrowed, and her expression changed from one that was unbalanced to suspicious. "Steven, you're not going to say anything, are you?"

Hell, no. He could be trusted to keep a secret. And he wanted her to know that.

"No, of course not. I'm not one to…" *Kiss and tell* came to mind, but that wasn't how he'd meant to finish the dumbstruck statement. "Don't worry, Ellie. I won't say anything to anyone."

"Thank you." Then she turned and snatched

her purse from the kitchen chair, where she'd left it when she arrived. "I really need to go before it gets too late. I want to drive over to my parents' house and level with them."

"Okay. I'll walk you out."

"Good," she said. "I'd probably get lost trying to find the front door."

He lifted his hand to touch her back, to guide her down the hall, but thought better about it.

"Thanks for dinner," she said as they made their way through the house to the foyer.

"No problem."

But Ellie clearly had one. A big one. And for some dumb reason, which didn't make any sense at all, her problem now seemed to be his.

From the moment Ellie had driven away last night, Steven knew he'd screwed up. He should have said something to set things back on track. But that was the problem. He'd been completely stumped and speechless.

A barrage of emotion had been tumbling inside him ever since she'd told him she was pregnant—mostly surprise and frustration, followed by sympathy and a wallop of guilt.

Steven didn't get ruffled easily. No matter what the problem, he'd always been able to think himself out of a corner. But not this time. One wrong word, one wrong move on his part would have only made things worse.

His first thought was to avoid her until the news got out and then to wait until her world righted itself on its axis. But he'd never taken the coward's way out, and he wouldn't start now.

By the time Sunday morning rolled around and he'd had his first cup of coffee, he was no closer to a solution than he'd been before going to bed. So he decided to go to the stable and saddle Big Red. A long trail ride on his favorite horse usually helped clear his mind.

After pouring the remainder of his second cup of coffee into an insulated mug, he stepped out of one of the side doors into the yard, only to run into Dillon.

The minute his brother noticed him, a crooked grin broke across Dillon's face, and he crossed the yard, obviously wanting to talk. But Steven wasn't in the mood.

"So...?" Dillon asked. "How'd it go?"

"Fine."

Dillon's grin created a single dimple in his cheek. "Crashed and burned, huh?"

Steven wanted to smack what looked more like a smirk than a smile off his brother's face, which wasn't cool. Nor was it fair. Dillon had crashed and burned a few times himself.

Letting it go, Steven continued toward the stable. He had to get moving before everything began to close in on him.

"You going to saddle up Big Red?" Dillon asked.

"Yeah."

"You want to talk about it?"

"Nope. Ellie and I had a nice dinner. Then she went home."

"As simple as that?"

Steven shot him a frown. "Don't worry about it. Okay?"

Dillon lifted both hands as if in surrender, then took a dramatic step back, giving him a wide berth.

Good. He needed to have some time alone. He'd think about apologizing later.

The long trail ride seemed to help Big Red more than Steven. By the time he'd cooled down the horse and returned to the yard, Callum and Becky were climbing out of their car after their trip to Austin. The couple looked happy but exhausted.

Becky waved at Steven, then pressed her index finger to her lips, signaling him to be quiet right before she retrieved one sleeping twin from the car seat and Callum got the other.

Steven didn't mind being silenced. He didn't feel like talking to anyone right now anyway, especially about babies and outings to the zoo.

After Becky carried Luna into the house, Callum lingered, a sleeping Sasha in his arms, her head resting on his shoulder.

"How's it going?" Callum asked, his voice soft and low.

"Okay," Steven whispered.

"Don't worry about waking this one." Callum grinned. "Once Sasha's asleep, she's out."

"Did you guys have a good trip?" Steven asked, doing his best to appear remotely interested. "You look worn-out."

"I'm beat. But we had a lot of fun. It was a great trip. The kids slept all the way home."

"Good." Steven turned toward the house, eager to slip into his private living quarters.

"Hey," Callum called to his back.

Steven looked over his shoulder. "What?"

"Something's bothering you. What's up?"

"Nothing."

Callum furrowed his brow. "Like hell. Is there something going on I ought to know about?"

"Nope."

"I don't believe you."

Steven never had kept too many secrets from his brothers, especially Callum, who was good at reading him. "I've got stuff on my mind, but it's not business related, if that's what you're thinking. And it's no big deal. I spent some time riding Big Red, and now I've got it figured out."

Callum nodded as if he believed him.

Steven wished it were true. But he was a far cry from figuring anything out, and his foul mood continued to dog him all night long.

On Monday morning, it followed him to the Paz construction site, where they'd moved their modular office. Even his employees noticed, but most of them knew better than to approach him.

Fortunately, by the time he got home and turned in for the night, he'd finally realized what was actually bothering him, which led to a partial solution.

He couldn't stay away from Ellie any longer. Hell, he didn't want to. They were friends, even if that's as far as it would go. And she deserved more from him than he'd given her. Once he wrapped his mind around that, his mood lightened.

First thing tomorrow morning, he'd stop by the mayor's office bearing gifts and an apology that was long overdue.

Chapter Six

Ellie, who almost never cried, had bawled her eyes out all the way home from the Fame and Fortune Ranch.

"I can't believe how stupid I was," she'd told Daria when she got home. "I actually thought I could practice on Steven before telling my parents."

"How'd that work?" Daria asked.

Ellie pointed to her watery eyes, puffy from tears. "I couldn't walk into their house looking like this. They'd never believe that I have things under control."

"And what about the attraction? Did telling Steven stifle it?"

"You can say that again." Ellie rolled her eyes and plopped down on the recliner. "It certainly dashed Steven's feelings for me."

"But not yours for him?"

"Oh snap, Daria. I have no idea how I feel." She raked a hand through her hair. "I take that back. I feel stupid. It's got to be the pregnancy hormones. They've completely chased off my common sense."

"Did you kiss him?"

"Not really. I mean, he sort of kissed me. Briefly. It was sweet and tentative, but it wasn't a real one." Ellie let out whoosh of air and sat back in the chair.

"Ellie," Daria said, "if his lips lingered on yours for a couple of heartbeats, it was a kiss. Maybe not a let's-get-naked one. But he kissed you. And no matter how long it lasted, you liked it."

Yes, that was true. It would have been an amazing kiss—if she hadn't bolted. But she had. And she'd blasted him with the news of her pregnancy, shocking him senseless and chasing any and all lingering pheromones completely out of his breathing range.

And then she'd left in a rush, nearly tripping over her own feet.

For the rest of the weekend, guilt and embarrassment had hovered over her like a dark cloud ready to release a flood of rain on her at any moment.

Could she have botched things any worse?

Finally, on Monday, a bell-ringing thought struck. What about Steven? It's not like he was a victim in all of this. Ellie's revelation might have shocked him, but for a man who always had a charming smile and a ready response, he'd been dumbstruck. And when he did speak, he could have been a little more understanding and a lot kinder.

Even after shifting the blame onto Steven, she slept like crap again, and on Tuesday morning, she woke up tired and out of sorts. So she put off a visit to her mom and dad yet again. She'd made a mistake by dating Mike in the first place and would own up to it. But she wanted to assure her parents that she was happy about the baby and that she had a game plan for the future.

After she showered and blow-dried her hair, she used a little extra makeup, especially concealer under her eyes to hide the darkened, puffy bags. Then she dressed in a pair of black slacks, pulling the zipper up but leaving the top button undone. She chose a loose-fitting blouse and topped it off with a colorful scarf that would draw the eye to her face instead of her waistline.

She'd no more than entered the city hall lobby, her flats clicking against the Spanish tile flooring, when she spotted Steven standing near the water fountain holding a bouquet of yellow roses in one hand and a large pink box in the other. And wouldn't you know it? He looked just as gorgeous as ever.

What was he doing here?

His sheepish gaze, which seemed to look into the heart of her, suggested he'd come to see her. As he crossed the floor to approach her, any doubt faded.

"I brought you something," he said, handing her the flowers.

She raised the palm of her hand to stop him. "I'm not allowed to accept gifts from anyone."

"Even flowers?"

"I don't want anyone to think I'm taking a bribe."

Steven's lips quirked into a playful grin. "Do you always play that strictly by the rules?"

"Yes, I do. And apparently, you're in the habit of bending them."

"If I was trying to bribe you, I'd use more than flowers and sweets." He lifted the lid on the pink box, revealing a variety of doughnuts—glazed, chocolate, twists and a pink cake one with colorful sprinkles.

"They look yummy," she said, "but I take my job seriously. I also took an oath to uphold the law."

Still, she peered into the box. She'd only had a light breakfast, and as she got a whiff of the sweet sugary smell, she was tempted.

She reached into her purse and pulled out one

of the dollar bills she kept tucked in a small pouch inside. "I'll tell you what. I'll buy that one with the pink frosting and candy sprinkles."

"Are you serious?" Steven laughed. "You think I'm a doughnut vendor now?"

"That's the only way I'll agree to take one."

For a moment, she thought he might lower the lid, but he took the dollar and waited for her to snatch the one she wanted.

She didn't wait to take a bite. "Hmm."

"You realize this never was meant to be a bribe."

"Then what is it?" she asked.

"A peace offering. I handled things badly on Saturday night, and I'm sorry."

She scanned the nearly empty lobby. "I'd rather not talk about that here."

"I realize that. Can we go for a walk?"

She lifted her arm to glance at her wristwatch, a college graduation gift from her parents. She had a meeting scheduled at ten, but she supposed it wouldn't hurt to take a few minutes to talk to him.

Steven nodded toward the glass door that led to the rose garden, a memorial for one of the beloved town founders, the first of many mayors who'd preceded her in office.

As they strolled toward a cement bench, Steven said, "I'm sorry for being a jerk the other night. You opened your heart to me, and I was so taken by surprise that I didn't offer you the support you deserved."

"I should have said something earlier, before…" She glanced at him, and when he nodded, she knew finishing her sentence wasn't necessary.

"Have you told anyone else yet?" he asked.

"I was going to talk to my parents, but I… haven't gotten around to it." Again, she glanced at Steven, and he nodded.

"Would you mind telling me more about the baby's father?" he asked.

"Why? I told you he's completely out of the picture."

"Yes, I know. But I'd like to be a better friend, a better listener."

So he wasn't going to run for the hills? They'd still be friends?

Ellie took a quick scan of the garden to assure herself no one was lurking nearby, that she was free to speak. "Mike and I had been dating for a while, and things got serious. But we'd been on different paths for months. He was doing a lot of traveling for work, and I was involved with local politics. We might have stuck it out, more as a habit. But…" She shook her head and continued. "One night, he told he me didn't want kids—ever. And that was a game changer for me. I mean, it's not like motherhood was at the top of my priority list, but eventually I would have wanted to have at least one child. So we broke up."

"When was that?"

"Four months ago. And I didn't even shed a tear. He flew to South America for an extended photo shoot, and I focused on Rambling Rose, as usual. But before long, I began counting the days and realized I'd gotten pregnant. He'd been downright adamant about not wanting a kid to screw up his life, so I knew he wouldn't be happy about it, but I figured I'd better tell him."

"What did he say?"

"He told me to get rid of it. I refused, and he said he was out, that I couldn't expect anything from him."

"Wow. What an ass."

"I realize that now. And I'm embarrassed by it. I mean, I should have picked up on his character flaws sooner than I did."

"Don't beat yourself up," Steven said. "We've all misjudged people. It happens."

"I know. I guess you could call it a lesson learned."

"Are you happy?" he asked. "I mean, about the baby?"

"Actually, I am. Some days I still can't believe it. By the middle of August, I'll be a mother."

"And a good one." Steven blessed her with a wink. "There's no doubt in my mind."

At times, she had a few doubts herself, even though her adoptive mom had set an amazing example, the best ever. Yet in spite of the outward sign of confidence Ellie had mastered years ago, she always felt as if she struggled between the past and the present.

It didn't happen very often these days, but occasionally a memory, a conversation, a voice would creep up on her and cause her to remember that her biological mom was a druggie who hadn't been married to her dad. And not just because he was serving a life sentence.

Thankfully, she'd been rescued from that dark world, but every now and then her adoptive father's question would come back to haunt her, to make her wonder if she'd ever be able to put it all behind her.

Honey, Ellie's a sweet kid. But do you think she inherited any bad genes from her biological parents?

From day one, Ellie had done her best to prove that she hadn't. Instead, she'd tried to be a reflection of the loving couple who'd adopted her—George Hernandez, a hardworking mechanic, and his wife, Alma, a devoted schoolteacher.

"Earth to Ellie."

She turned to Steven, who'd called her back to reality with a teasing grin.

"What's on your mind?" he asked. "I hope

you're not struggling about whether you should forgive me or not."

"I'm sorry. My mind drifted off, but don't worry. You're forgiven."

"Good." He studied her for a moment with eyes the color of the Texas sky. "Do you know whether it's a boy or a girl?"

Warmth filled her heart, and she placed her hand on her baby bump. "It's a boy."

"That's cool. Does he have a name?"

"Not yet. Daria, my friend, and I have been calling him Peanut ever since my first ultrasound, because that's what he looked like on the screen. But I'll probably name him George, after my dad."

"I'm sure that would make him proud."

"That's the plan." Her parents were pretty conservative. Still, she suspected their shock and disappointment wouldn't last very long. Daria was right. They'd be good grandparents.

"By the way," Steven said, "I gave away all but two of the tickets to the talent show at the high school on Thursday night. I thought you might want one."

"Actually, I would. Thanks."

"We could go together," he said.

Like a date? Probably not, but she'd better make it clear that she hadn't made that jump. "Can I meet you there?"

He seemed to ponder the question a little too long, then shrugged and said, "Sure. Why not?"

She glanced at her wristwatch, then at the glass door that led inside city hall. She needed to check in with Iris, the newly hired receptionist, and make sure that her ten o'clock meeting was still on.

"I'll let you go," Steven said. "Take the doughnuts. They're not what you'd call a personal gift. They're for you to share with the office staff. You can do whatever you want with the roses, although I hope you'll keep them for yourself."

She glanced at the bouquet she still held, lifted them to her nose and took a sniff, relishing the strong fragrance. "They're beautiful. And they smell amazingly good."

They were also yellow, the color that signified friendship. A peace offering, he'd called them. She supposed she could live with that.

She and Steven were still friends. But for some reason, knowing that's all they'd ever be left her a little uneasy. And a wee bit sad.

At a quarter to seven on Thursday night, Steven waited for Ellie in front of the high school auditorium. He'd been tempted to ask her to get a bite to eat with him before the talent show started, but that would have made the evening seem more like a date. And it wasn't.

It did kind of feel like one, though. As he stood

outside the open double doors, scanning the families and friends who were arriving to support the kids, his pulse kicked up a notch in anticipation. And the minute he spotted her approach, his heart damn near battered his chest.

As she hurried toward him, her cheeks flushed, he couldn't help but grin. She certainly had a thing about being on time, if not early. She also had a way of lighting up a room, no matter what she wore, be it a business suit or something more casual, like the black jeans and the long-sleeved pink blouse she had on tonight.

She might be pregnant, but he still found her attractive as hell. And while they weren't actually dating, that didn't mean they couldn't be friends. Right?

"I'm sorry I'm late," she said.

"You're ten minutes early," he argued, but he knew it was pointless.

"Daria's car wouldn't start. Her boss scheduled an unexpected meeting, so I had to drop her off first."

"No problem." Did that mean Ellie would have to cut their evening short to pick up her friend? "How's she going to get home?"

"She told me she'd catch a ride."

"Then let's go inside." Steven placed his hand on the small of Ellie's back to guide her toward the entrance. But touching her seemed a little too date-like, a little too intimate. So as she moved ahead of him, he let his fingers trail away.

Moments later, they were sitting in the two seats closest to the aisle, about six or seven rows from the stage.

Ellie leaned toward him, giving him an alluring whiff of her citrusy scent, and whispered, "I know this is a far cry from a Broadway show, but I had a good time last year. And I think you'll enjoy it."

She was right. Each performance was unique and entertaining.

A red-haired ventriloquist was a big hit, and so was a gymnast dressed in a clown costume who did flips and cartwheels across the stage. A couple of singers did a great job. Another tried hard but needed more practice. Several musicians played a variety of instruments, including the piano, a guitar, a trumpet and even a set of drums.

A barefoot girl wearing a white karate gi and a black belt showed off her martial arts skill. And a kid dressed in full cowboy garb, including chaps, carried a lariat onstage and performed rope tricks. But it was the last act that Steven liked best. A teenage boy and girl sang a duet from the Broadway musical *Annie Get Your Gun* that was worthy of a standing ovation. Their interaction on stage reminded him of the verbal banter he and Ellie often had. Not that either of them was all that competitive with the other, but he could imagine them singing "Anything you can do, I can do better."

As the oldest of the eight Fortune siblings, Steven was used to being the boss. And Ellie took her role as mayor seriously. She was tough and often underestimated, something he'd come to admire. It seemed only natural that two leaders like them often felt compelled to try and top each other.

The audience clapped and cheered at the end, then they all began to file out of the school auditorium. Steven figured he ought to offer to walk Ellie to her car, but he wasn't ready to say goodbye and send her off.

"I've got a real hankering for a hot fudge sundae," Steven said.

"A hankering, huh? I don't know, Mr. Fortune. You're starting to sound like a real Texan."

"Well, thank you, ma'am." He nodded toward the sidewalk that led to the shopping district. "The ice cream shop is just a couple of blocks down the street. Are you up for a short walk?"

Ellie brightened. "That actually sounds good to me. I have a real sweet tooth."

"You don't say." He laughed. "I guessed as much on Tuesday morning, when you zeroed in on that pink doughnut with candy sprinkles."

They moved through the throng of people and made their way across the street, which was unusually busy, thanks to the departing cars.

"By the way," Steven said, as they walked, "I've been thinking about all the people I met at Mariana's Market, and you're right. The longtime residents of Rambling Rose should be proud of the Fortune Brothers' development projects, and I want them to feel as if their voices have been heard." He glanced at Ellie, eager to see her reaction.

"Really?" Her eyes widened as if she could hardly believe the sudden turnaround. "You're going to alter your plans for the hotel?"

"Not exactly. I'm still one hundred percent behind the project. And I've heard nothing but positive reactions from the people who live in Rambling Rose Estates, but I really need to expand our support base. The way I see it, all I have to do is convince Mariana's crew that it's a good idea. Then it's only a matter of time before the planning commission gives us the green light."

Ellie grabbed him by the arm, pulled him to a halt, then circled in front of him and frowned. "Are you kidding me? You're more interested in persuading the people at Mariana's Market that you're right. I can't believe you're not going to consider their point of view at all."

Damn, she was pretty when she was worked up like that. But he wasn't going to bend to her—or to anyone—when it came to his personal project.

Steven sighed. "Have you even considered that I *could* be right?"

"No." She crossed her arms. "Not even *once*."

They stood like that for a moment, clearly at an impasse. Just like the song that had wrapped up the talent show. He almost made a joke of it. *Any stance you can take, I can take better.*

Something told him she wouldn't find it funny, though. And since they'd just become friends again, it wouldn't be wise to rock the boat.

He cast what he hoped was a disarming smile. "Like we've said before, Ellie. Maybe we should just agree to disagree."

Her expression softened, then she uncrossed her arms and returned to her place at his side. As he moved forward, she fell into step and they continued to walk along the sidewalk.

His arm brushed her shoulder a couple of times. If they'd been on an actual date, he would have reached for her hand.

Hell, he was tempted to do it anyway.

But he wouldn't.

"Will you meet me at Mariana's Market again this weekend?" he asked. "I'd like to set up a table where I can sit down with the locals and help them understand what the Fortune family has in mind for the project."

"I'll probably be there on Saturday. I like hanging out and talking to people. But I'm not going to sit at that table with you. I need to remain neutral, and I can't have even the appearance of favoritism where you and Fortune Brothers Construction are concerned. After all, optics are everything."

At that, he chuckled. "May I remind you that you're not the least bit neutral, and just about everyone in town knows how you really feel about the construction company and the hotel?"

"You do have a point there."

As they reached the Sweet Freeze, he opened the door for her, and she stepped inside. They weren't the only ones who'd had the idea of wrapping up their evening with an ice cream.

Moments later, Steven had ordered a triple fudge sundae, and Ellie chose a strawberry cone.

"And give her two scoops," he told the clerk.

They carried their desserts to a table at the rear of the shop and took a seat.

"Okay," Ellie said. "I'll stop by your display at Mariana's on Saturday."

He blinked in mock surprise. "All it took was a strawberry cone to convince you? I wish I would have known that sooner."

"I do love strawberries."

A grin tugged at his lips. "Does that mean you're going to be open-minded for a change?"

"What do you mean *for a change*? I'm always willing to look at both sides of a problem." She took a taste of her cone and then closed her eyes.

A rapturous expression crossed her face as she relished the taste, drawing his attention away from his own frozen chocolate concoction.

As he watched her lick that cone, his senses reeled, triggering thoughts of sex. If she continued to eat like that, as if she were making soft, breathless mewling sounds, he would end up watching her until his sundae melted into a soupy mess.

She drew the cone away from her mouth, then pointed the pink scoops at him. "Just for the record, you haven't swayed me in the least. But I'm curious about how you're going to reach out to the community—and how they'll take it. So count me in."

Oddly enough, he hadn't wanted to count her out. Even when they didn't see eye to eye, he was drawn to her. Under the circumstances, he ought to run like hell.

But he wasn't about to go anywhere, especially while she licked that blasted strawberry cone.

Ellie hadn't been to the Sweet Freeze in years, but she had a lot of nice memories here. Her mom used to teach school in Greenly, which was about twenty miles away, and she did a lot of tutoring after class and on Saturdays. So Ellie and her dad had spent a lot of time here—usually after a day at the playground, an afternoon matinee or following a softball game at the park.

She'd always had a fondness for ice cream, especially strawberry, but she couldn't remember it ever tasting this good. The sweet, cool treat really hit the spot. And it seemed to make her worries feel more like a couple of dust bunnies under the bed—still there but out of sight.

Steven leaned forward and lowered his voice. "I'd like to do something like this with you again."

Her lips parted, and she nearly dropped her cone onto the table. What was he suggesting?

"You want to meet at the Sweet Freeze?" she asked.

"Yes. I guess so. Or whatever."

She still wasn't sure what he meant. She had an idea, though. But she sure as heck wasn't going to make a guess, one that was more likely to be wrong.

So she skirted the question and delayed a response. "It's been a nice evening, hasn't it?"

Surely he didn't take the women he usually dated to high school talent shows and ice cream shops. She had to have connected the wrong dots. And, she admitted, that was actually a relief. A romantic liaison was out of the question, but the friend thing she could do.

"I had fun tonight," she added, against her better judgment.

He leaned back in his seat and smiled. "Surprisingly, I did, too."

The way he looked at her prickled her nerves and sent her blood racing. Was her deduction wrong? Was he actually talking about them going out, publicly? Okay, she was back to square one. And she wasn't sure what to say.

I'm pregnant. Remember?

And I'll soon look like I swallowed a basketball.

"So maybe we could go to a movie and have dinner?" he asked. "What do you think?"

"I think we should enjoy our ice cream." She scanned the immediate area, spotted a family placing their order up front, then lowered her voice. "It's one thing for us to be seen at community events, but I don't want people thinking we're... getting too chummy."

"Why should anyone care?"

She arched a brow. "Because I'm the mayor. And you and your family are at odds with the town."

"We're only at odds with some of the towns-people, although we're working on that."

"I hope so." She again scanned the ice cream shop, which was now close to empty. She doubted anyone could hear their conversation, but she didn't want to risk it and lowered her voice as a precaution. "There's one other reason. And when word..." She let her voice trail off, but he knew what she meant.

"You know," he said, his voice soft, low and

barely discernible, "the sooner you make the announcement, the better you'll feel."

He was right, she supposed. The pressure would be off, but she wasn't so sure she'd actually feel *better*. Not right away.

"So what did your parents say when you told them?" he asked. When she hesitated and looked down, he said, "You didn't tell them, did you?"

"Not yet."

"You do realize the cat will be out of the bag soon?"

"I know."

"Then you're better off telling them before they hear it from someone else."

Her eyes opened wide, and her heart raced. "Are *you* going to tell them?"

"No. Of course not. I gave you my word. What kind of guy do you think I am?"

In truth, she really had no idea. But she knew what kind of man he wasn't. One she should get involved with. Yet when he smiled at her like that, when he offered her friendship and support, not to mention his promise to keep her secret, her better judgment went up in smoke.

"On Saturday evening, after we spend the day at Mariana's Market, I'd like to take you out to dinner," he said. "Nothing fancy. Some place low-key and quiet. What do you think?"

That it was a crazy idea. Yet she was tempted beyond measure. She might be sorry for this later, but she gave a little shrug and said, "Sure. Why not?"

But after they left the Sweet Freeze and he walked her back to her car, after she turned on the ignition and headed home, she hoped she hadn't made another big mistake.

Chapter Seven

On Saturday morning, Steven and his brothers arrived at Mariana's Market early to set up a table before the shoppers arrived. Several tripods displayed photos of their completed projects and sketches of those still in the works. They also had a stack of colorful, glossy pamphlets ready to pass out to those who were interested or just plain curious.

An exhibit alone wasn't enough to draw much attention, so Steven decided to tempt passersby to stop at the table by offering complimentary refreshments—glasses of sweet tea and lemonade, along with platters of cookies he'd purchased from

Picard's Patisserie, the new French bakery that recently opened at the Shoppes.

After the successful grand opening nearly two weeks ago, one would think that shoppers would've flooded the specialty stores and eateries, something both Fortune Brothers Construction and the vendors had expected. Unfortunately, that hadn't been the case.

In an effort to boost sales and turn things around, Steven went out of his way to support and promote the various stores and businesses, which was why he'd placed a large order with Picard earlier that week.

"Fifteen dozen cookies ought to be enough," he'd told the short, balding baker. "I'd like a variety, but keep it simple. Nothing too fancy."

Steven hadn't wanted the people who frequented Mariana's Market to turn up their noses at something Picard had put his heart and soul into baking.

"I know just the thing," Picard said with a smile. "A lot of my specialties come from my *grandmaman's* recipes. She made cookies for me when I was a boy. You wait and see. Everyone will love them."

Last night, after Steven had picked up the carefully packed boxes from the bakery and climbed behind the wheel of his SUV, he'd tried one. Picard had been right; they were delicious. But they might be more elegant and worldly than Mariana's patrons were used to.

Now, as it neared ten o'clock on Saturday morning, people had begun to stop by the Fortunes' table to check out the multicolored macarons, French butter cookies and lemon madeleines, a costly purchase, even with the loyalty discount Picard had given them.

An older man wearing worn denim overalls and a red baseball cap—a farmer, Steven suspected—squinted as he peered at the table. "What the hell are those?"

"Cookies," Callum said. "Give 'em a try."

"How much?" the guy asked.

Steven lifted one of the trays so the man could get a better look at the variety of cookies. "No charge. They're complimentary. Go ahead and have one. Or take a few."

The farmer grunted, picked up a pink macaron, studied it for a moment and popped it into his mouth.

Steven reached for one of the pamphlets to give him, but the man slowly shook his head, lifted a weathered hand and waved him off. "Don't need it, Mr. Fortune. I'll take a free cookie, but I ain't buyin' what you're trying to sell." Then he turned and walked away.

Steven was still holding the unwanted pamphlet when Ellie approached the table. She'd dressed casually today in a pink-and-white-striped blouse, black denim jeans and a pair of sneakers. She also wore a pretty pout, which, for once, wasn't directed at Steven. Instead, she seemed a bit annoyed with the gangly black puppy she'd brought with her.

Ellie gave a gentle tug on the red leash to encourage the little rascal to come her way, but the distracted pup was more interested in its surroundings and the people milling through the marketplace.

Steven set down the pamphlet, left Callum at the table and strode toward Ellie, glad to see her.

"This must be Tank," he said.

She blew out a sigh and tucked a long, glossy strand of dark hair behind her ear. "I'm puppy-sitting. Daria's boss asked her to attend a business meeting with him in Houston, and Tank gets into too much trouble when he's left home alone. So I thought I'd better bring him with me."

"Didn't she have a business meeting with her boss last night?" Steven had never met Daria and didn't know anything about the relationship she had with her employer. Not that it was any of his business. Didn't Ellie find it odd that they would meet out of town—and on a weekend?

"Actually," Ellie said, "her boss called all of his employees together to announce that he's selling the car wash. Daria is the bookkeeper, so he asked her to go to Houston with him to meet the buyers. He thought she'd be able to answer any financial questions they might have."

"That makes sense. Hopefully, the new owners will let her keep her job."

"Daria doesn't think they will. They have several other car washes, so they probably already have a bookkeeper or accountant in place."

"That's too bad. Tell her that once the hotel nears completion, there will be a lot of job opportunities. In fact, that's what we've been telling people who stop by our table."

Ellie cut a glance at their display, where Callum was talking to two women in their mid-forties. The ladies appeared to be more interested in choosing a couple of cookies from the platters than they were in listening to anything Callum had to say about the hotel.

They were going to need community support if they wanted to get approval from the planning commission, which was the reason they'd set up the table in the middle of the marketplace in the first place. But it wasn't a good idea to open with the hotel. If Steven had been the one talking to them, he first would've tried to interest them in Paz, the spa that would be opening in a few weeks. Then he'd point out the restaurant they were building for his sisters, which would open in May. After he'd gotten their attention, he would have introduced the prospective hotel.

Sharing that strategy with his brother could wait. Now that Ellie was here, Steven was eager to steer away from the company/business chatter.

"How's your effort to kumbaya with the locals going?" she asked. "Have you made any new friends yet?"

Not really, but he didn't tell her that. He didn't want to hear her say *I told you so.* "It's early yet. The day's just getting started."

Ellie twisted the loop end of the leash, bit down on her bottom lip then asked, "Can I talk to you for a minute?"

"Sure."

"Privately?" She nodded to the right, away from any people walking by.

Steven took the first step, but Ellie's tug of the leash didn't faze Tank, so she stooped, picked up the noncompliant puppy and walked a few feet until they were out of earshot.

"What's going on?" Steven asked.

"Something's come up, and I can't go out to dinner with you tonight."

He might have let it go at that and asked if they could try again later in the week, but her eye twitched and tension stretched across her brow. He zeroed in on her big brown eyes and tried to read the subtext behind her words, but he wasn't having any luck. "What aren't you telling me?"

"Nothing. Not really. I…" She tore her gaze away from his and bent to place Tank back on the ground. After giving the pup a scratch behind the ear, she returned to an upright position and shrugged. "I already told you. I'm puppy-sitting, remember?"

Yes, but there had to be more to it than that. He suspected that she was having second thoughts about having dinner with him, about being seen with him in a social setting. He couldn't be sure, though. "There's a place on the corner of Main and Jefferson that serves burgers and salads. They have a few tables set up curbside and a sign out front that says they're pet friendly. So Tank can come along, too. That is, if he's the only reason you're dragging your feet."

She didn't answer right away, and while he waited, studying the silky strands of her hair, the thick dark lashes that framed her big brown eyes, the tilt of her chin, sexual awareness slammed into him and sent his blood pounding.

Did she feel it, too? Were the same arousing thoughts zapping through her brain?

She sucked in a deep breath and blew it out. "Okay, Steven. Here's the deal. Going out to dinner with you would be cool. And fun. But it would feel like a date, and there are a hundred reasons why that isn't a good idea."

He'd already considered each one. Yet none of them seemed to matter right now, even if they should.

"What's holding you back?" he asked.

She placed her free hand on her stomach, caressed the slight bulge for a moment, then let her fingers trail away.

The baby. Okay. She had a point. And it should give him pause, but it didn't. For some reason, he liked her. And he wanted to spend more time with her.

Before he could respond, a loud, angry voice sounded behind them, coming from the Fortune Brothers' table.

A big man in his late thirties shook his finger at Callum. "You good-for-nothing piece of crap. You Fortunes think you can pass out treats and sweet-talk the good folks of Rambling Rose into believing that you're on our side. But that's a crock. You only have your own interests and profits at heart."

Steven and his brothers could hold their own in a fight, even with a hulk who looked as if he'd once been a linebacker for the Dallas Cowboys. But he'd better stand beside Callum anyway, ready to offer backup, whether it was calm words or a physical stance.

Ellie stopped him before he could take a step and handed him the end of the leash. "Take this." Then she marched toward the hothead.

She reached him just as he pointed to the platters and said, "You can take those cookies and shove them up—"

"Jackson!" Ellie called out in a voice nearly as strong and loud as the one she'd just quieted.

The bulky, broad-shouldered giant turned to the mayor and folded his arms across his chest, resting them on what appeared to be the start of a beer belly.

"You're making a scene," she said.

"Maybe I am, but somebody's got to stand up to the Fortunes and tell them how it is. You've seen how they've moved into town and started buying up property and turning things upside down. Hell, they're acting as if they own the whole damn place."

"They've done some good things, too," Ellie said.

Jackson chuffed. "I can see they've already got to you and worn you down."

"Slow down," Ellie said. "Just the other day, I talked to your sister. Her son, *your nephew*, was treated for the intestinal flu and severe dehydration at the Rambling Rose Pediatric Center."

Jackson let out a half-assed snort. "The doctors

and nurses helped Joey. Not the Fortunes. They just prettied up the building."

"Come with me," Ellie told the red-faced man. "I want to talk to you. Away from the crowd."

Jackson held his ground for a moment. Then he turned and reluctantly followed the much smaller mayor out of the hearing range of anyone near the table. But still close enough for Steven to be privy to their conversation.

"No one loves this town more than I do," she told Jackson. "But as your mayor, I need to look out for *all* the townspeople. And that means those who live in Rambling Rose Estates, as well as the store owners at the Shoppes and Fortune Brothers Construction."

"Yeah, Ellie. I know. But you can't let 'em ruin our town."

"The Fortunes have done more than just 'pretty up' Rambling Rose. They've put our friends and neighbors to work, either directly or indirectly."

The man's brow furrowed, and he glanced down at his feet.

"Jackson, you trusted me with your vote. Now you need to trust me to lead Rambling Rose, to make compromises when necessary and to stand firm when bottom lines matter."

When Ellie looked up and realized Steven had been listening, she took Jackson aside, placed her hand on his shoulder and spoke privately with him.

The chat didn't last long. Maybe only a minute or two. Then Jackson nodded and walked away, his big, broad shoulders slumped.

Ellie remained where she stood and watched his retreat. Then she returned to Steven's side and reached for Tank's leash.

He handed it to her. "That was unbelievable."

Her brow twitched. "What was? Jackson's tirade? He's not the only one in town with strong feelings about your projects and the changes that are being made in the community."

"Actually," Steven said, "I was talking about *you*. I'm amazed at the way you handled that guy. Your persuasive techniques are your superpower. I saw you do it at the grand opening of the Shoppes, when you stopped the protest. And now this. So thank you. Again."

"You're welcome. But that wasn't anything special. It was just me. And what I do."

No, it was more than that. A lot more. And he suspected she knew it, too. "You went to bat for us, and I want to thank you by taking you to dinner."

"You don't owe me anything. Jackson has a loud mouth, and he gets worked up easily when he thinks there's been an injustice done. He doesn't always think before getting angry, but he has a big heart, especially when it comes to his family. So I took him aside and asked what his mother would think about him raising a ruckus in public. As I suspected, he backed right down."

"You really know your neighbors."

"Yes, I do. Anyway, it wasn't a big deal."

"I think it was," Steven said. "I don't like public altercations. You and I may not agree on many things, but we both want peace in our community. And a blowup at Mariana's Market, especially today, would make the company look bad. Believe it or not, the Fortunes are well thought of in Fort Lauderdale. I might not be a Fortune by blood, but I'm proud to bear the name. And I don't want my family and the construction company to be frowned upon in Rambling Rose."

She arched a single brow, clearly skeptical of his claim.

"All right," he said. "I'll admit that some of the townspeople don't like us—or trust us. But we're working on that."

She offered him a smile, then glanced down at the ground, where Tank was resting his head on his paw. Surprisingly, he looked to be taking a nap.

"So how about dinner tonight?" Steven asked again. "I'll pick you up. Or you can meet me there."

"I don't know…" she said.

"Over the last few weeks, we've become friends. Most of the community is beginning to see that, too. So don't worry about being seen with me in a social setting. Friends do things together all the time, and that includes sharing a meal."

She glanced down at the puppy sleeping at her feet, then looked up and grinned. "I'll ask one of the neighbor kids to look after Tank. So it doesn't matter where we eat. I'm up for burgers, Italian or whatever."

"Since you're giving me a choice, then let's go to Osteria Oliva."

Ellie furrowed her brow. "I've never heard of that. Where is it?"

"It's the new Italian restaurant that opened at the Shoppes. And before you object and say it's too trendy or ritzy, I have a good reason for wanting to eat there. Carla Vicente, the new owner, lost her father a few months ago. The restaurant had been his dream, and now she's determined to make a go of it as a tribute to him. But it's been a struggle."

"Why?"

"Carla doesn't have many customers yet. Hopefully, once the foot traffic at the Shoppes picks up and word spreads, she'll do all right."

"So you're trying to help."

Steven shrugged. "I guess you could say that helping is *my* superpower."

"Apparently, there's a lot I don't know about you." She studied him for a moment, her eyes twinkling with an unspoken thought. He'd give anything to know what she was thinking. Or feeling.

"Just for the record," she added, "you can be pretty persuasive, too."

"I have four younger sisters, so that's a skill I had to hone early. But I have to admit, you're not easy to sway."

"I know." She offered him a smile. "But in this case, you did. I'd like to support Carla, too. So tell me what time, and I'll meet you there."

"How about six? I'm sure she'll be thrilled to have the Rambling Rose mayor eat at her restaurant."

"Sounds good." Ellie stooped to pick up the sleepy puppy. "I'll see you tonight."

As she turned to walk away, her arms full with a squirming puppy, Steven couldn't help but shake his head and grin. He and Ellie might be at odds most of the time, but she actually had become his friend, and he was really looking forward to spending the evening with her.

And if he played his cards right, maybe they'd become more than friends.

After parking at the Shoppes, Ellie made her way into the lobby, a smile on her lips and a zing in her steps. She continued past the specialty shops on the first floor to the far end, where Osteria Oliva was located. She hated to admit it, but she was looking forward to having dinner with Steven.

He'd been right. The two of them had, surprisingly, become friends. And good ones, it seemed.

As she neared the restaurant, footsteps sounded behind her. She glanced over her shoulder to see Steven approach, a dazzling grin on his face. She stopped to wait for him to catch up.

From the black Stetson on his head to the boots on his feet, her newfound friend was looking more like a cowboy every day. And more handsome than he had a right to be.

He placed a hand on her shoulder, and the warmth of his gentle touch sent a coil of heat spiraling to her core, stirring up feelings that were a far cry from platonic.

"Thanks for waiting up," he said, as they continued on together. "I think you'll like this place, especially since it's special and trendy, but not fancy."

As they stepped through the arched entry, Ellie scanned the sunflower-yellow walls adorned with colorful European-style artwork, each with a dark frame that matched the wooden tables and chairs. A hand painted mural on the side wall depicted a vineyard and a quaint cottage. To the right of the cash registers, a small grocery section displayed imported products, such as olive oils, dry pasta, sauces, herbs and Italian wines.

There was a lot to like about Osteria Oliva, but Steven hadn't stretched the truth when he'd mentioned the lack of patrons. For a Saturday night, the new eatery was practically dead.

A matronly woman, her silver-threaded dark hair pulled into a neat and tidy bun, greeted them at the door. "It's nice to see you again, Steven."

"This time I brought a friend." He turned to Ellie, his hand still lingering on her back, his touch sending tingles down her spine. "This is Ellie Hernandez, the mayor of Rambling Rose."

Carla extended her arm and gave Ellie's hand a warm, two-handed shake. "It's nice to meet you. Thank you for coming."

"Steven raves about the food, so I'm glad to be here."

Carla swept her arm out toward the nearly empty room, where one older couple sat near the mural. "Please, sit anywhere you like."

Steven ushered Ellie to the back of the room, where they took their seats at a table for two.

A waiter dressed in black slacks and a crisply pressed white button-down shirt stood off to the side. He gave them a moment to settle in before approaching their table with two menus.

"Can I get you something to drink?" he asked.

"I'll have a glass of your Chianti Classico Reserva," Steven said.

Ellie smiled at the waiter. "Just water for me."

He nodded. When he left them to look over the menus, Ellie checked out the offerings—salads, sandwiches and European-style pizza. She suspected the locals who'd lived in town all their lives would find the food appealing. The prices weren't especially steep, either. But those people weren't shopping at the high-end stores, which meant they weren't going to stumble upon Osteria Oliva.

Moments later, when the waiter returned with a basket of fresh focaccia sprinkled with rosemary, they placed their orders—a sausage calzone for Steven and the vegetarian antipasto salad for Ellie.

"So what's new at Fortune Brothers Construction?" Ellie asked. "Any recent land grabs? Any new renovation projects in the works?"

"Not at the moment." He picked up the bread basket, offered it to her and waited until she chose a piece. "We're going to have to plan a retirement party, though. I knew it was coming. Our office manager made the official announcement this morning. I'm happy for him, but he's been an incredible asset, especially during our move to Texas. It'll be hard to replace him."

Ellie opened her mouth to recommend Daria for the position, but she didn't like the idea of her best friend going to work for the enemy—even though Steven no longer felt like one. Then again, Daria had student loans to pay back and would be out of a job once the car wash sold.

"Let me know when you start looking to replace the office manager. Or if you have to shuffle people around and another position opens up. My friend Daria doesn't have a ton of experience, but she has a college degree. She's also a hard worker and loyal. I'm sure she'd like to apply."

"Tell her to give me a call next week," Steven said.

Once their dinner was served, they continued to talk. And this time, for a change, without their usual bickering.

Steven told her about growing up in Fort Lauderdale, especially when he was a teenager. He might have done well academically, played sports and had a weekend construction job, but he'd still managed to have fun—and to get into mischief.

"How'd you manage to stay out of trouble?" she asked.

"It wasn't so hard in high school, but I got in plenty of trouble when I was in eighth grade." He tossed her a playful grin. "One day, we had a substitute teacher in math, and the guy didn't appreciate my sense of humor. So he sent me to the principal's office. More often than not, during P.E., the coach used to make me run extra laps for being a wise-ass. But the last time I got into trouble, my dad grounded me, and that was a real game changer for me."

"What did you do?"

"One of my buddies invited me to his family's country club to play golf. I was driving the cart a

little too fast and ran it into a tree. My dad wasn't
happy about it. He paid for the repair bill, but I
had to pay him back—with interest." Steven rested
his elbows on the table and leaned toward her, his
blue eyes glimmering with mirth. "Now it's your
turn. I admitted to a lot of stuff, and you just sat
there smiling, taking it all in as if you'd never met
such an entertaining hellion. Didn't you ever get
into trouble?"

Ellie glanced around the empty restaurant, pretending to watch for eavesdroppers, then leaned
forward and lowered her voice. "Don't tell anyone,
but I got a B-plus one semester in chemistry, which
screwed up my chance to be the valedictorian."

Steven feigned surprise, placed a hand on his
chest and gasped. "Seriously? That bad, huh?"

They both laughed, but it was true. That's about
the worst thing she'd done while in school. And if
truth be told, she'd cried when she'd realized that
B-plus had lowered her GPA enough to allow Jose
Rivera to snag the coveted award.

Funny how it seemed a little insignificant now.
And she found it even funnier that she'd really enjoyed her evening with Steven tonight.

After he paid the bill and left a tip, they headed
toward the lobby doors that would take them to
the parking lot.

"Thank you for dinner," Ellie said. "Now I owe
you one."

"Sounds good to me. Just tell me where and when. Or, better yet, give me your address, and I'll pick you up at your house."

She didn't want anyone to think they were dating, and while they really weren't, they sure seemed to be tiptoeing around it. So she came up with a better option—if he was interested. "There's an event in San Antonio I need to attend on Tuesday afternoon. If you can get the time off and don't mind hanging out with me for a boring hour or two, we could have an early dinner in the city."

"Sure. I don't have a lot going on Tuesday. What time do you want to leave?"

"One o'clock. It shouldn't last too long—an hour or two at the most. And if we don't dawdle over dinner, we should be back in Rambling Rose before it gets too late."

"Sounds good." Steven scanned the nearly empty parking lot. "Where's your car?"

"It's just to the right, next to the gray Lexus."

"I'll walk with you," he said.

When they reached her trusty Honda, she thanked him again for dinner and a nice evening.

"I'm glad you enjoyed it. I hope you'll help Carla out by spreading the word about her restaurant at Mariana's Market."

"Will do."

Ellie was about to turn away to reach for the door handle when Steven cupped her cheek. His gaze locked on hers like a laser, startling her. Tempting her.

He leaned forward, and while she ought to stop him, she couldn't seem to move. Her lips parted, and her heart raced. He kissed her lightly, sweetly—almost like a friend—at first. But as his tongue slipped into her mouth, seeking and finding her own, her hormones spun out of control.

Thankfully, after a surreal moment of sexual bliss, her brain kicked into gear. She placed her hand against his broad chest, felt the strong, steady beat of his heart, and pushed back, breaking the kiss almost as quickly as it started.

"We can't," she said. "I can't..."

"Why? Are you worried that someone will see us?"

"There's that. Yes."

And so much more.

It was too much. Too fast. Too soon.

"Ellie," he said, "you didn't do anything wrong. If you're worried about appearances, you shouldn't be. Even public figures are allowed to have a private life."

"It's not that simple." She stepped back and lowered her voice. "It's one thing to be an unwed mother, but I don't want to be one that's dating." Talk about flitting from one man's bed to another. Not that she'd planned to jump into bed with Steven, but she'd certainly kissed him. And she'd liked it. A lot.

"This is the twenty-first century, Ellie. People have children out of wedlock all the time. It's not a big deal."

"I know. But to me, it is."

"What makes you different?" he asked.

"It's hard to explain. I guess you could say that, try as I might, I still carry a little baggage from my early childhood years."

"Like what?" he asked.

The question sparked memories she'd like to forget. The shabby apartment where she once lived. The stained, threadbare green carpet. The knocks at the front door. The men who stopped by daily to visit her mother, a woman she'd dubbed Liz once she'd gotten a real mom.

Child Protective Services had taken her out of that apartment and that life when she was six, but she still recalled the neighbors' disapproving whispers and felt her mother's shame as if it had been her own.

That's why it mattered what people thought of her and how they'd react to her news. What would they say if she were to date a man who wasn't her baby's father, a man who bore the Fortune name?

"I'm sorry," she said. "I really like you, Steven, but under the circumstances, I think we should remain friends. At least for the time being."

He studied her for a moment, as if he hadn't heard her, then he tossed her a carefree grin. "Okay. Friends it is. I'll meet you at city hall a little before one on Tuesday."

Stunned that he still intended to go with her to San Antonio, she merely nodded as she climbed into her car and closed the door.

Steven Fortune was the last man in the world she ought to be attracted to, especially now.

Just friends, he'd said. And that sounded good. But how was that ever going to work when she couldn't deny his strong sexual appeal?

Chapter Eight

I really like you, but...

Some might consider a comment like that to be a brush-off, a way for a woman to let them down easy, but Steven knew Ellie had feelings for him. He'd seen it in her eyes, heard it in her laugh and felt it in her touch.

He liked her, too—as a verbal sparring partner and as a friend. And he certainly found her attractive. It was too early to tell if anything romantic would develop, but he felt drawn to her, and the chemistry was definitely there. Oddly enough, her reluctance to date or to be seen with him in public made him all the more determined to see her privately.

The way he saw it, the only thing standing in their way was political in nature. That's why it had both surprised and pleased him when she'd asked him to go with her to that event in San Antonio.

Now that Tuesday had rolled around, he took a cue from her and arrived at city hall at a quarter to one, which was on time by her standards. Rather than enter the building and ask for her, which seemed like the proper thing to do, he opted to respect her privacy and call her cell.

When she answered, he said, "I'm in the parking lot."

"I'll be right there."

And she was. He'd hardly shut off his ignition when he spotted her coming out the door and striding toward his SUV.

She was dressed in her typical business attire—a black suit and heels. She hadn't buttoned the blazer, nor had she tucked in the white blouse. Probably to hide her baby bump, which seemed a bit pronounced today. A good sign that her son was growing, that she had a healthy pregnancy.

As she climbed into the passenger seat, the hem of her skirt lifted and provided him with a glimpse of her shapely legs. The alluring sight didn't surprise him. His visceral reaction did.

"You look nice." He tossed her a smile. "As usual."

"Thanks." She adjusted her seat belt and tugged at her blouse.

As he pulled out of the parking lot and headed out of town, he said, "So tell me. What kind of event is this?"

"It's a gathering of mayors and other city officials from several nearby counties. The idea is for us to join forces in a cooperative effort to increase tourism in this part of the state."

"That's interesting. And a little ironic, don't you think?" A smile tugged at his lips, and he stole a glance across the seat. When he caught her eye, he winked. "Do you plan to join that effort or oppose it?"

"Very funny. But I suppose that's a fair question, since I haven't given you any reason to think I'm pro-tourism. Actually, I am. I just don't want to draw in the wrong kind of tourist to our town. I'd like to hear what they have to say, but don't worry. After the initial speeches, I'm going to leave. That way, we can have an early dinner."

Just as Ellie predicted, the few speeches didn't last much longer than an hour or so, although Steven suspected that he'd found them to be more interesting than Ellie had.

At the end of the presentation, the San Antonio mayor thanked them all for coming. "If you'll step through the open door into the adjoining room, you'll find several displays of various businesses within our counties and interesting places that visitors might like to see while in the area."

Steven leaned toward Ellie and whispered, "I know you said you'd be ready to cut out early, but would you mind if I took a look in that room?"

"Not at all. I'd like to see the displays, too."

As they entered what appeared to be a small exhibition hall, one business caught Steven's immediate attention. The Mendoza Winery out of Austin had set up four wine-tasting booths in each corner of the room. "Well, I'll be darned. I didn't expect to see any of my relatives here. Come on, I'd like to introduce you to my cousin Schuyler and her husband, Carlo Mendoza, the vice president of the Mendoza Winery. I met them last year, when we attended a wedding."

"Who got married?" Ellie asked, as she followed Steven to one of several wine bars.

"Jerome Fortune, once known as Gerald Robinson. He finally married the love of his life, a woman he'd dated forty years earlier. It's a little complicated. I'll explain more later."

When Steven and Ellie approached the booth where Carlo and Schuyler had displayed several bottles of red wine, Steven called out, "Fancy meeting you two here."

Carlo looked up, and when he spotted Steven, he flashed his trademark grin and extended his hand. "Our new motto is 'Have winery, will travel.'"

Schuyler, who looked especially pretty today in a classic red dress, smiled brightly. "Hey, Steven. It's good to see you. I didn't realize you were involved in politics."

"Only by association," he said. "Let me introduce you to my friend Ellie Hernandez, the mayor of Rambling Rose."

After the three took turns shaking hands, Steven turned to Ellie and said, "Before Schuyler married Carlo, she was a Fortune, although her family went by the name of Fortunado."

"We're offering each city official a case of Mendoza wine," Carlo said. "So Ellie, if you'll let me know when you're leaving, I'll have it carried out to your car."

"Thank you," Ellie said. "That's very generous."

Carlo placed his hand on his wife's back. "I wish I could take credit for the brilliant promotional idea, but Schuyler is always coming up with new ways for us to spread the word about our wines."

"When Carlo and I met last June," Steven told Ellie, "we found out we had a lot in common. We both hail from Florida."

"They also love wine," Schuyler added. "And they're huge Miami Dolphins fans."

Ellie let out a little gasp, feigning surprise at the audacity. "Keep your voices down. Everyone here is either a staunch fan of the Dallas Cowboys or the Houston Texans. I'd hate to see y'all get thrown out of here."

"Speaking of getting thrown out," Carlo said to Steven, "or rather cuffed and dragged out of town, what'd you think of Charlotte Robinson's final act at Jerome and Deborah's wedding?"

"What a wedding crasher." Steven let out a little whistle, then offered an explanation to Ellie. "Charlotte is Jerome's ex-wife. She was an angry, deceitful woman before they divorced, but she became completely unhinged afterward and took out her vengeance on a lot of people in the Fortune family."

"That's right," Carlo said. "In fact, now that I think about it, Ellie, you probably either know or have heard of Paxton Price. He used to be the sheriff, but he was recently elected mayor of Paseo."

"We've met a couple of times. He's a nice guy. I believe he was once a Dallas detective."

"That's right," Schuyler said. "During the ceremony, Charlotte came in screaming and waving a gun. After firing it in the air, she took Pax's future wife, Georgia Fortune, hostage."

"Oh no." Ellie's eyes grew wide. "That's horrible."

"It *truly* was," Schuyler said. "But luckily, Georgia was rescued unharmed, and Jerome and Deborah were able to get married the next day."

"I hope Charlotte is still in that psychiatric hospital," Steven said.

"I'm sure she is." Carlo reached for an uncorked bottle of merlot and poured a couple of ounces into each of two wineglasses. "After the fire, vandalism, cut brake lines and then a kidnapping, she'll probably remain there or in prison for a very long time."

Schuyler took the wine and handed it to Ellie. Steven expected her to decline, but she took it. Probably to be polite—or to put up a facade. He didn't think she'd drink it.

"That wedding was very nice," Schuyler said, "but it was the craziest one I've ever attended. And the biggest. Each and every known Fortune was invited to a two-week-long celebration leading up to the ceremony in Paseo."

"Seriously?" Ellie took a sip of wine, although she barely made a dent in the small pour. "Where'd they all stay? I mean, Paseo isn't a large town."

"Believe it or not," Steven said, "we camped out in a field on Deborah's ranch. You should have seen all the travel trailers, tents and luxury motor homes."

Schuyler handed Steven a glass of merlot. "Wasn't it cool to meet all the Fortune relatives?"

He wouldn't call it cool. There'd been a lot of them, and it had taken a while to learn their names and connections, especially since he and his family had always kept to themselves.

"It was definitely interesting," he said.

"Have you heard anything from Gary Fortune's side of the family?" Schuyler asked.

"I've been approached by Adam and Kane, two of his sons. They're hoping to get involved in some of the projects my brothers and I are spearheading in Rambling Rose."

Moments later, Paxton Price approached the wine bar. The tall, broad-shouldered man with a stocky build first greeted the Mendozas, then Steven. When he spotted Ellie, he grinned. "How're things going in Rambling Rose?"

"Other than being a little overrun by the rich and the famous?" She gave Steven a playful nudge. "We're hanging in there."

Pax chuckled. "I hear you. Same thing happened in Paseo, but it's not so bad, especially when you fall in love with one of them."

Ellie, who'd never seemed to be at a loss for words, flushed, her cheeks a pretty shade of pink.

"If I'd known this was going to turn out to be a family reunion," Pax said with a grin, "I would have asked Georgia to come with me."

Before anyone could respond, a couple others moseyed up to the wine bar, and Schuyler gave them her full attention.

Steven placed his empty glass on a tray set off

to the side and then addressed Carlo. "Ellie and I had better move on and let you two get back to work. But you can expect a call from me next week. I'd like to order a case of that merlot. It was amazingly good."

"You got it," Carlo said.

As Steven and Ellie turned to walk away, Schuyler called him back. "Steven, why don't you plan a visit to Austin one of these days?"

"I just might do that. I'd love to tour the winery."

"And bring Ellie," his cousin added. "I'll take her around the city and show her all the hot spots."

"Sounds like fun. I'll talk to you later." Steven stole a glance at Ellie. He wondered how she felt about being included in the invitation. He couldn't tell by looking, but there'd be time for them to talk about it over dinner—or on the way home.

As he scanned the city officials studying the displays that had been set around the room, he realized Schuyler wasn't the only one who'd assumed Steven and Ellie were a couple.

Unlike Schuyler, who seemed so accepting, the two women standing near a display of the San Antonio River Walk were eyeing them a little too carefully, a hint of disapproval in their expressions.

As Ellie and Steven walked around the room, she clutched the stem of her wineglass, pretending that she was actually drinking when she'd only taken a single sip. The merlot was good, though. Very good.

It might be fun to go with Steven to Austin and tour the Mendoza Winery. But being the mayor kept her busy. Her calendar was pretty full. And once the baby came…well, she wouldn't have much free time at all.

She took another scan of the displays that had been set up around the room and headed toward one that highlighted San Antonio's famous River Walk. She wanted to check out the nearby restaurants. It would be nice to eat near the water.

As she crossed the room, she spotted two well-groomed women looking at her and whispering. She recognized the snooty brunette wearing black slacks and a red blazer, although she couldn't remember her name. They'd probably run across each other a couple of times but had never been formally introduced.

"Like I told you before," the middle-aged brunette said to the blonde standing beside her, "she might be young and pretty, but no one takes her seriously."

Blondie let out a little snort, then lowered her voice, but she didn't speak quietly enough. "The men do, but for all the wrong reasons. All they can talk about is how beautiful she is, how sexy they find her. And they seem to agree that it'd be worth a move to Rambling Rose, just to see her more often."

Ellie's hearing had always been good, which had come in handy more times than not. Steven wasn't too far from the women. Had he picked up their conversation?

"She's not that sexy anymore," the brunette added. "Check out her waistline. She's getting thick in the belly."

"You're right. She didn't tuck in her blouse. Probably because she can't button her pants these days." Blondie covered her mouth to stifle a laugh. "Too much fast food. Or too many trips to the bakery."

Ellie's cheeks warmed, and her stomach clenched. Normally she had pretty thick skin, but pregnancy hormones must have gotten the better of her, pushing her to react. Instead of letting the rude comments pass, she approached the two catty women.

"Body shaming is frowned on these days," she said. "It actually makes those doing the shaming look bad. And that's not wise, especially if either of you has political aspirations. I suggest you take a class on how to be more PC. And while you're at it, you should learn how to conduct yourselves at public events. A little tact and kindness goes a long way."

"I'm sorry," Blondie said. "We didn't mean for you to hear that. We thought we'd kept our voices down."

"You didn't. But that's not the point. You shouldn't judge a person's character on their outward appearance. You're more apt to be wrong than right."

Ellie was about to turn away when Steven placed his hand on her shoulder, bolstering her with his presence, providing his support.

"Ellie Hernandez is the most beautiful woman in this room," Steven said, "inside and out. Unlike you two, she doesn't have a mean or jealous bone in her body."

Blondie seemed noticeably chastised—and perhaps a bit sorry.

On the other hand, the brunette lifted her finger and pointed at Ellie as if she were a parent scolding a child. "You're not going to be able to hide it forever, Ms. Hernandez. I can see the signs. How long before Rambling Rose realizes that the mayor has a bun in the oven?"

Shock and mortification struck Ellie like a wallop to the diaphragm, sucking the air out of her lungs. It took her a moment to recover, then she gathered up her battered pride and stood tall. "My private life is none of your business. Nor is it your concern."

Then she turned and walked away, leaving Steven with the two horrid women. She had no idea what he'd do or what he'd say—if anything—but she wasn't going to stick around to find out.

A couple of beats later, he was by her side.

"Are you okay?" he asked.

"Yes, I'm fine. But I need to get out of here. *Now.*"

Ellie hadn't mentioned a word about going out to an early dinner. She'd just insisted that they leave. But Steven couldn't blame her for that. The gossipy women had turned his stomach, and even though he'd had a light lunch, he wasn't hungry, either.

As he pulled his SUV out of the parking lot and began the drive back to Rambling Rose, he glanced across the seat at Ellie. "You doing okay?"

"Yes."

He didn't believe her, but he held his tongue and let silence fill the cab. He didn't blame Ellie for retreating from San Antonio. Her secret was out—or at least, someone had noticed her pregnancy.

Each time he stole a glance her way and saw her troubled expression, he wanted to reach out and take her hand, tell her it was going to be okay. But she leaned her head against the passenger window, pulling away from him. He figured he'd better give her some space.

By the time they reached the city hall parking lot, where she'd left her car, he couldn't hold his tongue any longer. "There's something I want to tell you."

She turned to him, but she didn't speak. Instead, she questioned him with her eyes.

"Those women were rude, and their comments hurt you and were totally uncalled-for. But you held your head high, and that's not always easy to do when people are mean and poke their noses where they don't belong. I'm proud of you, Ellie."

"Thanks." She gave a slight shoulder shrug. "I can handle the cattiness, the smirks and the laughter when it's directed at me personally. But I don't want my past or my private life to distract people from what's important."

"What's *really* important," he said, "is that you take care of yourself. You have a baby on the way, and you need to focus on that."

She looked up at him like a startled doe in a thicket. Her lips and chin trembled. Tears welled in her eyes, and for once, her gaze held no resistance, no argument, no objection. Rather, her vulnerability peered out at him, turning him to mush and leaving him vulnerable, too.

In an effort to show his support, he leaned across the seat and cupped her jaw. Then he drew her face toward him and placed a kiss on her brow. He wasn't sure how he expected her to react. A smile, maybe. But she burst into tears, shocking the hell out of him.

You'd think that he'd have mastered how to deal with a crying female, especially after he helped to raise four little sisters, but this situation was different. Ellie was different.

"Aw, honey. Don't…" Words failed him. The tough, sharp politician he could handle. This soft, sweet, hurting woman left him at a loss.

Ellie sucked in a deep breath, then swiped the tears from her eyes with both hands. "I'm sorry. Believe it or not, I never cry. You must think I'm a blithering mess."

"There's nothing for you to be sorry for. You're an amazing woman who's carrying a heavy load." He glanced around the parking lot, searching for bystanders who might have seen them arrive and witnessed her crying jag. Thank goodness, he didn't see any.

She sniffled and swiped her eyes once again, using the backs of both hands, but the tears continued to stream down her pretty face.

Steven had no idea what to say, but there was no way he'd just drop her off in the city parking lot like this and go on his own way. "Give me your address. I'm not going to let you drive home right now. I'll bring you back for your car later, when you're feeling better."

He expected an argument, a show of strength and determination, but she surprised him by saying, "Four eighteen Pumpernickel Court. It's a small subdivision near the elementary school. And you don't have to take me back to pick up my car. Daria should be home soon. I'll have her drop me off after dark. Or maybe even in the morning."

He nodded, then drove across town.

When he turned down the quiet, tree-lined street, Ellie said, "It's the white house with red-brick trim. The one with the big elm tree in the front yard."

Steven parked along the curb, then walked with her to the front porch and waited for her to unlock the door. She hadn't sent him on his way yet, and unless she did, he planned to stick around until her friend got home.

Ellie had no more than turned the key when a whine sounded from inside. "Tank must be home. I asked one of the neighbors to look after him while I was gone." She opened the door and stepped into a small, cozy living room as the scruffy black pup ran to her full throttle, nearly taking her out at the knees.

"Did you think we abandoned you, Tank?" She stooped to give the little mutt a scratch behind floppy ears.

When she straightened, Tank sat on his haunches and looked up at Steven, who stooped to greet him, too. "Hey there, little guy. Or should I say big guy? He's going to be a moose when he grows into those paws."

"I know. Right?" Ellie shut the door.

"He's not what I'd call cute," Steven said, "but he's friendly. There's something likable about him."

At that, for the first time since they'd left San Antonio, Ellie smiled, and his heart went out to her.

"We've been trying to housebreak him," Ellie said, "but he's still learning. Have a seat while I let him out in the backyard."

As the pup trailed after Ellie, Steven sat on the brown leather sofa and scanned the small living area, with its pale green walls and redbrick fireplace. A colorful area rug adorned hardwood floors.

Moments later, Ellie returned without Tank. "I'm sorry for falling apart at the seams."

"No problem."

She combed her fingers through her hair, then plopped down in a matching leather recliner. "I'm tired of hiding my pregnancy, although I can't do that much longer."

"Don't worry. People will adjust to the news. And life will go on."

"I know. You're right. But I've worked so hard to prove to some of my older and more conservative constituents that I'm a capable leader. I might be a young woman, but I want them to realize that my age and gender are assets, not liabilities."

"I agree completely," Steven said. "You're tough, but you also have heart." It was a nice combination.

"When the townspeople learn that I not only got involved with the wrong guy, but that I'm expecting his baby, they'll forget all the good I've done and focus on the mistakes. Not that I consider the baby a mistake. It's just that…" She blew out a ragged breath.

"You championed several big projects in the community," Steven said, "like the new park next to the lake. Thanks to you, Rambling Rose now has a beautiful greenbelt, and the children have a place to play. No one is going to forget that."

"Maybe not, but I don't want anything to jeopardize the work that still needs to be done." The long black strands, somewhat messy now from her meltdown, slid over her shoulder. *How could her ex-boyfriend just walk away from her?*

Steven sat quietly while she talked, mostly about being judged for having two X chromosomes and for being a millennial.

"You saw it today," she said. "Can you believe that those two women were so critical of me? You'd think they'd be happy to see one of their own take on a leadership position."

"They might be women," Steven said, "but they're nothing like you. They're clearly jealous. And they should be."

"Thanks, but now that they suspect I'm pregnant, they're going to spread the word. And then everyone will start asking questions I don't want to answer, especially about my personal life."

"Welcome to the world of politics," he said. "People are always going to have questions."

He'd do anything to help her, but there wasn't much he could do. Or was there?

She zeroed in on him with those big brown eyes, still a bit puffy, yet just as pretty as ever. "Don't you, Steven? Have questions, I mean?"

"Actually, I do. A lot of them. But I also have a suggestion." It elbowed itself front and center, then rolled right off his tongue. "Let's get married."

Chapter Nine

Ellie's jaw dropped. *Married?* He had to be kidding. "Don't make jokes."

"It's not a joke. The way I see it, if we were married, people wouldn't ask nosy questions."

"They'll also think the baby is yours."

He shrugged. "So what?" Then he laughed. "Hell, Ellie, having my baby might even bump up your poll numbers!"

At that, she rolled her eyes and frowned.

"Come on," he said. "Now, *that* was a joke."

She studied him for a couple of beats, then slowly shook her head. "We can't get married. We barely know each other. And after all the times we've bumped heads over one thing or another, who'd ever believe that we fell in love?"

"People who like to gossip, most likely. But you have to admit that marriage would solve at least part of your problem."

"And create a brand-new one."

"Nothing we couldn't fix together. After the baby is old enough, we can separate and get a quiet divorce."

Dang. He *was* serious. She tilted her head slightly, waiting for him to come to his senses. But he continued to sit there.

"What's in it for you?" she asked.

"Your friendship, I guess. I just want to help. Besides, it's not like either of us is dating anyone else right now."

"I don't know what to say. It sounds so…simple. Yet devious."

"It might be a sneaky ploy, but who would get hurt? The way I see it, you don't have too many options right now."

"So you're proposing a marriage of convenience?"

"If that's what you want to call it, sure. Why not?"

"Because there'd be nothing convenient about it." She studied him, expecting him to laugh off the sweet but ridiculous idea, but he didn't.

"Ellie, I just want to help."

She combed her fingers through her hair again, as if that might help her come to a decision. "It seems so…impulsive. Can I think about it?"

"Sure. But don't wait too long. I might get a better offer." She looked at him skeptically for a moment, and he laughed. "That was another joke."

"This isn't a laughing matter."

"No, it's not. But think it over. We can talk more about it in the morning."

Then he left her to ponder his offer. And that was exactly what she did. She stewed over the wacky proposal from the moment Steven walked out the front door until twenty minutes later, when her roommate and confidante came home.

Daria had no more than set down her purse when Ellie blurted out the latest twist in her current dilemma.

"Married? No kidding?" Daria asked. "He can't be serious."

"Those were my thoughts exactly. But he seems sincere."

"So talk to me." Daria plopped down on the sofa, taking the same cushion on which Steven had sat when he'd suggested the wild-ass solution to her problem. "I'm listening."

That was one of many things Ellie appreciated most about her best friend. Daria understood the way Ellie's mind worked, the way she talked out loud as she pondered a solution to a problem. And right now, she had a big one.

So Ellie chattered on, and Daria listened. When she finally took a break, her mind still reeling, Daria offered up an opinion. "It sounds to me as if Steven has fallen in love with you."

"Oh no. That's not it. We're just friends."

"Ellie." Daria blew out a sigh. "Friends tell me when I have a piece of spinach in my teeth. They listen to me complain about the jerk who claimed to be single and asked me out for drinks. Then, when he went to the restroom and spotted his wife, he left me sitting on a bar stool like a jilted fool."

True. Ellie and Daria had been through a lot together. "Friends also stand beside me while I puke my brains out each morning. And then they wipe my face with a damp cloth."

"That's right," Daria said. "And you're welcome. But friends don't offer to marry you just to save you from temporary embarrassment."

Ellie slunk back in her seat on the recliner, her hands on the armrests. "I know. But there's no way Steven is in love with me. He's just being nice. Besides, he said we'd get a quiet divorce after the baby gets here."

"I repeat," Daria said. "Friends don't offer to marry you. I'll bet you a nickel to a doughnut that Steven Fortune has fallen for you."

"That's impossible." Steven did care about her, though. And there was definitely some sexual attraction at play. He'd even kissed her. *Twice.* Of course, they'd been friendly kisses. Sort of. She'd been tempted to kiss him back, too. And if she had let loose the way she'd been tempted to, those kisses wouldn't have been so friendly.

That evening, Ellie continued to talk out her dilemma while Daria drove her to the city hall parking lot to pick up her car. And then again, after they got home and ate dinner.

By the time bedtime rolled around, Ellie had come to the conclusion that Steven had offered her an easy way out, and she'd be a fool not to take him up on it. But each time she decided to call him and tell him her decision, she'd go sideways.

How could she marry a man she didn't love?

Sure, she had feelings for Steven. What woman wouldn't? He was drop-dead gorgeous, smart and funny. But marriage was a big step. And so was a divorce.

Ellie prided herself on being an overachiever, a winner. And she'd hate for anyone to think she'd failed at holding a marriage together, even if it was fake.

Needless to say, by the time she arrived at city hall the next morning, she still hadn't touched base with Steven. How could she, when she didn't know what to tell him?

Doing her best to shake off her worries, she breezed into the lobby as if this were just another day in Rambling Rose.

"Good morning," Iris Tompkins, the receptionist, said. "The newspaper was delivered a few minutes ago. I put it on your desk."

"Thanks, Iris."

Before Ellie ran for mayor, her news source was either the internet or an app on her phone. But during the campaign, she'd begun reading a hard copy because she thought it gave her a better glimpse at the business world, especially when she looked at various ads. Besides, when she read the news off her phone, people at the coffee shop probably thought she was checking social media or playing a stupid game.

She'd no more than taken a seat behind her desk and started to flip through the pages when she spotted a write-up about the mayors' conference to promote tourism. She read it carefully, relieved that it didn't mention her name.

She continued to scan the newspaper for other articles, intending to skip the gossip page, but a photograph jumped out at her. No wonder that brunette at the conference had looked familiar. Her picture had to have been taken ten years ago—and had clearly been touched up—but she was the blasted columnist.

What Texas politician and media darling's recent weight gain has nothing to do with a fondness for fast food and desserts? We won't name names, but let's just say we expect the truth to pop out any day now...

Ellie's breath caught, and her gut clenched. The gossip columnist hadn't mentioned her by name, but it was pretty obvious. Her secret was out. She'd better drive over to her parents' house and give them the news in person before they heard it elsewhere.

But did she dare take the time to do it now?

Since Steven and Ellie had agreed to talk in the morning, he hadn't expected a call from her last night, but it was a workday and already past ten o'clock. Shouldn't he have heard something from her by now?

He strode the length of modular office they'd set up at the Paz job site, turned and walked back again. When he realized he was pacing like a nervous fool, he swore under his breath and stopped.

Why in the hell was he anxious for an answer to his proposal for a marriage that wasn't even going to be real? It was nuts. Yet he looked at the clock once again.

How long did it take a woman to make up her

mind? All she had to do was give him a one-word answer. A simple yes or no. How hard could that be?

Ellie might be a strong woman, but she feared telling her parents, which meant she had a chink in her armor, leaving her vulnerable. He'd seen the look on her face when that nasty brunette launched her attack. Were there other people out there who were eager to tarnish Ellie's reputation and ruin her political career?

Steven wasn't going to hang around waiting in the office all day, feeling like a caged animal, ready to snap at anyone who knocked at the door. He grabbed his keys off the desk and headed out the door, stopping long enough to tell the retiring office manager that he was going to be out of pocket for a while. Then he drove to city hall.

Once inside the lobby, he marched right past the receptionist, who tried to call him back. He ignored her and strode all the way back to Ellie's office. He probably ought to knock, but the door was ajar, so he pulled it open.

Ellie sat at her desk, her back to the doorway, the telephone receiver pressed to her ear.

"It's an invasion of privacy," she snapped, "and it's an example of low-life quasi journalism."

Steven took a repentant step back, planning to shut the door quietly and slip off without her noticing when her chair turned and he saw her expression and realized she was clearly disturbed, if not angry.

He assumed it was due to his unannounced arrival until her chair turned again and she spoke directly into the receiver. "I'm canceling my subscription, and you'd better hope that's all I do." Then she slammed down the phone, ending the call without saying goodbye.

"I'm sorry," he said. "I didn't mean to interrupt you. The door was open, but I should have knocked."

Ellie let out an unladylike sound and waved him in. Then she handed him the newspaper and pointed to an article in the gossip column.

After reading it, he realized why she'd called the paper to complain. "Who wrote that crap?"

"An anonymous junior reporter, I was told. But check out the picture of the columnist on the top. It was probably taken ten years or more ago and Photoshopped, but I know exactly who wrote it."

He did too. He recognized the woman in the photo. The rude, loudmouth brunette they'd seen in San Antonio.

"I'm sorry," he said.

"And I'm furious. I ought to make the official announcement and get it over with. But I'd hate to have a bad decision I made a year and a half ago dog me all over town."

He figured she was referring to the day she'd

met the father of her baby. "How long are you going to beat yourself up for misjudging someone's character?"

"As long as it takes."

He wasn't sure what she meant by that, but her frustration was evident when she combed her fingers through her hair, only to make a cute mess of the tidy topknot she wore in professional situations.

"I offered you a solution," he said. "Are you going to take me up on it?"

Ellie pushed her chair away from the desk, got to her feet and crossed her arms. "As much as I appreciate the kindness behind it, I can't marry you. I'm not going to saddle you with a wife and child."

"It would only be temporary. Besides, we're friends, right? You wouldn't be a burden."

"Don't you think marriage is a good way to ruin a friendship?"

"I won't let it," he said. "I give you my word."

She furrowed her brow—pondering his offer, he hoped.

"Ellie," he continued, "I really like you. And even when we bump heads about one thing or another, I respect you. Believe me when I say that I don't want to lose that. I give you my word, when this is all over, we'll still be friends—maybe even better ones than we are now."

"You make it sound so easy. But it's a wild and crazy solution." She slowly shook her head, but stopped abruptly. She blinked a couple of times. Her breath caught, and she paled. Then she placed both hands on her desk, bracing herself.

Steven hurried toward her, watching her sway, and reached her just as she crumpled against his side.

He glanced at the phone, prepared to hold her tight with one hand while dialing 9-1-1. The fire department was just down the street. It wouldn't take paramedics long to get here.

"Are you okay?" he asked, his heart pounding like a jackhammer at a construction site.

"I…feel a little…faint."

That was normal, right? Something pregnant women experienced all the time? Nothing to be concerned about?

He helped her take a seat. "Let me get you some water. Are you going to be okay if I leave you sitting there?"

"I'll be fine. I just got a little light-headed. That's all."

"No, that's not *all*. The stress is getting to be too much, and your body is rebelling. You've got to relieve some of the pressure, and I suggested a way for you to do that. Wait here. I'll be back."

Moments later, Steven returned with a disposable cup filled with water. He handed it to her, then knelt at her feet, watching until she drank half of it.

"Thanks." She managed a weak smile and set the cup on the desk.

"You're welcome. But just for the record, Ellie, I asked you a question. And I'm not going to take no for an answer."

She didn't respond right away, but by the look of resignation in her eyes, he could tell she was about to agree. That is, until she gazed at the open doorway and gasped. Her expression morphed into one of mortification.

Steven glanced over his shoulder and spotted an older Hispanic couple standing in the doorway, their brows furrowed, their eyes clearly troubled.

"Papa," Ellie said, her voice soft. "Mama."

Damn. What were her parents doing here? She clearly hadn't expected to see them. Had they read the gossip page in the newspaper and connected the dots?

Steven had no idea what thoughts were running through their minds, but he wasn't going to remain on his knees. He got to his feet, rose to his full height and said, "Mr. and Mrs. Hernandez. We haven't been formally introduced, but I'm Steven Fortune, one of the owners of Fortune Brothers Construction."

"I know who you are," Ellie's father said. "Most people in town do. And they're aware of the business you've brought to town. But they're not all happy about it."

Whether the older man was for or against the new businesses that had popped up, he didn't say. He merely looked Steven up and down, assessing him. Or maybe he was assessing the awkward situation he'd just walked in on—his daughter pale and uneasy, a man kneeling beside her.

"Ellie is an amazing woman," Steven said. "And she's a good mayor. The townspeople love her. You must be very proud of her."

Mr. Hernandez didn't speak, but his wife did. "Ellie has been nothing but a joy and a delight. She's been a real blessing to our family. We've always been proud."

"And up until today," Mr. Hernandez said, "she's never kept any secrets from us."

Steven glanced at Ellie, who appeared to be a little too overwhelmed to speak. And why wouldn't she be? First she'd read that shocking article, then she'd had the argument with the newspaper editor. She'd nearly fainted after that. And now her parents had arrived, their moods not difficult to discern.

"Mija," Mr. Hernandez said, "I can see what's going on in here."

"I know it looks a little odd, Papa, but I can explain. Steven stopped by city hall unexpectedly, and…" She looked first to Steven then back to

her father, whose face had reddened to the point
he might explode.

"Stopped by to *what*?" Mr. Hernandez asked.
"Do all your constituents kneel at your feet, pressing you for an answer?"

She sucked in a deep breath. "Steven isn't just
a constituent, Papa. He's my f—"

When she paused, Steven stepped in to help her
out. "I'm her fiancé. I asked her to be my wife,
and she agreed."

Chapter Ten

Ellie hadn't wanted to go along with Steven's scheme, but she'd just fallen into it. Now here she was, sitting behind the mayor's desk, nodding in agreement like a dumbstruck schoolgirl rather than a competent city leader.

"You're *engaged*?" Papa asked, his voice sharp, his brow furrowed. "And you haven't even introduced your mother and me to the man?"

Mama eased a step closer, her soft brown eyes wounded. "Why didn't you? Were you ashamed of us?"

"Oh God. No, Mama. I've never been ashamed of you! I never will be. It's just that…" Flustered,

Ellie shot a tight-lipped frown at Steven that all but said, *You and your big ideas. Now what?*

As if reading her thoughts, Steven placed his hand on her shoulder and gave it a gentle squeeze. "Ellie and I wanted to surprise you."

"When?" Papa remained in the doorway, his shoulders straight, his chest expanded, his expression a cross between anger and disappointment. "After the wedding?"

"Later today," Steven said.

Papa shot Steven a look of disapproval. "My wife and I don't run in the same wealthy, highfalutin social circles as you, so I don't know how you people handle things. But in my family, in my culture, a man is expected to approach a young woman's father first and ask for his blessing."

"I'm sorry, sir. You're right. I should have done that." The contrite expression Steven wore was one Ellie hadn't seen before. She rather liked it today, especially since his crazy idea had just blown up in his face. Hers, too. Yet at the same time, sympathy fluttered in her heart and up to her throat.

"Steven planned to ask for my hand, Papa. But things happened rather quickly. I'm afraid it's a little complicated."

Papa nodded at her desk, where the newspaper lay open to the gossip column. "I can see how things got complicated."

Guilt warmed Ellie's cheeks. Her parents had

read the morning paper and then they'd marched right over to city hall to ask her if it was true.

"Are you really expecting a baby?" Mama asked.

Ellie tried to hold her head up while kicking herself for not telling them sooner. "Yes, it's true. I'm so sorry you had to find out like this."

"When were you going to tell us?" Mama asked, her eyes watering.

Soon. Maybe tonight. But before Ellie could respond, Iris, the lobby receptionist, peered around her father's back and said, "Excuse me. I don't mean to interrupt."

Ellie cringed. How long had she been standing there? How much had she heard? "What do you need, Iris?"

"I wanted to remind you of that meeting at the water district this morning. It's at eleven."

Ellie didn't forget meetings, although that one might have slipped her mind today. "Thanks. I didn't forget. It's on my calendar."

Iris scanned Ellie's office, taking in the three people who stood in the room while Ellie sat at her desk. "Is everything okay?"

Heck no. Ellie's fairy-tale life had taken another hit. A big one. And she didn't want the Rambling Rose rumor mill getting wind of it. "Everything is fine, Iris. Please close the door on your way out."

The friendly—sometimes overly so—receptionist took a step back. "Oh. Of course."

When the office door snapped shut, Steven cleared his throat. "Mr. and Mrs. Hernandez, this is partially my fault."

Papa chuffed. *"Partially?"*

Undaunted, Steven continued. "Ellie wanted to tell me about the baby before she told you, but we hadn't been dating very long. We'd also kept it on the down low for political reasons. And even though we had strong feelings for each other, she wasn't sure how I'd feel about her pregnancy—or how she wanted to break the news to me. So she's been dragging her feet."

"How *do* you feel about it?" Mama asked him.

"I'll admit, the baby took us both a little by surprise. But I'm happy. We both are. In fact, I got on bended knee and proposed just before you two arrived."

Mama looked first at Ellie, then at Steven. "Have you set a date?"

"Not yet," Steven said, "but under the circumstances, I don't think we should wait very long."

"The sooner the better, I'd say." Papa raked a hand through his thinning gray hair.

"A wedding takes time to plan." Mama took another step into the room. "You'll need a dress. And invitations will need to be ordered. Then there are the flowers. Cake tastings. It can get expensive, *mija*. But don't worry. We've been setting money aside to pay for your wedding, just like we did for college. It's there for you now."

Another pang of guilt struck Ellie. Her parents had been saving and going without vacations, new cars and God only knew what else to provide for what they assumed would be a special day. "Thank you, Mama. I promise not to use it all. It's going to be a small wedding. Just family and a few close friends."

Papa chuffed. "The Fortune family alone will take up the entire church."

Mama had softened and gotten on board, but Papa was clearly not happy and still had a long way to go. If this was his reaction to a fiancé on one knee, how would he have reacted if she'd faced him without a husband in sight and told him she was pregnant?

"Will you let me help you plan it?" Mama asked.

"Of course. I'd love that. Daria is going to be my maid of honor. So the three of us can plot and shop together. It'll be fun."

Mama's sweet smile offset the tension in the room. "I can't wait. I've been dreaming of this day for a long time. I've also dreamed of holding a grandbaby in my arms. When is it due? Have you seen a doctor yet?"

Ellie smiled, happy to have her mother's full support. "The baby is due in mid-August, and the doctor said everything is going well. I have another appointment next week. Would you like to go with me?"

"I'd *love* that!" Mama turned to Papa, her eyes watery but bright. "*Mi amor.* We're going to be *abuelitos*. Isn't that wonderful?"

Papa let out a humph, announcing that he wasn't as delighted as Mama. At least, not now. He could be tough at times, but he had a good heart.

"I can't wait to tell my bunco group," Mama said. "They'll want to throw a shower for you. Actually, two of them. One for the wedding and then for the baby."

Ellie looked at Steven, wishing they could speak telepathically. If they could, she'd tell him that his solution to her problem had gotten way out of hand. And now she felt like Sandra Bullock onboard that runaway bus with Keanu Reeves. She just hoped that the two of them would end up living through it all and saving the other unwitting passengers.

Like Keanu, Steven might be a gorgeous, sexy hunk. But that didn't mean he could help her save the day. They'd have to talk more later, when they were alone and could put their heads together to slow the bus and steer it in a better direction.

"Mama," Ellie said, "for political reasons, I'm not ready for the news to leak out until I have a solid game plan in place. So would you and Papa please keep it to yourselves for a few days?"

"Of course, although it's going to be hard to keep quiet. It's all so exciting."

Papa didn't look too excited, but hopefully, after Mama worked on him and he had a chance to cool down, he'd come around.

"By the way," Ellie said, "you didn't ask, but I found out two weeks ago that the baby is a boy."

Mama lifted her hands to her face, placed them together as if in prayer, then she gave a muffled little clap and turned to Papa. "Did you hear that, George? We're having a grandson. Now you'll have someone to take fishing. Maybe he'll help you fix up that old car you've been storing in the garage."

Papa had wanted to restore that 1973 Bronco for ages, but since he couldn't seem to tell his boss at the auto repair shop that he was going to retire, Mama had feared it would sit there for years.

Ellie got up from the desk chair, slowly and carefully so she wouldn't risk getting light-headed again. Then she crossed the office to embrace each of her parents. "I love you both so much. I hope I haven't disappointed you too badly."

"We were a little taken aback at first," Mama said. "But we're not disappointed. Are we, George?"

Papa offered up a smile. "No, Ellie. You've always made us proud." Then he turned and eyed

Steven carefully. "You're the one who'd better not disappoint me, young man."

"I won't, sir."

Steven's lie didn't sit well with Ellie. When the time came for them to announce their divorce, Papa wouldn't be pleased at all.

She glanced at the clock on the wall. "I hate to rush everyone off, but I have a meeting at eleven. Can we talk more about this later?"

"Yes, of course." Mama kissed Ellie's cheek. "Call me tonight after you talk to Daria. Then we can plan our first shopping trip."

"I'll do that."

"Mr. Hernandez," Steven said, drawing her father's attention. He extended his arm, and Papa, thankfully, took his hand to shake. "You've raised a fine daughter, and we both have the utmost respect for you. When the baby gets here, we're going to name him George."

Papa blinked back his surprise. Or was it a tear welling his eye? "That would…" He cleared his throat. "That'd be… Well, I'm honored."

Ellie had known her father wouldn't stay angry very long, and he seemed to be feeling better about the situation already, which was a huge relief. At least the hardest part of the announcement had been made. And tomorrow morning, she'd call a press conference and ask Steven to stand beside her.

His phony marriage plan wasn't going to work out in the long run, but they were too deep into the pretense to change course now. Still, she wasn't looking forward to facing the community.

George and Alma Hernandez weren't the only Rambling Rose residents who read the San Antonio newspaper, and not all of them were on Team Fortune. At Mariana's Market, Jackson had implied that Ellie was a traitor for fraternizing with the Fortunes. So news of their upcoming marriage might not go over very well. And when everyone learned she was pregnant, they'd conclude that she'd actually slept with the enemy, even though she and Steven had barely kissed.

On the upside, Ellie always had been able to charm the press, as well as the community at large. So she wasn't overly worried, especially if Steven was at her side.

If he could handle Papa, the rest of the town would be a piece of cake.

After Ellie hurried to her meeting at the water district, Steven left city hall and returned to his office at Fortune Brothers Construction, where he spent the afternoon going over spreadsheets and blueprints, meeting with the accountant, and then taking part in several lengthy conference calls.

Finally, at a quarter to six, he called it a day, locked his office door and headed to his SUV.

He'd barely reached the parking lot when a tall, lanky reporter and a short, squat photographer rushed toward him.

"Is there any truth to the rumor that you asked Mayor Hernandez to marry you?" the reporter asked.

Oh, for Pete's sake. He'd known that word of his and Ellie's engagement would get out, but he hadn't expected it to happen so quickly. "No comment."

The camera flashed.

As Steven continued toward his vehicle without missing a beat, the reporter tried to match his strides. "Mr. Fortune, have the two of you set a date for the wedding?"

Ignoring the men and that blasted camera, Steven climbed into the SUV and drove away, his grip tight on the wheel. He'd like to throttle that damned gossip columnist. This was all her fault.

Ellie ought to sue the newspaper for printing that woman's salacious words, although the case would probably get thrown out based on a technicality. The columnist hadn't actually mentioned Ellie by name.

He suspected that Iris, the city hall receptionist, had contributed to the spread of gossip. She'd been curious when Steven had breezed past her on his way to Ellie's office this morning. And when George and Alma arrived with troubled expressions, her interest had probably been piqued, so she'd followed them.

She'd claimed to be standing outside the doorway so she could remind Ellie of a meeting, but Steven didn't buy that lame excuse. And now the Rambling Rose rumor mill was running amok.

If the newshounds were bothering him, he couldn't imagine what Ellie must be dealing with, so he called her cell.

She answered on the second ring.

"How's it going?" he asked.

"It's been a rough day, to say the least. That blasted gossip columnist has been stalking me. And apparently, there's a reporter camped in front of my house, too. Daria told me to stay away until he leaves, but he's not going anywhere until he get some answers."

"You're right. They're not just after you. When I left the office, a reporter and a photographer tried to corner me."

"This is getting out of hand," Ellie said. "We need to talk and work out a game plan."

"Where are you?" he asked.

"In my car. I was going to spend the night with my parents, but my mom told me there are a couple of local bloggers parked in front of their house. Apparently, the fact that a small town mayor is going to marry into the Fortune family has set off local interest. So I've been driving around town until I figure out where I can have some privacy."

"Come to the ranch. It's not only remote and a little difficult to find, we also have security. No one can get in the front gate without us knowing about it."

"Is your family okay with that? I mean, do they know what's going on?"

"Not yet, but they will. I'm going to call them now and give them a heads-up."

Ellie sighed. "This thing is snowballing on us, Steven."

True. They'd have to do some fast thinking. "Don't worry, Ellie. It'll be okay. We'll work it out."

"I hope you're right."

To be completely honest, so did Steven. But he'd always been able to think himself out of a corner.

"I have a guest bedroom," he said. "You should stay with me until we get everything figured out."

Silence stretched across the line for several pensive beats. Finally, she said, "Okay. I'll see you shortly."

With Ellie on her way to the ranch, Steven called Callum and briefed him on the upcoming wedding, as well as the nosy press. He'd expected his brother to be surprised, but he seemed to take the announcement in stride.

"I realize things came together pretty quickly," Steven said, "but don't worry. I know what I'm doing."

"It didn't take me long to fall for Becky," Callum said. "And we all saw the sparks between you and Ellie."

Sure, there was chemistry, along with physical attraction. But they'd bumped heads since day one for political reasons. Even their arguments and disagreements were passionate, in the broadest sense of the word.

Ignoring his brother and the suggestion he didn't want to deal with tonight, Steven said, "Ellie's right behind me. She's going to be staying with me."

"I'll let Becky and Dillon know."

Ten minutes later, Steven arrived at the gate-house, where he greeted Stan Hawthorne, the guard.

"I've invited Ellie Hernandez up to the house again tonight. She's a few minutes behind me. There might be some snoopy reporters on her tail, but don't let them through."

"They won't get past me, Mr. Fortune."

Steven thanked him and drove up to the house. He hadn't told Callum everything. So, for all the family knew, the marriage would be the real deal, and they'd assume that Ellie would be sharing his bed. Instead, she'd sleep in his guest room, just across the hall.

The sleeping arrangements could prove to be a challenge, though. Their chemistry was strong. Hopefully, unlike the news of their engagement, his attraction to Ellie wouldn't get out of hand.

After parking next to the expansive main house at the Fame and Fortune Ranch, Ellie popped open her trunk to get the spare outfit and toiletries she carried with her for emergencies. A change of clothing and makeup had come in handy on more occasions than one, but she'd never been so glad to be prepared for the unexpected as she was today.

She removed the canvas gym bag she used for yoga and her aerobics class, as well as a garment bag that held another outfit. She had enough to get her through the night and the next day. Daria had promised to pack a suitcase tomorrow and bring it to the ranch.

Hopefully, she wouldn't need to be here long. Once the news was out, the reporters and bloggers would back off, she could go back to her house and life would go back to normal. Only trouble was, with a fake wedding and a baby on the way, her life was changing at Mach speed. And she was going to have a new normal, whatever that might be.

When she reached the front entrance, she shuffled the bags she carried, giving herself a free hand to ring the bell, but she didn't need to. The door swung open, and Steven greeted her with a warm smile that lit his blue eyes.

"Here," he said, reaching for her tote bag. "Let me carry that."

"Thank you." She stepped into the large foyer that opened to a formal living room, but rather than scan her surroundings, she studied the man who'd offered her refuge.

His hair was still damp from a recent shower, and the clean and musky scent of soap and man filled her lungs. He'd shed the Western wear he'd had on earlier, replacing them with a casual look— a black T-shirt and a pair of worn jeans. He'd kicked off his shoes, too.

She tore her gaze from the gorgeous sight and scanned the empty room. "Where is everyone?"

"I told them you'd had a rough day and that we needed some privacy tonight."

She hated to admit it, but she really would appreciate some peace and quiet.

"I don't want you passing out on me again," Steven added.

"I didn't pass out. Not all the way."

"Close enough to worry me." Steven nodded toward the hall that led to his quarters. "Come with me."

"I would like to have some quiet time," she   .

said, as she followed him down the hall, "but I feel bad about chasing everyone off."

"You didn't. Dillon's busy working on a project in his quarters, and since the twins didn't get a good nap today, Callum and Becky are getting them ready for bed." Steven stopped and opened the door for her. "If it makes you feel better, Becky told Manny, the cook and caretaker, that he could sleep in tomorrow morning. She wants to fix breakfast for us. That is, if you don't mind."

"No, that's fine. We'll need to face them together soon, and we may as well get it over with." Ellie entered Steven's small living room, with its leather furniture and southwestern artwork on the pale green walls.

"You didn't see the guest room when you were here last," he said. "It's across the hall from me." Steven led her to the room in which she'd be sleeping and placed her bag on a queen-size bed covered with a white goose-down comforter. She would've found it to be cozy and restful if Steven hadn't been standing so close, if his warm gaze and blood-stirring scent weren't so alluring.

"Do you want to take a rest before dinner?" he asked.

"Actually, if you don't mind, I think I'll take a shower and put on something more casual."

"No problem. I hope you don't mind sharing a bathroom with me."

"I'm just glad to have a peaceful place to stay tonight."

"It might be a little steamy in there, but I left clean towels on the counter. Let me know if you need anything."

"Thanks, but I have everything I'll need." She pointed to the bag on the bed. "I came prepared."

"I can see that." He offered her a heart-strumming smile, then left her on her own.

Twenty minutes later, she came out of the bathroom clean and refreshed. She wore black yoga pants and a white T-shirt, which she'd have to wear to bed tonight. Her emergency preparedness kit didn't cover sleepovers. She left her sneakers in the gym bag, opting to go barefoot.

She padded down the hall and found Steven in the kitchen, chopping lettuce for a salad.

He turned and smiled as his gaze swept over her from head to toe. "I've never seen you without shoes. Pretty toes."

Her cheeks flushed, embarrassed by the compliment, by the intimacy of their new living arrangement, but she stood tall. "I can dress casually when I want to."

"I'm glad you did."

He'd kicked back for the evening, too, and if anything, the barefoot cowboy was even more appealing that way. And sexier than ever.

"What's for dinner?" she asked.

"Nothing fancy. Just turkey sandwiches, a tossed salad and chips. I hope that's okay."

"That's fine." In fact, it was perfect. He was perfect. And the friend she'd come to appreciate more than she'd ever expected. "Need some help?"

"Nope. I got it all under control. I thought we'd eat indoors tonight. The sandwiches are made, and the salad is almost done. It'll just be a minute." Steven turned back to add cherry tomatoes to the greens.

Ellie pulled out one of two bar stools, then glanced out onto the patio and into the backyard. The same small white lights twinkled on the trees outside, and yet again she couldn't help but think how the whole scene appeared to be more romantic than it should.

"I've been thinking about the wedding," he said. "We need to set a date, and the sooner the better. What about next Sunday?"

Talk about soon! But he was right. She sighed. "All right. That'll work. But there's so much to do. Where do you suggest we have it?"

"Let's have it here. There's bound to be a few newshounds trying to crash the ceremony, and we can easily step up the security. I'll just add a second guard at the gate that day."

He had a point. A good one.

"There's a large grassy area behind the main

house," he added. "We can rent chairs and a gazebo. It's up to you, though."

"That would be a nice touch, I guess. But I don't want the guest list to get out of hand."

"I can keep my number at a dozen or so," Steven said. "My parents will want to be here, and I'm sure Wiley, Ashley, Megan and Nicole will come with them. Then there's my sister Stephanie and her fiancé, Acton Donovan. And, of course, Dillon, Callum and Becky."

"There aren't too many people I'd need to include. My parents have a lot of friends and coworkers, not to mention my mom's bunco group, but I'll insist that we keep it a family affair. And, of course, Daria. She's like a sister to me."

"And she'll be the maid of honor." Steven reached for a pair of tongs and placed them in the salad bowl.

"Who will you ask to stand up with you?" Ellie asked.

Steven set the bowl on the bar, between the two stools. "If I go with one of my brothers, it would be a hard choice to make. I might ask my dad."

"That's kind of cool."

"I think so. I don't have a favorite brother, although I do have only one father."

Steven set two place mats on the bar, as well as silverware and a couple of napkins. He then took a bottle of water from the fridge and filled two glasses.

"Have you set up a shopping trip yet?"

"I would have done that this evening, but when I was talking to both my mom and Daria, we'd been more focused on avoiding the snoopy reporters. But I'll call the office and let them know I'm taking a few days off work. Hopefully, we can go shopping tomorrow."

"There's a store that sells formal wear at the Shoppes. It'd be nice if you can find a dress there."

To support the store owner, she assumed. And it was a nice thought. "I'd do it, but I don't think I'd be able to afford anything there."

He circled the edge of the bar to take his seat next to her, but he paused for a moment, just inches away, his eyes locked on hers. "Consider the dress my treat."

The offer, as well as the way he was looking at her, sent her senses reeling and her thoughts scampering to keep up. "Stop trying to be so nice."

"Can't help it." He grinned, then winked. "I *am* nice. You'll see."

They remained like that for a moment, bonded by an invisible tie, gazes locked, her heart thumping.

He reached out and cupped her jaw. His thumb skimmed her cheek, caressing her skin. She should stop him, push him away, jump out of her chair and run for the hills. But for the life of her, she couldn't move. As his lips brushed hers, she leaned into him and kissed him back.

His tongue swept into her mouth, and a wave of desire nearly knocked her to the floor. This was not good—the kiss, the desire for more, their current living situation.

Ellie let the heated kiss continue until her brain finally took control over her body, and she drew back. "I'm sorry, Steven. This isn't a good idea. We can't let it happen again."

He raked a hand through his hair, sucked in a deep breath, then slowly let it out. "You're probably right."

Then he winked at her again. "But you have to admit, it was nice."

It had been better than nice. And if things were different, she might be tempted to kiss him again, right here, right now. But the last thing she needed to do was fall for her fake fiancé.

And something told her she was getting too damned close to doing just that.

Chapter Eleven

The next morning, after Ellie dressed for the day and while she was making the bed in the guest room, Steven's deep, mesmerizing voice sounded from the open doorway.

"Becky and Callum made breakfast. Are you hungry?"

She placed the last pillow sham on the bed then turned to the door. "Yes, but I'm a little nervous about facing the troops. What, *exactly*, did you tell them about us?"

"Just that we'd been seeing each other for a while and that we tried to stay under the community's radar. Things got serious, and I asked you to marry me. You agreed, and now the press is hounding us."

"Okay. Got it." They'd touched upon that subject last night, but after they'd kissed, she'd gotten uneasy and made a quick retreat. But it was a new day now. She couldn't very well avoid the issue any longer. Nor could she avoid facing Steven's family.

"Is it okay to tell them about the baby?" he asked.

"We may as well." She rested her hand on her growing belly. "In fact, we really should."

Steven leaned a shoulder against the doorjamb. He'd never looked so handsome, so relaxed, so...

The memory of last night's kiss ricocheted in her mind. Try as she might, she couldn't seem to shake the blood-stirring yearning it provoked, the desire for more.

"I like seeing you do that," Steven said.

She took a step away from the bed, which was now made and a little too inviting, and eased closer to the doorway. It might be time to make another quick exit. "See me do what?"

"Rubbing your stomach like that. Caressing the baby."

The sweet sentiment, along with the appreciative way he studied her, darn near sucked the air from her lungs.

He lifted his hand toward her tummy. "Do you mind...?"

She didn't mind, but the question came as such a surprise that she could hardly speak. When she nodded, he leaned forward, placed a splayed hand on her baby bump and gave it a gentle, almost reverent stroke. Then he withdrew it and shrugged a single shoulder. "I'm sorry. I was…curious. I've never—"

"No," she said, her voice whisper soft, as she placed her own hand where his had been. "It's okay. I understand."

"This might sound lame, but I like seeing the maternal side of you. It adds a whole new dimension to the strong woman I've come to know and admire."

His sincerity, his praise, warmed her heart.

"Just so you know," he said, "I didn't mean to make you feel uncomfortable last night—when I kissed you."

The kiss itself hadn't made her uncomfortable. It was the feelings it stirred up, feelings that had been much too real for a fake engagement. "I got a little uneasy afterward, but it was nice while it was happening."

His head tilted slightly. "It was only *nice*?"

She crossed her arms and shifted her weight to one hip. "That's how you described it."

"I wasn't being entirely honest." He tossed her a playful grin that could easily turn her brain to mush again—if she'd let it. But that kiss had been too hot for comfort.

She couldn't remain in the same small room with the sexy man, close enough to breathe in his woodsy scent, and only a few steps from the bed. "This isn't going to work."

"What isn't?"

"Kissing. Touching. Pretending that we're romantically involved."

"Don't you think people will expect us to be affectionate?"

"In public? Probably. But being affectionate when we're behind closed doors will only make it seem real. And with a divorce on the horizon, we shouldn't complicate things. Right?"

"Good point."

"So you're not going to press for more kissing or touching or…anything more?"

He held up his hand in Boy Scout fashion. "I promise."

"Good." She'd won that round, although she didn't get the usual satisfaction she could expect when coming out on top of a deal. "I'm hungry. Come on. Let's go face the troops."

Steven followed her out of the room. When they reached the foyer, they walked side by side to the large, functional kitchen with state-of-the-art appliances and black marble counters. The warm

aroma of breakfast filled the room, providing tan-
talizing whiffs of fresh-brewed coffee and bacon.

Two adorable toddlers sat in their high chairs,
each of them with a sippy cup in hand. Callum
stood beside them, placing chunks of banana on
their trays, while Becky operated the griddle on
the stove, flipping hotcakes.

Ellie had met Callum's future wife a couple of
times, but only at ribbon-cutting ceremonies. They
really hadn't talked very much, but Ellie found the
brunette with sparkling brown eyes to be sweet
and likable—nice qualities for a nurse.

"Good morning," Steven said from the doorway.

Becky turned and blessed them both with a
warm smile. "Breakfast is almost ready. Can I get
you a cup of coffee, Ellie? We have orange juice,
too."

"OJ sounds good," Ellie said. "Thank you."

"Where's Dillon?" Steven asked Callum.

"He cut out early. Said he had to meet with one
of the suppliers in town."

Steven strode to the cupboard, pulled out a
white mug and poured his own coffee. "Ellie and I
had a chance to talk a little more last night. We decided to get married at the ranch on Sunday. Nothing big or fancy. Just a small, private ceremony."

One of the twins slapped her hand down on the
tray, mashing a banana chunk in the process, and

squealed with glee at the goo on her hand. Her sister grinned and smashed one of her own.

Steven laughed at the messy antics.

"Hey, bro," Callum said, "wait until you have a toddler or two. You might not find their messes so funny."

"I won't have to wait long for that," Steven said. "Ellie's having a baby in August."

At that, Callum's gaze dropped to Ellie's belly, then he cut a furrowed-brow look at Steven. "Your wedding announcement didn't surprise me a bit, but I didn't see *that* coming. Now I can see why you're in a hurry to tie the knot."

"What he means," Becky said, "is that we couldn't be happier for you two—the wedding, the baby and the whole nine yards. Welcome to the family, Ellie."

"She's absolutely right," Callum said. "It's a happy surprise."

"If there's anything I can do," Becky added, "whether it's to help you settle in at the ranch or get ready for the wedding, just let know."

"Thanks." Ellie's cheeks warmed at Becky's kindness, at her obvious acceptance. "I appreciate that."

While the two precious toddlers sat in their high chairs, making quite the mess of their meal, the adults took their seats at the large kitchen table and ate their fill of blueberry pancakes, scrambled eggs and turkey bacon.

Becky chatted about the pleasures of pregnancy and the joys of childbirth, her words more enlightening because of her medical background. She couldn't have been sweeter or more accepting.

Yet the more kindness the couple showed to her, the guiltier Ellie felt. She hated deceiving people who'd welcomed her into their home and family with open arms. But she had to continue to keep up the pretense.

She and Steven were in too deep to do otherwise.

Ellie had made it plain to Steven that she intended their relationship to remain platonic, although he wasn't so sure her hormones agreed with her. His certainly didn't.

He had no intention of breaking his promise not to push for more, but it was killing him. And so were the cold showers.

For the past couple of nights, climbing into bed alone and knowing that Ellie slept just across the hall had been a hell of a lot harder for him to handle than he'd expected. The woman grew prettier and sexier each time he laid eyes on her. And since she'd decided to work remotely, he saw her daily.

He tried to avoid her by spending more time on the jobsite or at the office, but that didn't help. Not when he constantly envisioned her back at the ranch, wandering through his quarters, barefoot, her long hair hanging loose and glossy over her shoulders and down her back. What guy wouldn't be distracted?

And then there was the wedding talk and all the chores. Ellie had sent out a press release two days ago, announcing their engagement and upcoming marriage without providing any details. Then she'd slipped off the property to meet her mom and Daria, who'd taken her to shop in San Antonio so they could avoid the rumor mill in Rambling Rose. Fortunately, they found a dress and ordered the flowers that afternoon.

Steven didn't ask to be included in the shopping trips, but he insisted on taking part in the cake tasting that Picard's Patisserie hosted at the ranch.

Picard outdid himself with the samples he set out on the table in the main kitchen. Then the short, balding baker proudly stood by as Steven, Ellie, Alma, Daria and Becky studied the miniature cakes he'd placed in front of them.

"What's this?" Steven pointed to the most decadent sample.

"That's the Black Forest," Picard said. "It's a chocolate cake with kirsch, whipped cream and topped with tart cherries."

"And this one?" Ellie asked.

"It's a white cake with Grand Marnier flavor and a raspberry buttercream filling."

After a couple of bites, the ladies began to rave about Picard and his cakes, much to the delight of the French baker. Steven wondered if they'd be able to settle on a favorite. At least, until he tasted the last sample in front of him.

"Ellie." He reached for her fork, cut into the small cake and offered her a bite. "Try this."

She opened her mouth, and he gave her a taste. Her eyes lit up. "Oh, yes. This one. I love it."

As she licked the frosting from her lips, Steven forgot about the almond-flavored cake with a filling that tasted like crème brûlée.

All he cared about was Ellie, and getting a sweet taste of her.

The other women quickly agreed that they'd chosen the perfect cake.

Picard happily took the order and promised to deliver it himself on Sunday morning, prior to the ceremony that afternoon.

As far as Steven knew, everything was set. They'd only invited immediate family and a few close friends, but with a few extra additions made here and there, Steven had to call the party-rental people to increase the number of chairs they'd need to deliver.

In the meantime, he'd done a little shopping of his own at his favorite Western-wear shop, picking up a black jacket and slacks as well as a fancy white shirt.

An hour ago, he'd left the office early to pick up his jacket from the tailor. He'd considered going back to work but decided to call it a day and went home instead. Ellie had been spending a lot of time in seclusion, having taken some days off from city hall, and deserved to go out to dinner for a change. So he decided to surprise her.

He entered his living quarters and, finding them quiet and empty, assumed Ellie was with Becky on the other side of the house. So he went to the bedroom, hung his jacket in the closet and kicked off his boots. He'd no more than stepped back into the hallway when the bathroom door opened, and Ellie walked out wrapped in a fluffy white towel.

She gasped and nearly jumped out of her skin. "Oh my gosh. *Steven.* You scared me."

And she mesmerized him. Whether dressed in business attire or rocking a pair of jeans, Ellie Hernandez was a beautiful woman. But wearing only a towel? He couldn't find words to describe her.

"I'm sorry," he said. "I didn't mean to frighten you."

"That's okay. I just didn't expect you. I mean, this is your house." She pointed at the open door to her room, nearly losing her grip on the towel in the process. "I forgot to bring a change of clothes into the bathroom with me…" She studied him for a moment, nearly as closely as he watched her.

"You're making me crazy," he said. And if she dropped the towel, he'd be toast.

She'd told him twice that she was conflicted about kissing or getting too close, even if her body language was giving him a much different spin. Only a jerk would push her now, no matter how badly he wanted to.

"It's not that I don't want to," she added.

"I know. I do, too. But I get it." The political stuff had gotten in the way.

For a moment, a sense of apprehension settled over him. Would making love hurt either of them in the long run?

How could it? They were both going into the fake marriage knowing that it had an ending date. As long as they both kept that in mind, everything would be fine.

Steven might have repeated the rules, but he wasn't a jerk. If they were going to make love, Ellie would have to make the first move, which she apparently was reluctant to do.

He was about to retreat to his bedroom, the living area or even to the stable when she eased toward him.

Was she changing her mind about getting in too deep? He hoped to hell that's what was happening, but he'd made her a promise. And he'd be damned if he'd break it.

She continued to close the gap between them. "This is crazy, Steven."

Yes, it was. The tall, willowy brunette, her dark brown eyes doe-like, was making him nuts. And so was her springtime scent as it burrowed deep in his nostrils, making a memory.

"We're not supposed to do this."

"If it makes you feel better," he said, "everyone already thinks we're lovers. And we'll be married on Sunday afternoon."

"I know, but making love will only complicate things."

"Maybe so." But if she was game, he was. "Our engagement might be fake, but the chemistry between us is the real deal. I don't know about you, but a cold shower isn't going to help me this time."

"Damn you, Steven."

Her lips parted, and he cupped her jaw, his fingers extending to her neck, her hair draping over his knuckles. "Say the word, Ellie, and I'll walk away."

When she didn't raise an objection, he kissed her, deeply and thoroughly, sending a rush of heat through his veins, his blood pounding in need. She swayed slightly then reached for his shoulder to keep her balance.

He didn't feel all that steady himself, so he scooped her into his arms and carried her to his bed, where he laid her down, her long black hair splayed upon the pillow sham, her beautiful body stretched out on top of the matching comforter.

He paused for a beat, drinking in the angelic sight, until a shadow of insecurity crossed her brow.

She placed a hand on her belly and worried her bottom lip. "I'm not usually this...round."

"Don't say that, Ellie. Don't even think it. You're the prettiest, sexiest expectant mother I've ever seen."

She clicked her tongue and all but rolled her eyes. "Oh, come on, Steven. How many pregnant women have you seen naked?"

"Just you. And believe me, I like what I see." He nodded at the bed where she lay. "Do you mind...?"

She rolled to the side, making room for him. And that was the only encouragement he needed. He removed his clothes. All the while, she watched him with passion-glazed eyes—as eager as he was, it seemed, to feel his skin against hers.

With a straining erection evidence of his arousal, he slowly joined her on the bed. Yet as eager as he was to make love with her, he wanted to take it slow and easy, taking his time to please her—and to ensure he didn't do anything that might hurt the baby.

He placed a gentle hand on her belly. "I'll be careful."

"I know you will, but don't worry. You won't hurt me or the baby."

He kissed her again—long and deep. As their bodies pressed together, their hands stroked, caressed, explored until they were both caught up in the throes of passion. His only thought, his only concern was to please her the way she was pleasing him.

His thumb skimmed across her taut nipple, and when her breath caught, he bent his head and took the sweet tip into his mouth, tonguing it, sucking it, until she gripped his shoulders, sending a rush of heat pounding through his blood.

He couldn't seem to get enough of her. Looking. Touching. Tasting. He stroked her skin, so soft. And he studied the flecks of gold in her eyes, saw the desire brewing there. He spotted something else, too. Emotions he'd never seen, never sensed, churned in her gaze. It ought to scare the hell out of him, but it intrigued him, drew him in.

"I hope I'm not sorry about this later," she said, yet her grip on his shoulder didn't ease.

"You won't be," he said. "I'll make sure there's nothing to regret."

He brushed his lips across her brow, holding back, allowing her to change her mind, although it would probably kill him if she did.

"I want you," Ellie said, her voice barely a whisper as she cupped his face with both hands. "I need to feel you inside me."

He didn't want to prolong the foreplay any longer, either. He entered her slowly at first, getting the feel of her, the feel of them. Her body responded to his, and she arched up to meet each of his thrusts. In and out. Taking and giving.

Should he slow the pace, take it a little easier?

Her breath caught, and she gripped his shoulders, her nails pressing into his skin. "Yes. Oh, yes..."

That was all he needed to hear. He increased the tempo until she reached a peak, crying out with her climax and sending him over the edge. He let go, shuddering as he released with her in a sexual explosion that had him seeing stars spinning in the night sky.

He held her close, relishing each wave of pleasure, too overcome to speak. He'd known making love with her would be amazing, but he hadn't expected it to be quite like this.

They'd forged a bond, it seemed, one that most friends never had. And while he meant to keep his promise to her, that he wouldn't let them get in too deep, he had to admit that sex had never felt so good, so right.

The scent of their lovemaking swirled around them as he relished the sweet afterglow. When his heart rate finally began to slow to a normal pace, he rolled to the side, taking her with him. He brushed a strand of hair from her brow and looked down at her.

She smiled leisurely, and he kissed the tip of her nose. "Who would've ever thought that being friends with benefits would be as incredible as this?" he said.

She flinched, then slowly eased out of his embrace.

"What's wrong?" he asked.

"Nothing. Not really. It was definitely good. I just wish we wouldn't have acted on our impulses. There's too much at stake, and I don't want to screw up our friendship."

Then she rolled to the side, grabbed her towel and headed out of the room, messing with his pride and leaving him more than a little bewildered.

Ellie returned to the guest room, snatched the clothes she'd left on the bed and went to the bathroom to freshen up and get dressed. All the while, she kicked herself for being so impulsive.

She was a bright, capable woman who always weighed the options and thought things through. But not today. She'd let sexual attraction and desire run amok. And letting her brain take the back seat had knocked her off balance.

She'd spent years proving that she was a born

leader who could accomplish anything a man could do—and she'd often done it better. But she'd just taken a giant step backward when it came to proving anything.

To make matters worse, not only was Steven an amazing lover, the best she'd ever had, he'd also become a kind and supportive friend, one who'd gone so far as to offer to marry her, just so she could save face.

But friends didn't sleep together. Nor did they stir up the yearnings and romantic feelings Ellie had begun to have. And that left her uneasy and a little disoriented.

The bathroom walls began to close in on her, and all she wanted to do was escape to a quiet place where she could think herself out of the corner she'd just backed into. But where could she go? Reporters and bloggers were just waiting to pounce on her, so she would probably end up driving around town until she came up with a better game plan.

After running a brush through her hair and applying some lip gloss, she slipped into a pale green T-shirt and a pair of black yoga pants, her baby belly stretching the waistband to the limit. She opened the bathroom door and stepped into the hall, only to find Steven standing there, shirtless and wearing a pair of jeans, the top button undone. She stopped dead in her tracks, like a possum facing an oncoming car in the street, heart pounding and having nowhere to run.

Guilt and insecurity—feelings she rarely, if ever, experienced—slammed into her.

"Ellie," he said, his voice soft yet husky. "What's wrong?"

Nothing.

Everything.

It's hard to put it into words.

"We need to talk," he said.

He was probably right, but not now. Not until she'd had some time to think. And not until he put on a shirt and covered that broad chest and those taut abs.

She looked everywhere but at him. "There's not much to say. I shouldn't have let that happen. I wasn't thinking clearly." She still wasn't. Making love with Steven had jumbled every thought in her head.

What's worse, it had messed with her heart, too.

He folded his arms across his bare chest, not nearly hiding it from view, and shifted his weight to one hip. "Didn't you enjoy what we just did?"

Her cheeks warmed, and she winced. He had to have heard her moaning softly, had to have realized she'd connected deeply with him as he'd climaxed along with her. If she told him she hadn't taken any pleasure in their lovemaking, he'd know she was lying.

"I enjoyed it as much as you did, but that's not the point." She combed her fingers through her hair, snagging a nail on a tangle she'd failed to brush out. Why hadn't she taken the time to pull it into a neat, tidy bun? Her brain worked better when she dressed professionally, and her words came much easier.

But she'd be darned if she could sound the least bit coherent while the man she'd just made love with stood half-naked in front of her. But she may as well spit it out. "Making love, as good as it was, only makes things worse. This is supposed to be a fake engagement, Steven. We had an agreement, and what we just did makes it feel more real."

"We're both consenting adults. What's wrong with acting on the attraction that's been brewing between us?"

He had a point, but she was about to make another romantic mistake, this one worse than the one she'd made with Mike, because it could lead to heartbreak—*hers* and obviously not his.

Steven opened his arms, clearly expecting her to walk into his embrace, to lay her head on his shoulder, but she couldn't seem to move. The Rambling Rose mayor insisted that she stand firm, while the child who lived within, the frightened little girl who'd once had to fend for herself in a run-down apartment, urged her to go to him, to accept the comfort he offered.

But Ellie no longer needed anyone to rescue her. Nor did she let people take care of her, like Steven had been doing the past couple of weeks. His compassion appeased the inner child, but it flustered the hell out of the city leader.

Steven wasn't giving up, nor did he lower his arms, but their face-off didn't last long. For some damned reason, she couldn't resist him. She eased forward and stepped into his embrace, accepting his comfort, just as she'd done when he'd offered his hospitality and friendship.

As she breathed in his woodsy scent, as his strong, warm arms enveloped her, she couldn't seem to absorb the peace and security she needed, and the whole fake marriage idea seemed more ludicrous than ever.

How could she only pretend to be in love with Steven when she was falling in love with him for real? And to make matters worse, she felt awful about misleading people, deceiving them.

Especially him.

Steven held her close and caressed her back. When he whispered, his warm breath stirred her hair. "Feeling better now?"

"A little." But not nearly enough.

He pressed a kiss against her temple, which helped a wee bit more. "Then I'll hold you until you're back on track and ready to tackle the world again."

Would she ever be back to normal? There was a big struggle going on in her brain. Love versus friendship. Right versus wrong. Truth versus lies.

She knew what she needed to do. Her parents had taught her well.

It's always best to tell the truth. It's easier to keep your story straight.

Papa's words echoed in her head, spurring her on, telling her exactly how to proceed.

"This whole marriage thing has gotten way out of hand," she said.

"The wedding is on Sunday, Ellie. It's too late to backpedal now. But I don't think that's the only thing troubling you."

He was right. But did she dare admit that she no longer knew the woman she'd become? That she was uneasy about being pregnant with another man's baby, caught up in a marriage of convenience and falling for a fake fiancé who thought sex was only meant for fun?

But their ruse had gathered too much steam already. The flowers and cake had been ordered. Steven's family from Florida was flying into San Antonio on Saturday evening. Mama had bought the perfect dress.

And so had Daria, who should be saving her money rather than spending it. Even Papa had gotten on board sooner than anyone had expected him to and had asked a guy he knew to play the guitar during the ceremony.

No, Steven was right. It was too late to do anything about it now. Not unless she wanted to turn a big mistake into one hot mess.

Chapter Twelve

Last night, at a quiet dinner party in the main part of the house, Steven had introduced Ellie to his parents, brother and sisters who'd traveled from Florida to attend the wedding. Ellie had been a little nervous about meeting them, but she shouldn't have been. They'd been nothing but kind, friendly and accepting.

David Fortune, who'd made millions in the video game industry, had silver-streaked hair and wore wire-rimmed glasses. The tall, well-dressed man appeared to be a little nerdy, but he was friendly and seemed genuinely happy about the wedding.

His wife, Marci, was an attractive woman in her mid-fifties. She seemed a bit shy and reserved, but greeted Ellie with a warm smile. "It's nice to meet you. I wish David and I could stay longer than a couple of days. But we'll be back to visit in the upcoming months. We're looking forward to getting to know you."

Wiley, Steven's younger brother who'd also been adopted by David, had arrived on the same flight. The triplets, however, were moving to Rambling Rose, so they'd rented a trailer and driven out. With the restaurant opening in May, the three sisters were eager to get settled so they could oversee the construction of Provisions, the trendy new eatery, and make sure it was built to their specifications. At twenty-three years old, they were pretty young to be taking on such a big project, but they seemed to know what they were doing.

The triplets were also identical, with straight blonde hair, blue eyes and nicely curving figures. Their parents and siblings had no problem telling them apart, but Ellie doubted if she'd ever be able to do so. Even though they'd had on different outfits last night, she'd still had trouble remembering who was wearing what.

"Megan, Nicole and I would like to hang with you guys this evening," Ashley had said about twenty minutes after their arrival, "but we need to unpack. We have a lot to do in the morning."

They would be busy, all right. Steven had asked them to whip up an after-wedding meal, and they'd jumped at the chance to show off their cooking skills.

It hadn't taken long for Ellie to decide that she liked Steven's family, and the evening had gone well. They'd wholeheartedly welcomed her into the fold, wishing her and Steven a lifetime of happiness, which left her feeling awkward and guilty. How would they feel when they learned the marriage wouldn't last?

Still, the sun came up on Sunday morning, and the wedding plans began to take shape.

At three o'clock, Ellie stood at the open sliding door and scanned the lawn, where the wedding guests sat in white rental chairs, facing the gazebo that had been adorned with greenery and yellow roses.

Papa stood on the patio, waiting to walk her down the grassy aisle, his brown eyes glistening as if holding back tears. "You make a beautiful bride, *mija*," he told her when she made her way out to him. "I always knew you would."

"Thank you, Papa." She kissed his cheek. "You look so handsome in that new suit. You're the perfect father of the bride."

"I wasn't so perfect at first. I'm sorry I wasn't more supportive."

"That's okay. I should have come to you and Mama months ago. I'm sorry, too."

"That's all behind us, *mija*." He nodded toward the gazebo, where the ceremony would take place. "Wiley walked your mother down the aisle and escorted her to our seats in the front row. And Daria's taken her place up front, although I can't believe you let her bring that dog, let alone walk him down the aisle on a leash."

Ellie smiled. "Don't you think Tank looks cute with that yellow Western bandanna tied around his neck?"

Papa clucked his tongue, but not in a disapproving way. "At least he matches the wedding party."

"He should," Ellie said. "He's a part of it."

Papa offered his arm. "Are you ready to do this?"

No. She wasn't at all ready. She wanted to bolt, to run for the hills and escape. But when she looked at the man who'd rescued her from foster care and provided her with affection, a happy home and everything a child could ever need, tears filled her eyes. "I love you, Papa. I don't know how to thank you for all you and Mama have done for me."

He pressed a kiss on her brow. "You've already thanked us by growing up to be a beautiful young woman with a heart for your family and for the community."

As they started across the yard to the grassy aisle, Ellie looked at the gazebo. The yellow roses that adorned it were pretty, but she'd chosen the color that represented friendship. At least there was one wedding prop that reflected truth and reality.

She glanced at the yellow rosebuds in her bouquet, another reminder of the bittersweet situation she'd agreed to, the fake union she was about to take part in.

Her heart stalled for a moment, then it began to rumble, sending a rush of adrenaline coursing through her veins.

She ought to stop the madness here and now. Yet she pressed her lips together and clutched Papa's arm as if it might be the only thing keeping her on the straight and narrow.

As they took the short walk from the house to the grassy aisle, the guitarist began to strum an instrumental melody. Mama stood, and the wedding guests got to their feet, too. Ellie did her best to smile, while she focused on the gazebo, where Pastor Ecklund, a short, gray-haired man with a ruddy complexion, stood front and center, facing her with a happy smile.

Daria, who'd chosen a floral-print sundress with a yellow background, stood to the minister's right, with Tank sitting at her feet, the Western bandanna giving the black pup a splash of color.

Steven and his father stood on the minister's left. David Fortune looked classy in his dark suit and yellow boutonniere. But it was Steven, who'd never looked more handsome in his black Western jacket and slacks, white shirt, and bolo tie, who drew her full attention. When an appreciative smile crossed his face, a bevy of butterflies took flight in her tummy.

What were they doing? Was there any way to stop the madness before it was too late?

"Who gives this woman away?" Pastor Ecklund asked.

"Her mother and I," Papa said as he handed her off to Steven.

The two of them turned to face the minister. They'd asked him to keep things short and sweet. And he did just that. In a matter of minutes, they'd made the vows they'd never keep—to love each other, for better, for worse, for richer, for poorer, in sickness and in health...as long as they both should live.

Tears sprung to Ellie's eyes. People would think they were tears of joy, rather than sorrow. Because she actually meant the vows she spoke.

"If anyone here has a reason why these two shouldn't be married," Pastor Ecklund said, "speak now or forever hold your peace."

Ellie had a reason. A big one. This wasn't a marriage based on love. It was based on a lie, and it would end in divorce. Should she speak now? This was her chance—the last one she'd have.

Her lips parted to object, but when she looked at Steven, when she saw the radiant smile on his face and the sparkle that lit up his blue eyes, the words wouldn't form.

"I now pronounce you man and wife," Pastor Ecklund said.

Like any loving, eager groom, Steven took her in his arms and blessed her lips with a sweet, husbandly kiss, ending the ceremony.

As far as anyone knew, the wedding had turned out to be everything a bride could hope for.

Too bad it had all been a sham.

After the ceremony, the bride and groom greeted their guests together, thanking them for their support and good wishes. Then they split up to mingle separately.

There'd been times when Steven had wished that he hadn't proposed to Ellie as a way to help her avoid a sticky political situation. But that wasn't because he had any regrets himself. Ellie, however, seemed to be plagued with them, and he hated to see her so uneasy. He'd thought making love the other night would have made her feel better, but she claimed it had made things worse.

He supposed that's why he felt compelled to stick so close to her during the reception. Even now, as he stood off to the side with his brothers and dad, he was so damned focused on the bride that he was having a difficult time following the conversation.

His father made a comment, and his brothers laughed. Steven managed to smile and nod as if he'd actually heard him speak and caught the joke.

As a man who'd always tried hard to earn the name he shared with Callum and Dillon, he usually listened intently and carried his own weight in a family conversation. But he couldn't seem to do that today.

He scanned the yard again and spotted Ellie talking to Daria, that goofy little pup tethered to a yellow leash and sniffing at the grass. Both the women wore smiles, so he assumed Ellie was holding up okay.

"Steven," his father said, finally drawing his full attention. "You did well."

At what? Was he talking about business? If he questioned his dad, everyone would know he'd been lost in thought. And he wasn't about to explain why.

"Ellie isn't just bright," his father added, "she's beautiful, too. You picked a good one. I hope you'll both be as happy as your mother and I are."

"Thanks," Steven said, his gaze returning to

his bride, who was a vision in her white dress, one she'd chosen because it only revealed a hint of her baby bump.

"I'm a little surprised that you didn't buy her an engagement ring," his dad said. "You found time to pull of a beautiful wedding in record time. You even went so far as to buy a plain gold band."

"Ellie wanted something simple."

His father's head tilted, and his brow creased. "She doesn't seem like a keep-it-simple gal to me."

She wasn't. She was beautifully complex, and she deserved an engagement ring, even if the marriage didn't last. "I'm going to surprise her with a diamond at Christmas," he said.

Would they still be married then? He'd once thought so, but after the past few days, he wasn't so sure. She might be smiling and wearing white, but she was still on edge, still uneasy. That's why he hadn't let her out of his sight.

He'd actually suggested they go on a honeymoon, which would have given them a good reason to cut out early, but Ellie said that was out of the question. She'd been away from city hall for too long as it was. In fact, she planned to return to the office tomorrow morning. Hopefully, she was ready to face the press.

Neither of them mentioned the wedding night, but Steven looked forward to having one. They hadn't made love since the first time, but he couldn't see why she'd object.

Either way, he'd like to take her away from the crowd. But that would have to wait. Ashley, Megan and Nicole were in the main kitchen, putting the finishing touches on the post-wedding meal, which was yet to come, along with the cake.

"If you'll excuse me," Steven told his father and brothers, "I'm going to get something to drink. It's been a long day."

As he strode toward the portable bar the rental company had set up, he scanned the yard again.

Ellie and Daria still stood off to the side, away from most of the wedding guests and talking quietly. He liked Daria, and she'd proven to be a good friend to Ellie, the perfect maid of honor, it seemed.

Manny, the family cook and caretaker, approached the bar and stood beside Steven. "Nice wedding."

"Thanks."

"What can I get you?" the attractive blond bartender asked.

"I'll have a glass of red wine," Manny said.

The bartender reached for a bottle of the Mendoza Winery merlot. "And what'll you have, Mr. Fortune?"

"A cold beer."

While he waited, Steven glanced over his shoulder and saw his sister Stephanie approach Ellie and Daria. Funny, but instead of returning to his dad and his brothers, he'd much rather join that conversation.

As Ellie and Daria chatted, Stephanie Fortune approached them. The pretty blonde seemed to glow with excitement over her engagement to Acton Donovan. From what Ellie had heard, she and Acton had recently announced that they'd be having a baby soon.

Stephanie zeroed in on Tank. "Would you look at that sweet puppy. He looks so cute wearing that yellow bandanna." She stooped to give the rascally pup a scratch behind the ears. "How're you doing, buddy? I'm so glad you found a good home."

"He certainly did," Ellie told her new sister-in-law. "He's a little spoiled and can be a rascal at times, but he's sweet and lovable. He's also doubled in size since Daria adopted him."

Stephanie straightened just as Becky approached them with a grin. "What's going on over here?"

Ellie had come to like Callum's wife and tossed her a smile. "Not much. Just a little girl talk. Please join us."

"It was a lovely wedding," Becky said. "And you rock that wedding dress."

"Thank you." Ellie's hand lifted to her belly, but she caught herself before drawing any attention to her baby bump.

Becky turned to Stephanie. "How're you holding up? I know it hasn't been easy."

A wisp of sadness crossed the vet assistant's face. "Okay, I guess. I miss baby Linus."

"Baby Linus?" Ellie asked.

"He's the baby Stephanie fostered," Becky said. "During the grand opening of the pediatric center, a woman named Laurel went into premature labor. She was stabilized, and Dr. Green sent her to the hospital in San Antonio to deliver, because they have a NICU. Then, not even a month later, Laurel left Linus on the doorstep of the pediatric center with a note that mentioned keeping her child safe and something about finding his rightful home at Fortune's Foundling Hospital."

Ellie furrowed her brow. "But the foundling home isn't there anymore. You'd think everyone would know that. In fact, Steven purchased an old scrapbook at Mariana's Market that has a newspaper article in it about the hospital and its closing."

"Apparently Laurel wasn't thinking clearly," Becky said.

Stephanie rubbed her tummy, much the way Ellie found herself doing these days and, in a wistful voice, said, "I loved that baby."

"I know you did." Becky placed a gentle hand on Stephanie's shoulder. "I'm so sorry you had to let him go."

Stephanie's eyes filled with tears. "It's weird,

though. Laurel had implied that Eric, the father, wouldn't be pleased about the baby, but he was actually thrilled. I wasn't prepared for that. And it broke my heart to let him go."

"You'll never forget that sweet baby," Becky said, "but at least you and Acton will have one of your own soon."

Stephanie sniffled, blinked back her tears and offered a wistful smile. "That's true."

"Whatever happened to Laurel?" Ellie asked.

Stephanie shrugged. "We may never know. The authorities haven't been able to find her. And I hate to say it, but I don't have a good feeling about her disappearance."

Ellie cringed at the thought of a baby being abandoned and of something happening to the young mother, even if things seemed to have turned out okay in the long run.

"How's Linus doing?" Becky asked. "Have you talked to Eric?"

"Yes, I have. And to be honest, I'm a little worried."

"Why?" Becky asked.

"Eric thinks Linus isn't growing fast enough."

"That could be due to his prematurity," Becky said.

Stephanie sighed. "Maybe so. I sure hope that's all it is."

So did Ellie. Compared to what Baby Linus had been through, and whatever his birth mother had gone through or might still be going through Ellie's worries about her own situation paled. And it seemed to put things back into perspective. Ellie had her health. She also had a loving family and loyal friends. And she would soon have a baby to hold and to love. She and Steven may have entered a fake marriage, but Baby George was real.

For the first time since learning she was pregnant, she decided not to worry about what people might think or what the press might print. Nor did she care if the community learned that she'd entered a fake marriage with a man who only wanted to be friends.

She stole a glance across the lawn and spotted Steven near the bar, holding a long-neck bottle of beer. As he talked to the bartender, an attractive blonde in her late twenties or early thirties he laughed at something she said, and a twinge of jealousy gripped Ellie.

On the outside, he might look like a happy groom. But he was rich, handsome and still single at heart.

She should be thankful for his friendship, as well as his efforts to help her face her parents and the community. And she was. But she'd fallen head over heart for a man who didn't love her. Not the way a real husband should.

This was supposed to be a happy day, and dammit, Ellie would force herself to look on the bright side—and there was one.

After all, she told herself, *it's not about me. Nor is it about Steven.*

Right now, the only thing that mattered was the very real little boy she'd be bringing into the world in four and a half months. And she could certainly be happy about that.

Chapter Thirteen

For a fake wedding that had been pulled together in record time, the ceremony, as well as the entire afternoon and evening, had turned out a lot nicer than Ellie had expected it to. And even more surprising, the Fortunes not only had welcomed her into the fold, they'd accepted her parents as well.

The two families, one ultra wealthy from Fort Lauderdale and the other blue collar from Rambling Rose, had very little in common, yet they seemed to hit it off.

If they hadn't, and the laughter and friendly conversations had only been for show, then they were better actors than the bride and groom.

The triplets had put on an amazing wedding dinner that included lobster and filet mignon. Nicole, the self-taught sous chef, was every bit as talented as Steven had said she was. And Ellie had no doubt that Provisions, their restaurant, would be popular and jam-packed once it opened in May.

In fact, the wedding had gone so well that Ellie could almost believe their marriage would last. That was, if Steven were to fall in love with her. If he didn't, then the divorce they'd planned to get in the future was the only option.

By the time the evening festivities wrapped up, Ellie had been ready to retreat to the guest room and call it a day. But before she could start down the hall, Steven had tossed her a dazzling, sexy smile, and her energy level rose.

"Your bed or mine?" he'd asked.

She hesitated, but only for a moment. "Yours."

He took her hand and led her to his room, where he stopped near the bed. He cupped her face with both hands and kissed her softly. Then he reached up and unpinned her once elegant twist, letting her hair tumble down, over her shoulders.

She turned her back to him and, using her right hand, she swept the loose tresses to one side, giving him access to the buttons. "I'm going to need some help."

"That would be a pleasure." He slowly and deliberately undid each tiny pearl button. When the fabric gapped, he pressed a kiss on her shoulder, his breath warm against her skin. Then he helped her remove the gown.

Wearing only a pair of white lace panties and a matching bra, she turned to face him again. Their eyes fixed on each other as they removed the last of their clothing, one piece at a time.

When they were both naked, Ellie couldn't help scanning her husband's handsome face, his broad shoulders and taut abs. Steven Fortune was a hottie on any given day of the week. But standing naked, just steps from his bed, he was an arousing sight to behold.

When he opened his arms, she stepped into his embrace—skin to skin, her breasts pressed against his chest.

He kissed her deeply, thoroughly, as if this was a real wedding night, as if she was his real bride and he was her groom. His tongue swept into her mouth, meeting her own, twisting, dipping, tasting with a hunger that couldn't be sated with a kiss.

As if sensing her need, her desire, Steven lifted her in his arms and laid her on top of his bed. He joined her, and they took up where they'd left off—tongues mating, breaths mingling, hearts racing, hands seeking and caressing.

A thrill of excitement shivered through her, and an empty ache settled deep in her core.

"I want you," she said. She needed him, too.

And even though the events leading up to today had been based on a lie, her words were true, her hunger undeniable.

As he hovered over her, ready to give her what she asked for, yet not all that she wanted, she opened for him. He entered her, filling her, pleasing her with each thrust, each stroke.

Yet at the same time, she held back, afraid to put her heart and soul into their lovemaking.

How could she give him her all, when their wedding night wasn't real, and their marriage wouldn't last?

He drove into her, and she arched up, again and again until they both reached a peak. She let go, and they came together in a glorious, star-bursting climax that nearly knocked the earth off its axis.

Ellie didn't dare speak, didn't dare move, as they lay amid tangled sheets, the scent of their lovemaking in each breath they took. Even as her world seemed to right itself, she lay cradled in his arms, her head resting on his chest, his hand on her hip.

Making love had been good, but the something she'd held back had been missing.

If Steven sensed anything was off, he didn't say. He might have assumed that she was exhausted from a long, stressful week. And that was certainly true because she fell asleep and didn't wake up until morning.

Ellie hadn't set an alarm, but she hadn't needed to. The sunlight peeking through the shutter slats woke her at eight. After a stretch and a yawn, she climbed out of bed and padded to the bathroom, where she showered and got ready for the day. She dressed in her favorite business suit, although this was the last day she'd be wearing it for a while. Her belly felt as if it had doubled in size in the last week.

She wasn't sure when Steven left. He'd said he had an early meeting at the Paz job site. Dillon was concerned the building might not pass the electrical inspection, so they'd called in the foreman and one of the contractors to discuss the problem.

Before leaving the privacy and comfort of Steven's living quarters, she fixed a healthy breakfast of yogurt, granola and fruit. Then she headed to the foyer to let herself out.

"Ellie?" Steven's mother called out from the main part of the house. "Is that you?"

Her steps slowed just short of the front door. "Yes, Marci. It's me."

The sweet, middle-aged woman approached with a coffee cup in hand. "I was hoping I'd get to see you before you left for work."

Ellie's radar went on high alert. Things had been almost too perfect over the last twenty-four hours, so she waited for the other shoe to drop.

"Is something wrong?" she asked.

"No, not at all. I just wanted to let you know how nice it is to see my son so happy. And so much in love."

Marci reached out, took Ellie's hand in hers and gave it a gentle squeeze. A warm smile brightened her face. "We wouldn't have missed your special day for the world, honey. I'm just sorry we have to return to Florida this afternoon. I'd love to get to know you better. But don't worry. I'm sure we'll be back soon. I can't wait to get to know the twins better. Aren't they precious?"

"They sure are."

"And I suspect Stephanie and Acton will be getting married soon." Marci burst into a rosy-cheeked, bright-eyed smile. "Can you believe it? They'll be having a baby, too. I can't wait to go home to my friends and boast about my grand-children."

Accepting Stephanie's child was a given. But would Marci accept Ellie's son as easily and un-conditionally as she had Becky's daughters? That was, if her marriage to Steven lasted more than a few months.

Ellie liked to think that Marci would. Taking care not to bump the cup in the older woman's hand, she gave Steven's mother a hug and thanked her again. "Have a safe flight home, Marci."

"Thank you, honey. Have a good day."

Ellie let herself out of the house and headed

to her car. Twenty minutes later, she arrived at city hall and parked in her reserved space. She'd no more than entered the building when a short, heavyset reporter rushed to her.

"Mayor Hernandez," the reporter asked, "rumor has it you and Steven Fortune got married over the weekend. Any truth to that?"

Ellie answered without slowing her pace. "Yes, that's true. We had a small wedding yesterday. Just family and a few close friends were there."

Undaunted, the reporter lifted his iPhone, no doubt wanting a picture, and dogged her through the spacious lobby. "Is it true that you're expecting a baby? And that you're already five months along?"

The question struck a low blow, and while Ellie wanted to breeze right past the guy and enter the privacy of her office, the time had come to face facts and the community at large.

She stopped abruptly, turned and faced him, just as the camera flashed. "Steven and I are looking forward to the birth of our son in mid-August."

The camera flashed again, but she ignored it and strode to the reception desk, where Iris sat, taking in the scene. "Do I have any messages?"

"Yes, three of them." The receptionist reached for several pink slips that sat next to the While You Were Out pad. "Gosh, Ellie—I mean, Mayor Hernandez—I had no idea you were dating Mr.

Fortune until just recently. Things sure happened fast between you. I'm surprised you were able to keep your relationship a secret."

Ellie stiffened. "My personal life is none of your business, Iris. And if you'd like to keep your job, you'd better remember that."

The nosy receptionist let out a little gasp. "I'm sorry. I didn't mean to overstep."

Yeah. Right. Ellie snatched her messages and continued to her office. Unfortunately, Iris wasn't the only one who'd be making assumptions and doing the math. But it was too damned late to worry about that now.

As the days passed, there'd been mixed reactions to Ellie's announcement about her marriage and the upcoming birth of her son. Her Q ratings had never been higher. And from what she'd heard, most of her constituents considered her and Steven to be local celebrities and an attractive couple. Those were the friends, colleagues and townspeople who embraced the news and considered the wedding and the upcoming birth of her son to be blessed events. But there was still a vocal minority who believed that she'd sold out.

At times, Ellie had to agree with them. Not that she'd compromised her principles when it came to her position as the Rambling Rose mayor. In that respect, she never wavered and continued to look out for the city's best interests. But when it came to her personal life, it was a completely different story.

Against her better judgment, she'd married a man who didn't love her, a decision that betrayed every marital value she espoused.

On the outside, things seemed to be working out okay. She and Steven were more than compatible in bed. On top of that, he was kind, considerate and fun to talk to. She had to admit he was the best fake husband ever, and with each passing day, she grew to love him more. But he hadn't given her any reason to believe that his feelings for her had changed at all, and Ellie couldn't continue in a relationship like that. It was time to confront him and ask how long he intended to keep up the charade, the pretext. Did he expect them to remain friends and lovers indefinitely? Or had something changed between them?

If he couldn't give her the right answers, the ones she hoped to hear, then she would just have to make it easy on them both.

That morning, while Steven brewed a pot of coffee before leaving for one of the job sites, Ellie appeared in the small kitchen. "I'm glad you haven't left yet."

"Hey, you're up early." He turned and blessed her with a bright-eyed grin. "It's only five o'clock, and the sun isn't even up yet."

"I need to talk to you, and I didn't want to wait until this evening."

"All right. What do you want to talk about?"

"About us. Our marriage." They'd spent nights making love and falling asleep in each other's arms. Surely she wasn't the only one who felt it, who cherished it.

"There's not much to talk about," he said, as he removed a disposable heat-resistant cup from the pantry and filled it with coffee. "I'm happy."

She folded her arms across her chest. "What does that mean?"

He placed the lid on top of his to-go cup and snapped it in place. "It means I like having you here. I'm comfortable with the situation and I'm not in a hurry to do anything differently."

"You're *comfortable*?" she asked.

He set the cup back on the counter and turned to face her. "You're not?"

Ellie didn't like words that translated to mediocre, words like *nice* and *comfortable*. She'd always been an overachiever and never settled for just so-so.

"No," she said, "I'm having a problem with it."

"Wow. I didn't see that coming. You aren't happy?"

"It's not that. It's just that I don't like facing an uncertain future. I need to know what to expect and how to plan for it. And I don't have any idea how long this relationship will last."

"You're thinking too hard," he said.

"That's what I do, Steven. I think. I plan. I make lists and follow them to a T. I don't like open-ended solutions."

"If you're worried that I'll back out on our agreement, don't be. I have no intention of break-ing it." He reached for her hand, lifted it to his lips and kissed her fingers. "I'm not going anywhere."

Maybe not yet. But how long would he stick around?

When she didn't respond, he released her hand and furrowed his brow. "Now I'm getting worried. Do you want out? Are you ready to end things?"

Not if he loved her. But the unspoken words twisted her heart into a knot, and she opted to provide him with a half-truth. "No, I'm not ready for it to end."

"Good." He swept her into his arms and gave her a quick kiss.

She kissed him back, although as far as she was concerned, it felt a little cool. A little stiff.

Apparently he hadn't noticed, because he re-leased her, turned back to the counter and picked up his cup as if nothing had happened, as if noth-ing was wrong.

She'd try to do the same thing by pretending that they were back on an even keel, which wasn't easy to do when the small boat she seemed to be riding on was being tossed to and fro, making her seasick.

"What do you have planned today?" Steven asked.

"I have to go to city hall this morning, and this afternoon I have a doctor's appointment."

"Is your mother going with you again?"

"Not this time."

He seemed to think about her answer.

She felt compelled to ask if he wanted to go with her, but why would he? She wasn't his real wife. And she wasn't having *his* baby.

"I have another meeting," he said. "This one is at Provisions. So I'd better get on the road."

That must've been where his mind was just moments ago.

"I'll talk to you later," he added.

She nodded, but she wasn't so sure they had any more to talk about. He'd made his feelings clear, even if he hadn't come right out and admitted it. He liked being her friend and lover. But that was it.

And she couldn't go on this way much longer. She'd eventually blurt out her feelings and voice her regret.

Still, just as she'd done every workday since she'd moved in with him, she followed him to the foyer, where he gave her a kiss goodbye. "I'll see you tonight," he told her. "Don't worry about dinner. I'll pick up something in town and bring it home."

She nodded, although dinner was the last thing on her mind. And so was spending another night at the Fame and Fortune Ranch. Against all odds, she'd fallen in love with a man who considered their marriage a temporary arrangement.

It wasn't Steven's fault, though. They'd made a deal, and he was sticking to it. How could she be angry at him for doing everything he'd said he would do?

She was the one who'd changed the rules. But that didn't mean she had to continue playing the game.

As she walked back to their living quarters— or rather, to Steven's living quarters—she placed her hand on her belly. Did she really want to drag her baby into a situation like this?

No, she did not. And she'd be insane to continue the ruse. She had to end things with Steven, and the sooner she did so, the better. She'd always prided herself on her honesty. But what a laugh that was. She'd been deceiving everyone she'd come into contact with for months, but no one more than herself.

She returned to the bedroom and packed her things. Before dragging her suitcase, garment bags and canvas tote out to the car, she stopped at the small desk in Steven's room, opened the drawer and pulled out a pen and paper.

A personal conversation was probably in order, but she could spell out her feelings on paper much easier than she could say them to his face. So she wrote a note to explain why she was leaving. Then she left it on the kitchen table, where he would be sure to see it as soon as he got home.

Tears welled in Ellie's eyes as she drove back to town, her suitcase and bags in the trunk, her wedding dress in the back seat. As badly as she wanted to hurry home so she could vent to Daria and lick her wounds, she drove straight to her parents' house instead.

She'd been lying to the two people who loved her more than anyone else in the world. And her mom and dad deserved better from her. They'd proven their love and loyalty for years, and it was high time she trusted them enough to admit her mistakes and share her heartache.

What was wrong with her? Why had it taken her so long to figure it out? She'd never wanted to disappoint them, but she had. And worse yet, she'd disappointed herself.

As the tears streamed down her cheeks, she swiped at them with the back of her hand and continued to drive to the one place in town where everything was familiar—the white clapboard church on the corner, the elementary school she'd attended, the park where she used to play.

She turned down the tree-lined drive and continued to the three-bedroom home in which she'd grown up. Her father's old green pickup and her mother's sedan were parked in the driveway, which meant she could face them both in one fell swoop.

After parking at the curb, she took a moment to study the well-manicured lawn, the colorful flowers that lined the walkway. Then she got out of the car and headed for the front porch. Birds chirped in the treetops, announcing that winter was over and spring had come to bring new life and hope.

Ellie knocked lightly on the door, then let herself in. "Mama? Papa? It's me."

"We're in the kitchen," her mother said. "We slept in this morning, so we're having a late breakfast. Come join us."

Ellie crossed the warm, cozy living room, taking note of the mantel over the redbrick fireplace that still displayed several framed photographs of her as a child and one of her in her cap and gown at her college graduation. That was just another sign of her parents' deep love for her.

As she entered the kitchen, she found her mother frying bacon and scrambling eggs while her father sat at the table sipping coffee and reading the sports page.

"This is a nice surprise," Mama said as she

removed the frying pan from the flame. When she turned and faced Ellie, her smile faded, and a frown took its place. "You've been crying, honey. What's the matter?"

"It's a long, complicated story," Ellie said. "And I need to get it off my chest."

Her father pulled out a chair. "Have a seat, *mija*. Your mother and I have all day."

Ellie wasn't sure where to begin, but if she intended to level with her parents, she'd have to start with Mike. So she told them about the mistake she'd made in thinking he was family material, only to find out the hard way that he wasn't. She admitted that he'd fathered her baby. And then she'd shared his coldhearted response to the news.

"Was Steven angry when he found out you were pregnant with Mike's baby?" Mama asked. "Is that why you're crying?"

"He knew. And it didn't bother him."

"Then I don't understand why you're upset," Papa said. "Are you afraid the press will find out that Steven isn't the father?"

Ellie blew out a sigh. "I don't even care about that. Not anymore."

Mama poured herself a cup of coffee and took a seat at the table. "Then why are you so unhappy?"

"Steven is my friend, and he asked me to marry him so that I could save face in the community. And, like a fool, I agreed to do it, even though I knew it would end up being one more mistake in the long run."

"You married a man you didn't love?" Mama asked.

"I went into the agreement thinking of Steven as my friend, but then I fell in love with him. Unfortunately, he doesn't feel the same way about me. And I can't keep living like that, pretending that the marriage is real and that my new husband fathered my baby." An ache settled in Ellie's chest, and tears filled her eyes again.

"Pastor Ecklund is an ordained minister," Papa said. "You might not feel like the marriage is real, but like it or not, you and Steven are legally wed."

"I know, and that complicates the matter. When this stupid charade started, we agreed to get a quiet, amicable divorce after the baby was born. But under the circumstances, I think it's best if we split up now."

"And Steven's okay with that?" Mama asked.

"Why wouldn't he be? He's not the one who will have to face the press and explain to the community that he lied to them." Ellie shot a glance at Papa, then at Mama. "Worse than that, I lied to you. And I'm so sorry. I hope you'll forgive me."

"Of course we will. At least you're being truthful now." Mama reached out and patted the top of Ellie's hand. "It won't be easy being a single mom and raising a child on your own, but your father and I will stand by you every step of the way."

"Thanks, Mama. You have no idea how much I appreciate that."

"Your mother's right," Papa said. "You mean the world to us, *mija*. And so does that little boy. Just tell us how we can best support you."

Ellie blew out a sigh as another onslaught of tears began to slide down her cheeks. "I'll let you know when I figure it out. In the meantime, people are going to talk. If anyone asks why I left Steven, just tell them that it didn't work out."

For once, she'd be telling the truth. Things hadn't worked out, even though Ellie wished with all her heart that they had.

Chapter Fourteen

"What a day," Steven muttered as he drove back to the ranch. It started early and ended late, but it had been productive. The spa building had passed its final inspection, which meant the grand opening was still on track.

After leaving the office, he stopped by Peking Palace and picked up Chinese takeout. He wasn't sure what dishes Ellie liked, so he ordered a variety from the menu. They'd end up having leftovers for days, but that didn't matter.

By the time he arrived at the ranch, the sun had nearly set. Ellie's car wasn't parked in her usual spot, but he didn't think anything of it. She probably had an unexpected meeting in town. Hopefully, she'd be home soon.

Once inside the foyer, he headed to his private quarters and stopped in the kitchen. He placed both bags on the counter, then opened the fridge and pulled out a bottle of water. He unscrewed the top and took a big swig, quenching his thirst.

He considered taking a shower before he spotted a note on the table addressed to him.

> *Dear Steven,*
>
> *I'm sorry, but I can't keep living a lie. I'm not angry with you. How could I be when you've never been anything but good to me? But it's time for me to go home. I need to set up a nursery and prepare for the baby.*
>
> *I value our friendship and appreciate all you've done for me. If our marriage had been real, things might have been different. But my highest priority right now is my son. He deserves to have a loving home, and one that's permanent.*
>
> *Ellie*

The words blindsided him, and he sat down to read them again.

She'd moved out? Just like that? And without talking it over with him first, without asking him how he felt about it?

Hell, how *did* he feel about it?

Angry came to mind. Hadn't she cared enough about him or his feelings to tell him to his face? He was disappointed to find her gone. He was hurt, too, he supposed.

His head spun with other emotions he couldn't quite put his finger on. Were they still friends? Had they gone back to being at political odds?

Damn. He found the whole thing confusing. And he wasn't sure what, if anything, to do about it.

And then there was the baby. His entire family and the whole damned town thought it was his. He'd been prepared to step up to the plate, but apparently Ellie hadn't ever considered him taking an active, paternal-type role. She'd taken her mom to one of her obstetrical appointments, and even though he'd thought she might ask him to go in Alma's place this afternoon, she hadn't.

At the time, he'd been afraid to ask, afraid he might be overstepping. He'd had a busy day, but he would have shuffled things around and found the time.

She clearly preferred to go alone, and that irritated him more now than it had this morning. And it shouldn't. Hell, he wasn't the baby's father.

Yet, in some odd way, he'd begun to think that he was. How was that for losing his head over his friendship with Ellie?

He sat at the kitchen table for the longest time, the note in his hand, his brain scrambling to make sense of it all. It wasn't until his cell phone rang that the fog began to clear.

Was Ellie having second thoughts? Was she on her way home?

He glanced at the lighted display and frowned. Then he swiped his finger across the screen to accept Callum's call.

"Yeah, what is it?" he asked, anger and frustration setting a sharp edge to his tone.

"Whoa," Callum said. "I didn't mean to bother you. Is this a bad time?"

It sure as hell wasn't a good one. "What's up?"

"Nicole is cooking again tonight and asked me to find out if you and Ellie are going to join us for dinner."

"No, Ellie's...not home."

"We can always keep a couple of plates warm for you."

"Don't bother. I'll... We'll fend for ourselves."

"Is something wrong?" Callum asked. "You seemed okay when we left the office this afternoon, but something must have set you off."

"Don't worry about it." Instead of going into any more detail than that, Steven ended the call.

He hadn't meant to take out his anger on his brother. But he wasn't about to share his mixed-up thoughts with anyone. He'd rather wallow in them on his own.

And that's just what he did. He stewed over the situation all night long, tossing and turning until dawn.

The next day, at the construction trailer on the Paz job site, his brothers tiptoed around him. It hadn't taken long for the office staff and the employees to pick up on his foul mood and to steer clear of him. And that was fine with him.

Before he left for the day, Callum and Dillon finally approached him, hands on hips, their expressions serious.

"We have no idea what happened last night," Callum said, "but we can connect a few dots, especially since Ellie's car wasn't in the yard again this morning."

Steven could have explained, starting at the beginning, but it wasn't that simple. And he wasn't sure why. It might help to talk it out, but he was the oldest brother. His siblings were supposed to come to him for advice, not the other way around.

"Have you talked to Ellie?" Dillon asked.

Steven couldn't believe this. Since when was Dillon the expert on relationships? His last two hadn't gone well. Or so he'd gathered. But Steven bit back a snappy retort. He might be angry and all kinds of mixed up, but he wasn't so off balance that he'd intentionally hurt his younger brother.

So he shook it off the best he could. "There's nothing to talk about, guys. Ellie and I just need some time apart."

Then he walked out the door and strode toward his pickup. It wasn't supposed to end this way. Nor was it supposed to hurt. For a fake marriage, the breakup felt pretty damned real.

It had been two long days since Ellie had left the ranch, and Steven still didn't feel any better about her leaving, about that damned note she wrote, about the way his queen-size bed had grown bigger and colder without her in it.

Even when he'd holed up at Fortune Brothers Construction and tried to keep his mind on work, he felt her absence. And that didn't make any sense.

A knock sounded at the door of the modular, drawing him from his thoughts. He would have let someone else answer, but everyone else had taken off early, no doubt chased off by his crappy mood.

"What is it?" he asked.

"It's Alma Hernandez."

Steven's heart jumped to his throat then dropped to his gut. Had something happened to Ellie or the baby?

He rolled back his desk chair, got to his feet and crossed the room in three steps. He swung open the door and found Alma standing there, holding her purse in both hands.

"I don't want to keep you from your work," she said, "so I'll make this quick."

"No problem. Please, come in." He stepped aside, and when she entered, he closed the door to give them privacy.

He strode to the chair that sat across the desk and moved a stack of files and a folded blueprint he'd piled on it.

"I'm sorry for the mess. I don't usually get visitors here. Please. Have a seat."

As the retired schoolteacher complied, he wheeled his chair around the desk and sat next to her. "What's going on? Is Ellie okay?"

"She's not sick, if that's what you mean. But she's not the least bit okay. She's concerned about the divorce."

Divorce. The harsh sound of the word slammed into him. They'd talked about separating down the road, and of course, they'd planned to do it legally and file the necessary paperwork with the court. But in Steven's mind, "down the road" hadn't meant a week after the wedding.

"What's she worried about? I won't fight her, if that's what she's afraid of. I just wish she would have talked to me. We might have…" He sucked in a deep breath, then blew it out. "We made a deal, and I'm willing to follow through on it."

"Is that what you want?" Alma asked. "To follow through on the agreement?"

"I don't understand why you're asking me that question," he said. "Ellie's the one who left, and I'll admit I wasn't happy about it. If she had something on her mind, she should've talked to me in person. Instead, she left a Dear John letter that didn't shed much light on her thoughts and feelings."

Alma studied him as if he were one of her students, as if he'd stayed on the playground after recess was over and the rest of the kids had returned to class. She seemed to be considering the proper punishment, only that wasn't necessary. Ellie had already given him the ultimate time-out.

"Do you care for my daughter?" Alma asked.

"Yes, of course I do. I wouldn't have married her if I didn't."

"Do you *love* her?"

The word crept into his chest and shimmied up and down his spine. He had feelings for Ellie. Deep ones. And it had hurt like the devil when she left.

"I might. I'm not sure. I…" Steven raked a hand through his hair. He sure as hell felt something for her.

"At the wedding," Alma said, "I saw you watch Ellie as she walked down the aisle. The expression on your face didn't seem fake. And neither did your smile or the happiness glimmering in your eyes. Unless you're bound for the Broadway

stage, I suspect you're feeling more than friendship for her."

She was right. His feelings ran deeper than that.
"I'm not supposed to feel more than friendship.
That was the deal."

"If you love her—or if you think it might come
to that one day—I suggest you fight for her."

Fight who? Steven's hand fisted, and his brow
furrowed. "Did that bastard come back from South
America?"

"No, and I don't expect he ever will. The battle
I was referring to is the one going on inside you."

He was definitely struggling. And it sounded
like Ellie was, too. But a man had pride. And she
was the one who'd thrown in the towel.

"What's holding you back?" Alma asked.

Steven merely sat there, pondering her words,
as well as his thoughts and feelings.

"Is it the baby? I know it isn't yours."

"No, that's not it. That poor little guy can't help
it if his biological dad is an ass."

"That's true. But a lot of men wouldn't want to
take on someone else's responsibility."

David Fortune had. He'd adopted both Steven
and Wiley, and he'd treated them both like his biological sons. Steven had appreciated being a Fortune and had wanted to prove himself worthy of
the name.

But in reality, what had he been trying to prove?

David had treated all the boys the same. He went to parent-teacher conferences, watched baseball games, sent them all to camp, paid for private lessons, listened to problems. And he'd never once complained.

Steven blew out a sigh.

"My daughter has a stubborn streak," Alma said. "And I can see that you do, too. She's in love with you, but I'm not sure if she'll be the first to admit it. And I'm fairly certain that you feel the same way about her. Don't let your pride get in the way of your happiness." Alma wheeled her chair back and stood. "I hope you'll forgive me for showing up uninvited. I'm usually not one to meddle, but I couldn't help myself this time. I'll go now—and leave you to think about what I said. But no matter what you decide or how this ends, my husband and I have the greatest respect for you. We think you're a good man, an honorable one."

"Thanks." He wasn't sure if he was thanking her for the compliment she left him with or for coming to talk to him. But he stood and walked her to the door.

Before she could exit, Steven stopped her. "If Ellie loves me, then why did she leave?"

Alma smiled softly. "You'll need to ask her that." Then she turned and walked away, leaving him stunned and with a lot to think about.

* * *

Ellie had gone to visit her parents again this afternoon, but her mom was just leaving to run an errand. Ellie told them she'd come back another day, but Papa insisted they focus on something else for a change.

"It'll be good for you to get out," he'd said.

When she agreed, he'd taken her window-shopping for baby furniture. Then he'd driven her to the hardware store to pick up some paint samples to take with them.

He'd been right. Spending the day with him had helped a lot. She still felt incredibly sad when she thought about Steven and what might have been, but her father had helped her to realize she had a lot to be thankful for, a lot to look forward to.

On the way home, Ellie called Daria to ask if she had given dinner any thought.

"Hey," Daria said. "I'm glad you called. I've got some news. And it's about to bubble right out of me. The CEO of the car wash chain that purchased Happy Suds just called me and asked if I'd like to work for them."

"That's great news. But I thought they already had an accountant."

"They do, but his wife is an officer in the army, and she just received orders to spend the next three years in Germany. So he and the entire family are going with her. He's leaving in three weeks, so the

CEO wants me to come to Houston now so I can work with him before he goes. That way, we can make a smooth transition."

"When are you leaving?"

"Actually, I'm already packed. The company is going to put me up in an apartment in Houston for the next couple of months. Then, once I get the lay of the land, I'll be able to buy a place of my own. Only thing is, I'll have to travel some. But I'm okay with that."

"You sound excited."

"I am. The pay is good. And they plan to buy more car washes, so there's a chance for upward mobility."

"I'm happy for you," Ellie said. "But I'll miss you."

"Houston isn't that far away. I can visit sometimes. And you can stay with me, too. But I have a favor to ask."

"What's that?"

"I can't take Tank with me."

Ellie couldn't tell her no. Besides, she liked the little rascal. "I might have to ask my parents to puppy-sit when I'm at work, but they probably won't mind."

"That would be great," Daria said. "I have a hair appointment in about ten minutes, so I need to run. Then I'm headed out of town. Can we talk more about this tomorrow?"

"Sure. I'm not going anywhere."

Five minutes later, Ellie arrived home and let herself into the house. Daria had already left, but Tank greeted her at the door, tail wagging.

She stooped to give him a scratch behind the ear. "Looks like it's just you and me, Tank. And the baby makes three."

Tank cocked his head to the side, clearly not understanding.

"Come on," Ellie told him. "I'll let you outside so you can go pee."

She'd just opened the slider to let the puppy into the backyard when the doorbell rang. It was probably the neighbor kids wanting to play with Tank. So she crossed the small living room, her bare feet padding on the hardwood floor, and opened the door.

Instead of the two red-haired children she'd expected to see, she spotted Steven standing on the stoop, his Stetson in hand. Her heart dropped to her feet, and she feared her lower jaw did the same dang thing.

"Can I come in?" he asked.

She stepped aside, her heart pounding to the beat of a rock band, and allowed him to enter.

"I've missed you," he said.

She'd missed him, too. But that didn't mean she'd move back to the Fame and Fortune Ranch.

She swept her hand toward the living room. "Come in and sit down."

He strode to the sofa, placed his hat on the coffee table and took a seat. She kept her distance. She'd be able to keep a clearer mind when she wasn't breathing in his musky scent, when he wasn't close enough to touch.

"How are you doing?" he asked.

"Fine. I saw the doctor yesterday, and he said everything's good—the baby's growing and healthy."

"I'm glad to hear that, but I was actually talking about your feelings."

His bluntness took her aback, and she realized he was talking about the goodbye letter she'd left him. It had seemed like the right thing to do at the time, but she suspected cowardice had played a large part in it.

Unwilling to show any vulnerability, any guilt, she shrugged a single shoulder. "I'm hanging in there. I had a nice talk with my parents the other day. And I spent yesterday afternoon with my dad. So I'm moving along."

"How are you feeling about me?" he asked. "About us."

She'd be darned if she'd blurt out how she really felt. That she missed him terribly. That her heart ached for him. Her body, too.

"You go first," she said. "How are *you* feeling?"

He sucked in a deep breath, then let it out in a long huff. "Honestly? I feel like crap, Ellie. I can't sleep, I can't eat. And I don't think any of that's going to change until you come home."

The revelation struck her like a freight train barreling down the track. She'd left without having a heart-to-heart, which she might have owed to him. But there was no way she'd roll over and return to what they'd had.

"I can't go back to the ranch. If I did, then I'd be the one who couldn't sleep or eat." In truth, she wasn't doing much sleeping or eating anyway.

"I'm sorry," he said. "And I hate to admit this, but I really let you down."

At that, her ears perked up. What had he done? Had he talked to the press? Had he managed to sneak around and get the planning commission to approve that blasted hotel he was dead set on building?

"I didn't mean for it to happen," he said.

Her heart battered her rib cage. "Steven, what did you *do*?"

"I didn't keep my promise. I couldn't." He got to his feet, reached into his pocket and pulled out a small black velvet box.

Tears welled in her eyes, and the words wadded up in her throat, making it difficult to breathe, let alone speak.

"I promised you that we'd be friends, that this

would be a marriage in name only. But—" He reached for her hand, and when she placed it in his, he drew her to her feet. "I don't want to just be friends. I don't want to get a divorce. Not now, not ever. I love you, Ellie."

Her heart stalled in her chest, and she tried to wrap her mind around what he was saying. What she hoped he was saying. "Are you sure about that?"

"I struggled with it long enough, but it's the only answer I have for my foul mood, for snapping at anyone who crosses my path. I just hope you're struggling for the same reason."

"I am. I love you, too. I didn't mean for it to happen, but it did. And I was afraid to tell you."

"Don't ever hold back, Ellie. I want to know it all. Be my friend, my lover and my partner in life."

He lifted the velvet lid, revealing a sparkling diamond, and her heart swelled to the point she thought it had filled with helium and would fly out of her chest.

"Will you be my real wife?" he asked.

She could scarcely speak, so she nodded. Somehow, the words seemed to bust their way through the lump in her throat. "Yes, I will."

He removed the ring and slipped it on her finger. "Our engagement might have started out fake, but our wedding was the real deal. And so is my love for you."

As he took her into his arms, she kissed him with all the love in her heart.

When they came up for air, he cupped her face and gazed into her eyes. "Since we're always going to be honest with each other, I have to admit something else. I felt a little hurt that you didn't ask me to go to the doctor with you. I want to be your baby's father in every sense of the word."

"My next appointment is in three weeks," she said. "I'd love to have you go with me. In the meantime… Wait here."

She hurried to the bedroom and went to the nightstand, where she'd left the small scrapbook she'd created after her first visit to the obstetrician and took it to him. "Look at this."

"What is it?" he asked.

"Open it and see."

He did, and a slow smile stretched across his lips as he saw the sonogram images she'd been saving. "This is amazing."

"Meet George Steven Fortune. You'll have to wait until August to see him in person, so these will have to do for now."

"This is awesome," he said. "Little George will be here before we know it. We'll have to get busy so we can turn my guest room into a nursery."

Ellie bit down on her bottom lip. "Would you mind if we lived here? In my house?"

"Don't you like the ranch?"

"I love it. But I'd like some private time while we create our family."

"I'd like that, too. Will Daria mind having a new roommate?"

"Actually, she got a new job and moved out. So it'll just be the two of us. And Tank."

"I'll live anywhere, as long as you're with me. Besides, it's closer to the construction office and several of our job sites. With the wellness spa opening in a week and the restaurant opening in May, I'll be busy. And I won't miss the commute from the ranch."

"What about the hotel?" she asked. "What's going on with that?"

"To tell you the truth, I'm not sure if it'll ever come to fruition, but that's okay. I don't mind putting that project on the back burner for a while. You and I have a baby to get ready for."

"My parents will insist upon helping. I hope you don't mind."

"Not at all. I'm going to like having them as in-laws, especially your mom."

Ellie kissed him again. "You are going to be the best husband ever."

"I thought I already was."

She laughed. "You've got that right."

"That reminds me, I owe you a honeymoon," he said. "Would it be okay if we started it today? Right now?"

"There's nothing I'd like better." Ellie took him by the hand and led him to her bedroom.

As they stood beside her bed, Steven kissed her again—long and deep—savoring the feel of her in his arms, the taste of her on his tongue. He slid his hands along the curve of her back and over the slope of her derriere.

"I love you," she whispered as she removed her green top, revealing a lacy white bra.

A surge of desire shot right through him, and he felt compelled to stake his claim, but they had the rest of the day and all night. And he intended to use every bit of it.

He watched as she peeled her yoga pants over her hips. *Pinch me*, he thought. Ellie was a dream come true—his dream. His wife.

Her gaze never left his as he removed his clothing, baring himself to her in a slow, deliberate fashion.

When they were both naked, she pulled the comforter from the bed, then lay down and opened her arms, silently inviting him to join her. And he gladly did.

She skimmed her nails across his chest, sending a shiver through his veins and a rush of heat through his blood. They continued to stroke, to touch, to taste until he thought they'd both go crazy if they didn't quench the fire the only way he knew how.

Unable to prolong the foreplay any longer, Steven hovered over her and gazed into her passion-filled eyes. "Are you ready?"

"More than ready."

He entered her slowly at first, and her body responded to his, up and down, in and out. As she met each of his thrusts, they came together in a sexual explosion that damned near took his breath away. And as they lay in the sweet afterglow, the reality of their union was staggering as they celebrated their real love, their real marriage and the promise of a very real happy-ever-after.

* * * * *

COMING SOON!

We really hope you enjoyed reading this book. If you're looking for more romance, be sure to head to the shops when new books are available on

Thursday 6th March

To see which titles are coming soon, please visit

millsandboon.co.uk/nextmonth

MILLS & BOON

Coming next month

ONE NIGHT WITH HER MILLIONAIRE BOSS
Kandy Shepherd

The rain was coming down so hard it had driven channels into the gravel, forming small gushing streams. The path was well lit, but it was getting more difficult to avoid the streams and save her shoes and she found herself jumping from side to side as if in a game of aquatic hopscotch. She cursed out loud when the umbrella suddenly turned completely inside out. She was left with only a light jacket over her dress for protection against the elements.

Then Ned was there. 'Seems like you could do with some help,' he said. He was sensibly encased in a long oilskin raincoat and held aloft an enormous black umbrella.

'This darn umbrella is useless,' she spluttered and threw it on the ground.

'Don't tell me—you chose it because it was purple.'

'It was the first one I saw,' she fibbed. Of course she'd been attracted to the pattern of purple iris. The possible sturdiness of the umbrella hadn't been a consideration.

'Come here,' he said.

Ned pulled her to him and under the shelter of his umbrella. Suddenly the stinging onslaught of the rain on her face stopped, but she was far too distracted by Ned's closeness to care. She was dry. She was warm. *He was hot.*

'It's great to get rain. We need it. Trouble is when it all comes down like this at once, so much of it runs off.'

'Hopefully it will ease off,' she said.

His chest was a wall of solid muscle. As he led her towards the house, steering her through the channels, she leaned in closer. Just, of course, to make sure she was completely under the shelter of his umbrella.

'We're almost there or I'd pick you up and carry you,' he said.

'*What!*'

'You're a little thing. Nowhere as heavy as a full-grown sheep to sling over my shoulder.'

Before she had a chance to reply, they reached the house. In one fluid movement, Ned ditched his umbrella, put his hands under her armpits, lifted her off the ground and up the steps, depositing her on the veranda. Freya was back on her feet, out of the rain, before she had time to protest.

'Did you just compare me to a sheep?' she said, mock glaring up at him, a smile twitching at the corners of her mouth. His hair was dark with damp and fat drops of water sat on his cheeks. He grinned. Her heart gave that curious lurch of recognition—she didn't know where it came from.

'A ewe, if I'm to be precise,' he said.

'I'm glad you at least amended that to be a lady sheep.' She couldn't resist his grin and responded with one of her own. 'Do you really lift and haul sheep around the place?' If so, no wonder the man was made of muscle.

'If needs be,' he said. 'I grew up learning to do everything that needed to be done with sheep. Rescue them, shear them, sometimes birth them. So yeah, I've had to haul around the odd sheep or two over the years. No special treatment for the boss.'

He sounded so laconic, so laidback, so *manly* she leaned up on tiptoe and kissed him on the cheek. 'Thank you, for rescuing me like a stray sheep caught in the rain.' She froze. *Why did she do that?*

Her lips tingled from the connection to his skin, cool with raindrops. For a crazy moment she'd wanted to taste them, taste *him*. Her gaze connected with his for a long, still moment.

Continue reading
ONE NIGHT WITH HER MILLIONAIRE BOSS
Kandy Shepherd

Available next month
www.millsandboon.co.uk

MILLS & BOON

THE HEART OF ROMANCE

A ROMANCE FOR EVERY KIND OF READER

MODERN

Prepare to be swept off your feet by sophisticated, sexy and seductive heroes, in some of the world's most glamorous an romantic locations, where power and passion collide.
8 stories per month.

HISTORICAL

Escape with historical heroes from time gone by. Whether yo passion is for wicked Regency Rakes, muscled Vikings or rug Highlanders, awaken the romance of the past.
6 stories per month.

MEDICAL

Set your pulse racing with dedicated, delectable doctors in th high-pressure world of medicine, where emotions run high passion, comfort and love are the best medicine.
6 stories per month.

True Love

Celebrate true love with tender stories of heartfelt romance, the rush of falling in love to the joy a new baby can bring, an focus on the emotional heart of a relationship.
8 stories per month.

Desire

Indulge in secrets and scandal, intense drama and plenty of hot action with powerful and passionate heroes who have it a wealth, status, good looks…everything but the right woman.
6 stories per month.

HEROES

Experience all the excitement of a gripping thriller, with an romance at its heart. Resourceful, true-to-life women and str fearless men face danger and desire - a killer combination!
8 stories per month.

DARE

Sensual love stories featuring smart, sassy heroines you'd war best friend, and compelling intense heroes who are worthy o
4 stories per month.

To see which titles are coming soon, please visit

millsandboon.co.uk/nextmonth

MILLS & BOON
MEDICAL
Pulse-Racing Passion

Set your pulse racing with dedicated, delectable doctors in the high-pressure world of medicine, where emotions run high and passion, comfort and love are the best medicine.

LET'S TALK
Romance

For exclusive extracts, competitions
and special offers, find us online:

- facebook.com/millsandboon
- @MillsandBoon
- @MillsandBoonUK

Get in touch on 01413 063232